Jill Mansell

an offer you can't refuse

headline
review

First published in 2008
by HEADLINE REVIEW
An imprint of HEADLINE PUBLISHING GROUP

First published in paperback in 2008
by HEADLINE REVIEW

18

ISBN 978 0 7553 4180 1 (A format)
ISBN 978 0 7553 2816 1 (B format)

Typeset in Bembo by
Palimpsest Book Production Limited,
Grangemouth, Stirlingshire
Printed and bound in the UK by
CPI Mackays, Chatham ME5 8TD

Headline's policy is to use papers that are natural, renewable and
recyclable products and made from wood grown in sustainable forests.
The logging and manufacturing processes are expected to conform to
the environmental regulations of the country of origin.

HEADLINE PUBLISHING GROUP
An Hachette Livre UK Company
338 Euston Road
London NW1 3BH

www.reviewbooks.co.uk
www.hodderheadline.com

To my daughter Lydia and all her friends and teachers at school, especially Mr Fielding, form tutor, and Miss Wilson, English teacher.

And (deep breath now . . .) Zainab, Mya, Kat, Louise, Pinki, Lacey, Hannah M., Sophia, Ellis, Ellie, Laura, Emily, Tash, Alice, Millie, Ella, Hannah O., Sophie, Charli, Anna and Harriet

What a lovely lot you are!

Chapter 1

Ten Years Ago

There are some places where you might expect to bump into your boyfriend's ultra-posh mother. At a Buckingham Palace garden party perhaps, or Glyndebourne, or turning her nose up at Ferrero Rochers at some foreign ambassador's cocktail party. And then there are other places you wouldn't expect to bump into her *at all*.

Like, for example, the Cod Almighty at the dodgier end of Tooting High Street.

'Blimey, it's Dougie's mum.' Instinctively wiping her hands on her green nylon overall and curbing the urge to curtsey – because Dougie's mum was *that* posh – Lola said brightly, 'Hello, Mrs Tennant, how lovely to see you!'

And how typical that she should turn up two minutes before closing, when all they had left to offer her was a tired-looking saveloy and a couple of overlooked fishcakes. Maybe Alf could be persuaded to quickly chuck a couple of fresh pieces of haddock into the fryer and—

'Hello, Lola. I wondered if we could have a chat.' Even for

1

a visit to a fish and chip shop, Dougie's mother's make-up was immaculate, her hair swept into a Princess Michael of Kent chignon.

'Oh, right. Absolutely. I'm just finishing here.' Lola glanced across at Alf, who made good-humoured off-you-go gestures. 'We close at half past two. So you don't want anything to take away?'

Was that a shudder? Mrs Tennant shook her head and said with a flicker of amusement, 'I don't think so, do you?'

Having retrieved her shoulder bag from the back room and shrugged off her nylon overall – youch, *static* – Lola ducked under the swing-top counter and took the king-sized portion of chips Alf had wrapped up for her, seeing as they had so many left.

'Bye, Alf. See you tomorrow.'

'I can drop you home if you like,' said Dougie's mother. 'The car's just outside.'

Lola beamed; free chips *and* a lift home in a brand new Jaguar. This was definitely her lucky day.

Outside on the pavement it was stiflingly hot and muggy. Inside the Jaguar the cool air smelled deliciously of expensive leather and Chanel No. 19.

'This is such a great car,' sighed Lola, stroking the uphol-stery as Dougie's mother started the engine.

'Thank you. I like it.'

'How could anyone not like it?' Lola balanced the steaming parcel of chips in her lap, careful to keep it away from her bare legs. Her stomach was rumbling but she heroically resisted the temptation to open them. 'So why did you want to see me? Is this about Dougie's birthday?'

'No. Actually it's about you and Dougie. I want you to stop seeing him.'

Bam, just like that.

Lola blinked. 'Excuse me?'

'I'd like you to end your relationship with my son.'

This couldn't be happening. Her shoulders stiffening in disbelief, Lola watched as Dougie's mother drove along, as calm and unconcerned as if they were discussing nothing more taxing than the weather.

'*Why?*'

'He's eighteen years old.'

'Nearly nineteen.'

'He's eighteen now,' Mrs Tennant repeated firmly, 'and on his way to university. He *is* going to university.'

'I know.' Bewildered, Lola said, 'I'm not stopping him. We're going to see each other whenever we can, take it in turns to do the journey. I'll catch the coach up to Edinburgh every other weekend, and Dougie's going to drive down here when it's his turn, then—'

'No, no, no, I'm sorry but he won't. This isn't the kind of relationship Doug needs right now. He told me last night that he was having second thoughts about going to university. He wants to stay here. And that's all down to you, my girl. But I won't stand by and let you ruin his life.'

The hot chips were burning Lola's legs now. 'Honestly, I'm not ruining his life. I want the best for Dougie, just like you do. We love each other! I've already told him, if we miss each other too much I'll move up to Edinburgh and we'll live together!'

'Oh yes, he mentioned that too. And the next thing we know, you'd be feeling left out because he'd have all his university friends while you're stuck working behind the counter of some backstreet fish and chip shop.' Mrs Tennant's lip curled with disdain. 'So to regain his attention you'd accidentally get yourself pregnant. No, I'm sorry, I simply can't allow this to happen. Far better for you to make the break now.'

Who did this woman think she was?

'But I don't want to.' Lola's breathing was fast and shallow. 'And you can't force me to do it.'

'No, dear, of course I can't force you. But I can do my best to persuade you.'

'I won't be persuaded. I love Dougie. With all my heart,' Lola blurted out, determined to make his mother understand that this was no silly teenage fling.

'Ten thousand pounds, take it or leave it.'

'*What?*'

'That's what I'm offering. Think it over. How much do you earn in that fish and chip shop?' Dougie's mother raised a perfectly plucked eyebrow. 'No more than five pounds an hour, I'm sure.'

Four pounds actually. But it was still a mean dig; working at the Cod Almighty was only a temporary thing while she applied for jobs that would make more use of her qualifications.

'And if I took your money, what kind of a person would that make me?'

'Oh, I don't know. The sensible kind, perhaps?'

Lola was so angry she could barely speak; her fingernails sank through the steamed, soggy chip paper, filling the air-conditioned interior of the car with the rank, sharp smell of vinegar. Something else was bothering her too; up until today, Dougie's mother had always been perfectly charming whenever they'd met.

'I thought you liked me.'

'Of course you did.' Mrs Tennant sounded entertained. 'That was the whole idea. I know what young people are like, you see. If a parent announces that they don't approve of their children's choice of partner, it's only going to make them that much more determined to stay together. Fuelling the flame and all that. Goodness no, far better to pretend everything's rosy and you think their choice is wonderful, then let the relationship fizzle out of its own accord.'

'But ours isn't going to fizzle out,' said Lola.

'So you keep telling me. That's why I'm giving it a helping hand. Goodness, this traffic is a nightmare today. Is it left down here at the traffic lights or straight on?'

'Left. And how's Dougie going to feel when he hears what you've said to me today?'

'Well, I should imagine he'd be very annoyed with me. If you told him.' Mrs Tennant paused for effect. 'But do yourself a favour, Lola. Don't say anything just yet. Give yourself time to really think this through, because you do have a brain. And ten thousand pounds is an awful lot of money. All you have to do as soon as you've made up your mind is give me a ring when you know Dougie isn't at home. And I'll write out the cheque.'

'You can stop the car. I'll walk the rest of the way.' No longer willing to remain in her boyfriend's mother's plush Jag, Lola jabbed a finger to indicate that she should pull in at the bus stop ahead.

'Sure? OK then.'

Lola paused with her hand on the passenger door handle and looked at Dougie's mother in her crisp white linen shirt and royal chignon. 'Can I ask you something?'

'Feel free.'

'Why don't you approve of me?'

'You risk ruining my son's future.' Mrs Tennant didn't hesitate.

'We love each other. We could be happy together for the rest of our lives.'

'No you *couldn't*, Lola. Do you really not understand what I'm trying to explain here? You're too brash and noisy, you have no class, you're not good enough for Dougie. And,' the older woman paused, her gaze lingering significantly over Lola's low-cut red vest top and short denim skirt complete with grease stain, 'you dress like a cheap tart.'

'Can I ask you something else?' said Lola. 'How are you going to feel when Dougie refuses to ever speak to you again?'

And, heroically resisting the urge to tear open the parcel of chips and fling them in Dougie's mother's face, she climbed out of the car.

Back at home in Streatham – a far more modest house than Dougie's, which his mother would surely sneer at – Lola paced the small blue and white living room like a caged animal and went over everything that had happened. OK, *now* what was she supposed to do? Dougie was currently up in Edinburgh for a few days, sorting out where he was going to be living come October and acquainting himself with the city that was due to be his home for the next three years. Doubtless Mrs Tennant had planned it this way with her usual meticulous attention to detail. Her own mother and stepfather were both out at work. The ticking of the clock in the kitchen was driving her demented. Bloody, bloody woman – how *dare* she do this to her? What a *witch*.

By four o'clock she could no longer bear to be confined. Deliberately not changing out of her *low-cut* top and *far-too-short* denim skirt, Lola left the house. What she was wearing was practically standard issue for teenagers on a hot summer's day, for heaven's sake – not tarty at all. And if she didn't talk to someone about the situation, she would burst.

'Ten thousand pounds,' said Jeannie.

'Yes.'

'I mean, ten thousand *pounds*.'

'So?' Lola banged down her Coke. 'It doesn't matter how much it is. She can't go around doing stuff like that. It's just sick.'

They were in McDonald's. Jeannie noisily slurped her own Coke through two straws. 'Can I say something?'

'Can I stop you?'

'OK, you say it's a sick thing to do. And you're going to say no. But what if Dougie comes back from Edinburgh on Friday and tells you he's met someone else? What if he sits you down and says, "Look, sorry and all that, but I bumped into this really fit girl in a bar, we ended up in bed and she's just fantastic"?' Pausing to suck up the last dregs of her Coke, Jeannie pointed the straw at Lola. 'What if he tells you you're dumped?'

Oh, for heaven's sake.

'Dougie wouldn't do that.'

'He might.'

'He *wouldn't*.'

'But he *might*,' said Jeannie. 'OK, maybe not this week, or even this month. But sooner or later the chances are that you two will break up. You're seventeen years old. How many seventeen-year-olds spend the rest of their lives with their first love? Let's face it, that's why it's called *first* love, because you go on to have loads more. You're too young to stay with the same person, Lola. And so's Dougie. I know you're crazy about each other now, but that's not going to last. And if Dougie *is* the one who finishes it, you can't go running to his mother crying that you've changed your mind and can you have the money now please? Because it'll be too late by then. You'll have lost out big time. Think about it, you'll be all on your own.' Mock sorrowfully, Jeannie clutched her chest. 'Heartbroken. No more Dougie Tennant *and* no ten thousand pounds.'

So that was the advice from a so-called friend. Well, what else should she have expected from someone like Jeannie, whose parents had fought an epic divorce battle and left her with a jaundiced view of relationships? Jeannie now despised her mother's new husband and was escaping all the hassle at home by moving to Majorca. The plan was to work in a bar, dance on the beach and generally have the time of her life. Sleep with lots of men but very definitely not get emotionally involved with any of them. Any kind of romantic relationship was *out*.

The memory of Dougie's mother continued to haunt Lola all the way home, that pale patrician face and disparaging voice letting her know in no uncertain terms why she was nowhere near good enough for her precious son.

Lola pictured the smirk on that face if Jeannie's cheery prediction were to come true. Then again, imagine how she'd react if she and Dougie defied her and got married! Ha, wouldn't *that* be fabulous?

Except . . . except . . .

I'm seventeen, I don't want to get married just to spite someone. I'm too *young*.

Back home again, Lola was overcome by an overwhelming

urge to speak to Dougie. No plan in her head, but she'd play it by ear. When she heard his voice she would decide what to do, whether or not to tell him that his mother was the world's biggest witch. God, how would he feel when he found out?

Dougie was staying in a bed and breakfast in Edinburgh. The number was on the pad next to the phone in the narrow hallway. Dialling it, Lola checked her watch; it was five o'clock. He should be there now, back from his visit to the university campus . . .

'No, dear, I'm afraid you've missed him.' The landlady of the B&B had a kindly, Edinburgh-accented voice. 'They came back an hour ago, Dougie changed and showered and then they were off. Said they were going to check out the pubs on Rose Street!'

'Oh.' Lola's heart sank; she'd so wanted to hear his voice. 'Who was he with?'

'I didn't catch their names, pet. Another boy and two girls . . . isn't it lovely to see him making new friends already? The boy's from Manchester and the pretty blonde one's from Abergavenny! I must say, they do seem absolutely charming. I'll tell him you rang, shall I? Although goodness knows what time he'll be back . . .'

Hanging up, Lola heard Jeannie's words again. It wasn't that she was overwhelmed with jealousy that Dougie had gone out for the evening with a group of new friends, two of whom happened to be female. It was just the realisation that this was the first of many hundreds of nights when she would be apart from him and—

Lola started as a floorboard creaked overhead; she'd thought the house was empty.

She called out, 'Hello?'

No reply.

'Mum?' Lola frowned. 'Dad?'

Still nothing. Had the floorboard just creaked on its own or was someone up there? But the house seemed secure and a burglar would have his work cut out, climbing in through a bedroom window. Taking an umbrella as a precaution, Lola made her way upstairs.

What she saw when she pushed open the white painted door of her parents' bedroom shocked her to the core.

Chapter 2

'Dad?' Lola's stomach clenched in fear. Something was horribly, horribly wrong. Her stepfather – the only father she'd ever known, the man she loved with all her heart – was packing a case, his face almost unrecognisable.

'Go downstairs.' He turned his back on her, barely able to speak.

Lola was shaking. 'Dad, what is it?'

'Please, just leave me alone.'

'No! I won't! Tell me what's wrong.' Dropping the umbrella, she cried, 'Why are you packing? Are you ill? Are you going to hospital? Is it cancer?'

Grief-stricken, he shook his head. 'I'm not ill, not in that way. Lola, this is nothing to do with you . . . I didn't want you to see me like this . . .'

It was such an unimaginable situation that Lola didn't know what to think. When she approached him he made a feeble attempt to fend her off with one arm.

'Daddy, *tell* me,' Lola whispered in desperation and tears sprang into his eyes.

Covering his face, he sank onto the bed. 'Oh Lola, I'm sorry.'

She had never been so frightened in her life. 'I'm going to phone Mum.'

'No, you mustn't.'

'Are you having an affair? Is that why you're packing? Don't you want to live with us any more?'

Another shake of the head. 'It's nothing like that.'

'So tell me what it *is* then.' Lola's voice wavered; they were both crying now. 'You have to, because I'm scared!'

Twenty minutes later she knew everything. Unbelievable though it seemed, Alex had been gambling and they'd never even suspected it. Through his twice-weekly visits to a snooker club he had been introduced to a crowd of card players and gradually, without even realising it, he'd found himself being sucked in. They had all met regularly at a house in Bermondsey to play poker and at first Alex had done pretty well. Now, he suspected that this had been the plan all along. Then the tide had turned, he had begun to lose and the genial group had made light of his run of bad luck. When the losses had mounted up to a worrying degree, Alex had confided in them that he needed time to pay back what he owed them. It was at this point that the genial group had stopped being genial and begun to threaten him. Terrified by the change in them, realising he was in way over his head, Alex had done the only thing possible and concentrated all his energies on winning back all the money he'd lost. Since his bank manager wouldn't have appreciated this as a sensible business plan, he'd borrowed the money from the friend who'd introduced him to the poker group in the first place.

A week later he'd lost it all.

He borrowed an emergency sum from a money-lender, tried again.

Lost that too.

Meanwhile his family was oblivious. When Lola's mum asked him if he was all right, he explained that he was just tired and she told him he shouldn't be working so hard. The following night, as he was leaving the garage where he worked as a mechanic, he was stopped by two heavies in a van who explained in graphic detail what they would do to him if he didn't repay every penny he owed by this time next week.

This time next week was now tomorrow and desperate times called for desperate measures. Sick with shame and in fear for his life – the heavies had been phoning him regularly, reminding him that the countdown was on – Alex had decided to disappear. It was the only answer; he couldn't admit to Blythe what he'd done, the hideous mess he'd made of his life. She and Lola meant everything in the world to him and he couldn't bear it any longer. If Lola had arrived home half an hour later he would have been gone for good.

'I wish you had,' he said heavily. 'You told us you were going shopping in Oxford Street this afternoon. I thought I was safe here.'

Shopping in Oxford Street. She'd completely forgotten about that after Dougie's mother had dropped her bombshell.

Lola, her face wet with tears, said, 'But I didn't, and now I know.'

'I still have to go. I can't face your mother. I'd be better off dead,' said Alex in desperation. 'But I'd rather do it my way than stay to find out what those bastards have in store for me . . . oh God, I can't believe this is happening, how could I have been so *stupid* . . '

Hugging him tightly, Lola already knew she had no choice. Her biological father, an American boy, had done a bunk the moment he'd found out that Blythe was pregnant. But it hadn't mattered because Alex had come along two years later. He loved Lola as if she were his own daughter. He had made her boiled eggs with toast soldiers, he'd taught her to ride a bike, together they had made up silly songs and driven her mother mad, singing them over and over again; she had run to him when she'd been stung by a wasp, he had driven her all the way to Birmingham to see a boy band who were playing at the NEC. His love for her was absolutely unconditional . . .

'I can help you,' said Lola. 'You don't have to leave.'

'Trust me, I do.'

Dry-eyed − this was too important for tears − she said, 'I can get the money for you.'

'Sweetheart, you can't. It's fifteen thousand pounds.'

Her stomach in knots, Lola didn't allow herself to think of the repercussions. 'I can get you most of it.'

And when Alex shook his head in disbelief she told him how.

When she'd finished he shook his head with even more vehemence. 'No, no, I can't let you do that. No way in the world, *absolutely not.*'

But what was the alternative? For him to disappear from their lives? For her to lose the only father she had ever known? For her mother's world to be shattered?

'Listen to me.' Although her own heart felt as if it were breaking in two, Lola played her trump card. 'Mum would never need to know.'

'Lola. How nice to see you again.' Adele Tennant opened her front door and stepped to one side. 'Come on in.'

Following her across the echoing, high-ceilinged hall, Lola

felt sick and dizzy but grimly determined. Mustn't, *mustn't* pass out. She'd barely slept last night, hadn't been able to eat anything either.

'I'm glad you've seen sense.' Adele sat down at the desk in her study and reached for her chequebook. Next to her, morning sunlight bounced off the glass on a silver photo frame. Shifting position to avoid the glare, Lola saw that it was a photograph of Adele and her children, Dougie on the left and Sally on the right. The photo had been taken a couple of years ago while they were on holiday somewhere unbelievably exotic, with palm trees and an ocean the colour of lapis lazuli, because Adele Tennant didn't take her holidays in Margate. Dougie, tanned and grinning in a white shirt, was looking carefree and heartbreakingly gorgeous. Sally, the older sister Lola had never met, was blonde and pretty in a flamingo-pink sarong. Now twenty-six and engaged to an Irish landowner, she was living with him in the Wicklow Mountains outside Dublin. Dougie adored his sister and Lola had been looking forward to getting to know her.

Her throat tightened. That wouldn't be happening now.

'You won't regret this.' Adele crisply uncapped a fat black fountain pen and hovered the glinting nib above the cheque.

The old witch couldn't wait.

'Hang on a minute.' Lola briefly closed her eyes, wondering if she could do this. Yes, she could. 'Ten thousand isn't enough.'

'I beg your pardon?'

'It isn't enough.' She had to say it. 'I need fifteen. Then I'll leave Dougie alone. I'll never see him again.'

'The cheek of you!'

Lola's mouth was bone-dry. 'Otherwise I'll move up to Edinburgh.'

Adele shot her a look of utter loathing. Frankly, Lola didn't blame her one bit.

'You are beyond the pale.'

Lola felt sicker than ever. 'I need the money.'

'Eleven thousand,' Adele retaliated. 'And that's it.'

'Fourteen,' said Lola. What if she threw up all over Adele's Persian rug?

'Twelve.'

'Thirteen.'

'Twelve and a half.'

'Done.' That was it, she'd haggled her way up to twelve and a half thousand pounds. As far as Dougie's mother was concerned, she was now officially despicable beyond belief. But it was enough to get Alex out of trouble; his boss at the garage was able to loan him the rest.

'I hope you're proud of yourself.' Adele dismissively wrote out the newly agreed sum.

Lola could so easily have burst into tears. She willed herself to stay in control. 'I'm not. I just need the money.'

'And hallelujah for that.' Adele, for whom twelve and a half thousand wasn't that much money at all, smiled her chilly, unamused smile. 'So what are you going to be spending it on?'

As she said it, her gaze slid disparagingly over Lola in her turquoise vest, jeans and flip-flops.

It was all over now. No more Dougie. She no longer had to try to impress his mother. 'Moving abroad,' said Lola. 'New bikinis. Silicone implants. Isn't that what you'd expect?'

'It's your money now. I don't care what you do with it, so long as you keep out of my son's life.' Adele paused. 'Will you tell him about this?'

'No.' Lola shook her head and took the cheque which Alex

would pay into his account this morning. He had arranged an overdraft to cover the days before it cleared. In exchange she handed over to Adele the letter she'd written this morning, the hardest letter she'd ever had to write. 'I'm just going to finish with him. You can give him this when he gets home. I'll be out of the country by then.'

'Delighted to hear it. Dougie will be over you in no time, but I agree it's best to put some distance between you. Well, I'll show you out.' Adele rose to her feet and ushered Lola back through the house. Evidently relieved that Dougie wouldn't be discovering the part she had played in seeing off his undesirable girlfriend, she smiled again at the front door and said, 'Goodbye, Lola. It's been an education doing business with you.'

This was it, this was really it. Lola's throat swelled up and for a moment she considered ripping the cheque into tiny pieces.

It was what she wanted to do. But then what would happen to Alex?

'I do love Dougie.' Her voice cracked; she still couldn't imagine living without him. 'I really, really do.'

Opening the door with a flourish, Adele said cheerfully, 'But you love money more.'

The moment he arrived home three days later, Dougie had only one thing on his mind.

'Hi, Mum, you OK?' He dumped his rucksack in the hall and kissed Adele on the cheek. 'Just going to shoot over to Lola's.'

Adele hugged her clever, handsome eighteen-year-old son, the light of her life. 'Actually there's a letter here for you from Lola.'

It had almost killed her not to steam open the envelope.

Now, as Dougie scanned the contents and she saw the colour drain from his face, Adele knew she'd been right to do as she had. He was far too fond of the girl for any good to come of it; at his age it was ridiculous to have let himself get so involved with any girl, let alone one as unequal socially as Lola Malone, the cheaply dressed daughter of a mechanic.

'What does it say?'

'Nothing.' Pain mingled with disbelief in Dougie's dark eyes as he crumpled the letter in his fist and headed upstairs.

Adele didn't want to see him hurt, but it was for his own good. It was for the best. Calling up after Dougie she said, 'Are you hungry, darling? Can I get you something to eat?'

'No.' He turned abruptly, his jaw set. 'How did you know the letter was from Lola?'

Adele thought fast. 'I was upstairs when I heard something coming through the letterbox. When I looked out of the window she was running up the road. Why don't I make you a roast beef sandwich, nice and rare?'

'Mum, I'm not *hungry*.'

Adele's heart went out to him. 'Sweetheart, is everything all right?'

'It will be.' Filled with resolve, Dougie nodded and said evenly, 'I'm going to my room, then I'm going out. And yes, everything *will* be all right.'

But it wasn't, thank God. Lola had kept her part of the bargain. The moment Dougie left the house, Adele infiltrated his room and found the crumpled-up note under the bed.

Dear Dougie,

Sorry to do it like this, but it's easier than face to face. It's over, Dougie, I don't want to see you any more. We've had fun and I don't regret our relationship but my feelings for you have changed recently, the magic just seems to have gone. I don't want to move up to Edinburgh with you, it's not my kind of place, and the thought of all that travelling up to see you is just too much. It'd never work out – we both know that, deep down. So I've decided to go abroad, somewhere hot and sunny. Don't bother trying to contact me because I've made up my mind. You'll find someone else in no time, and so will I.

Have a good life, Dougie. Sorry about this but you know it makes sense.

Cheers,

Lola x

Adele nodded approvingly, crumpled the note back up again and replaced it under the bed.

Good girl. She couldn't have put it better herself.

Together-forever, together-forever, together-forever. The words sang tauntingly through Doug's head in time with the rhythmic rattle of the tube train over the tracks. Just last week – seven *days* ago – he and Lola had taken a picnic up to Parliament Hill. Lola had let out a squeal of mock outrage when he'd pinched the last sausage roll. He'd run off with it, she'd caught him up and wrestled him to the ground and he'd given the sausage roll to her. They'd shared it in the end, laughing and kissing the crumbs from each other's lips. It was a warm sunny day and new freckles, baby ones, had sprung up across Lola's tanned nose. He'd rolled her onto her back and teased her about them, holding her arms above her head so she couldn't dig him in the ribs. And then they'd stopped laughing and gazed into each other's eyes, both recognising that what they were experiencing was one of those perfect moments you never forget.

'Oh Dougie, I love you.' Lola had whispered the words, her voice catching with emotion. 'We'll be together forever, won't we? Promise me we'll be together forever.'

And he had. Furthermore he'd meant it. Now, sitting in the swaying carriage gazing blindly out of the window as the train clattered along singing its mocking song, Doug wondered what could have happened to make it all go so wrong.

'She's gone, love. I'm so sorry. You know what Lola's like once she makes up her mind about something – whoosh, that's it, off like a rocket.'

Dougie couldn't believe it. Lola had left. It was actually happening. One minute everything had been fine and they'd been completely, deliriously happy together, the next minute she'd disappeared off the face of the earth. It wasn't manly and it wasn't something he'd admit to his friends in a million years, but the pain of loss was so devastating it felt as if his heart might actually break.

Instead, struggling to retain his composure, Dougie swallowed the golf ball in his throat. 'Did she say why?'

'Not really.' Blythe shrugged helplessly, as baffled as he was. 'Just said she fancied a change. Her friend Jeannie was moving to Majorca, they met up for a chat and the next day Lola announced that she was going out there with Jeannie. To *live*. Well, we were shocked! And I did ask her if she'd thought things through, what with you two having been so close, but there was no stopping her. I really am sorry, love. She should have told you herself.'

It didn't help that Lola's mother was looking at him as if he were an abandoned puppy in a cardboard box; she was sympathetic but there was nothing she could do.

'Do you have a phone number for her? An address?'

'Sorry, love, I can't do that. She doesn't want you to contact her. I think she just feels you have your own lives to lead.' Lola's mum struggled to console him.

As if anything could. Dougie raked his fingers through his hair in desperation. 'Is she seeing someone else?'

'No.' Vigorously Blythe shook her head. 'Definitely not that.'

He didn't know if that made things better or worse. Being dumped in favour of someone else was one thing, but being dumped in favour of no one at all was an even bigger kick in the teeth. Controlling his voice with difficulty, Dougie said, 'Can you do me a favour? Just tell her that if she changes her mind, she knows where I am.'

'I'll do that, love.' For a moment Blythe's blue eyes swam and she looked as if she might be about to fling her arms around him. Terrified that if she did he might burst into tears and ruin his street cred for life, Dougie hurriedly stepped away from the front door.

'Thanks.'

Chapter 3

Seven Years Ago

'Oh Lola, look at you.' Squeezing her tightly, Blythe slipped instantly into mother hen mode. 'It's February. You'll catch your death of cold!'

'Mum, I'm twenty, you're not allowed to nag me any more.' But secretly Lola enjoyed it. Hugging her mother in return, she then teasingly lifted the hem of her top to show off her toffee-brown Majorcan tan.

'You'll be frostbitten once we get outside.' Taking one of Lola's squashy travelling bags, Blythe began threading her way through the crowded airport to the exit. 'Are you sure you don't want to pull a jumper out of your case?'

'Quite sure. What's the point of being browner than anyone else and covering it all up with a jumper? Oh Mum, stop a moment, let me hug you again. I've missed you so much.'

'You daft thing. How's it going with Stevie?'

'It's gone. I'm not seeing him any more. We drifted apart.' Lola smiled to show how little it mattered. Stevie had been fun but their relationship had never been serious. Patting her stomach she said, 'And I'm starving. Are we going straight home or shall I pick up a burger here?'

'No burgers today. We're eating out. Alex is treating us to lunch,' said Blythe. 'He's booked a table at Emerson's in Piccadilly.'

'Whoo-hoo, lunch at Emerson's. There's posh,' Lola marvelled. 'What have we done to deserve this?'

Blythe gave her arm a squeeze. 'No special reason, love. It's just wonderful to have you back.'

Her mother had been lying. There was a special reason. Alex waited until they'd chosen their food before ordering a bottle of champagne.

'Alex, have you gone mad?' And it was real champagne. This was plain reckless; when Lola had been growing up she'd never even been allowed proper Coca-Cola at home, only the pretend kind because it was cheaper.

'I'm out of the business,' said Alex as the waiter brought the bottle to the table.

'Oh no.' Lola's heart sank; then again she'd always known it was a risky venture. Following her departure from home three years ago, Alex had given up gambling, just like that. Since that terrible time when they'd almost lost him he hadn't so much as joined in a sweepstake on the Grand National. He had given up visiting his snooker club too. Instead he had stayed at home every night, becoming more and more interested in the business opportunities being offered up by the fast-expanding internet. When he'd come up with a germ of an idea for a web-based hotel booking service, Lola had listened and nodded politely without really understanding how it might work. As far as she was concerned Alex could have been yabbering away in Elvish. All this internetty stuff sounded pretty far-fetched to her; she'd had very little to do with it herself.

23

But Alex had persisted, eventually setting up a company and working on it in his spare time. Then last year he'd given up his job at the garage in order to devote more hours to it. Lola had been under the impression that things were going rather well.

Oh God . . . she hoped he hadn't slipped and gone back to gambling.

'So.' Here came the sick feeling of dread again. 'What went wrong?'

Alex's eyes crinkled at the corners, the lines emphasised by the light from the candle on the table.

'Nothing went wrong. It was too much for me to handle. I'd have needed to take on staff, find proper offices . . . I couldn't deal with everything myself.'

Lola nodded. 'Mum said you were working all hours.'

'I never imagined it would take off like that. It was incredible, but it was scary. Then another company approached me,' Alex explained. 'They offered to buy me out.'

'Oh! Well, that must have been a relief.' As long as Alex wasn't gambling again, she was happy.

'It is a relief.' Alex gravely nodded in agreement and raised his fizzing glass. 'So here's to us.'

'To us.' Lola enthusiastically clinked glasses with them both and took a big gulp of delicious icy-cold champagne.

'By the way,' said Alex, 'I sold the business for one point six million.'

Luckily the champagne had already disappeared down her throat, otherwise she'd have sprayed it across the table like a garden sprinkler.

'Are you *serious*?'

'It's true!' Blythe's eyes danced. 'You don't know how hard

it's been for me not to tell you. I nearly blurted it out at the airport!'

'My God,' Lola breathed.

'And this is for you.' Alex took a folded cheque from his inside pocket and passed it across the table.

'My *God*.' Lola's hands began to tremble as she counted the noughts, then recounted them. For several seconds she couldn't speak. Her mother had never found out about the traumatic events of three years ago, which made it all the more difficult to say what she wanted to say. But Alex, although he hadn't needed to, was paying her back many, many times over. It was too late, but he so badly wanted to make amends for what she had been forced to do in order to save her family.

Finally, unsteadily, Lola said, 'Alex, you don't need to do this.'

Their eyes met. He smiled. 'You're my daughter. Why wouldn't I?'

'I said it was too much,' Blythe chimed in proudly, 'but he insisted. Now, you're not to fritter it away!'

'You can afford to move out of that poky little rented apartment of yours,' said Alex, 'and buy yourself a villa up in the hills. That wouldn't be frittering.'

Unable to contain herself, Lola jumped up out of her chair and threw her arms around him. Never mind a villa up in the hills; now she could afford to move back to London and buy herself somewhere to live here.

Because Majorca might be brilliant in many ways, but there really was no place like home.

'*Lola*.' Appalled by the attention she was receiving, Blythe frantically attempted to tug down her daughter's short skirt. 'Stand up straight, for heaven's sake. Everyone's looking at your pants!'

*   *   *

There was always something deliciously disorientating about emerging from a dark, candlelit restaurant at three thirty in the afternoon and discovering that it was still daylight outside, albeit chilly grey city daylight.

But the greyness didn't matter, because it only made the brightly illuminated shops all the more enticing. Like a human magnet Lola found herself being drawn irresistibly in the direction of the biggest, sparkliest shops.

'We'll leave you to it.' Her mother and Alex couldn't be persuaded to join her. 'Don't spend too much.'

'Mum, I haven't been home for four months! I've got some catching up to do.'

'Maybe a nice warm coat.' Blythe could never resist a dig.

When they'd headed back to the car, Lola threaded her way through the narrow back streets of Piccadilly until she reached Regent Street. Oh yes, here they were, the department stores she'd missed so much, with their elegant beauty halls and perfume departments and escalators that led to other floors awash with yet more gorgeous things to lust over . . .

Better still, here was Kingsley's.

Lola paused at the entrance, savouring the moment. Department stores were fabulous but they still came second to bookshops in her heart. Alcudia in Majorca had many things going for it but the sad collection of battered and faded English-language paper-backs on the rickety carousels in the beachfront souvenir shops wasn't one of them. She craved a proper bookshop like an addict craves a fix. There really wasn't much that could beat that gorgeous new-book smell, touching the covers and turning the pages of a book whose pages had, just possibly, never been turned before.

And if it was weird to feel like that, well, she just didn't care. Some people were obsessed with shoes and loved them with a passion. Shoes were fine but you couldn't stay up all night reading one, could you?

Anyway, it was freezing out here on the pavement; she might as well be naked for all the good her clothes were doing. With a delicious shiver of anticipation Lola plunged into the welcoming warmth of Kingsley's.

Oh, look at them all. So many books, so little time. All those piles and piles of delicious hardbacks with glossy covers, crying out to be bought and devoured. Lola ran her fingers over them, prolonging the moment and not realising she had a dopey smile on her face until another customer caught her eye and smiled back.

'Sorry.' Several glasses of champagne over lunch had loosened her tongue. 'I live in Majorca, so it's been a while since I saw so many books.'

The man's ears promptly glowed pink. 'Lucky you. So, um, whereabouts in Majorca?'

'Alcudia, up on the north side of the island.'

'I know Alcudia!' The man, who was middle-aged, blurted out, 'I go there with my mother every year. We stay in an apartment in the old town. What a coincidence!'

Hmm, not *that* much of one, seeing as a zillion holiday-makers invaded Alcudia each year, but Lola was touched by his enthusiasm. 'Well, I work in a restaurant down by the harbour. So if you fancy some great seafood next time you're there, you'll have to drop by for a meal.'

The man's face was by this time so scarlet with excitement that she began to fear for his blood pressure. 'That sounds most enjoyable. Mother isn't tremendously keen on seafood, but I daresay chef could whisk her up an omelette as a special favour to you.' He hesitated. 'Unless . . . um, are you very expensive?'

'Not expensive at all. In fact, very reasonable. And you can ask for anything you like. We're very obliging,' Lola assured him with a smile. 'You'll have a great time, that's a promise.'

The man, who clearly didn't get out much, said eagerly, 'What's the name of the place? And whereabouts exactly are you? You'd better give me directions.'

'I can do better than that.' Flipping open her silver handbag, Lola fished out one of the restaurant's business cards and handed it over.

'Thanks.' The man beamed. He squirrelled it away and checked his watch. 'It's a date, then. Gosh, is that the time? I need to get to a cashpoint before—'

'Excuse me,' barked a voice behind them, 'that's *quite* enough. I'm going to have to ask you to leave.'

Bemused, Lola turned and saw that she was being addressed by a big-boned, grey-haired female member of staff who was positively aquiver with disapproval.

'I'm sorry, are you speaking to me?'

'Ha, don't give *me* any of your smart talk. Come on, off you go, leave our customers alone.' The woman stuck out her arm, pointing to the door like a traffic cop. 'Out, out. We don't need your sort in here.'

'*What?*' Lola's mouth dropped open; was the woman completely deranged? Half laughing in disbelief, she turned to the man next to her but he was backing away, petrified.

'Plying your filthy trade in here, pestering genuine customers,' the woman went on furiously. 'It's disgusting and I won't have it happening in this shop.'

'Plying my *trade*?' Lola's eyebrows shot up. 'What are you talking about? I'm not a prostitute!'

'Don't argue with me, young lady. I heard what you were saying to that gentleman. Look at you!' The woman jabbed an accusing finger at Lola's skimpy white top, abbreviated lime-green skirt and long bare legs. 'It's perfectly clear what you are!' She turned to the man for back-up. 'What did you think when you saw her?'

'Um . . . well . . .' In an agony of embarrassment he stammered, 'I s-suppose she is r-rather exotically dressed.'

Oh, for crying out loud.

'I live in Majorca! I just flew back today! I didn't know it was going to be this cold here! Tell her what we were talking about,' Lola demanded, but it was too late. Mortified, the man had scurried out of the shop.

'And you can get out too, before I call the police.' The woman wore a look of triumph. 'This is a respectable shop and we don't need people like you coming in here, reeking of drink and propositioning innocent men.'

Walking out now wasn't an option; it simply wasn't in Lola's nature. If someone said, 'don't touch that, it's hot', she had to touch it to discover how hot. If they said, 'don't jump off that wall, you'll hurt yourself', she was compelled to jump off the wall to find out just how much it would hurt.

The woman, she now saw from the name badge, was an assistant called Pat.

'I came in here to buy books and I'll leave when I've bought them.' Refusing to be intimidated, Lola said coolly, 'But before I go, I'll be having a word with your manager.'

Fifteen minutes later she made her way to the till with an armful of books, aware that word of her set-to with Pat had spread around the store. Pat was no longer anywhere in sight. Other members of staff were covertly observing her from a distance. The young lad on the till rang up Lola's purchases and did his best not to look at her legs.

'Could I speak to the manager please?' said Lola.

He nodded, picked up the phone and muttered a few words into it.

Lola waited.

Finally a door at the back opened and a slender woman in her forties emerged.

It was like the gunfight at the OK Corral.

The woman approached Lola and said, 'I'm so sorry about Pat, she's just been telling me what happened and I'd like to apologise on behalf of Kingsley's. The thing is, Pat's retiring in six weeks and if you make a formal complaint it'll spoil everything for her.'

'I—'

'And I probably shouldn't be telling you this but she does have a bit of a bee in her bonnet about, um, working girls.' Lowering her voice to a whisper the woman said, 'Her husband, you see, ran off with one and Pat was beside herself, especially when she found out she used to be a man. The girl I mean. Not Pat. Poor thing, she was devastated. So that's why she over-reacted. I'm really, really sorry. I've had a talk with her and she'll never do it again.'

'Well, good,' said Lola. 'I'm happy to hear that.'

The manager looked hopeful. 'So does that mean everything's OK? You won't make an official complaint?'

'No, I won't.'

'Oh thank you! Thank you *so much*.' She clasped Lola's hand in gratitude. 'That's so good of you. Poor old Pat, I know she shouldn't have said those dreadful things, but she's had a tough time and in a way I'm sure you can understand why she'd get upset—'

'I'm not a prostitute,' said Lola.

This stopped the manageress in her tracks.

'Oh!' Covering her surprise, the woman hastily backtracked. 'Of course you aren't! I didn't mean it to sound like that! Heavens, of *course* I didn't think that!'

Lola grinned because an outfit that wouldn't merit so much as a second glance in Alcudia clearly held other connotations in a London bookshop in chilly November. Maybe the time had come to start modifying her wardrobe.

'I think you did. Don't worry about it. And you haven't asked me yet why I wanted to see you.'

The woman looked flustered. 'Right. Sorry, I'm in a bit of a muddle now. So why did you want to see me?'

'This.' Lola tapped the sign on the counter, identical to the one she'd spotted in the window earlier. 'It says you have a vacancy for a sales assistant.'

'We do. To replace Pat when she leaves.'

Better and better.

'Do you need many qualifications for that?'

'You need to love books.'

'I love books,' said Lola.

The manageress looked stunned. 'You mean *you're* interested? In *this* job?'

It was clearly an extraordinary request. 'Sorry, would I not be allowed to work here?'

'It's not that! I just thought Pat said you lived abroad.'

Lola smiled at the woman and said, 'I think it's time I moved back.'

Chapter 4

Present Day

'You work where? In a bookies?'

'In a book*shop*.' Even as she yelled the words above the blaring music, Lola wondered why she was bothering. 'Kingsley's. I'm the manager of the Regent Street branch.'

'God, rather you than me. Books are boring.' The boy winked and leered over the rim of his beer glass at Lola, evidently convinced of his own irresistibility. He had super-gelled hair and a knowing grin. Having subjected her to a slow, apprecia-tive once-over he said, 'Nah, you're having me on. You don't look like the manager of a bookshop.'

What she *could* have said in reply to this was, 'Well, you don't look like a dickhead, but you clearly are one.'

'Well, I am,' Lola said patiently. 'I promise.'

'You should be wearing granny glasses and, like, a scuzzy old cardigan or something. And no make-up.'

Lola knew what she should be doing; she should be punching the stupid smirk off his face. Aloud she said, 'I'm guessing you don't go into many bookshops.'

'Me? No way.' Proudly the boy said, 'Can't stand reading, waste of time. Hey, fancy a drink?'

'No thanks. Can't stand drinking, waste of time.'

He looked shocked. 'Really?'

'Not really. But drinking with you would be a huge waste of time.' Lola excused herself and made her way over to the bar where Gabe, whose leaving party it was, was chatting to a group of friends from work.

'Gabe? I'm going to head home.'

He turned, horrified. 'No! It's only nine o'clock.'

'I know. I just feel like an early night.'

'An early *what*? Hang on, where's the real Lola?' Gabe inspected her face closely. 'Tell me what you've done with her.'

Lola grinned, because she was as mystified as he was; she absolutely wasn't the early night type. Parties were normally her favourite thing.

'I know it's weird. Maybe I'm going down with something. Anyway, you have a great time.' Reaching up and giving Gabe a hug she said, 'I'll knock on your door with tea and Panadol in the morning.'

He looked even more alarmed. 'Make it tomorrow evening and I might be awake.'

Lola left the bar, shivering as a splatter of icy rain slapped her in the face. If it was raining, the chances of managing to flag down a cab were slim to nil so she set off in the direction of the tube, tugging her cropped velvet jacket around her in an attempt to huddle up against the cold and click-clacking along the pavement in her pink sparkly heels.

It wasn't as if it was Gabe's only leaving party; this was just a motley collection of people from the offices where he worked as a chartered surveyor. *Had* worked there, anyway, for the past four years, although as from today he was out of a job and ready for the adventure of a lifetime in Australia.

Lola made her way down the street, pleased for Gabe but aware of how much she would miss him. When she'd moved back to London seven years ago with the unexpected windfall from the sale of Alex's business burning a hole in her bank account, she had fallen in love with the third flat she'd visited.

She'd felt a bit like Goldilocks on that eventful day. The first flat, in Camden, had been too small. The second, in Islington, had been larger but too dark and gloomy and had smelled of mushrooms.

Happily, the third had been just right. In fact it had exceeded Lola's wildest dreams. Radley Road was a pretty street in Notting Hill where the houses were multicoloured – like Balamory! Yes! – and number 73 was azure blue and white. On the second floor was Flat 73B, a spacious one-bed apartment with a view from the living room over the street below and windows big enough to let the sun stream in. The kitchen and the bathroom were both tiny but clean. The moment Lola had stood in that flat she'd known she had to have it. It was calling her name.

Never one to take her time and ask sensible probing questions, she had swung round to the estate agent with tears of joy in her eyes, clasped her hands to her chest and exclaimed, 'It's perfect. I want to buy it! This is The One!'

Whereas what she *should* have said was, 'Hmm, not too bad I suppose. What are the neighbours like?'

But she hadn't, thereby allowing the super-smooth estate agent to send up a silent prayer of thanks for hopelessly impulsive property buyers everywhere and say jovially, 'That's what I like to see, a girl who knows her own mind!'

And Lola, who now knew just how gullible she'd been, had beamed and taken it as a compliment.

But neighbours were an important factor to be taken into consideration, as she had duly discovered on the day she'd moved into Flat 73B. Sharing the second floor, directly across the landing from her, was Flat 73C. Ringing the doorbell that afternoon in order to introduce herself, Lola had been filled with goodwill and happy anticipation.

It had come as something of a shock when the door had been yanked open and a scrawny old man in his eighties had appeared, filled with malevolence and bile.

'What d'you want? You woke me up.'

Lola exclaimed, 'Oh, I'm so sorry, I just came to say hello. I'm Lola Malone, your new neighbour!'

'And?'

'Um, well, I just moved in across the hall. This afternoon!'

The man eyed her with naked dislike. 'So I heard, all that bloody racket you made getting your stuff upstairs.'

'But—'

Too late. He'd already slammed the door in her face.

His name was Eric, Lola later discovered, and while he wouldn't put up with any noise from her, he wasn't averse to making plenty himself. He played the trumpet, quite astonishingly badly, at any hour of the day or night. He liked his TV to be on at full blast, possibly so he could carry on listening to it while he was playing his trumpet. He also cooked tripe at least three times a week and the smell permeated Lola's flat like . . . well actually, quite a lot like boiled cow's stomach.

Oh yes, she'd gone and got herself a living, breathing nightmare of a neighbour. Too late, Lola realised why the estate agent, upon handing over the key on completion, had given her that cheery wink and said, 'Good luck!'

Having respect for one's elders was all very well, but Eric was a filthy-tempered, cantankerous old stoat who'd done everything in his power to make her life a misery.

After two years of this, Eric had died and Lola was just relieved he'd been out at his day centre when it happened; as her co-workers at Kingsley's had pointed out, if he'd been found dead in his flat, everyone would have suspected her of bumping him off.

But the reign of Eric was over now, the flat had been cleaned up and put on the market, and Lola crossed her fingers, hoping for better luck this time.

And it had worked. She'd got gorgeous Gabe – hooray! – and like magic the quality of her home life had improved out of all recognition, because he was the best neighbour any girl could ask for.

Better still, she hadn't fancied him one bit.

Gabriel Adams, with his floppy blond hair and lean slouchy body, had been twenty-nine when he'd moved into the flat across the landing from her. And this time *he* had been the one who'd knocked on Lola's door to invite her over for a drink on his roof terrace.

Which meant she liked him already.

'I never even knew there was a roof terrace.' Lola marvelled at the view from the back of the house; it was like discovering a tropical island complete with hula girls in your dusty old broom cupboard.

'It's a suntrap.' Gabe grinned at her. 'I think I'm going to like it here. Does this T-shirt make me look gay?'

Since it was a vibrant shade of lilac, clearly expensive and quite tight-fitting, Lola said, 'Well, a bit.'

36

'I know, it's too much. I'm super-tidy and a great cook. I can't wear this as well.' Pulling off the T-shirt to reveal an enviably tanned torso, Gabe held it towards her. 'Do you want it or shall I chuck it away?'

It wasn't just expensive, Lola discovered. It was Dolce and Gabbana. Liking her new neighbour more and more she said, 'I'll have it. Are you sure?'

'Sure I'm sure. The colour'll suit you. Better than me chucking it in the back of a drawer and never wearing it again.'

Except it wasn't, because a week later as she was on her way out one evening, Lola bumped into Gabe and his girlfriend on their way in. The girlfriend, who had flashing dark eyes and an arm snaked possessively around Gabe's waist, stopped dead in her tracks and said, 'What are you doing wearing my boyfriend's T-shirt?'

'Um . . . well, he g-gave it to . . .' Catching the look on Gabe's face, Lola amended hastily, 'I mean, he *lent* it to me, because I, um, asked if I could borrow it.'

The girlfriend shot her a killer glare before swinging round to Gabe. 'I bought you that for your birthday! Don't go lending it out to some girl just because she's cheeky enough to ask to borrow it.'

The thing was, Gabe hadn't done it on purpose. He hadn't meant to cause trouble, he was simply thoughtless and so generous himself it didn't occur to him that some people might not appreciate his actions.

But he broke up with that particular girl shortly afterwards and Lola had been able to start wearing the T-shirt again. From then on a stream of girlfriends came and went, entranced by the fact that Gabe was an entertaining, charming commitment-phobe. Each of them in turn was utterly convinced they would be the one to make him see the error of his ways and suddenly yearn for a life of monogamous domestic bliss.

Each of them, needless to say, was wrong.

Or had been, up until three months ago when Gabe had met an Australian backpacker called Jaydena on the last leg of her round-the-world trip. Jaydena had bucked the trend and been the one to leave Gabe, returning to Sydney when they'd only known each other for a couple of weeks and were still completely crazy about each other. Back in Australia, she emailed Gabe every day and he emailed her back. Within weeks she'd persuaded him to jack in his job and fly out to join her.

Lola was stunned when she heard. 'But . . . *why*?'

'Because I've never been to Australia and everyone says it's an incredible place. If I don't go now I could regret it forever.'

'So I might never see you again.' It was a daunting prospect; Gabe was such a huge part of her life. And not only for the fun times. When Alex had died five years ago – suddenly, and desperately unfairly, of a heart attack – Lola had been distraught, unable to believe she'd never see her beloved father again. But Gabe had been a rock, helping her through that awful period. She'd always be grateful to him for that.

'Hey, I'm not selling the flat, just renting it out for a year. After that I could be back.'

Lola knew she would miss him terribly but alarm bells were ringing for another, far less altruistic reason. 'Where are you going to find a new tenant? Through a lettings agency?'

'Ha!' Gabe gleefully prodded her in the ribs. 'So it's only yourself you're worried about, panicking at the thought of who your new neighbour might be.'

'No. Well yes, that too.'

'Already sorted. Marcus from work just split up with his wife. He's moving in.'

Oh. Lola relaxed, because she knew Marcus and he was all right, if a bit on the boring side and inclined to yabber on about motorcycles. Which could well have had something to do with his marriage breaking up.

'So no need to panic,' said Gabe. 'All taken care of. You two'll get along fine.'

'Good.' Visualising Marcus in his oil-stained, unfashionable clothes, Lola said, 'But I can't see me borrowing his T-shirts.'

Ugh, it was raining harder than ever now. Wishing she was wearing flatter shoes, Lola hurried along the road with her jacket collar up, then turned left down the side street that was a short cut to the tube station. She winced as her left foot landed in a puddle and—

'Get off me, get off! Noooo!'

Chapter 5

Lola's head jerked up, her heart thudding in her chest at the sight of the violent scene unfolding ahead of her. The woman's piercing screams filled the air. as she was dragged out of the driver's seat of her car by two men who flung her roughly to the ground. One of them knelt over her, ripping at something on the woman's hand. When she struggled against him he hit her in the face and snarled, 'Shut *up.*'

But the woman let out another shriek of fright and he hit her again, harder this time, bouncing her head off the road. 'I said *shut* it. Now give me your rings.'

'No! *Owww.*' The woman groaned as he wrenched back her arm.

'Leave her alone!' bellowed Lola, punching 999 into her phone and gasping, 'Police, ambulance, Keveley Street.' Filled with a boiling rage, she kicked off her shoes and raced down the road to the car. 'Get off her!'

'Yeah, right.' The man sneered while his cohort revved the engine of the woman's car.

'Come on,' bellowed the cohort, 'hurry up, hurry up.'

'Stop it!' Lola grabbed hold of the attacker's greasy hair and yanked his head back hard, shocked to see in the darkness that the face of the woman was covered in blood. 'Leave her alone, I've called the police.'

'Let go of me,' roared the man, fighting to free himself.

'No, I won't.' Grappling with him on the ground, Lola smelled alcohol on his fetid breath and felt ice-cold rain seeping through her tights. The woman was lying on her side facing away from her, curled up and moaning with pain. The man swore again and twisted like an eel to escape but Lola had him now and she was damned if she'd let him go before the—

CRRRACKK, an explosion of noise and pain filled Lola's head and she realised the other attacker had hit her from behind with some kind of weapon. Then everything melted and went black and she slumped to the ground.

As if from a great distance Lola heard the screech of tyres as the car accelerated away. Close to, the woman groaned. Without opening her eyes, Lola stretched out an arm, encountered the woman's foot and clumsily patted it.

'S'OK, you're all right, just hang on and the police'll be here.' God, she felt so sick. The pain at the back of her head was intense. But the woman next to her in the road was now sobbing hysterically, in need of reassurance and comfort.

'Th-they tricked m-me, I th-thought someone was hurt . . . then when I stopped the c-c-car they d-dragged me out . . .'

'Hey, hey, don't be upset.' Lola stroked the woman's leg, the only part of her she could reach. 'I can hear sirens, someone's coming, you're OK now.'

'I'm not OK, there's b-blood everywhere, he punched me in the face and b-broke my n-nose.'

'Sshh, don't cry.' Squeezing the woman's calf and shivering

41

with cold, Lola forced down a rising swell of nausea. 'Here's the ambulance. I hope they don't run over my shoes . . .'

The next twenty minutes were a confusing blur. Lola was dimly aware that she was having trouble answering the questions put to her by the paramedics and the police. She hoped they didn't think she was paralytic with drink. Blue flashing lights gave the otherwise pitch-black street the look of an eerie disco but no one was dancing. Requested to hold out an outstretched arm then touch her nose with her forefinger, Lola missed and almost took her eye out. Asked to name the Prime Minister she struggled to put a name to the face floating around in her mind. 'Hang on, don't tell me, I know it . . . I know it . . . is it Peter Stringfellow?'

The other woman had already been whisked off to hospital in the first ambulance. When a second arrived in the narrow, suddenly busy street and a stretcher was brought out, Lola waved her hands and protested, 'No, no, I can't go to the party, I've got work tomorrow.'

'You need to be checked over, love. You were knocked out.'

'I know I'm a knockout.' Lola beamed up at the curiously attractive paramedic . . . OK, so he was in his fifties and resembled a pig but he had lovely eyes. 'Will you dance with me?'

'Course I will, love. Just as soon as you're better.' He grinned down at her.

'You're gorgeous.' How on earth had she never found big double chins and enormous stomachs attractive before?

'I know, I know. Johnny Depp, that's me.'

'No you're not, you're way better than him.' As she was expertly lifted onto the stretcher Lola gazed adoringly up at the paramedic and wondered why he was swaying back and forth. 'You look like Hagrid.'

'Mum, I'm fine. They've X-rayed my skull and checked me out all over. It was just a bash on the head.' Gingerly Lola leaned forward in bed to show her mother the egg-sized bump. 'They're discharging me later. They only kept me in overnight because I was knocked out for a few seconds and when I came round I was a bit muddled.'

'So I've just been hearing in the nurses' office,' said Blythe. 'Apparently you were hilarious, propositioning one of the poor ambulance men. I can't believe you did something so ridiculous.'

'It wasn't my fault! I was concussed!'

'I don't mean that. I'm talking about you launching yourself into a dangerous situation. You could have been killed.'

This had occurred to Lola too; at the time she'd simply acted on impulse although in retrospect it had been a bit of a reckless thing to do. 'But I wasn't. And I'm OK.' Apart from the blistering headache. 'Could you give work a ring and tell them I should be in tomorrow?'

'I most certainly will not. I'll tell them you might be in next week, depending on how you feel.'

'Mum, how are *they* going to feel if you tell them that? It's December! Everyone's rushed off their feet!'

'And you were knocked unconscious,' Blythe retorted. 'Anything could have happened. My God, for once in your life will you listen to me?'

A man who'd been walking up the ward stopped and said genially, 'It always pays to do as your mother tells you.'

He was in his sixties, well-spoken and smartly dressed in a

suit. Was this her consultant? Lola sat up a bit straighter in bed and smiled expectantly, all ready to convince him that she was well enough to be allowed home. After last night's debacle with the paramedic she'd better put on a good show.

'Miss Malone?'

'That's me.' Eagerly Lola nodded. To prove her brain was in good working order, he'd probably ask her the kind of questions doctors used on old people when they wanted to find out if they were on the ball. OK, what was the capital of Australia? What was thirty-three times seven? Yeesh, don't let him ask her to name the Shadow Chancellor of the Exchequer.

'Hello.' He moved towards her, smiling and extending his hand.

'Hi!' Quick, was it Melbourne? Victoria? Lola's brain was racing. People always thought it was Sydney but she knew it definitely wasn't. Might he give her half a point for that, at least?

The man shook her hand warmly. 'It's very nice to meet you. I'm Philip Nicholson.'

He even smelled delicious. Watching him turn to shake her mother's hand, Lola breathed in his expensive aftershave. Goodness, what charming manners, this was like being in a private hospital and getting – *ooh, was it Perth?*

'I just had to come and see you,' he went on.

'Well, I suppose you couldn't avoid it. All part of the job description!' Lola beamed at him, aware that he was looking at her head. Touching the tender area she said, 'Bit of a bump, that's all. I'm absolutely fine. Except, can I just quickly tell you that I'm rubbish at capital cities?'

Philip Nicholson hesitated and glanced over at Blythe, who shrugged and looked baffled.

44

'In case that's what you were going to ask me,' Lola hurriedly explained. 'I mean, some are all right, like Paris and Amsterdam and Madrid, they're easy, and I *do* happen to know that the capital of Azerbaijan is Baku, but in general I have to say that capitals aren't my strong point.' To be on the safe side she added, 'Neither's politics.'

Carefully Dr Nicholson said, 'That's not a problem. I won't ask any questions about either subject.'

'Phew, what a relief.' Lola relaxed back against her piled-up pillows. 'I'd hate to be kept in just because I couldn't name the leader of the Liberal Democrats.'

Dr Nicholson cleared his throat and said, 'I'm sure that wouldn't happen.'

'Well, hopefully not, but sometimes you *do* know the answer and you just can't think of it. Someone fires a question at you, you know it's important to get it right and – boom! – your mind goes blank!'

'Of course it does.' He nodded understandingly.

'Like, let's try it with you.' Lola waggled an index finger at him. 'Capital of Australia.'

Dr Nicholson hesitated. Blythe, never able to resist a quiz question, let out a squeak of excitement and raised her arm. Lola swung the pointing finger round and barked in Paxmanesque fashion, '*Yes*, Mum?'

'Sydney!'

'No it *isn't*.' Lola returned her attention to Dr Nicholson. 'Your turn.'

He was looking somewhat taken aback. Opening his mouth to reply, he—

'Brisbane!'

'Sshh, Mum. It isn't your go.'

45

'Um . . .'

'Melbourne!' squealed Blythe.

'Mum, control yourself. It's Dr Nicholson's turn.'

At this, his shoulders relaxed and his mouth began to twitch. 'It's Canberra. And I've just worked out what's going on. I'm not Dr Nicholson, by the way.'

Bemused, Lola said, 'No?'

He smiled. 'Entirely my fault. I knew the police had told you our name last night and I kind of assumed you'd remember. But you were concussed. I'm sorry, let's start again. My name's Philip Nicholson and I'm here to thank you from the bottom of my heart for coming to my wife's rescue. You did an incredibly brave thing and I can't begin to tell you how grateful we are.' His voice thickened with emotion. 'Those thugs could have killed her if you hadn't gone to help.'

Lola clapped her hand over her mouth. 'I thought you were my consultant, coming to check whether I was compos mentis.'

Philip Nicholson looked amused. 'I realise that now.'

'Phew! Just as well I didn't think you were here to examine my chest.' God, imagine if she'd whipped her top off, that would've given him a bit of a start.

'Quite.'

'How's your wife this morning?' said Lola.

'Well, still shocked. Battered and bruised. Two broken fingers.' There was a hard edge to his voice now. 'Where they tried to wrench her rings off.'

'Did they get them?'

'No. Which is also thanks to you. She's pretty shaken up, and her face is swollen. But physically it could have been a lot worse.' Philip Nicholson shook his head and slowly exhaled. 'My wife and I owe you so much.'

46

Lola squirmed, embarrassed. 'Anyone would have done the same.'

'No they wouldn't,' Blythe retorted. 'Most people would have had more sense.'

Their visitor nodded. 'I'm inclined to agree. Though very grateful, of course, that your daughter wasn't—'

'Hello, hello! Morning, all!' A little man wearing a maroon corduroy jacket over a green hand-knitted sweater came bouncing up to them. Pumping Lola's hand and simultaneously pulling closed the curtains around the bed, he said, 'I'm Dr Palmer, your consultant. Let's just give you a quick once-over, shall we? If you two could leave us alone for ten minutes that'd be marvellous. I say, that's a fair-sized bump on your head. How are you feeling after your little adventure last night?'

'Great.' Lola watched as with mesmerising speed he began testing her reflexes, her eyes, her co-ordination. 'Are you going to be asking me questions?'

'Absolutely.'

She couldn't help feeling a bit smug. 'The capital of Australia is Canberra.'

'Good grief, is it really? Always thought it was Sydney. Never been much good at capital cities, I'm afraid. When I'm checking out my patients I prefer to ask them sums. What's twenty-seven times sixty-three?'

'Uh . . . um . . .' Lola began to panic; seven threes were twenty-one, carry two and—

'Only kidding.' Mr Palmer's eyes twinkled as he snatched up her notes. 'What day is it today?'

'Wednesday the fourth of December.' Phew, that was more like it, that was the kind of question she could answer.

'Cheers.' He wrote the date on a fresh page then added o/e NAD.

'What does NAD mean?' Lola peered at it. 'Please don't say Neurotic and Demented.'

The consultant chuckled. 'On examination, no abnormality detected.'

'My mother might not agree with you there. So does that mean I can go home?'

'I think we can let you go.'

Beaming, Lola wiggled her feet. 'Yay.'

'What a charming man.' Blythe, evidently quite bowled over by Philip Nicholson, found Lola's glittery shoes in the bottom of her bedside locker. 'And so grateful. His wife's on Ward Thirteen, up on the next floor. Poor thing, from the sound of it her face is a terrible mess. I think they're going to be sending you flowers, by the way. He asked for your address.'

'If they're that grateful they might send me chocolates too. Did you phone work?'

'I did. Told them you wouldn't be in until next week.'

'Who did you speak to? What did they say?'

'It was Cheryl.' Blythe held out the cropped velvet jacket as if Lola were six years old. 'And it was quite hard to hear what she was saying. Everyone was cheering so loudly when they heard you were going to be away, I could hardly make out a word.'

'Cheek. Everyone loves me at work. Honestly,' said Lola, 'if Philip Nicholson wants to get me something really useful, a new mother wouldn't go amiss.'

Chapter 6

'This is fantastic. I feel like the Queen.' Being at home and having a fuss made of her was a huge novelty and Lola was relishing every minute. Once you'd been officially signed off work by the doctor, well, you may as well lie back and make the most of it. Friends called in, bringing chocolate croissants and gossip from the outside world, a couple of police officers had dropped by to tell her that the muggers hadn't been caught, and Blythe had come over yesterday and spring-cleaned – well, winter-cleaned – the flat.

Best of all, she had Gabe at her beck and call.

'You're a fraud.' He brought in the cheese and mushroom toasted sandwich he'd just made. 'You don't have to be in bed.'

'I know.' Lola happily patted her ultra-squishy goosedown duvet, all puffed up around her like a cloud, and wriggled into a more comfortable sitting position. 'But I get so much more sympathy this way. It's like being back at school and staying home with tonsillitis. All cosy, watching daytime TV, everyone being extra-nice to you and knowing you're missing double physics. Ooh,' she bit into the toasted sandwich and caught a string of melted cheese before it attached itself to her chin.

'*Mmmmpphh,* this is heaven. Oh Gabe, don't go to Australia. Stay here and make toasted sandwiches for me forever.'

Gabe found her toes and tweaked them. 'What did your last slave die of?'

'Nothing. I've never had a slave before, but now I definitely know I want one.' At that moment the doorbell rang downstairs. 'Like when the doorbell rings,' said Lola. 'And you just ask someone else to run down and see who it is.'

'That'll be me, then.'

'Sorry. I'd do it myself if I could.' Lola shrugged regretfully. 'But I'm an invalid.'

He was back a couple of minutes later with a great armful of white roses tied with straw and swathed in cellophane. 'Flowers for the lady. From a *very* upmarket florist. Here's the card.' Gabe tossed a peacock-blue envelope over to Lola. 'Unless you want me to read it for you because you're too ill.'

'I'll manage.' Since she didn't have any friends who would use such a glitzy company, Lola had already guessed the identity of the sender. And she wasn't wrong. 'They're from Philip Nicholson. He hopes I'm feeling better. His wife was discharged from hospital yesterday.' She paused, reading on. 'He's inviting me to a party at their house so I can meet her and they can thank me properly.'

'You can't go to a party. You're an invalid.'

'It's not until next Friday; that's seven days away. I'll be fine by then. It's nice of them to invite me.' Lola hesitated, pulled a face. 'But won't it be a bit embarrassing?'

'Spoken by the girl who once superglued her finger to her forehead and had to wait in casualty for six hours before the nurse could unglue it.'

OK, that had been more embarrassing.

'I'm still not sure. They live in Barnes.' Lola checked the address. 'Sounds posh.'

'You'd hurt their feelings if you didn't turn up.'

This was true.

'And they must want me to go.' She showed Gabe the hand-written letter. 'He's even organised a car to come here and pick me up on the night. Crikey, now I *really* feel like the Queen.' Having finished her toasted sandwich, a thought struck Lola. 'Is there any of that apricot cheesecake left?'

'No, you ate it.'

'Oh. Well, could we buy some more?'

Gabe rolled his eyes. 'You really should get back to work. You're turning into Marie Antoinette.'

Five days later Lola was back. She adored her job and she loved her customers − dealing with the public was her forte − but sometimes they were capable of testing her patience to the limit. Especially in the run-up to Christmas, when vast hordes of people who didn't venture into bookshops at any other time of year came pouring through the doors with a great Need to Buy coupled with Absolutely No Idea What.

It could be an enjoyable challenge. It could also be the road to madness. Lying in bed watching lovely Fern and Phil and dunking marshmallows in hot chocolate seemed like a distant dream.

'No, no, it's none of them.' The woman with the plastic rain hat protecting her hair − why? It wasn't raining today − rejected the array of books Lola had shown her.

'OK, well, that's everything we have in stock about insects. If you like, I can look on the computer and—'

'It's nothing like *any* of these,' the woman retorted. 'There's no pictures in the one I'm after.'

A book about insects containing no illustrations of insects. Hmm, that would probably explain why they didn't stock it.

'Would you recognise the cover if you saw it?'

'No.'

Lola tried for the third time. 'And you really can't remember who wrote it?'

The woman frowned. 'No. I thought you'd know that.'

She was clearly disappointed, feeling badly let down by the incompetence of Kingsley's staff. 'I'm so sorry,' said Lola, 'I can't think how else to do this. I'm afraid we're not going to be able to—'

'Oink, oink!'

Okaaaay. 'Excuse me?'

The woman said triumphantly, 'There's a pig in it!'

A pig. Right. A pig in a book about insects. Zrrrrr, went Lola's brain, assimilating this new and possibly deal-clinching clue. Zzzzrrrrrrrr . . .

'Is it *Lord of the Flies*?'

'Yes! That's the one!'

Lola exchanged a glance with an older male customer currently leafing through a book on the subject of kayaking down the Nile. For a split second she saw the twinkle of suppressed laughter in his eyes and almost lost it herself.

But no. She was a professional. To the woman in the rain hat Lola said cheerfully, 'It's a novel by William Golding. Let me show you where to find it,' and led her off to the fiction section.

When she returned, Kayak Man was waiting to speak to her.

'Hi. Well done with your last customer, by the way.'

'All in a day's work. You nearly made me laugh.'

'Sorry.' He put down the kayak book. 'Anyway, I'm hoping you can help me now.'

Lola smiled; he had a lean, intelligent face. 'Fire away. I like a challenge.'

'Jane Austen. My wife's read all her books. I was wondering, has she written any new ones this year?'

Lola waited for his eyes to twinkle. They didn't. Her heart sank.

'I'm sorry, Jane Austen's dead.'

'She is? Oh, that's a shame, my wife *will* be sorry to hear that. We must have missed her obituary in the *Telegraph*. What did she die of, do you know?'

'Um . . .' What *had* Jane Austen died of? Multiple injuries following a parachuting accident, perhaps? Had she crashed her jet ski? Or how about—

'Lola, there's someone here wanting to speak to you.' It was Cheryl, sounding apologetic. 'A crew from a TV station are interviewing store managers about Christmas shopping and they wondered if you could spare them five minutes. If you're too busy, Tim says he'd be happy to do it.'

'I bet he would.' Tim was besotted with the idea of being on TV; it was the reason he went along to all the film premieres in Leicester Square, why he'd dressed up as a chicken to audition for the *X Factor* (the judges had told him to cluck off) and what had propelled him to stand up while he'd been in the audience on *Trisha* to announce that as a baby he'd been found abandoned in a cardboard box at Victoria station and he was desperate to find his mother. His mum, who'd been ironing a pile of his shirts when the TV programme aired, had given Tim a good clump round the ear when he'd arrived home that afternoon.

'It's OK, I'll do it myself.' When you were having a good hair day it was a shame to waste it. 'Cheryl, can you help this gentleman? His wife's read everything by Jane Austen so I'm wondering if she might enjoy one of the sequels by another author.'

Having excused herself, Lola made her way over to the young male reporter waiting at the tills with a cameraman and his assistant. 'Hi, I'm Lola Malone. Where would you like to do this?'

The reporter said, 'Oh. We're meant to be doing the interview with the manager.'

'I'm the manager.'

'God, are you really?' The male reporter – who looked exactly like a male reporter – eyed Lola's sleek black top, fuchsia pink skirt and long legs in opaque black tights. 'You don't look like the manager of a bookshop.'

'Sorry. Were you expecting someone more frumpy?'

He looked abashed. 'Well, yes, I suppose I was.'

It was a preconception that drove Lola mad and made her want to rattle people's teeth. 'I could run out and buy a grey cardigan if you like.'

'You're joking, no, you look *fantastic*.' He spread his hands in admiration. 'Crikey, I just didn't think . . .'

'You should get out more.' Lola winked, because it was also a preconception she enjoyed shattering. 'Try visiting a few more bookshops. You might be surprised – nowadays, some of us don't even wear tweed.'

Chapter 7

The piece aired on the local evening news two days later. It lasted less than ninety seconds and the reporter had asked some pretty inane questions but Lola, watching herself on TV as she set about her hair with curling tongs, felt she'd acquitted herself well enough. It wasn't easy to be witty and scintillating whilst responding to, 'And here we are, in Kingsley's on Regent Street, with less than a fortnight to go before Christmas! So, just *how* busy has it been here in this store?'

The urge to stretch her arms wide like a fisherman and say, '*This* busy,' had been huge.

'Well?' Still wielding the tongs, Lola turned to look at Gabe when the piece ended.

'Yes, that was definitely you.'

'Was I OK?'

Gabe was busy unwrapping a Twix bar. 'You answered his questions, you didn't burp or swear, or take a swig from a bottle of vodka. That has to be good news.'

'But did I *look* nice?'

'You looked fine and you know it. What time's this car coming?'

'Seven thirty. Should I wear my red dress or the blue one?' Curling completed, Lola bent over and gave her head a vigorous upside-down shake. 'I feel quite jittery. I'm not going to know anyone else there. What if it's all really embarrassing and I want to escape but they won't let me leave?'

'OK, you'll get there around eight. Leave your phone on and I'll ring you at nine,' said Gabe. 'If you're desperate to get away, tell them I'm your best friend and I've gone into labour.'

'My hero. The things you do for me. How am I going to manage without you when you're gone?' Vertical once more, Lola hugged him then made a lightning lunge for the Twix in his hand. She was fast, but not fast enough.

'I'm sure you'll cope.' Gabe broke off an inch and gave it to her. 'You'll soon find some other poor guy's Twix bars to pinch.'

By seven fifteen Lola was ready to go – OK, it was uncool to be punctual but she simply couldn't help herself – and peering out of the window.

'Wouldn't it be great if they sent a stretch limo?'

Gabe looked horrified. 'That would be *so* naff.'

'Why would it? I love them!' OK, she was naff *and* uncool.

'Don't get your hopes up. From the sound of him, this guy has better taste than you. In fact,' Gabe went on as a throaty roar filled the street outside, 'that could be your lift now.'

It was Lola's turn to be appalled. Flinging the window open as the motorbike rumbled to a halt outside, she watched as the helmeted rider dismounted. Surely not. If someone said they were sending a car they wouldn't economise at the last minute and send a motorbike instead. Would they? Oh God, her hair would be *wrecked* . . .

'Hi there, Lola.' Phew, panic over, it was only Marcus.

'Hi there, neighbour-to-be! Come on up,' said Lola. 'Gabe's in my flat at the moment.'

Upstairs in Lola's living room, clutching his motorcycle helmet and looking sheepish, Marcus said, 'All right, mate? The thing is, I've got some good news and some bad news.'

'Go on then,' prompted Gabe.

'Well, me and Carol are back together, she's giving me one last chance. And I'm taking it. Turning over a new leaf. Cool, right? So that's the good news.' An embarrassed grin spread across Marcus's shiny face. 'But that means I won't be moving in here after all, mate. Sorry about that.'

Gabe shrugged, having already pretty much guessed what Marcus had come here to say. 'Well, I suppose I can't blame you. Bit short notice, seeing as I'm off next week.'

'I know. Sorry, mate.'

'I'll have to register with a lettings agency now.'

'I might know someone who could move in.' Eager to help, Marcus said, 'There's a guy at my motorcycling club whose parents are keen to get rid of him. He could be interested.'

Lola pictured a spotty gangly teenager inviting hundreds of his spotty gangly mates round for parties. 'How old is he?'

'Terry? Early fifties. Don't look like that,' Marcus caught the face Lola was pulling at Gabe. 'Terry's a good bloke. And he works in an abattoir,' he went on encouragingly, 'so you'd never go short of pork chops.'

The car, a gleaming black Mercedes, arrived at seven thirty on the dot. It wasn't a stretch limo, but it was without a doubt the cleanest, most valeted car Lola had ever been in, and knowing that you wouldn't have to pay a huge taxi fare at the end made it an even more pleasurable journey. She sat back as the car purred along, feeling like royalty and quite tempted to wave graciously at the poor people trudging along the pavements on the other side of the tinted glass.

The house, when they reached it, was a huge double-fronted Victorian affair in Barnes, as impressive as Lola had imagined. There were plenty of cars in the driveway and discreet twinkling white Christmas lights studding the bay trees in square stone tubs that flanked the super-shiny dark blue front door. Lola was hoping to be sophisticated enough, one day, to confine herself to discreet white Christmas lights; as it was, she was more of a gaudy, every-colour-you-can-think-of girl and all of it as über-bling as humanly possible.

She tried to tip Ken, the driver, but he wouldn't accept her money. Which felt even weirder than not having to pay the fare.

Even the brass doorbell was classy. Lola clutched her Accessorize sequinned handbag to her side – as if anyone was likely to steal it *here* – and took a couple of deep breaths. It wasn't like her to be on edge. How bizarre that attempting to beat up a couple of muggers hadn't been nerve-wracking, yet this was.

Then the door opened and there was Mr Nicholson with his lovely welcoming smile, and she relaxed.

'Lola, you're here! How wonderful to see you again. I'm so glad you were able to come along tonight.' He gave her a kiss on each cheek. 'And you look terrific.'

Compared with the last time he'd seen her, she supposed she must. Not having uncombed, blood-soaked hair was always a bonus.

'It's good to see you too, Mr Nicholson.'

'Please call me Philip. Now, my wife doesn't know I've invited you. You're our surprise guest of honour.' His grey eyes sparkled as he led her across the wood-panelled hall to a door at the far end. 'I can't wait to see her reaction when she realises who you are.'

Philip Nicholson pushed open the door and drew Lola into a huge glittering drawing room full of people, all chattering away and smartly dressed. A thirty-something blonde in aquamarine touched his arm and raised her eyebrows questioningly; when he nodded, she grinned at Lola and whispered, 'Ooh, I'm so excited, this is going to be great!'

'My stepdaughter,' Philip murmured by way of explanation. Nodding again, this time in the direction of the fireplace, he added, 'That's my wife over there, in the orange frock.'

Orange, bless him. Only a man could call it that. The woman, standing with her back to them and talking to another couple, was slim and elegant in a devoré velvet dress in delectable shades of russet, bronze and apricot. Her hair was fashioned in a glamorous chignon and she was wearing pearls around her neck that even from this distance you could tell were real.

Then Philip said, 'Darling . . .' and she swivelled round to look at him. In an instant Lola was seventeen again.

Adele Tennant's gaze in turn fastened on Lola and she took a sharp audible intake of breath.

'My God, what's going on here?' Her voice icy with disbelief, she turned pointedly back to Philip Nicholson. 'Did she just turn up on the doorstep? Are you mad, letting her into the house?'

Poor Philip, his shock was palpable. Lola, who was pretty stunned too, couldn't work out who she felt more sorry for, him or herself.

'How did you find out where I live?' Adele's eyes narrowed

suspiciously. 'How did you track me down? My God, you have a nerve. This is a *private party*—'

'Adele, stop it,' Philip intervened at last, raising his hands in horrified protest. 'This was meant to be a surprise. This is Lola Malone, she—'

'I know it's Lola Malone! I'm not senile, Philip! And if she's come here chasing after my son . . . well, I can tell you, she's got another think coming.'

Yeek, Dougie! As if she'd just been zapped with an electric cattle prod, Lola spun round; was he here in this room? No, no sign of him unless he'd gone bald or had a sex change.

'I'm so sorry.' Philip Nicholson shook his head at Lola by way of apology. 'This is all most unfortunate. Adele, will you stop interrupting and listen? I don't know what's gone on in the past but I invited Lola here tonight because she's the one who came to the rescue when you were mugged.' His voice breaking with emotion he said, 'She saved your *life*.'

And what's more, thought Lola, she's starting to wish she hadn't bothered.

OK, mustn't say that. At least Philip's pronouncement had succeeded in shutting Adele up; while her brain was busy assimilating this unwelcome information her mouth had snapped shut like a bronze-lipglossed trap.

'I thought you'd like the opportunity to thank her in person,' Philip went on, and all of a sudden he sounded like a head-master saddened by the disruptive behaviour of a stroppy teenager.

People were starting to notice now. The couple Adele had been talking to were avidly observing proceedings. The blonde who was Philip's stepdaughter – crikey, that meant she was Dougie's older sister – came over and said, puzzled, 'Mum? Is everything all right?'

'Fine.' Recovering herself, Adele managed the most frozen of smiles and looked directly at Lola. 'So it was you. Well . . . what can I say? Thank you.'

'No problem.' That didn't sound quite right but what else could she say? *My pleasure?*

'It was such a brave thing you did,' exclaimed Dougie's sister. What was her name? Sally, that was it. 'I can't bear to think what might have happened to Mum if you hadn't dived in like that. You were amazing!'

Lola managed to maintain a suitably modest smile, while her memory busily rewound to that eventful night ten days ago. Euurrgh, she had stroked Adele's ankle, she had *squeezed* Adele Tennant's *thigh* . . .

Except she wasn't Adele Tennant any more. She was Adele Nicholson.

'So you remarried,' said Lola, longing to ask about Doug and feeling her stomach clench just at the thought of him.

'Four years ago.' Adele was being forced to be polite now, in a through-gritted-teeth, I-really-wish-you-weren't-here kind of way.

'Congratulations.' Lola wondered what Philip, who was *lovely*, had done to deserve Cruella de Vil as a wife. Presumably Adele did have redeeming qualities; she just hadn't encountered them yet.

'Thank you. Well, it's . . . nice to see you again. Can we offer you a drink? Or,' Adele said hopefully, 'do you have to rush off?'

Rushing off suddenly seemed a highly desirable thing to do. Excellent idea. Since every minute here was clearly set to be an excruciating ordeal, Lola looked at her watch and said, 'Actually, there is somewhere else I need to—'

'Here he is!' cried Sally, her face lighting up as she waved across the room to attract someone's attention. 'Yoohoo, we're over here! And what sort of time do you call this anyway? You're *late*.'

Lola didn't need to turn around. She knew who it was. Some inner certainty told her that Dougie had entered the drawing room; she could *feel* his presence behind her. All of a sudden every molecule in her body was on high alert and she was no longer breathing.

Dougie. Doug. Whom she'd thought she'd never see again.

'Sorry, I was held up at a meeting. Some of us have a proper job. Hi, everyone, how's it going? What have I missed?'

Chapter 8

Lola was zinging all over; now she'd completely forgotten *how* to breathe. Except how embarrassing if she keeled over in a dead faint in front of everyone; when a woman had done that in the shop last summer she'd lost control of her bladder.

Imagine coming round, surrounded by Dougie and his family, and discovering you were lying in a puddle of wee.

But this was the kind of situation you needed time to prepare yourself for, time she hadn't been allowed, and now she was doing her usual thing of being inappropriately flippant. Whereas in reality she was filled with a mixture of giddy excitement – maybe twenty per cent – and eighty per cent fear and trepidation. Because as far as Dougie was concerned, she'd left him without a word, dumped him and run off abroad without a proper explanation. Had ten years been long enough for him to forgive her for that?

'*Well.*' Winking at Lola, Sally spoke with relish. 'Philip invited along a surprise guest . . .'

Who turned out to be one very surprised guest. Lola dug her nails into her palms – welcome the pain, welcome the pain and *don't* pass out – and turned round to look at him.

'Hello, Dougie.'

For a split second their eyes locked and it was as if the last decade had never happened. Doug looked the same but taller, broader, *better*. He'd always had the looks, the ability to stop girls dead in their tracks, and now here he was, having that exact same effect, doing it to her all over again.

Except it would be nice if he could be smiling, looking a bit less stony faced than this.

OK, maybe not very likely, but nice all the same. Even if just to be polite.

'Lola.' Doug's shoulders stiffened as if she were a tax inspector. Taking care to keep his voice neutral he said, 'What brings you here?'

Oh God, this was awful, all the old tumultuous feelings were flooding back. She'd never been able to forget Dougie; he'd been her first love.

What's more, seeing as it had never really happened again since, her One and Only.

'I did,' said Philip. 'Sorry, I hope this isn't awkward, but I had no idea you two knew each other. Anyway, surely that's irrelevant now.' He cast a warning glance at Adele with her mouth like a prune and rested a hand reassuringly on Lola's shoulder. 'Under the circumstances I'm sure we can put the past behind us. Doug, this is the young lady who came to your mother's rescue when she was attacked.'

Dougie's expression altered. 'God, really? That was *you*? We didn't know. That's incredible.'

'The police told me her name was Lauren something or other,' Adele said prunily and with a hint of accusation, as if Lola had done it on purpose.

'It is, but I've been called Lola since I was a baby. It was a nickname that just stuck.'

'Well, thanks for doing what you did.' There was a warmth in Dougie's eyes now, breaking through the initial wariness. 'From what I hear, you were pretty fantastic.'

Oh, I *was*. Shaking inwardly, Lola did her best to look fantastic but at the same time incredibly self-effacing. Dougie was gorgeous and now fate had brought them back together. The break-up had happened a decade ago; they'd practically been children then. Surely Doug would forgive her for chucking him. 'Well, when someone needs help you just go for it, you don't stop to wonder what—'

'Ooh, I've got it now!' Sally let out a mini-squeal of recognition and pointed excitedly at Lola. 'You're the one I never got to meet! You were going out with my little brother when I was living in Dublin with Tim the Tosser! Then you did a bunk and broke his heart!'

Oh don't say that, *please* don't say that. I'm so sorry, I didn't want to do it, Lola longed to blurt out. It broke my heart too!

Doug said drily, 'Thanks, Sal.'

'Oh, come on, it was years and years ago, all in the past now. And she did break your heart.' Sally gave him a jab in the ribs, visibly relishing his discomfort. 'You were a complete pain, don't you remember? All because you couldn't believe your girlfriend had given you the elbow and buggered off abroad.' She nudged Lola and added cheerfully, 'Did him the world of good, if you ask me.'

'That's funny,' said Doug, 'because I don't remember anyone asking you.'

'That's enough.' Adele intervened before the bickering could start. 'Doug, the Mastersons have to leave very soon but they really want to see you before they go.'

'I'll do that now. As soon as I've got myself a drink.' Evidently glad of the reprieve, Doug glanced at Lola and Sally, and said, 'Excuse me. I'll see you later.'

They watched Doug cross the room with Adele, while Philip went in search of a waiter.

'That's one rattled brother,' Sally observed gleefully. 'God, I love it when that happens!'

Guilt and pain swirled up through Lola's stomach. 'Did I really break his heart?'

'Too right you did! Talk about miserable! Ooh, is that yours?'

Lola's phone was chirruping in her bag. She took it out and Gabe's name flashed up at her.

'Feel free.' Sally made encouraging answer-it gestures.

'Thanks. Sorry, I'll just take it outside for a minute.' Longing to confide in Gabe, Lola excused herself and escaped the party. She crossed the hall, quietly let herself out of the house – better safe than sorry – and answered the phone.

'I know, I'm early,' said Gabe. 'Couldn't wait. So how's it going? Are they showering you with diamonds?'

She grimaced in the darkness. 'Diamonds, wouldn't that be nice. More like bullets.'

'What? Why?'

'You won't believe what's happening here.' Lola kept walking to warm herself up, around the side of the house and along a narrow stone path leading beneath a hand-carved wooden pergola into a rose garden. 'The woman who was mugged only turns out to be the mother of an old boyfriend of mine. And she loathed me! If I'd known it was her I'd have run in the other direction. You should have seen her face tonight when she found out I was the one who'd gone to help her!'

'So you're leaving? Do I feel a contraction coming on?'

'Hang on, don't start boiling kettles just yet. I *was* going to

66

leave,' said Lola. 'God, it was awful, I couldn't wait to get out of here. And it went without saying that the Wicked Witch couldn't wait to be shot of me.' She paused, reliving the moment her stomach had done a Red Arrows swoop-and-dive. 'But then it happened. *He* turned up. Oh Gabe, I can't describe how it felt. I thought I'd never see Dougie again, but now I have. And he's more gorgeous than ever. It's like a miracle, I can't believe he's here. So I'm not going to leave now, even though his hateful mother wishes I would. I've got to talk to Doug properly, he's only just arrived and it's been a bit awkward so far. We're all pretty stunned at the moment. But . . . oh God, it's just so amazing seeing him again, I haven't been this excited since—'

'Hey, hey, calm down, do you not think you're getting a bit carried away? If this guy dumped you before, what makes you think he's going to be thrilled to see you again?' As a heterosexual man who had dumped hundreds of weeping females in his time, Gabe said warningly, 'What makes you think he'll even want to *talk* to you?'

'Gabe, you don't understand. He isn't *an* ex-boyfriend. He's *the* ex-boyfriend. Plus, he didn't dump me. I was the one who left him.' Lola swallowed. 'According to his sister I broke his heart.'

'And now you've taken one look at him and decided you want him back. Trust me,' said Gabe, 'that's a recipe for disaster. You can never go back. Whatever annoyed you about this guy before will only annoy you again.'

'For heaven's sake, will you stop lecturing me? This is my first love we're talking about here! We were crazy about each other. Dougie was about to start at Edinburgh University,' Lola paced up and down the flagstoned path in an attempt to keep warm, 'and we planned to visit each other every weekend, but if that wasn't enough I was going to move up there to be with him. You have no idea how happy we were together.'

She heard Gabe snort with derision. 'So happy that you finished with him. That makes sense.'

'But that's just it, I didn't *want* to finish with him. His bloody mother made me do it!' Lola squeezed her eyes shut as the long-ago hideous encounter in Adele Tennant's car swam back into her brain; the smell of expensive leather upholstery had haunted her ever since. 'She hated me, thought I was a bad influence on her precious golden boy . . . she was terrified I'd put him off his studies or, even worse, persuade him to jack in university altogether.'

'So she asked you to stop seeing her son. Erm,' said Gabe, 'did it ever occur to you to say no?'

'She didn't ask me. She made me an offer I couldn't refuse.' Lola hated even thinking about that bit; had spent years doing her best to banish it from her mind.

'You're not serious!' At last she had Gabe's full attention. 'You mean, like swimming with the fishes? She actually threatened you with a concrete overcoat and a trip to the bottom of the Thames?'

'Not that kind. She offered me money. I was seventeen years old.' There was a bitter taste in Lola's mouth now; no matter how compelling the reason, the inescapable fact remained that she had betrayed her boyfriend. 'And she offered me ten thousand pounds if I'd stop seeing Dougie.'

'Which you *took*?'

'Which I took.' The bitter taste was guilt; it wasn't an action she was proud of, hence never having mentioned it to Gabe before.

He let out an incredulous bark of laughter. 'You let her buy you off?'

Lola shivered as a blast of icy air wrapped itself around her stomach. 'I didn't want to, but I had to.'

'Bloody hell! Ten *grand*. What did you spend it on?'

Lola hesitated, but it was no good; she couldn't tell him. Racked with remorse, Alex had begged her never to reveal their secret to another living soul and it was a promise she had to keep. Alex might be gone now but her mother must never find out what had happened. Which meant she must never tell anyone. Choking up at the memory, she said, 'I just needed it. You don't understand what a—'

Crackkk.

She froze at the sound of a dry twig snapping underfoot behind her. Swinging round with her heart in her throat, Lola saw the tall figure just visible in the darkness at the entrance to the rose garden.

Not just any old tall figure either. That silhouette was instantly recognisable.

'Ten thousand pounds,' said a quiet voice every bit as incredulous as Gabe's.

Oh God.

'I don't understand what?' complained Gabe, for whom patience wasn't a strong point. 'Don't stop there! What is there to not understand?'

'I'll call you back.' Her hand suddenly trembling with more than cold, Lola ended the call and dropped the phone back into her bag.

Chapter 9

'Ten thousand pounds,' Doug repeated, shaking his head.

Lola swallowed. 'Your mum was desperate to split us up.'

'I can't believe I'm hearing this.' He moved towards her. 'You wrote me a letter and left the country.'

'Because that's what she wanted me to do. Don't you see? All that stuff I said in the letter wasn't true!' Lola knew she had to make him understand. 'I still loved you! It broke my heart too, I was miserable for *months*.'

'Oh, don't give me that.' Doug's tone hardened. 'I've heard some lines in my time, but—'

'Dougie, I'm not lying! And I'm sorry, *so* sorry I hurt you. But it was your mother's idea – she was the one who offered me the money. And trust me, she *was* desperate,' Lola pleaded. 'If I'd turned it down she'd only have found some other way to get rid of me.'

'Jesus! You could have mentioned it! Did it not even occur to you to tell me what was going on? Did you not think it might have been fair to ask me how *I* felt about it?'

'I was going to.' Lola's fists were clenched with frustration; not being able to tell him the truth meant he was always going

70

to think she was a mercenary bitch. Helplessly she said, 'But you were moving up to Edinburgh, you'd have started social-ising with all those girls up there . . .'

'*What?*'

'We were so young! What were the chances, realistically, of us staying together? I knew I loved you,' Lola rattled on in desperation, 'but what if I'd said no to the money then a few weeks later you'd met someone you liked more than me? How stupid would I have felt if you'd sent me a Dear John letter then?'

In the darkness Doug raised his hands. 'Fine. You did absolutely the right thing. Let's just forget it, shall we?'

Did he mean that? 'Let's.' Lola nodded eagerly, wondering if now might be a good moment for a lovely-to-see-you-again kiss. 'From now on all that stuff's behind us, right? We can start afresh.'

'Start afresh?' There was a smidgeon of sarcasm in his voice. 'No need to go that far, surely. You'll be leaving soon enough.'

'I don't have to.' Hurrying after him as he abruptly turned and headed down the path leading back to the house, Lola said, 'I've only just got here! Dougie, it's fantastic to see you again, we've got so much catching up to do.'

'Trust me, we haven't.'

'But I want to know what you've been doing!' Desperation made her reckless. 'And you came outside, so that means you wanted to talk to me too.'

Dougie reached the front door and paused to look at her. 'I came outside for a cigarette.'

'You smoke now?'

'Not a lot.'

'You should give up,' said Lola.

A muscle twitched irritably in his jaw. 'I did give up. Six weeks ago.'

So her sudden reappearance had jolted him. Lola sniffed the air but could only detect cold earth and aftershave. 'I can't smell smoke.'

Dougie pulled a single cigarette and Bic lighter from his shirt pocket. 'I was about to light it when I heard you talking on the phone.'

'So you didn't smoke it, you listened to me instead. See? I'm coming in useful already.' Reaching out and snatching the cigarette from his hand, Lola snapped it in two and tossed it over her shoulder into a lavender bush.

Dougie heaved a sigh and pushed open the front door. 'If you hadn't been here I wouldn't have been tempted in the first place. If you want to do something really useful you'll leave.'

'There you are.' Adele, flinty eyed, was standing in the hall with Sally beside her. 'We were wondering what had happened to you.'

'We've been catching up.' Dougie's tone was brusque. 'I've just been hearing about the ten thousand pounds you paid Lola to stop seeing me.'

Adele shot Lola a look capable of shrivelling grapes. 'So she told you, did she? Ten thousand pounds, is that what she said?'

Lola's heart sank like a dropped anchor.

'What's that supposed to mean?' Doug demanded.

'I offered ten thousand. But that wasn't enough for her. She demanded fifteen.' Adele shrugged elegantly. 'And then, when I refused, she started haggling.'

Oh God.

'So did you,' Lola whispered.

Doug shook his head. 'I don't believe this. How much did you end up with?'

'Twelve.'

'Twelve and a half,' said Adele the hateful witch.

'OK, but I *needed* that—'

'Stop.' Dougie held up his hands. 'I've heard enough. Now I definitely need a drink.' He turned and strode back into the drawing room.

Lola watched him go. It probably wasn't the moment to be thinking this, but he was even more irresistible when he was angry.

'Now see what you've done,' said Adele. 'Why don't you leave before you ruin the entire evening?'

It might have been a tempting proposition earlier but that was before Dougie had turned up. Since leaving was no longer an option – because what if she never saw him again? – Lola said, 'Look, I'm not as bad as you're making out. I only took that money because there was an emergency and I desperately needed it. I'm actually a really nice person. Can't we just forget about all that old stuff?'

I patted your thigh, for God's sake.

Adele exhaled audibly. 'None of us was expecting this to happen this evening. I'm grateful for what you did the other night, obviously. But I can't pretend I'm happy to see you again. Giving you the money was what I needed to do at the time, but I never wanted Doug to find out.'

'Trust me, neither did I. He overheard me on the phone and I really wish he hadn't. That's why I need to talk to him properly, to explain. Don't worry, I won't slag you off.' As Lola said this she saw Adele wince at the turn of phrase, proving as it did how common she was and how wildly unsuitable for someone as well brought up as Doug.

'Well, let's just get through the rest of the evening without any more unpleasantness.' Adele shook her coiffured hair slightly as if dismissing the thought of it from her mind. Cracking a thin pseudo-smile she said, 'Shall we go through and join the others?'

'I'll follow in a minute, when I've just, um . . .' Lola pointed to the downstairs loo, dithered over what the polite word for it was, then wondered why she was bothering. 'After I've had a quick wee.'

The cloakroom was small but stylish, all ivory marble and tasteful lighting. A bit too tasteful actually; Lola, touching up her make-up, had to lean right across the sink to get close enough to the mirror to check she didn't have speckles of mascara on her cheeks.

Lost in thought about Doug and how she might win him over against his better judgement, Lola jumped out of her skin when her phone suddenly rang. Losing her precarious balance and about to topple nose first into the mirror, she put out a hand to stop herself and sent her make-up bag flying off the side of the sink.

'Noooo!' Lola let out a shriek of horror as the bag landed with a splosh in the toilet bowl. Not her make-up . . . oh God . . .

It was too late, the contents of her cosmetics bag were already drowned. All her favourite things – lovely eyeshadows, bronzing powder, eye pencils, her three *very* best lipsticks – were sitting there submerged in the bottom of the loo. And to add insult to injury her bloody phone was still ringing.

'Gabe, I know you're trying to help, but NOT NOW!' Switching the phone off again, Lola surveyed the scene of devastation and let out a groan of despair. 'Oh *hell* . . .'

Then she jumped again, because someone was tapping cautiously on the cloakroom door.

'Hello? Everything OK in there?' It was a worried female, possibly Sally.

'It's all right. I'm fine.' At the sight of her all-time favourite Urban Decay super-sparkly mocha eyeshadow, Lola could have cried.

'Lola? Is that you? What's happened?'

Seeing as it was Sally, Lola unlocked the door.

She didn't have to say a word.

'Oh no, poor *you*! Crikey, no wonder you let out a screech. I had my handbag stolen once.' Sally squeezed her arm in sympathy. 'I mean, having to replace my credit cards and stuff was a pain in the neck. But losing my make-up was just traumatic. When I found out my favourite mascara had been discontinued I practically had a nervous breakdown right there in Harvey Nicks.'

Despite everything, Lola grinned. 'You're making me feel so much better.'

'Oh, sorry!'

'And we can't leave it in there.' Bracing herself, Lola bent down and gingerly picked the unzipped make-up bag out of the toilet bowl then dropped it – splat – into the waste bin beneath the sink. 'Typical that it had to happen before I had a chance to do my mouth.'

'Well, I can help you there. You want to borrow lipstick? Just come upstairs with me.'

Everything in Sally's bedroom was yellow and white and super-tidy. Sitting on the king-sized bed and gazing around, Lola said, 'This is a great room.'

'It'd be more great if it wasn't in my mother's house.' Sally grimaced. 'Not that I don't love her, but it's hardly ideal, is it? I'm thirty-six. I was living with my boyfriend in Wimbledon until a fortnight ago but we broke up so I moved in here temporarily.'

'What happened with you and the boyfriend?'

'Oh God, nightmare. I'm a walking disaster when it comes to men.' Sally shook her head. 'I paid for him to have his teeth bleached as a birthday present because that's what he wanted. Next thing I know, he's telling me he's seeing the dental nurse. So that's it, I'm single again, back with my mother and giving up on men. I'm going to buy myself a dear little cottage somewhere in the country and breed llamas instead. Knit my own socks and grow my own jam. Wouldn't that be idyllic?' She paused, holding up a fuchsia-pink Chanel lipstick and scrutinising Lola's mouth. 'What kind of colour are you after?'

'Something rusty-bronzy rather than pink, if you've got it. Can you knit?'

'Well, no, but I could always pay some sweet little old lady to do that for me. Rusty-bronzy, rusty-bronzy . . .' Sally was busily rummaging through the boxes on her dressing table.

'If you'd rather live in Notting Hill, my neighbour's off to Australia next week. He's letting his flat out for a year.' Lola couldn't help herself; it was worth a shot and at least Sally didn't work in an abattoir.

'Is he? I haven't been to Notting Hill for years. Oooh, I know the one you need . . .' Sally flitted out of the bedroom, returning moments later with a lipstick in a bullet-shaped gold case. 'Here you go, it was on the bathroom shelf all the time. Is this more you?'

Lola took it with relief. Versace, no less, and a gorgeous, distinctive shade of russet-red with a brownish-gold lustre. 'This is exactly me.' Peering into the dressing-table mirror, she applied it with a flourish and smacked her lips together.

'Perfect. Now I can face the world again. Does Dougie have a girlfriend?'

'D'you know, I'm not sure. He *was* seeing someone a while back, but I don't know if it's still going on. You know what men are like, they don't talk about that kind of stuff like we do.' Sally fluffed translucent powder onto her nose and said, 'Why? Do you still fancy him?'

Only an older sister could say it quite like that, as if it was on a par with fancying Quasimodo.

Lola said regretfully, 'He's gorgeous. We were so happy together once and I messed that up. It was all my own fault, I know that, I made a mistake but at the time I didn't . . . I just couldn't . . .'

'Oh please, I didn't mean to make you feel worse. You were only seventeen,' Sally exclaimed. 'We all make mistakes at that age. And, OK, Dougie was miserable but he recovered. It's not like he joined a monastery!'

Grateful for Sally's understanding, Lola managed a wobbly smile. 'I'm glad he didn't. Sorry, seeing him again like this has been a bit overwhelming. But who knows, maybe I can persuade him I'm irresistible and he'll forgive me . . .'

The bedroom door, which hadn't been shut, swung further open. 'Look,' Doug said curtly, 'I really wish I didn't have to keep overhearing this stuff, but Philip wants to make a speech and he asked me to round everyone up.'

'OK, we're done here.' Sally gaily flipped back her hair and headed for the door.

'And can I just say,' Doug fixed Lola with a steely knee-trembler of a gaze as she passed him in the doorway, 'don't waste your energy with the being irresistible bit, because I'm not interested.'

Hang on, what were the qualities he'd always admired in her when they'd been a couple? Her eternal optimism and refusal to take no for an answer?

'You might change your mind,' Lola said bravely. 'I'm very lovable.'

'Not to me.'

'I could be. If you'd just give me a chance.'

'Lola, don't even bother to try. Nothing is going to happen between you and me. After this evening we won't see each other again and that's fine by me. So let's just go downstairs, shall we, and get this farce over with. The sooner it's done, the sooner you can go home.'

Everyone gathered in the drawing room for Philip's speech. It was sweet, if hard to believe, hearing this nice man speak so movingly about the happiness Adele had brought into his life. Everyone raised their glasses to Adele, then Philip went on to talk about Lola and her actions on the night of the mugging. He concluded by announcing that they were all indebted to her, and that from now on she was part of the family. Cue applause, a toast and – hilariously – another brittle hug from Adele. It was like being embraced by a Ryvita.

Then the embarrassing bit was over and everyone went back to drinking and chatting amongst themselves. Everyone except Adele, who looked at Lola's mouth and said, 'What an extraordinary coincidence, you appear to use the same lipstick as me.'

Oh bugger, *bugger*. And she *knew*.

'Sorry.' Lola couldn't believe she hadn't recognised it earlier. 'I . . . um, lost mine and Sally offered to lend me one. I didn't realise it was yours.'

'You may as well take it with you when you leave.' Adele

shuddered as if Lola had just spat on the hors d'oeuvres. 'It's not as if I'd use it again now.'

'Everything OK?' Doug joined them.

'Lola used my lipstick.' With an incredulous half-laugh Adele said, 'I must be old-fashioned. It just seems an incredibly brazen thing to do. So . . . *personal*.'

Lola opened her mouth to protest but now Dougie was surveying her with equal distaste, as if she were Typhoid Mary going around spreading her vile germs on other people's lipsticks. There came a time when you simply had to accept that winning someone over wasn't an option.

When Lola's phone trilled for the third time that evening, Adele's mouth narrowed with fresh annoyance.

'Will you stop hanging up on me?' Gabe demanded. 'I do have better things to do with my time than keep trying to get through to you. It's not that complicated,' he rattled on. 'I just need to know if everything's going OK. A simple yes or no will—'

'Are you serious? The contractions are *how* far apart? Just wait there and stay calm,' said Lola. 'Boil the kettle and take deep breaths. I'm on my way.'

Chapter 10

'I dreamt about him last night,' said Lola.

Cheryl was restocking the bestseller shelves at the front of the shop. Pausing to gaze at the book in her hand, she frowned and said, 'Dreamt about who? Harry Potter?'

'As if. I'm talking about Dougie, you dingbat.'

'Oh. You mean you're *still* talking about Dougie. Do the words "not a hope in hell" mean anything to you?'

Honestly, just because Cheryl's marriage had ended in a bad way; now forty and happily divorced, she was enjoying a man-free life. Doggedly, Lola said, 'Failure is not an option.'

'Flogging a dead horse?' Cheryl persisted. 'Chasing rainbows? Expecting a miracle?'

'Don't be such a pessimist. I dreamt I was rowing a boat down Portobello Road and I lost one of my oars, but all of a sudden Dougie swam up to me and jumped into the boat.'

'And tipped you out?'

'And rescued me! He showed me the hidden switch that turned on the engine.' Lola felt herself growing misty-eyed at the memory. 'And the next thing I knew, we were whizzing along like something out of a James Bond film, all through the streets with people screaming and diving out of our way, and Dougie was sitting next to me with his leg pressing against mine . . .'

'Is this about to turn into one of those mucky dreams?'

'Sadly not. We didn't have time. My alarm went off.' Lola passed Cheryl a handful of Dan Browns; it was Monday afternoon, three days since the party, and Dougie had taken up more or less permanent residence inside her head. It wasn't going to be easy, making someone love you again when they didn't even want to see you, but she'd never felt this way about anyone else; having him reappear in her life like this was just—

'By the way, someone's watching you,' said Cheryl.

'They are? Who?' It didn't take long to conjure up a fantasy; in less than a split second Lola had the whole Officer-and-a-Gentleman scenario rolling. When she turned round, Dougie would be making his way across the shop floor towards her like Richard Gere. OK, maybe he wouldn't actually be wearing that white officer's uniform but he'd still sweep her effortlessly up into his arms and carry her out, while staff and customers alike clapped and cheered, whooping with delight and calling out, 'Way to go, Lola.'

'That one over there by autobiographies.'

Lola turned slowly and another delicious fantasy was dashed. For crying out loud, the man was in his fifties; why would she even want him to carry her out of the shop?

'That's not Doug.'

Cheryl rolled her eyes. 'I didn't say it was. He's been looking over at you, that's all. *Really* looking.'

'Probably saw me on TV last week and now he's trying to pluck up the courage to ask for my autograph.' Lola prepared to smile in a cheery, down-to-earth fashion and prove that fame hadn't gone to her head – God, wouldn't it be fantastic if he really did ask? – but the man had turned away. Oh well. Ooh, unless he was a private detective hired by Dougie to find out if she was a nicer person now than she'd been ten years ago . . . he'd done his best to put her out of his mind but hadn't been able to . . . maybe he could forgive her after all . . .

'Are you daydreaming again? Tim's waving at you,' Cheryl pointed out. 'They're short-handed over at the pay desk.'

Ten minutes later Lola's fan arrived at her till. Up close he was younger than she'd first thought; in his mid-forties probably. His hair was dark and just that bit longer than usual, and he was wearing a striped mulberry and olive shirt with well-cut black trousers. Quite trendy for a man of his age. Nice grey eyes too.

'I've never read one of these before.' He passed over the book, a thriller by a prolific American author. 'Is he good?'

'Seriously good. You won't be able to stop reading even when you want to. You'll be holding your breath for hours.' Lola rang the book up, aware that the man was studying her name badge.

'Sorry.' He saw that she'd noticed. 'Nice name. Unusual.'

'Thanks.' She took his ten pound note and scooped the change out of the till. He was way too old for her to be interested in him in any romantic way but he had an attractive smile. 'There you go. Hope you enjoy it. Don't blame me if you get sacked for not being able to stay awake at work tomorrow.'

His smile broadened. 'And if I do enjoy it, I'll be back to buy another one.'

There was something about the way he was looking at her that made Lola wonder if this was how it felt to be famous. She said lightly, 'Do you recognise me?'

He looked startled. 'What?'

'I was interviewed on TV the other night. I thought maybe you'd seen it.'

The man's expression cleared. 'No, I'm afraid I missed that. I just came in to buy a book.'

Damn, she wasn't famous after all. 'Sorry.'

'No problem.' He relaxed visibly. 'I'm sorry I missed it. Were you good?'

'I was brilliant.' As Lola passed him the bag containing his thriller a thought struck her: *Why* was he now visibly relaxed? Innocently she said, 'Does anyone ever recognise you?'

Ha, that surprised him.

'Excuse me?'

'I just wondered if people ever realised who you are.'

Another pause. 'Why would they?'

'Maybe because they're very clever and they've worked it out.' Lola flashed him a sunny smile.

He looked at her. 'Worked what out?'

'That you're a private detective.'

'Me?' He pointed to his chest, shaking his head in amused disbelief. 'Is that what you think? I'm not a private detective.'

Luckily there was a lull at the tills; no other customers were waiting to be served.

'Ah,' said Lola, 'but you would say that, wouldn't you?'

'I suppose so. But I'm still not one.'

'Except that could be you covering your tracks, like any good private detective would.'

He tilted his head to one side. 'So *if* I was, which I promise I'm not, who would I be spying on?'

'Ooh, I don't know. Anyone in this shop.' Lola shrugged playfully. 'Me, perhaps.'

'You. And why would a private detective be tailing you?' Another brief pause. 'Are you in some kind of trouble?'

'Not at all.' She'd only said it on the spur of the moment – nothing ventured, nothing gained – but Lola knew now that this man was no more than a charming stranger, albeit a slightly bemused one, thanks to her interrogation. 'OK, you're not a private detective. I believe you.'

He nodded gravely. 'Thank you.'

Out of nowhere a queue for the tills had materialised. Lola said, 'Enjoy your book.'

The man left, clutching his dark blue Kingsley's carrier bag and wearing the kind of expression that people have when they think they've handed over a ten pound note and been given change for twenty.

Chapter 11

Weren't Toastabags the greatest invention in the whole world *ever*?

The toaster popped up and Lola hooked out the bag, tipping the gorgeous crispy toasted cheese and tomato sandwich onto a plate. Possibly her favourite food, and to think that when she'd first clapped eyes on a Toastabag she hadn't believed it could work, because how could a plasticky baggy-type thing go into an electric toaster and not melt?

OK, toasted sandwich: check.

DVD in DVD player: check. She'd treated herself to the latest release starring Tom Dutton, one of her favourite actors.

Box of tissues: check. When she'd dragged Gabe along to the cinema to see the film she'd honked like a big goose during the weepy bits and shown herself right up.

Remote control for DVD player: check.

Remote control for TV . . . bum, where was it? Oh, under the sofa cushions. Check.

Now she was all ready to go . . .

The doorbell rang as she was about to take the first heavenly bite of toasted sandwich. Someone had a sense of humour.

Lola looked at her make-up-free reflection in the kitchen window, teamed with dripping wet hair and lime-green towelling dressing gown, and really hoped Tom Dutton hadn't chosen this moment to pitch up on her doorstep.

She pressed the intercom. 'Yes?'

'Lola?'

A female voice. 'Who's that?'

'It's me! Sally Tennant!'

Good grief. *Sally*. *Doug's sister*. As Lola pressed the buzzer, her stomach gave a little squiggle of excitement. 'Come on up.'

Sally, wrapped in a glamorous cream coat and black patent high-heeled boots, was looking glossy and stylish. She would have looked even more stylish if there hadn't been a pair of sparkly red plastic antlers flashing away on top of her head.

'Oh sorry.' She pulled a face when she saw Lola's hair and dressing gown. 'Bad time?'

'Of course not. I can't believe you're here.' Lola ushered her into the living room, switched off the TV. 'Is this something to do with Doug?'

'Doug.' Sally looked blank. 'No. Haven't seen him. Why, have you?'

'No.' Lola swallowed her disappointment.

'I asked Philip for your address. I'm here about that flat you told me about.'

The flat. Lola hadn't thought for a moment that Sally would take her up on the offer – she hadn't appeared to be even listening when she'd mentioned it. And now she was actually here. Talk about cutting it fine. But at the same time, how *brilliant*.

'You're really interested? That's fantastic. Gabe's off to Australia tomorrow . . . he's out saying goodbye to his friends tonight,

God only knows what time he'll be back. But I've got a key. I can show you the flat now.' Tightening the belt of her dressing gown, Lola said, 'You'll love it, I promise!'

'Gabe? Can you hear me?' At the other end of the phone Lola could make out yet more noisy celebrations. 'I've just found someone for your flat. Remember I told you about Sally, Doug's sister? Well, she's here and she's had a look round, and it's just what—'

'What?' hissed Sally when Lola abruptly stopped and listened. 'Doesn't he want me to move in? Why, what's wrong with me? Tell him he won't find a better tenant *anywhere*. Look, I can pay the deposit now, money isn't a problem . . . Lola, tell him how much I want this flat!'

Lola said slowly, 'Yes . . . OK, right . . . no, of course I under-stand.' She finished listening to Gabe then hung up.

'What?' wailed Sally. 'Why can't I have it? I want it!'

Lola felt a twinge of guilt; she was the one who'd begged Gabe not to take on Terry-the-abbatoir-worker.

'It's not you. Gabe registered the flat this morning with a lettings agency. He's signed a contract with them. And they rang him a couple of hours ago to tell him they were bringing a client round tonight. If this guy says he wants it, there's nothing we can do. He's got first refusal,' she explained. 'And he's keen to find somewhere fast.'

'Oh.' Sally looked crestfallen. 'Well, maybe he won't like it.'

'Everyone likes Gabe's flat. Damn it,' Lola said frustratedly, 'I want you to be my neighbour, I don't want some smelly *boy* moving in next door . . .'

'What?' Sally eyed her with curiousity as Lola's voice trailed off. 'What are you thinking?'

'Gabe says they're due round at eight.' Lola checked her watch. 'I'm just wondering what time the corner shop shuts.'

With a glimmer of a smile Sally said, 'Has anyone ever told you you're a little bit weird?'

'Excuse me.' Lola raised her eyebrows. 'You're the one with the flashing antlers on your head.'

The corner shop was still open. If Sanjeev wondered why his best customer when it came to magazines, chocolate and ice cream was all of a sudden buying up cabbages, he didn't ask. By ten to eight the evil stench of boiled cabbage was thick in both Lola's flat and Gabe's. When the saucepans had been removed from Gabe's kitchen Lola found a music channel on the TV in her own flat and turned the volume up to maximum. Eminem blared out and Sally took off her antlers, shaking out her hair and kicking off her shoes.

At three minutes past eight they heard the front door being opened downstairs, then two people entering Gabe's flat. Lola gave it a few seconds then crossed the landing and thumped on the door.

It was opened by a man in a suit. 'Yes?'

'Hi there, is he in?'

'Excuse me?'

'The Angel Gabriel.' Lola raised her voice to be heard above the sound of the music. 'Mr Let's-Complain-About-Everything.'

The letting agent said frostily, 'If you mean Mr Adams, he isn't here.'

'No? Best news I've heard all day.' Grinning at the potential tenant behind him – gangling, thirties, spectacles, accountanty-looking – Lola said, 'Well, can you just pass on a message from Lola and Sal across the hall, tell him we're having a few friends

88

round tonight. They'll be turning up after the pub and we'd appreciate it if he didn't give us the usual grief, seeing as this time we're warning him in advance.' Leaning forward conspiratorially, she added, 'To be honest, the police are fed up with him calling them and whingeing about us. I mean, talk about a Neddy No-Mates! If you can't have a party and a laugh with your friends, what's the point of living, eh?'

'Maybe you could leave a note for Mr Adams.' The letting agent spoke brusquely, keen to close the door on a potentially deal-breaking neighbour.

'Hang on.' The gawky accountant-type behind him raised his voice above the thudding hip-hop beat that was now making the floor vibrate. 'How often do you have parties?'

'Not often. Two or three times a week, that's all.'

'And the smell,' said the accountant. 'What *is* that?'

'Hmm? Oh, can you notice it?' Lola shrugged. 'No idea. It comes and goes in waves – something to do with the drains, I think. Cost us a fortune to have everything checked out but it didn't do any good. We thought maybe Neddy No-Mates had buried someone under his floorboards.' She paused and said, 'Why do you want to know?'

'This flat's been registered with a lettings agency.' The accountant blinked rapidly. 'The owner's moving to Australia.'

'You're kidding. Hey, fantastic!' Hearing footsteps behind her, Lola turned and said to Sally, 'Hear that? Neddy No-Mates is off to Oz!'

'To get away from us?' All of a sudden nine months pregnant beneath her coat, Sally nodded approvingly. 'Cool. So does that mean you're going to be our new neighbour?'

'I, um . . .' Was that a glint of terror behind the geeky spectacles? 'Well, I'm not . . .'

'Because if you ever fancy a spot of babysitting, I've got just the thing for you right here!' Sally gave her swollen stomach a pat. 'I mean, just because we're having a baby doesn't mean we have to stop doing what we want to do, does it? Whoo-hoo!' Eminem had given way to Snoop Dogg. Sally, clutching her stomach with one hand and waving the other in the air, executed some enthusiastic hip-hop-esque dance moves. 'Whoo-*hooooo*!'

It was a sight to make a grown man nervous. Two grown men, in fact. The geek and the lettings agent edged nervously away. Lola, filled with admiration, prayed that Sally wouldn't get carried away and attempt to shake her booty.

Imagine the embarrassment if her cushion fell out.

'How many of you are there living in that flat?' said the geek.

'Just me and Lola and this little creature when he gets here.' Still energetically gyrating along to the music, Sally pointed gaily at her stomach.

'Who needs a man when you've got a turkey baster?' said Lola, winking at the lettings agent. 'Our baby's going to have two mothers who *know* how to have fun.'

When the agent and the geek had left the building, Lola turned off the ear-splitting music and threw open the windows in both flats to disperse the nostril-curling boiled-cabbage smell.

'Gosh, that was fun.' Sally pulled the balled-up velvet cushion out from under her coat and flung it onto the sofa. 'Think it'll do the trick?'

'It'd do the trick if I was the one looking for a flat.' Lola took a bottle of white wine from the fridge and poured out two glasses.

'Poor bloke, he did look a bit stunned. I suppose we just have to wait now. Should I be drinking that in my condition?'

'You could always have water instead.'

'Water? Yeurgh, nasty wet *watery* stuff. No thanks.'

Lola's phone rang ten minutes later and she leapt on it.

'What did you do?' Gabe came straight to the point.

Innocently Lola said, 'Sorry?'

'No you're not. I've just had a call from the lettings agent,' said Gabe, 'telling me that in view of the Situation, I'm going to need to drop my rental price.'

'Oh Gabe, that's *terrible*.'

'Quite significantly, in fact.'

'You poor thing!'

'He also said getting rid of that putrid smell had to be a priority.'

'Oh dear.'

'So this friend of yours, this sister-of-Doug,' said Gabe. 'I'm assuming she's there with you now.'

Lola looked over at Sally. 'Might be.'

'And she wants my flat.'

'Definitely. More than anything.'

'What caused the smell?'

'Four big saucepans of boiled cabbage.'

'Here, give me the phone.' Reaching over, Sally grabbed it and said, 'Gabe? Hi, please let me be your new tenant! I'm super-housetrained, I promise. I'd really look after your flat and I'm completely trustworthy, I'll pay the full rent by direct debit and leave the deposit with Lola now, you won't regret it . . . what? Oh, OK.'

'What did he say?' demanded Lola when Sally put down the phone.

'That I was giving him earache.'

'And?'

'That moving to Australia was beginning to seem like the best decision he'd ever made.'

'And?'

'That you and I deserve each other and he feels sorry for our baby.'

Since Sally was currently sitting on the sofa with one elbow digging into the abandoned velvet cushion, Lola felt quite sorry for it too. 'So that means . . . ?'

Sally beamed and clinked her glass against Lola's. 'I can move in as soon as I like.'

Chapter 12

'Oh, I'm going to miss you *sooo* much.' Lola blinked and hiccuped; she hadn't expected to feel this emotional but actually saying goodbye to Gabe was hard.

'Hang on, you're strangling me.' He prised her off him. 'It's like being hugged by a giant koala.'

'That's to get you into practice. Oh bugger, what do I look like?'

'A panda in a pink dress.' Gabe watched her mopping up mascara. 'I can't believe you're crying. I'm only going for a year.'

'I know, I know I'm being stupid.' Lola blew her nose like a trumpeting elephant. 'But what if you change your mind? You might decide to stay there for good and I'll never see you again. You're my best male friend in the world and you're about to fly off to the other side of it. What if you and Jaydena get married and buy a house and settle down and have loads of Aussie kids?'

She expected Gabe to burst out laughing at such a ridiculous idea, but he didn't.

'If that happens, you can always come out and visit us.'

Oh God, he really meant it! He was that besotted with Jaydena. Had he never even *watched* Kath and Kim?

Apart from anything else, Lola knew they had particularly evil spiders in Australia, the kind that hid under toilet seats and bit your bum. So she definitely couldn't go.

'You could come back and visit me,' she offered.

'What, with all those kids?' Gabe grinned. 'Are you crazy? We couldn't afford it.'

He was in love. Lola did her best to feel happy for him. She looked at her watch. 'I'm going to be late to work.'

'And my cab's due in ten minutes.' Gabe gave her a kiss on the cheek and pushed her towards the door. 'Go on, get yourself out of here. You've got your new friend Sally moving in tonight – you won't even notice I'm gone.'

'You were right,' said the man who wasn't a private detective.

'Oh, hi.' Recognising him, Lola dumped the pile of hardbacks she'd brought out from the stockroom and said cheerfully, 'Right about what?'

'Last night. I couldn't put that book down. I was awake till four this morning finishing it.' He shook his head in baffled disbelief. 'I didn't know reading could be like that, I had no idea. I've just never been a booky person. All these years I've been missing out.'

'Ah, but now you've seen the light.' Lola loved it when this happened; witnessing a conversion never failed to give her a thrill. 'You've become one of us. Welcome to our world; you're going to love it here.'

'I need another thriller and I don't know where to start.' The man was wearing a navy suit today, with a burnt-orange shirt and a turquoise silk tie. 'There are so many to choose from. Can you recommend an author?'

Could she recommend an author? Ha, it was only the favourite bit of her job!

'You'd like this one.' Lola picked up a book with a gunmetal grey cover. 'Or this.' Eagerly she reached across the table for another. 'Now he's a *gripping* writer.'

The man looked more closely at Lola. 'Are you OK?'

Bugger, she'd redone her make-up on the tube on the way into work. Clearly not thoroughly enough.

'I'm fine. It's just . . . nothing.' Lola checked herself; he was a complete stranger. 'Look, see how you get on with this one. When you've tried a few different authors we can work out which others you might like, then—'

'Beano!'

'Excuse me?' She turned to face the hatchet-faced woman who had just barked in her ear.

'I need a *Beano Annual* for my grandson!'

'Sorry,' the man in the suit shook his head apologetically and took the book with the grey cover from her. 'You're busy. Thanks for this. I'll let you know how I get on with it.'

'Come on, come on,' bellowed the woman, spraying saliva. 'I haven't got all day!'

By the time Lola fought her way back through the crowds with the *Beano Annual*, the man in the suit was gone. The hatchet-faced woman didn't even say thank you. But then people like that never did.

Twenty minutes later Lola felt an index finger irritably poking at her left shoulder blade. 'Excuse me, excuse me,' came an irritated female voice. 'I want the new book by that Dan Black.'

Lola turned. 'You mean Dan Brown.'

'Don't tell me what I mean, missy. I don't care what the man's name is, just get me the book.'

'I tell you what,' said Lola, 'why don't you stop expecting me to wait on you hand and foot, and get it yourself?'

Outraged, the woman sucked in her breath. 'You impertinent creature! How dare you? I shall report you to the manager and have you sacked!'

'And I'll have you arrested for crimes against colour coordination. Because pink,' Lola curled her lip at the woman's fluffy scarf and padded jacket, 'does *not* go with orange.'

Then they realised they were being watched by a bemused elderly man clutching a biography of Churchill.

'It's all right.' Lola winked at him. 'She's my mother.'

'Hello, darling.' Blythe gave her a quick hug and kiss on the cheek and tucked a stray strand of hair behind Lola's ear. 'Can't stop, I'm racing to finish all my Christmas shopping then I've made an appointment to have my hair done this afternoon. Just popped in to show you what I've bought for tonight. Tell me which outfit I should keep and I'll take the other one back.'

Lola didn't get her hopes up; being allowed to choose was Blythe's attempt at compromise. Sadly it was like telling someone they were about to be thrown into deep water and generously giving them the choice between a concrete straitjacket and lead diving boots. Blythe had as much fashion sense as a chicken, coupled with a hopeless predilection for mixing and matching things that Really Didn't Go. Somehow it hadn't seemed to matter when Alex had been alive – between them, they had regarded Blythe's manner of dressing as no more than an endearing quirk. But it was five years now since Alex had died and during the last eighteen months Blythe had tentatively begun dating again. All of a sudden clothes had become more important. Keen for her mother to make a good impression on the outside world, Lola had begun attempting to steer her into more stylish waters.

But it had to be said, this was on a par with trying to knit feathers. Lola braced herself as her mother rummaged in a pink carrier bag and pulled out a silky beige top.

With purply-blue satin butterflies adorning each shoulder strap.

And a purply-blue frill around each armhole.

And scattered multicoloured sequins across the cleavage area.

Lola bit her lip. If it had been *just* a silky beige top, it would have been perfect.

'Okaaay. Now the other one.'

'Ta-daaa!' Having stuffed beige'n'silky back into its bag, Blythe produced the second top and held it up against herself with a flourish, indicating that this, *this* one, was her favourite.

As if Lola couldn't have guessed. Top number two was brighter – a retina-searing geranium red – and much frillier, with jaunty layered sleeves, sparkly silver buttons down each side and a huge red and white fabric flower – bigger than a Crufts rosette – at the base of the V-neck.

'Hmm,' said Lola. 'Is this for when you run away to join the circus?'

'Don't be so cruel! It's beautiful!'

'Right, so what would you wear it with?'

Her mother looked hopeful, like a five-year-old attempting to spell her name. 'My blue paisley skirt?'

'No.'

'Green striped trousers?'

'No!'

'Oh. Well, how about the pink and gold—'

'*Noooo!*'

Blythe flung up her hands in defeat. 'You're so picky.'

'I'm not, I just don't want people pointing and saying, "There goes Coco the Clown". Mum, if you really want to keep the red top, wear it with your white skirt.'

'Except I can't, because it's got a big curry stain on the front. Ooh,' Blythe exclaimed, her eyes lighting up as inspiration struck, 'but I could snip the red flower off this top and superglue it to the skirt instead, that'd cover the mark! That's it, problem solved!'

People would point and laugh. Lola opened her mouth to protest but her mother was busily stuffing the tops back into their carriers, checking her watch and saying, 'Gosh, is that the time? I must fly!'

'Where are you going tonight?'

'Oh, it's just our quiz team having a Christmas get-together, something to eat followed by a bit of a bop. Malcolm's driving, so I can have a drink.'

Hardly the Oscars. Lola let it go. Trinny and Susannah would have a field day with Malcolm, who was bearded and bear-like, with a penchant for baggy corduroys and zigzaggy patterned sweaters. Since Malcolm was to sartorial elegance what John Prescott was to ice dance, he was unlikely to object to an over-sized flower attached to the front of a skirt. If you told him it was the latest thing from Karl Lagerfeld, he wouldn't doubt it for a minute.

But Malcolm wasn't what Lola had in mind for her mother. Sweet though he was in his bumbling teddy-bear way, she had her sights set several notches higher than that. Because Blythe deserved the best.

Chapter 13

The eye-watering, throat-tightening boiled-cabbage smell had gone, thank goodness. Loaded up like a donkey, Sally struggled through to the living room then dumped her belongings on the floor.

Excitement squiggled through her stomach. This was it, her new home for the next twelve months at least. New flat, new resolutions, whole new life.

Chief resolution being: no more having her heart broken by boyfriends who were nothing more than rotten no-good *hounds*.

And where better to start than here? Sally gazed around, taking in the unadorned cream walls, ivory rugs and pale minimalist ultra-modern furniture. There was no denying it looked like a show home. Even the light switches were minimalist. What with the total lack of clutter, it also exuded an air of bachelor-about-town.

Oh well, soon sort that out.

'In here, love?' Huffing and puffing a bit, the taxi driver appeared in the doorway with several more cases.

'Just chuck them down. Thanks.' He was in his fifties, grey-haired and ruddy-cheeked, wearing a wedding ring. Was he a lovely man, completely devoted to his wife, the kind of husband who put up shelves and mowed the lawn without having to be nagged into doing it? Or was he a shy conniving cheat who promised to do those things then sloped off to the pub instead and came home hours later reeking of other women's perfume?

Actually, he probably didn't. Sally softened and gave him the benefit of the doubt. And she'd never know anyway, because you weren't allowed to ask complete strangers personal questions like that. Which was, as far as she was concerned, a big shame. Why couldn't there be a law passed, making it compulsory? Imagine meeting a man for the first time, finding him attractive and being allowed to inject him with a truth drug:

'You seem very charming, Mr X. But if we were to have a relationship, how long would it be before you started treating me like a piece of poo on a shoe?'

'Well, usually about a month.'

'Thanks. Next!'

The taxi driver gave her an odd look. 'You all right, love?'

'Me? Oh yes, fine.' Sally hastily collected herself . . . ooh, though, how about if you could also wire them up to a machine capable of delivering painful electric shocks when the response warranted it? 'Sorry, miles away. How much do I owe you?'

When he'd left, Sally shrugged off her coat, pushed up her sleeves and set to work opening the first couple of cases. She was going to be happy here in Radley Road. Happier still, once she'd made the flat her own.

Left standing at the altar was a lonely place to be. It sounded like a line from a country and western song. Worse still, when it had actually happened, it had *felt* like being trapped in a country and western song. Some memories faded but humiliation on that scale was never going to go away.

And that had just been Barry the Bastard. There'd been loads more over the years, more than any girl should have to endure, ranging from Tim the Tosser whom she'd lived with in Ireland for over a year, to Pisshead Pete seven Christmases ago. Culminating, needless to say, in her latest calamitous choice, William the Wanker. And in truth he was no great loss; the dental nurse he'd run off with was welcome to him. His gleaming, too-white teeth had looked weird anyway, like something out of a Disney cartoon.

'Hellooo?'

Sally was looping multicoloured fairy lights around the fireplace when the bell buzzed and she heard Lola's voice. Eagerly she rushed to open the door.

'Wow,' said Lola, gazing around the living room. Wow was an understatement. 'This is . . . different.'

'Isn't it?' Sally beamed with pride. 'I can't believe how much I've got done in three hours! Nothing like a splash of colour to cheer a place up! You know, I really think I have a flair for interior design – I should do it for a living. The world would be a happier place if we all did our homes like this.'

The world would definitely be full of people wearing sunglasses. The floor was littered with empty bags and cases, not to mention several packets of biscuits. There were bright paintings adorning Gabe's cool cream walls, with five . . . no, six . . . no, *seven* sets of fairy lights draped around the frames. The brushed-steel lampshade from the Conran shop had been taken down; in its place was a hot-pink chandelier. The ivory cushions on the sofa sported new fluffy orange covers. A sequinned pink-and-orange throw covered the seat below the window. And a fountain of fake sparkly flowers exploded out of a silver bowl on top of the TV.

'Good for you,' said Lola. 'If Gabe could see this, he'd have a fit.'

'Good job he's in Australia then.' Unperturbed, Sally reached into one of the cases and pulled out a swathe of peacock feathers awash with iridescent blue and green glitter. 'Pass me that gold vase, over there, would you? At the weekend I'm going to paint my bedroom to match these!'

'Paint the bedroom?' Lola felt she owed it to Gabe to look dubious; he'd spent a fortune having his flat redone just three months ago.

'It's too plain as it is! Like being in a prison cell! I'm here for a whole year,' said Sally. 'Anyway, it's only a couple of coats of paint – if your friend really hates it, I'll slosh some cream over the walls the day before he gets back.'

'Sorry. Gabe's a bit fussy, that's all. He had the colour specially mixed.'

Sally's eyebrows shot up. '*This* colour? Are you serious? How hard is it to go down to B&Q and buy a vat of emulsion?'

'I know, I know.' Lola raised her hands, disclaiming responsibility. 'He's just . . . particular.'

'Is he gay?'

'Trust me. Gabe's the opposite of gay.'

'He's also fifty zillion miles away. So what I think is, you don't mention to him that I'm repainting his flat, and neither will I.'

'Go on then.' Relenting, Lola opened her bag. 'I'll drink to that.'

'Oh my God, champagne!'

'Not quite. It was either one bottle of the proper stuff or two of pretend.' Lola held one bottle in each hand.

102

'And we wouldn't want to run out.' Seizing them, Sally said joyfully, 'Come on, let's pop these corks – whoops, don't step on the Garibaldis!'

'. . . I mean, I'm thirty-six years old and this is the first time I've been able to do out a room just the way I like. How crazy is that?'

By ten o'clock the first bottle had been upended into the waste bin (parrot-pink, trimmed with marabou) and the second was three-quarters empty. Sally was cross-legged on the rug (purple, speckled with biscuit crumbs), waving her glass dramatically as she ran through her life history. With the chandelier switched off, the many strings of fairy lights gave the room the kind of festive multicoloured glow that had Lola half expecting to be given a present. She frowned, puzzled by Sally's statement. 'What, you've never been allowed to do it before? What about when you were a teenager?'

'God, especially when I was a teenager! My mother sent the cleaner into my bedroom every morning to tidy everything up and make my bed. I was allowed to have three posters on my wall.' Sally paused to scoop another biscuit from the packet on the floor next to her. 'As long as they were posters of horses. I was more of a Spandau Ballet, Duran Duran kind of girl, but she wouldn't let me put them on the walls. Ghastly creatures, she called Duran Duran. And Spandau were yobs. I think she was terrified I'd find myself a boyfriend who wore ruffled shirts and make-up.'

Lola pictured Adele's horror at the prospect. 'So what happened next?'

'Daft question. I found myself a boyfriend who wore ruffled shirts and make-up.'

'And you were how old when you left home?'

'Eighteen. But I've never lived on my own, it's always been either flat-sharing or moving in with boyfriends. Which means there's always been someone around to moan about my decorating plans. I've spent the last eighteen years having to compromise. Well, not any more.' Sally's exuberant gesture encompassed the room and caused the contents of her glass to spill in an arc across the rug. 'From now on I'm going to do what I want to do and no one's going to stop me. No more Tim the Tosser, no more Pisshead Pete, no more boring men telling me I can't have leopard-print wallpaper in my kitchen. Bum, my glass is empty.'

'That would be because you just swung it upside down.'

'Did I? Bum, now *this* is empty.' Tipsily aghast, Sally gave the second bottle a shake. 'OK, don't panic, I've got a bottle of white burgundy in the fridge – whoops, my foot's gone to sleep, I hate it when that happens.'

'Shall I get it?' Lola jumped up, because Sally's attempts to stand were of the Bambi-on-ice persuasion.

'Excellent plan. But you'll have to hunt around for a corkscrew.'

In the kitchen, Lola took out the chilled burgundy and rummaged through drawers in search of Gabe's corkscrew. Surely he hadn't taken it with him.

The doorbell rang and she heard Sally say perplexedly, 'Who can that be?' But she must have limped over to the intercom because twenty seconds later the door to the flat was opened and Sally exclaimed, 'I wasn't expecting you here tonight!'

Friend?

Mother? *Please no*.

Old boyfriend?

Lola's hands froze in mid-corkscrew search as she heard the visitor say, 'I know, but I have to meet a client in Oxford tomorrow morning, so this was the only time I could bring the stuff over. I tried to call but your phone's switched off.'

Oh, that voice, it was like warm honey spreading through her veins. Not one of Sally's old boyfriends then, thought Lola. One of mine!

'That would explain why George Clooney hasn't rung. Thanks, just dump the cases against the wall.' Bursting with pride Sally said, 'So what d'you think of my new flat?'

Lola listened, holding her breath.

'Bloody hell. It's like a cross between Santa's grotto and a Moroccan souk.'

'I know, isn't it fantastic?' Sally clapped her hands. 'I can't believe how gorgeous it looks!'

Doug said drily, 'I can't believe you're my sister.' Evidently spotting the empty wine glasses on the coffee table he added, 'Drinking for two now? Or has someone else been round?'

Sally giggled. 'Someone else is still round.'

OK, enough skulking in the kitchen. Lola stepped into the living room. 'Actually I wouldn't call myself round, more curvily girl-shaped.'

Chapter 14

'Oh, for God's sake.' Dark eyes narrowing, Doug said impatiently, 'Not you again.'

It hurt, but as far as he was concerned, Lola knew she deserved it. Just as well she was the optimistic type; maybe she could win him round. 'Dougie, I've already said I'm sorry.'

'I know you have. But what are you doing here?' he demanded.

'Dougie, don't be so *rude*,' wailed Sally. 'Lola's my *friend*.'

'I'm more than her friend.' Lola flashed him a playful smile and saw the split-second look of horror on his face . . . *Jesus, surely not* . . . 'I'm her next door neighbour.'

Doug shook his head in disbelief; being a neighbour might not be quite as alarming as being a predatory lesbian but it was evidently a close-run thing. He looked over at his sister. 'You didn't mention this.'

'Of course I didn't. If I'd told you I was going to be moving in next door to Lola, you'd have tried to talk me out of it.'

Exasperated, Doug retorted, 'Damn right I would. And I'm not the only one.'

'Well, too bad. I don't care what Mum says – it's not my fault she doesn't like Lola. You and Mum should put all that

106

old stuff behind you, it's irrelevant now. Anyway, this is my flat and I'm jolly well staying here.'

Overcome with gratitude, Lola longed to burst into applause, but the line of Dougie's jaw wasn't exactly forgiving. Instead she attempted to change the subject.

'Errm, I couldn't find the corkscrew.'

'OK, I think there's one in one of the cases in my bedroom. Hang on, I'll go and have a look.'

'You never know,' Doug said softly when Sally had left the room, 'play your cards right and you could land yourself another handy little windfall. My mother might be so keen to keep you away from Sal that she'd be prepared to pay you to move out.'

It hurt like a knife sliding in under her ribs. Lola said, 'Look, what do you want me to do? Fall on my knees and beg for forgiveness? I did a bad thing once and I'm sorry I hurt you, but at the time I didn't have any choice.'

Doug shook his head. 'Fine. Anyway, we're not going to argue about that again. I'm just here to drop off the rest of Sal's things. I'll fetch them from the car.'

'I'll help you.' Had Sally still not managed to locate the corkscrew or was she being discreet and keeping out of the way?

'No need.'

'I want to.' Lola followed him out into the hallway.

'I can manage.'

'But it's going to be easier if there's two of us.' She clattered down the stairs behind him. 'And I'm strong! Remember that time I beat you at arm-wrestling?'

Doug's shoulders stiffened. 'No.'

'Oh, come on. At Mandy Green's party. Her brother started this whole arm-wrestling competition out in the garden because

107

he said no girl could beat a boy. But he was wrong,' Lola said proudly, 'because I did, I beat him and I beat *you*—'

'That's because I let you win,' Doug said curtly.

'What? You didn't! *Ouch.*' As he reached the front door, Lola cannoned into his back.

'Of course I did.' Doug yanked open the door, shooting her a dismissive look over his shoulder. 'Did you seriously think you were stronger than me?'

'But . . . but . . .' Lola had spent the last decade – ten whole *years* – being proud of that achievement. And now Doug was shattering her illusions. This was like suddenly being told that Father Christmas didn't exist.

Woooooop went the dark green Mercedes on the other side of the road as Doug pointed a key at it.

Unless . . . unless he was lying when he said he'd let her win.

'Right, you can carry the bags with the clothes in. They're not so heavy.' He opened the boot. 'I'll deal with the boxes of books.'

Books. If there was one thing Lola was the queen of, it was carrying piles of books. Who needed to lift weights in a gym when you worked at Kingsley's?

Reaching past Doug she slammed the boot shut.

'Jesus!' He snatched his hand away in the nick of time. 'You nearly had my fingers off! What d'you think you're playing at?'

'I don't believe you lost on purpose. I think that's just your excuse.' Pushing up the sleeve of her sweater to give her elbow some grip, Lola angled herself up against the corner of the car's boot and waggled her fingers. 'So we'll just find out, shall we? On your marks, get set . . .'

'I tell you what,' said Doug, 'why don't we just carry my sister's things into the flat?'

'Chicken.'

'Lola, let me open the boot.'

'Clucka-lucka-luck.'

He gave her a raised-eyebrow look. 'What?'

OK, if she hadn't been a teeny bit squiffy she possibly wouldn't have done that. 'It's my chicken impression.'

'Not exactly Rory Bremner, are you?'

'Ooh, I saw Rory Bremner once,' Lola said excitedly. 'In a delicatessen.'

'He must have been thrilled. Can we get the stuff out now?'

She waggled her fingers once more. 'You're really scared I'll win, aren't you?'

'I don't believe this.' Heaving a sigh, Doug pushed up the sleeve of his pale grey sweatshirt, assumed the position against the car and clasped Lola's right hand. Her heart lolloped as his warm fingers closed around hers. She could feel his breath on her face, smell the aftershave he was wearing, see the glint of stubble on his jaw, imagine the way his mouth would feel if she were to kiss him right now . . .

Like premature ejaculation it was all over far too soon. *CLONCK* went the back of her forearm against the boot of the Mercedes.

'That's not fair,' Lola wailed. 'I wasn't ready.'

'Correction. You weren't strong enough.' He paused. 'What are you doing now?'

'Nothing. Just looking at you.' She'd seen a lot of eyes in her life but none more beautiful than Dougie's. He had the thickest, darkest eyelashes of any man she'd ever known.

'Well, stop it. I don't trust what's going on here. All of a sudden you're persuading my sister to move into the flat next to yours and I want to know why.'

'I didn't persuade her. It was her decision. But I'm glad she

109

chose to,' said Lola. 'Because I like Sally. We get on well together. And I'd rather have her living next door than the geeky nerdy type who would have moved in if she hadn't come along in the nick of time.'

'Is that the only reason?'

'Of course!'

'Now why don't I believe you? Oh yes, that's right, because you're a mercenary liar. Take these.' Having sprung open the boot once more, Doug dumped a huge pink canvas holdall in Lola's arms.

'How many times can I say I'm sorry?'

'Forget it. Not interested.' There was that muscle again, twitching away in his jaw as he hauled out two boxes of books. 'Just so long as you aren't still harbouring some kind of plan to persuade me to change my mind about you, because *that's* not going to happen.'

'I know. You told me that last week.' Honestly, whatever happened to forgive and forget?

'. . . then we went back to my flat and tore each other's clothes off. We had wild sex all night long and it was . . . ooh, fabulous!'

'Nice try, Pinocchio.' Cheryl carried on stacking books on a table in readiness for an author to come in and do a stock-signing. 'So what really happened?'

What had really happened was far less encouraging. Lola pulled a face and said, 'He emptied the car, dumped Sally's things in her flat and drove off.'

'Oh dear. So you won't be bringing him along to Bernini's tomorrow night. I was looking forward to meeting him.'

Tomorrow night was their works Christmas party. This year for some reason someone had suggested it should be fancy dress and in a moment of madness Lola had agreed. 'I wouldn't inflict that on Dougie. I'm not sure he's the dressing-up-like-an-idiot kind.'

'Plus,' Cheryl helpfully pointed out, 'he's not exactly your number one fan at the moment.'

'I know, I know.' Lola began folding the books' jacket flaps to the title pages to make signing speedier. Too ashamed to reveal the whole truth, she had left out the money aspect; as far as Cheryl was concerned, all that had happened was that Dougie had reacted badly to being chucked.

'Oh, cheer up,' said Cheryl. 'If anyone can win him round, you can. Think about it, meeting up with your first love again is fate! It's romantic! You made a mistake before, but there's no reason why you can't give things another whirl, especially if he's as gorgeous as you say he – oh, hello!'

Looking up, Lola saw that the man who wasn't a private detective was on the other side of the table.

'Hi.' He greeted them both with a friendly smile.

'How did you get on with . . . ?' Bugger, out of the books she'd recommended, Lola couldn't remember which one he'd ended up buying.

'It was great. I'm going to try the other author you mentioned. It's just that he's written a whole lot of them and I wasn't sure if I should start with the first in the—'

'Lola, there's a drunk guy trying to steal books.' Tim rushed up, his face puce with indignation. 'He's over in Mysteries, trying to stuff a load of Agatha Christies down his trousers. Quick!'

Euww. Dropping the book in her hand, Lola raced across the shop floor in Tim's slipstream, dodging customers and cursing shoplifters. Poor Agatha, what a grim thing to happen. She definitely didn't deserve this.

Chapter 15

'Where to, mate?'

'Airport,' said Gabe.

He sat back in the air-conditioned cab and didn't glance up at the window of Jaydena's apartment as the driver pulled away from the kerb.

That was it then. So much for happy ever after. Happy ever after, in fact, had disappeared right down the toilet.

How had he, of all people, managed to get it so wrong?

'It's not your fault.' Tears had been streaming down Jaydena's face last night as she finally came clean. 'You're a fantastic guy, really you are.'

I know, thought Gabe.

'And I'm so *sorry*, it's just that it never occurred to me that Paul would change his mind and want me back. But he's, like, the big love of my life, the one I could never forget. Oh Gabe, this is the best thing that's ever happened to me. Can you understand that? I don't want to hurt you, but there's no other way.'

It was almost a relief, on one level, figuring out at last why Jaydena had been as jumpy as a cat on a hotplate ever since he'd arrived last night.

On the other hand, discovering the truth still hurt like hell.

'You slept with me.' Gabe frowned. 'We had sex. If you and this guy are back together, why would you do that?'

'Oh God, because I felt so terrible,' Jaydena wailed. 'You flew all this *way*.'

He looked at her. 'And that was my consolation prize? Thanks a lot.'

'I already said I'm sorry!'

'Fine.' Gabe turned away; the last thing he was going to do was beg. 'I'm just saying you could have told me before I left London.'

'I know, but I couldn't, I had to wait for Paul to make up his mind and by the time he did, you were already on the plane.'

'Thoughtful of him.' In return, Gabe imagined taking Paul along for a day trip to a crocodile farm. Preferably bound and gagged.

'Look, I know it's not ideal,' Jaydena pleaded. 'But it's better that we do this now than next week or the week after.'

She'd sobbed some more after that, and apologised some more, and even ended up offering to sleep with Gabe one last time by way of making things up to him. 'So you have some kind of, like, closure, y'know?'

'No thanks.' He marvelled at his own idiocy; this was the girl for whom he'd given up his home, his job, his London life. And here she was, offering him a pity shag.

'Sure? I don't mind. Paul wouldn't either,' said Jaydena. 'I already asked and he said it's fine by him.'

What a hero. Gabe envisaged the feeding frenzy when he dropped Paul head first into the pool of crocodiles. 'That's very generous of him, but it's still a no. I'll use your computer, if that's OK, and get onto the airline.'

113

'Absolutely. Help yourself.' Nodding vigorously Jaydena said, 'Feel free.'

He'd managed to book a flight, then checked his emails. There was one from Lola saying, 'Hey, how's it going? Why haven't you been in touch yet? OK, maybe I can guess why – too busy doing other stuff with Jaydena. Text me when you have a few seconds to spare, you big tart. And remember, there's more to life than sex!'

Gabe paused. If only she knew.

There was no point emailing Lola now; he didn't have the words. Anyhow, she'd find out soon enough.

It hadn't been the easiest of nights. Gabe had slept fitfully on the sofa in Jaydena's living room and been up by six. The sensible part of him felt that after coming all this way he should stay on in Australia, for a while at least, to experience the lifestyle and the weather, see the sights and generally make the trip worthwhile.

The other pissed-off part of him just wanted to get the hell out of the damn place, put some serious distance between himself and Jaydena and head back home.

As the taxi made its way across Sydney towards the airport, he gazed out at the glittering ocean, the paintbox-blue sky and the scantily clad blondes on their way to the beach. Keen though he was to escape the country, it occurred to Gabe that when he reached London he'd barely have any proof that he'd even been here. Reaching over and unzipping the front compartment of his rucksack, he pulled out his digital camera and began taking photographs out of the window.

'Good holiday, mate?'

It wasn't the taxi guy's fault that his life had just taken a nosedive. Snapping a picture of a girl in a raspberry-pink bikini cycling along with a terrier on a lead in tow, Gabe said, 'Great, thanks.'

'Ah, it's a beautiful place, mate. Nowhere else like it. Bin here long?'

'Not too long. But you're right, it's a beautiful country.'

'The best.' The driver nodded with pride then pointed to the service station up ahead. 'OK if I pull in for a couple of minutes or are you in a rush to get there?'

'No rush at all.' Gabe's flight wasn't leaving for another five hours; he'd just been keen to get out of the flat. 'Do what you want.' *Everyone else does.*

The man drove into the service station, parked up next to the car wash and disappeared inside the shop. Gabe, in the back of the cab, scrolled through the half-dozen or so photos he'd taken and deleted one that was blurred because they'd been driving over a bump at the time. He glanced up as a slender brunette emerged from another parked car and made her way around the corner of the building. For a split second Gabe thought she seemed familiar, before remembering he was in Sydney, Australia. It wasn't like bumping into someone you knew in the supermarket back home.

Moments later his head jerked up again as another figure, male this time, emerged from a second car and headed in the same direction as the brunette.

Gabe frowned. Wasn't that . . . ? No, it couldn't be.

But as the man moved out of sight, curiosity got the better of Gabe. Opening the rear door of the cab, he climbed out. Ninety degrees of heat hit him in the face. Mystified, Gabe reached the side of the whitewashed building and saw . . . blimey . . . that he hadn't been mistaken after all. Except no wonder he hadn't twigged at first; it wasn't every day you saw

115

two members of Hollywood's A-list sneaking off down a narrow alley behind a service station in order to kiss each other senseless.

Unless it was for a movie and they were being paid millions of dollars to do it.

Which certainly wasn't the case here. This time they were doing it for free.

Click. Gabe hadn't even planned on taking their photo; somehow, the camera in his hand came up and there they were in the frame, so completely wrapped up in each other that they neither saw him nor heard the shutter close. Gabe took another photo, this time getting a clear shot of the girl's face. Then, realising what he was doing – God, what was he, some kind of snooper? – he turned and hurried back to the cab.

'All right there?' The taxi driver emerged from the shop with a bottle of iced water and a bag of toffees.

'Fine.'

'Off we go, then.'

As they waited to pull out onto the main road, the male half of the couple emerged from the alley. Tom Dutton, Oscar-winning actor, wearing faded denims and a red checked shirt. His long blond hair flopped over his forehead as he loped back to his car. Simply because it would thrill Lola, who had dragged him along to the cinema last summer and noisily sobbed her way through the weepy that had been Tom Dutton's most recent film, Gabe raised his camera and took one last photo.

Personally he'd thought the film was crap.

Chapter 16

Lola wasn't averse to a bit of untidiness but stepping into Gabe's flat was something of an eye-opener. The initial impression was of utter chaos, Selfridges Christmas department mixed with a charity shop the morning after an all-night party.

'Hi there, I was wondering if you had any black shoe polish—*whoops*.' Lola just managed to avoid stepping on a triangle of pepperoni pizza lying on an open copy of *Heat*. Something told her she wasn't going to be in luck. Most of Sally's clothes appeared to be strewn across the floor, along with a couple of damp bath towels. Just as well Gabe wasn't here to see this.

'I do, I do!' Sally gaily dropped her apple core onto Gabe's formerly pristine glass-topped coffee table and pressed her fingers, psychic-style, to her temples. 'Hmm, shoe polishes, shoe polishes. They're here somewhere . . . I remember taking them out of a case and putting them . . . ooh, I know! On the window sill in the kitchen!'

Where else? Following Sally into the kitchen, Lola saw a whole range of shoe polishes flung into a pink and gold flowerpot along with a Nicky Clarke hairspray, a zebra print alarm clock, a bag of satsumas and a skipping rope.

'Brilliant. I'll only be a couple of seconds.' Holding her favourite black stilettos, Lola squeezed liquid polish onto the toes. Instant magic. The scuffs disappeared and she recapped the tube. 'Shall I put this out of the way in the cupboard under the sink?'

'No need. I like things where I can see them.' Surveying her in her dressing gown, Sally said, 'Off out somewhere nice?'

'Wine bar in Soho. Works Christmas party.' Lola pulled a face. 'Fancy dress.'

'Ooh, I love fancy dress! What are you going as?'

'A Playboy Bunny. Don't laugh,' said Lola. 'Everyone had to put an idea into the hat and I drew the short straw. Tim from work has gone over to the fancy dress hire place to pick everything up. He'll be here any minute with my costume.'

'At least it's sexy. I always wanted to be a Playboy Bunny when I grew up. But Mum said over her dead body. Oh well,' Sally said cheerfully, 'you'll have to come and give me a twirl before you leave.'

'Blimey.' Coming face to face with Tim on her doorstep, lugging an enormous zip-up carrying case, Lola said, 'That can't all be for me.'

Her outfit was a skimpy affair, surely. Black satin swimsuit thing, white fluffy tail and a pair of ears. How much space could that take up?

'Been a bit of a mix-up.' Tim looked embarrassed.

'What kind of a mix-up?'

His cheeks flamed. 'When I ordered a Bunny outfit they thought I meant . . . well, a *bunny* bunny.'

'You mean . . . ? Oh God, let me see.' Lola unzipped the carrying case and was confronted by a full-size rabbit suit made of white nylon fur. 'I have to wear *this*?'

'Sorry,' Tim said miserably.

She pulled out the suit and gave herself a static shock. On the bright side, she wouldn't need to spend the evening holding her stomach in.

On the less bright side, what a waste of polishing her shoes. She was destined to spend the night with her feet encased in giant furry white rabbit's paws.

'I'm going to get hot in there.' The nylon fur crackled and gave Lola another zip of static as she stroked it.

'You can swap costumes with me if you want to,' said Tim.

The 'if you want to' part didn't fill her with optimism. 'Why, what's yours?'

'Well, I *was* going to be a gladiator. Kind of like Russell Crowe. But the breastplate snapped and they couldn't let me have it.'

'So you're not a gladiator. Instead you're . . . ?'

Tim mumbled, 'Barney the Dinosaur.'

Lola sighed. 'Thanks, but I'll stay with the rabbit. Purple was never my colour.'

'You're all pink!' Cheryl, looking glamorous and suitably exotic in her hula skirt, danced up to Lola.

All pink. Fancy that.

'Imagine how hot it feels, being trapped inside an all-in-one bunny suit.' Lola reached for a bottle of ice-cold water. 'Then double it. Actually,' she paused and glugged down several mouthfuls of the water, 'quadruple it.'

The DJ started to play 'Last Christmas' by Wham!, causing a stampede (why? *why*?) onto the dance floor.

'Fancy a dance?' said Cheryl, shimmying her hips.

'Not really, no.'

'Couldn't you take the bunny suit off now?' Cheryl tilted her head sympathetically to one side.

'I could, if I'd thought to bring a change of clothes with me.' Huffing her damp fringe out of her eyes, Lola couldn't believe it hadn't occurred to her. But beneath the nylon fur she was scantily clad and jolly though the crowd at Bernini's were, she didn't feel they were ready to witness her in her pink and green polka-dotty knickers and matching balcony bra.

Mind you, it was a salutary experience dressing up like a rabbit. Until tonight she hadn't realised how nice it was to be paid attention by members of the opposite sex. Being eyed up was something she'd pretty much taken for granted.

'You know, I feel as if I'm wearing an invisibility cloak,' said Lola. 'Nobody's looking at me.'

'Oh, that's not true.' Cheryl did her best to sound convincing.

'It is.' Lola could see the gaze of men sliding over her without pausing in their search for an attractive girl to flirt with. Tonight, she couldn't help noticing, the attractive girl was Cheryl in her undulating hula skirt.

'Look.' Eager to help, Cheryl pointed across the dance floor. 'Those people over there are looking at you.'

'They're laughing. That's different. They're pretending to clean their whiskers and lick their paws.' Lola took another swig of water. 'I don't mind. I'm just saying. Actually, those celebrities who whinge and moan about being pestered every time they go out could do a lot worse than get themselves a nice bunny suit.'

'Hey, at least you aren't Barney the Dinosaur.'

Poor old Tim, his outfit was even hotter and heavier than her own. Lola watched him attempting to dance like George Michael when he was still straight, wincing as his dinosaur tail swung lethally from side to side. Helen, dressed as Cleopatra, was gamely bopping around with Batman, aka Darren, who had legs like string beans. In the far corner of the dance floor a group of Hogwarts students with black bin-bag cloaks were climbing onto their broomsticks—

'I can see someone looking at you.' Cheryl gave her a nudge.

Lola didn't get her hopes up. 'Where?'

'Over there, just come in.' Cheryl nodded at the door. 'The one in the blue shirt, see him yet? He hasn't taken his eyes off you since he got here. Actually . . .' Her voice trailed off as she peered more closely at the new arrival. 'He looks familiar. Where have I seen him before? Ooh, and now he's coming over!'

Lola surveyed him, glad she hadn't got her hopes up. 'He's one of our customers.'

'God, you're right, it is. Did we invite customers along tonight?'

'No.' Mystified, Lola watched the man who wasn't a private detective. When he reached them she noticed that the usual easy smile was tinged with something else, possibly nerves.

'Hi.' As she nodded in recognition, one of the bunny ears flopped down into her field of vision, which didn't help.

'Hi there. I wasn't sure at first if it was you.' The smile became a grin. 'Nice outfit.'

'Thanks.' Lola paused as Cheryl melted tactfully away into the crowd. 'So is this a coincidence, you turning up here tonight?'

'No, it isn't. When I was in the shop yesterday I heard your friend talking about the party here tonight.'

At least he was honest. 'So are you a stalker?'

Another pause. Finally he shook his head. 'Not really. I mean, I suppose so, kind of. But for a reason. Not in a creepy way, I promise.'

That was the thing, he just didn't *seem* creepy. 'Well, good,' said Lola, indicating Darren on the dance floor, 'because otherwise I'd have to set Batman onto you.'

The corners of the man's eyes creased with amusement but beneath the surface he was still on edge. 'Look, is there anywhere we could talk?'

'About what?'

'Something important. Sorry, I know this place isn't ideal, but I didn't want to do it at the bookshop. There's a free table over there in the corner.' As he steered Lola gently towards it, he eyed the empty bottle of water in her hand. 'Can I get you another drink? Maybe a . . . carrot juice?'

Lola stopped, gave him a look.

He raised his hands. 'OK, sorry, sorry. I can't believe I said that.'

'I can't believe it either. So far this evening eleven people have asked me if I'd like a carrot juice. Eight have asked me if I'd like some lettuce. Four have made hilarious jokes about popping out of a magician's hat. Honestly, this place is just one huge comedy club *bursting* with Billy Connollys.'

'Sorry, I'm usually a bit more original than that. Put it down to nerves.'

They reached the table. The man pulled out a chair for Lola then sat down himself.

'Why are you nervous?' Her right ear was falling over her eye again; impatiently Lola tossed it out of the way.

'Sure I can't get you a drink?'

'I'd rather know what all this is about.'

Wham! finished playing and was replaced – surprise surprise – by Slade belting out 'Merry Christmas Everybody'. Noddy Holder's cheese-grater voice vibrated off the walls and everyone on the dance floor punched the air, pogo-ing madly and singing along not *quite* in time with the music. Having watched them for a few seconds, Lola turned her attention back to the man and said, 'Still waiting.'

In the dim lighting of this corner of the bar his expression was unreadable. 'Twentieth of May?'

Something squeezed tight in Lola's chest. 'That's my birthday.'

He sat back, exhaled, pushed his fingers through his dark hair then half smiled. 'In that case you're definitely my daughter.'

The furry white nylon ear flopped once more over Lola's face. Little stars danced in her field of vision as she fumbled with the Velcro fastening her costume at the neck. But her fingers couldn't manage it and heat was spreading inexorably through her body. Finally she managed to say, 'Please, could you help me take my head off? I'm feeling a bit . . . um, faint.'

Chapter 17

One minute you were in a wine bar more or less blending in with the twenty-two other people cavorting around in fancy dress, the next minute you were sitting in an all-night café with a mug of hot tea, attracting all manner of smirks and funny looks from everyone else in the place.

Lola still couldn't assimilate what had happened; her brain had stubbornly refused to believe what he was telling her. Apart from anything else, this man wasn't even American. Yet . . . why would he be here doing this if it weren't true?

'Sorry.' The man sitting opposite her said it for the third time. 'I knew it was going to be a shock but I couldn't think of any way of saying it that wouldn't be.'

'That's OK.' At least it was cooler in here. The urge to pass out had receded. Her head was still spinning but out of shock rather than syncope. 'You can't imagine how unexpected this is.'

He did that rueful semi-smile again. 'For me too.'

Lola sipped her tea, burning her mouth but appreciating the sugar rush. 'So you're . . . Steve?'

The semi-smile abruptly disappeared. 'No. That's not me.'

So. Not American, not called Steve. Something wasn't right here. But he seemed so genuine, so convinced . . .

'What's your name then?'

What's your name? What a question.

'Nick. Nick James.' Shaking his head, he said, 'I can't believe your mother didn't tell you that.'

'Tuh, that's nothing! She told me you were from New York.' She looked at him suspiciously. '*Are* you?' Was he, perhaps, *pretending* to be British?

His eyebrows went up. 'What else did she say?'

'Oh God.' Lola almost dropped her cup. 'Your eyebrows. That's just how mine go when I'm surprised . . .' Tea slopped onto the table as her trembling increased, because the similarity was almost uncanny. 'You've got my eyebrows!'

'Actually, you've got mine,' Nick James pointed out.

'That's incredible! And we have dark hair.'

'You have your mother's eyes and freckles.'

'But not her hair. Before you saw me, did you think I'd be a redhead?'

He shook his head. 'I knew you weren't. I visited you once, when you were a baby.'

Lola felt as if all the air had been squeezed from her lungs. 'You did?'

'Oh yes. Briefly.' He smiled. 'You were beautiful. Seeing you for the first time . . . well, it was incredible.'

Her eyes abruptly filling with tears, Lola said, 'And then you buggered off again.' The tears took her by surprise and she brushed them away angrily; it wasn't as if she'd had a miser-able life without—

'No, *no*. God, that's not what happened at all.' Horrified, Nick James said, 'Is that what you think, that I was the one who walked away? Because I didn't, I swear. I loved your mother and I wanted the three of us to be a family, more than anything. She was the one who wouldn't have it.'

'Hang on.' Lola stopped him, because this was just too surreal; there had to have been some kind of misunderstanding here. 'This is Blythe we're talking about?'

She had to double-check. Imagine if he sat back in dismay and said, 'No, not Blythe! I'm talking about *Linda*.'

And the eyebrows had just been an eerie coincidence.

But he didn't, he just nodded and said simply, 'Blythe Malone, that's right.'

'Anything to eat, love?' A waitress bustled over to their table, mopping up the tea Lola had spilled on the Formica.

'No thanks.' There was so much to take in, not least the discovery that her own mother had lied to her.

And in a pretty major way.

'Sure? We've got a lovely lamb hotpot.' The waitress helpfully pointed to the appropriate photograph on the laminated menu. 'Or faggots and chips, everyone likes our faggots.'

Normally Lola would have thought of something funny to say to this, but her brain was all over the place. 'I'm fine. Really.'

'She'd rather have a plate of carrots.' One of the men at the next table chuckled and nudged his friend, who broke into a buck-toothed Bugs Bunny impression.

'Sorry.' Nick James looked at Lola. 'I should have found somewhere better than this.'

Offended, the waitress sniffed and said, 'Charmed, I'm sure.'

'It doesn't matter.' Lola shook her head. 'I wish I wasn't wearing a bunny suit, but that can't be helped. And the tea's great.' She smiled up at the waitress. 'Actually, I'll have another one.'

'My flat's not far from here. We could go there if you want

126

to,' Nick James offered. 'But I thought that might seem a bit strange.'

'A bit.' Much as she'd have preferred to be wearing normal clothes, Lola had felt the same way about inviting him back to Radley Road.

He nodded in agreement. 'Neutral ground's better. For now, anyway.'

His voice was nice, well-spoken without being posh. He was wearing well-cut navy trousers and a mulberry and blue striped shirt. The watch on his wrist was a black and gold Breitling. And – she now knew it was true; believed him absolutely – he was *her actual biological father.*

'When I was little I always thought my dad was a film star,' said Lola, 'because the only Americans I knew were the ones I'd seen on TV.'

'And you got yourself an advertising exec instead. Bad luck.'

'That's OK. It's just weird, all these years imagining you being an American, *talking* like an American, and now having to lose that idea. I used to wonder if the dark one from *Starsky and Hutch* was my dad.'

'Sorry.'

'I never much liked his cardigans anyway. Or the guy from *Miami Vice*,' said Lola. 'Don Johnson.'

Nick said gravely, 'I promise I've never pushed up the sleeves of my suit.'

'Or Robert Wagner from *Hart to Hart*. Or John Travolta. Even thingummy with the dodgy moustache who was in *Smokey and the Bandit*.'

'If I'd known, I'd have brushed up on my American accent.' He shrugged, half smiled. 'I can't imagine why Blythe told you that.'

Lola glanced at her handbag, lying on the chair next to her and containing her mobile. There was nothing to stop her calling her mother right now and demanding an explanation. Or even using the camera on her phone to take a photo of Nick James, then sending it to Blythe along with a message saying '*Guess who?*'

But she couldn't bring herself to do that.

Ooh, Tom Selleck, he'd been another on her list of possible fathers. She'd evidently had a bit of a hankering for one with a moustache.

Except Nick James didn't have one.

God, this was so *weird*.

'How did you find me?'

'The piece you did on the local news,' he admitted. 'When I said I hadn't seen it . . . well, that was a lie. I was flicking through the TV channels that evening and there you were, with your name up on the screen. Lola Malone. You were Lauren when you were born.'

'I know,' said Lola.

'Sorry, I meant I knew you as Lauren. But the day I came round to your mother's house when you were a baby, she handed you over to a friend and said, "Could you take Lola out into the garden?"'

'Our next door neighbour's daughter couldn't say Lauren so she called me Lola. It stuck. Nobody calls me Lauren.'

He nodded. 'Well, anyway, I didn't know for sure if it was you, but it was an unusual name and you were the right age and colouring. So I had to come to the shop and see you.'

That was why he had engaged her in conversation.

'Hang on, so you didn't really like those books I recommended.' Lola's pride was wounded. 'You were just pretending.'

Nick smiled and shook his head. 'I loved the books. I read them because you'd recommended them. Don't worry, I'm definitely converted.'

He was telling the truth. That made her feel better. Lola took another sip of tea. 'I can't believe I'm sitting here talking to you now. Wait till I tell Mum.'

A flicker of something crossed her father's — *her father's!* — face. 'How is Blythe?'

'She's great. Living in Streatham. Having fun.'

'Married?'

'I had a fantastic stepdad. He died five years ago.'

Nick shook his head. 'I'm sorry.'

'But Mum's doing really well. She's started dating again. I'm trying to do something about her clothes. Did she have really weird dress sense when you knew her?'

He looked amused. 'Oh yes.'

'At least that's something I didn't inherit from her.' Lola patted her furry white nylon suit. 'I mean, I'd rather shoot myself than go out in public wearing something that people might laugh at.'

Nick nodded in agreement. 'Thank goodness for that. I have pretty high standards myself.'

He did, come to think of it. Each time she'd seen him he'd been wearing expensive clothes well. A million questions were bubbling up in Lola's brain.

'So what happened?' she blurted out. 'I don't understand. Why did you and Mum break up?'

He paused. 'What did she tell you?'

'Well. A big lie, obviously. But the story was that she met an American guy called Steve when he was working over here one summer. She thought he was wonderful, completely fell for him, discovered she was pregnant, told him she was pregnant and never saw him again after that day. When she went along to the pub he'd been working in, they told her he'd left, gone back to the States. They also told her his surname wasn't what he'd said it was. So that was that. Mum knew she was on her own. She'd fallen for a bastard and he'd let her down. She told me she never regretted it, because she got me, but that she'd learned her lesson as far as men were concerned. Then when I was four years old she married Alex Pargeter, who was the best stepfather any girl could ask for.'

'Good.' Nick sounded as if he meant it. 'I'm glad.'

'But none of that stuff was true, was it?' Lola's fingers gripped the now-empty mug in front of her. 'Your name isn't even Steve. So now it's your turn. I want to know what really happened.'

'What really happened.' Another pause, then Nick exhaled and shook his head. Finally, slowly, he said, 'What really happened is I went to prison.'

Chapter 18

'It was my own stupid fault. There's no one else to blame. Everything would have been different if I hadn't messed up.'

Having left the café, they were now heading in the direction of Notting Hill. It was a frosty night and the pavement glittered under the street lamps but Lola was protected from the cold by her bunny suit. She was getting a bit fed up, though, with groups of Christmas revellers singing 'Bright Eyes' at her. Or bellowing out 'Run, rabbit, run, rabbit, run run run' while taking aim with an imaginary shotgun. Or bawdily asking her if she was feeling *rampant* . . .

Which was the kind of question you could do without, frankly, when you were out with your dad.

Your *jailbird* dad.

God, look at me, I'm actually walking along the Bayswater Road *with my father.*

'Blythe knew nothing about it,' Nick went on. 'She was four months pregnant. We'd been together for almost a year by then. Obviously we hadn't planned on having a baby, but these things happen. We started looking around for a place to buy, so we could be together. That was an eye-opener, I can tell you. I was

131

only twenty-one; there wasn't much we could afford. I felt such a failure. If only we had more money. Are you cold? Because if you're cold we can flag down a cab.'

'I'm fine.' Lola's breath was puffing out in front of her but the rest of her was warm. 'So what did you do, rob a bank?'

'I got involved with a friend of a friend who'd set up a cigarette and booze smuggling operation. Bringing the stuff over from the continent, selling it on, easy profit.' Drily, Nick said, 'Until you get caught. Let me tell you, that wasn't the best day of my life.'

'You were arrested.' Lola tried to imagine him being arrested; she'd only ever seen it happen on TV.

He nodded. 'What can I tell you? I was young and stupid, and I panicked. Blythe would have been distraught, so I couldn't bring myself to tell her. I appeared at the magistrates court, still didn't tell her. Had to wait four months for the case to come up in the crown court. *Still* didn't tell her. Because I'd only been involved in the operation for a few weeks my solicitor said there was a chance I wouldn't go down and I clung on to that. I know it's crazy, but I thought maybe, just maybe, Blythe wouldn't need to know about any of it. That she'd never find out.'

Lola could kind of see the logic in this. Hadn't she once failed to hand in an entire geography project and pinned all her hopes on the school burning down before her teacher found out? Oh God, she *was* her father's daughter . . .

Aloud, she said, 'Good plan.'

'It would have been if it had worked. Except it didn't.' Nick shrugged. 'The judge wasn't in a great mood that day. I got eighteen months.'

They'd both gambled and lost. Except her punishment had

only been a trip to the headmistress and three weeks' detention. 'So how did Mum find out?'

'My cousin had to phone her. Can you imagine what that must have been like? She came to visit me in prison ten days later, said it was all over and she never wanted to see me again. I told her I'd only done it for her and the baby, but she wasn't going to change her mind. As far as she was concerned I was a criminal and a liar, and that wasn't the kind of father she wanted for her child. It was pretty emotional. Understandably, Blythe was in a state. Well, we both were. But she was nine months pregnant, so all I could do was apologise and agree with everything she said. That was the second-worst day of my life.' He paused. 'You were born a week later.'

Lola was beginning to understand why her mother had invented an alternative history.

'I served my time, behaved myself and got out of prison after nine months,' Nick went on. 'You and your mother were all I'd thought about. I was desperate to see you, and to make Blythe understand how sorry I was. If she still had feelings for me, I thought I might be able to persuade her to change her mind, give me another chance. So I came round to the house and that's when I saw you for the first time. It was incredible. You were . . . well, it's not something you ever forget. You were beaming at me, with your hair in a funny little curly topknot and Ribena stains on your white T-shirt. But your mother wasn't open to persuasion, she said she'd never be able to trust me. She also said I'd put her through hell and if I had an ounce of decency I'd leave the two of you in peace, because no father at all would be easier for you to deal with than a lying, cheating, untrustworthy one. She finished off by saying if I really wanted to prove how sorry I was, the best thing I could do was disappear. And you know what?' As they waited for the traffic lights to change, he gave Lola a sideways look. 'She meant it.'

'Hey, it's the white rabbit!' someone bawled out of a car window. 'Where's Alice?'

The lights turned green. Together they crossed the road. 'So that's what you did,' said Lola. Notting Hill tube station was ahead of them now.

'I didn't want to. But I was the one who'd messed up. I felt I owed Blythe that much. So I said goodbye and left.' He waited. 'That was the worst day of my life.'

Crikey, this was emotional stuff.

'I keep feeling as if I'm listening to you talk about some television drama.' Lola shook her head in disbelief. 'Then it hits me all over again; this is actually about *me*.'

'Oi, you in the fur,' roared a bloke zooming past in a van. 'Fancy a jump?'

'My flat's down here.' Loftily ignoring the van driver, Lola turned left into Radley Road. 'I've still got loads more questions.'

'Fire away.'

'Have you been in trouble with the law since then?'

Nick shook his head. 'No, no. Apart from three points on my licence for speeding. I learned my lesson, Your Honour.'

'Are you married?'

Another shake. 'Not any more. Amicable divorce six years ago.'

'Any children?'

He broke into a smile. 'No other children. Just you.'

Lola swallowed; God, this was really happening. Wait until she told her mum about tonight.

'Well, this is where I live.' She stopped outside number 73; they'd walked all the way from Soho.

'Nice place.'

'Thanks.' The events of the evening abruptly caught up with Lola; one minute she'd been strolling happily along, the next she was so bone tired all she wanted to do was lie down and sleep for a week. But this man – *her father* – had just spent the last hour walking her home . . .

'Right then, I'll be off.' Nick James watched her yawn like a hippo.

'I feel awful, not inviting you in for a coffee.'

'Hey, it's fine. I'll get a cab.' He raked his fingers through his hair. 'It's been a lot to take in.'

Lola nodded; gosh, and now she didn't know how to say goodbye. This was even more awkward than the end of a disastrous blind date. Was she supposed to hug him, kiss him, shake hands or what?

Nick James smiled and said, 'Tricky, isn't it?'

'Yes, it *is*.' Relieved that he understood, Lola watched him take out his wallet. 'Ooh, do I start getting pocket money?'

'I was thinking more of a business card.' The smile broadened as he handed over his card. 'I don't want to put pressure on you, so from now on I'll leave it up to you to get in touch with me. That's if you decide you want to.' Turning, he began to walk back down the street.

Lola watched him go, a lump forming in her throat. What a night, what a thing to happen out of the blue. Tucking the rabbit's head under one furry arm, she delved into her bag for her front door key.

Nick James was about to turn the corner when she cleared her throat and called out, 'Um . . . Nick? I will be in touch.'

He paused, turned to face her and raised a hand in acknowledgement. 'I hope so.'

135

Chapter 19

At four o'clock the following afternoon the taxi pulled into Radley Road. Gabe said, 'It's the blue and white house up there on the left.'

OK, he was back.

When the cab had disappeared he hauled his luggage up the steps and let himself in through the front door. Leaving the cases in the hall, he made his way upstairs. Then, bracing himself, he knocked on Lola's door.

So much for bracing. No reply.

Well, it wasn't as if she was expecting him. As far as Lola was concerned he was still on the other side of the world.

Gabe went downstairs and fetched his cases, piling them up outside Lola's. Then he crossed the landing and knocked on the door of his own flat.

The girl was out too. He knocked again to make extra sure. OK, it was his property and he had a right to enter it. Plus, drinking far too much water earlier meant he could do with using the loo. Exhausted after the flight and irrationally annoyed by the lack of welcome, Gabe twiddled the keyring around until he located the right key.

He fitted it into the lock, twisted it to the left and pushed open the door.

Jesus Christ, the place had been burgled. Stepping back in horror, Gabe surveyed the scene of devastation. Except if burglars had been here, wouldn't they have made off with that flat-screen TV? Or the expensive DVD recorder? Or that pile of money over there on the floor next to the plate of spaghetti bolognese?

What the bloody hell *was* this? Gabe ventured further into the living room, treading a careful path between abandoned clothes, CDs, magazines, opened packets of biscuits and half-full coffee mugs. Did the girl have some kind of stalker ex-boyfriend who'd been round to the house and trashed it?

But he knew that wasn't right either. The mess and devastation wasn't . . . vindictive, somehow. It was too casual to have been done in anger. Squeezing his eyes tight shut then opening them again, Gabe realised with a sinking heart what kind of a tenant had moved into his home. He investigated the rest of the flat and had his worst fears confirmed. The kitchen was beyond belief. The bedroom looked as if it had been ransacked. The bathroom resembled a small branch of Boots that had been caught in a hurricane. There was a packet of smoky bacon crisps in the sink. The bath brimmed with water that was emerald green and stone cold. There were at least six damp towels on the floor.

He'd been away for *four days*.

His beautiful flat, his pride and joy. The muscles in Gabe's temples went into spasm and his head began to ache. As if he didn't have enough to deal with right now.

Oh well, the sooner the girl was out of here, the better. Maybe it was just as well he'd come back.

That was when he heard the bang of the front door downstairs, followed by the sound of footsteps on the staircase. Was it Lola or the new girl, the Queen of Trash?

Gabe left the flat, closed the door behind him and waited on the landing to see which one of them it—

'Aaaarrrggh!' Lola let out a shriek of fright and almost lost her footing on the stairs. One hand grabbed the banister while the other covered her mouth.

'No, I'm not a ghost,' said Gabe. 'It's really me.'

Lola was clasping her chest now. 'But you're . . . you're . . . what's going on?'

'Didn't work out.' He loved Lola to death but still hated having to tell her, to admit he'd failed.

Her mouth dropped open. 'You changed your mind?'

'No.' Gabe briefly shook his head. 'She changed hers.'

Lola threw herself at him, knocking the air from his lungs. *Whoosh*, she was in his arms babbling, 'You mean you're back? Oh my God, that's fantastic! Is Jaydena completely mad? I can't believe it, I thought I was hallucinating! What a *cow*!'

This was why he loved Lola. 'I think so too. She got back together with an ex.'

'Oh well, her loss.' Lola gave him another rib-crushing squeeze. 'Come in and tell me all about it. Shall we leave your stuff out here? My God, you went all that way for nothing! Will you be able to get your job back? Where on earth are you going to *live*?'

'What are you talking about?' Following Lola, Gabe said, 'I'm back. I'll be living here, of course.'

'You mean in Sally's flat?'

'For crying out loud, it's not her flat! It's mine! I'll explain to her that I need it now, give her a week's notice. *And* I've just been in there,' he said incredulously. 'Have you seen the state of the place?'

'She's not terribly tidy.' Hastily, since she was the one responsible for Sally moving in, Lola added, 'Very nice though.'

'Not terribly tidy? That's like saying the Beckhams aren't terribly thrifty. She only moved in four days ago – imagine what it'd look like after four months! No,' Gabe shook his head, 'she has to go. As for a job, I've no idea. I haven't even thought about that yet. The last week hasn't exactly gone according to plan.' He took the can of lager Lola was offering him and pinged off the ring pull.

'No wonder you're a bit grumpy,' Lola said sympathetically.

'I'm not *a bit grumpy*. I went to Australia, I came back again and I didn't even have time to get a suntan.' Exasperated, Gabe glugged down ice-cold lager before wiping his mouth with the back of his hand. 'Dammit, I'm *pissed off*.'

'OK, you choose. Now, do you want to carry on talking about Australia or shall we change the subject?'

He surveyed Lola, who was evidently dying to unleash some gossip. Nodding in realisation he said, 'Right, of course, you've seen that guy again. Doug, isn't it? Has he forgiven you yet?'

Lola's face fell at the mention of her first love. 'Not even slightly.' Then she brightened. 'But something else has happened. I've met another man.'

'And to think they call you fickle.' Gabe regarded her with affection, because it wasn't her fault his own life was crap. 'Go on then. Who is he?'

'Actually,' Lola grimaced, 'this is the weird bit. He's my father.'

At seven o'clock they heard the front door open and close, then the sound of someone climbing the stairs.

'Here's Sally.' Lola stayed sitting, clearly not looking forward to the next bit.

'Right, I'll speak to her. The sooner this is sorted out, the better.' Gabe rose to his feet, ready to do battle with the bag lady who'd wrecked his flat.

'The thing is, she—'

'Don't worry, I know she's Doug's deranged sister, I won't yell at her.' Ha, *much*.

'But—'

'I shall be charm personified,' said Gabe, opening the door.

Except the girl he came face to face with on the landing was no bag lady. This girl was tall and curvaceous in a red wrap-around dress and an elegant cream coat. Her hair was baby-blonde and swingy, her eyes were the colour of chestnuts, accentuated by expertly applied eyeliner. Her mouth was curvy and painted red to match her dress. She was even wearing Jo Malone's Lime, Basil and Mandarin, which was Gabe's all-time favourite perfume.

This couldn't be the girl he'd spoken to on the phone last week, surely.

'Hello!' She smiled cheerily at Gabe and, key poised, headed for the door of his flat.

It just *couldn't*.

Gabe cleared his throat. 'Are you Sally?'

She stopped, turned. 'Yes! And you must be a friend of Lola's.' Her eyes sparkling, she indicated the mountain of luggage and said jokily, 'Are you moving in?'

'I'm Gabe Adams.' God, it *was* her.

'Gabe?' Sally looked puzzled. 'But that's the name of the one who moved to Australia.'

'I didn't *move* to Australia, I *went* to Australia. But things didn't work out,' Gabe said evenly, 'so now I'm back. Look, I realise this is inconvenient for you, but I'll help you pack up your stuff. And if you could be out by the end of the week, that'd be great.'

She stared at him. 'Excuse me?'

How could any girl who lived in such abject squalor look like this? How was it physically possible? 'Well, you'll be moving back in with your mother.' Ha, lucky old *her*. 'I'll even hire a van if you like.' Gabe felt he was being more than generous; with all the stuff she'd strewn around his flat he'd need a pantechnicon. 'And we can do it any time this week, whenever suits you best.'

'I don't understand,' said Sally. 'I'm not going anywhere.'

'But you have to. Because it's my flat and I need it back.'

Her eyebrows furrowed. 'And I'm saying you can't *have* it back because the agreement was that I could live here for a year *at least*.'

'OK, OK.' Gabe heaved a sigh; it had always been on the cards that she might dig her heels in, decide to be difficult. 'I'm giving you official notice as of today. That's in the contract. You have one month to find somewhere else. God knows where I'm going to stay until then, but—'

'Hang on,' Sally interrupted. 'What contract?'

'The one you signed with the lettings agency.'

'I haven't signed any contract,' said Sally.

Behind him, Gabe heard Lola's door click open. He turned and said evenly, 'What's going on here? Why didn't she sign the contract?'

Lola could feel her heart clattering away in overdrive. She'd been hiding behind the door listening to their heated exchange. Now it was time to face the music. Uncurling her clenched

141

toes, she took a deep breath and said reluctantly, 'I cancelled the agency.'

'*Why?*'

Oh God, Gabe had been dumped by his girlfriend, he'd just arrived back from Australia, and he was suffering from jet lag on top of jet lag. All in all, he wasn't in the sunniest of moods.

'OK, the thing is, I was trying to *help*.' When she went on the defensive, Lola knew she used her hands a lot; now they were going like a pair of wind turbines in overdrive. 'And you told me yourself that the lettings agency charges a fortune, so when Sally came along I thought I could save you a heap of money, which I *thought* you'd be happy about. Because I knew we could trust Sally, she obviously wasn't going to be giving you any trouble with the rent, so it made sense to just, you know, deal with her direct and cut out the middleman. She gave me the deposit and the first month's rent in cash and I paid them into your account.'

'No problem, I'll give it straight back,' Gabe retorted.

'This isn't fair.' Sally's tone was heated. 'You're being completely unreasonable.'

'*Me?*' Gabe jabbed at his own chest and yelled, '*I'm* being completely unreasonable? What about the state of my flat? Would you say the carnage you've reduced it to is *reasonable*?'

Sally stared at him. 'How do you know what I've done to it?'

'Because I went in and had a look!'

She gasped. 'You can't just let yourself in whenever you like.'

'You can't stop me.' Gabe was really losing it now. 'It's my flat!'

'Which you rented to me. And I like living here.' Sally's eyes abruptly brimmed with tears. 'What's more, I'm not going to move out.'

'Oh please.' Lola was by this stage feeling absolutely terrible. 'I'm sure we can arrange something. Who are you phoning? Not the police?'

Having pulled out her mobile, Sally was blindly jabbing at buttons. 'I'm getting Doug over here. He'll sort this out.'

Doug? *Yeek*, the very name was enough to set Lola's heart racing. Would Gabe and Sally think her shallow if she quickly washed her hair and re-did her face before he turned up?

Chapter 20

The answer to that was a resounding yes, but she'd gone ahead and done it anyway. When Doug arrived at her flat forty minutes later he surveyed the three of them and said levelly, 'What a mess.'

Lola really hoped he didn't mean her. If she said so herself, she was looking pretty good.

'You're telling me.' Gabe's tone was curt. 'Have you seen what your sister's done to my flat?'

'I don't need to. I can guess. She's not what you'd call tidy,' said Doug with heroic understatement.

'*And* she's a liar.' Gabe turned to Sally and said accusingly, 'When we spoke on the phone, you told me you were completely trustworthy.'

'I am!'

'You promised you were super-housetrained.'

'Oh God, you're so *picky*.' Sally rolled her eyes. 'That's just what people say when they want to rent somewhere. Like when you go for a job interview, you have to act all enthusiastic and tell everyone you're a really hard worker. If you said you were a lazy toad who'd be late for your own funeral, they wouldn't take you on, would they?'

Gabe threw his hands up in the air. 'So you lied.'

'It wasn't a lie. Just a little fib. It's not against the law to be untidy.'

Gabe addressed Doug. 'I just want her out.'

'I can see that,' said Doug. 'Right, tell me exactly what's going on.'

When they'd finished explaining the situation, Doug looked at Lola and said, 'So basically this is all your fault.'

'Oh, of course it is. I do my best to help people out and this is what happens, this is the thanks I get.'

'Legally,' Doug turned to the others, 'either of you can cause untold hassle to the other. If you ask me, that's a waste of everyone's time and money. Shall we go and take a look at the flat now?'

'Everyone put on their anti-contamination suits,' said Gabe.

Over in Gabe's formerly pristine living room, now awash with magazines and clothes and abandoned food and make-up, Doug nodded sagely. 'Oh yes, this is familiar.'

Defiantly Sally said, 'But it's still not an arrestable offence.'

'What I don't understand,' Lola was puzzled, 'is when I came to the house in Barnes, your bedroom was fine. Completely normal.'

'That's because I have a mother who nags for England.' Sally heaved a sigh. 'And because she has two cleaners who barge in and tidy my room every day. Which is why I was so keen to get out of there.' Glaring defiantly at Gabe she added, 'And why I'm definitely not going back.'

'How many bedrooms here?' Doug was exploring the flat. 'Two?'

There was a pause.

'I hope you're not thinking what I think you're thinking,' said Gabe.

Doug shrugged. 'Do you have any better ideas?'

'I have a very much better idea,' Gabe retorted. 'She's your sister. You can take her home with you.'

'Not a chance. Lola, could you have her?'

Sally complained. 'You're making me sound like a delinquent dog.'

'Trust me,' Gabe gestured around the room in disgust, 'a delinquent dog wouldn't make this much mess.'

'I would take her.' Keen though she was to scramble into Doug's good books, Lola couldn't quite bring herself to make the ultimate sacrifice and thankfully had a get-out clause. 'But I've only got the one bedroom.'

'Fine. So you two,' Doug turned back to Gabe and Sally, 'have a choice. You either hire yourselves a couple of solicitors to slug it out or you give flat-sharing a go for a couple of weeks.'

'I can't believe this is happening to me.' The stubble on Gabe's chin rasped as he rubbed his hands over his face.

'You never know,' Lola said hopefully. 'It might work out better than you think.'

'Ha! I'll end up strangling her, then I'll be arrested and slung in prison, then *neither* of us'll end up living here.' As he said the word prison, Gabe winced and looked apologetically at Lola. 'Sorry.'

'Right, decision time.' Doug pointed to Sally. 'Would you be willing to give it a try?'

Huffily she said, 'Oh great, be chopped up into tiny pieces and hidden *tidily* away in a black bin bag. Just what I always wanted.'

'So you'd prefer a solicitor. Expensive,' mused Doug. 'That's a lot of shoes.'

You had to admire his style. Sally was now looking like a sulky fourth-former being told her homework wasn't up to scratch. Lola kept a straight face as Sally shrugged and said, 'I don't see why I should, but I suppose I could give sharing a go for a couple of weeks.'

Doug swung back to Gabe. 'But you still want to stick with the legal route, or . . . ?'

What a pro. He was like an auctioneer juggling bids. Entranced by his masterful air, Lola watched and held her breath.

Gabe hesitated, then exhaled and threw up his hands. 'Oh, for God's sake. We'll try it, then. Seeing as I don't have any choice.'

'Good call,' said Doug.

'But only for a couple of weeks. Then she has to move out. And I'm not living like *this*.' Gabe gestured at the floor in disgust.

'We'll help you clear the stuff away, won't we?' Lola beamed hopefully at Doug; now she could impress him by showing him how great she was at tidying up.

But Doug just looked at her as if she'd gone mad. 'Me? Not a chance, I'm out of here. And *you*,' he instructed Sally, 'behave yourself and don't give him a reason to chop you into pieces. Just try and get along together, OK? And put your clothes away once in a while.'

'Not once in a while!' Gabe exploded. 'All the time!'

'Oh, don't start already,' Sally jeered. 'You sound like *such* an old woman.'

Doug forestalled their bickering. 'My work here is done.' His gaze fixed on Lola. 'You can show me out.'

Lola's breathing quickened; she so desperately wanted him to stop regarding her as the wickedest woman in Britain.

In the hallway downstairs Doug came straight to the point. 'What was that about prison, earlier?'

He didn't miss a trick.

'What?' Lola thought rapidly.

'Your friend Gabe mentioned prison. Then he looked embarrassed and apologised. Who's been to prison?'

'My father.'

'Really? God. *Alex?*' Doug frowned. 'What happened?'

Lola felt her throat tighten. 'Not Alex. My real father. His name's Nick James.' Her voice began to wobble. 'It's all been a bit strange really. I only met him for the first time yesterday. Well, that's not true, he's been coming into Kingsley's and chatting to me but it wasn't until last night that he actually told me he was my real d–dad. And there was me, dressed like a r–rabbit . . . God, sorry, I wasn't expecting this to h–h–happen. Must be having some kind of delayed reaction.' Hastily she pulled a tissue out of her bra and wiped her eyes. 'To be honest I think it's all c–come as a bit of a sh–shock.'

'OK, don't cry.' There was a note of desperation in Doug's voice; this was rather more than he'd been expecting and way more than he could handle. Lola realised he'd never seen her crying before. It was something she hardly ever did in public, darkened cinemas excepted, largely because some girls – the Snow White brigade – might be able to cry prettily but she always turned into a pink blotchy mess. In fact, the only way to hide her face from Doug now was to bury it in his chest.

If only he wouldn't keep trying to back away . . .

Finally she managed to corner him against the front door and conceal her blotchiness in his shirt. Oh yes, this was where she belonged, back in Doug's arms at last. She'd missed him so much. If she hadn't needed to take the money, would they still have been together now? It was heartbreakingly possible.

Gingerly he patted her heaving shoulders. 'Hey, sshh, everything'll be all right.'

The fact that he was now being nice to her made the tears fall faster. Nuzzling against the warmth of his chest, making the most of every second, Lola said in a muffled, hiccupy voice, 'All these years my mum lied to me about my f-father.'

'And he's only just come out of prison?'

'No, that was years ago. Cigarette smuggling, nothing too terrible. He went to prison just before I was born. Pretty ironic really. My mother decided he wasn't good enough to be my dad, so she refused to let him see me. And then seventeen years later, *your* mother decided I wasn't good enough to be your girlfriend.'

'That *is* a coincidence.' Doug paused. 'Did she offer him twelve thousand pounds to stay away too?'

OK, still bitter.

'I haven't even told Mum yet. Heaven knows what she's going to say when she finds out he's been in touch. It's just so much to take in.' Lola raised her face and wondered if he ever watched romantic movies, the kind she loved, because this would be the *perfect* moment for him to sweep her into his arms for a passionate Hollywood kiss.

'You've got mascara on your nose.' Doug evidently hadn't read the romantic-hero rules.

So close your eyes.

But that didn't happen. Even less romantically, his phone burst into life in his jacket pocket, less than three inches from her ear.

The spell was broken. Doug disengaged himself and answered

the phone. He listened for a few seconds then said, 'No, sorry, I was held up. I'm on my way now.' He ended the call and opened the front door. 'I have to go.'

'Mustn't be late. Or you'll get home and find your dinner in the dog.' She was longing – *longing* – to know who he was rushing off to meet, but all Doug did was give an infuriating little smile. Almost as if he knew she was fishing for clues.

'Why were you dressed as a rabbit when you met your father?'

Ha, he wasn't the only one who could smile infuriatingly. 'It's a long story.' Lola was apologetic. 'And you have to rush off.'

He had the grace to nod in amusement. 'Touché. So what's he like?'

'Nice, I think. Normal, as far as I can tell. We have the same eyebrows.' If he made some smart remark about the two of them having the same morals she might have to stamp on his foot.

'The same eyebrows? You mean you take it in turns to wear them when you go out?' Doug shook his head. 'You want to splash out, get yourselves a pair each.'

Chapter 21

'Look, I'm sorry about yesterday,' said Gabe.

Sally, just home from yet another pre-Christmas shopping trip, dumped her bags and took off her coat. 'Really? Yesterday you were like a grizzly bear with a sore head.' Actually that didn't begin to describe him; yesterday he'd been like a bear with a sore *everything*.

Gabe shrugged and smiled. 'Yesterday wasn't the best day of my life. Now I've slept for thirteen hours I'm feeling a lot better.'

Well, that was a relief.

'So I hope we can get along,' he continued, clearly keen to make amends.

'Me too. Can I ask you something?'

'Fire away.'

Sally eyed him in his falling-to-pieces Levi's, bare feet and ancient T-shirt full of holes. 'Don't you think it's a bit weird to *be* so tidy and nitpicky and go around *looking* such a scruffy mess?'

It had been a genuine question – she was *interested*, that's all – but Gabe instantly got his hackles up.

151

'No. Don't you think it's weird that you go around looking like you've stepped out of *Vogue*, yet at home you live in a tip?'

She pointed a warning finger. 'Look, we're stuck with each other, for better or worse. *Please* don't start being annoying again.'

For several seconds their eyes locked. Sally could tell he was struggling to control his irritation. Lola hadn't said as much, but she wouldn't be surprised if Gabe was a little bit gay on the quiet. He was exceptionally good-looking for a start. Obsessive-compulsive when it came to tidiness. And what straight man would ever have eyelashes that long?

'Right. Sorry.' Evidently having reminded himself that he was supposed to be making amends, Gabe said, 'How about a cup of tea?'

Oh well, she could be conciliatory too. 'Great. White please, one sugar.'

'And I'm making fettuccine Alfredo if you're hungry.'

Ha, absolutely without a question gay. Bisexual anyway. The Australian girl must have found out – caught him flirting with some leathery-wiry Crocodile Dundee type or something – and packed him off on the first flight home.

But who cared, if he was a good cook? Sally slipped out of her shoes and removed her silver drop earrings. 'I love fettuccine Alfredo. OK if I have a shower first?'

'Fine.' But the way the word came out, it didn't sound fine.

'What? Why are you looking at me like that?' From the way Gabe was acting, you'd think she'd just ripped the head off a baby bird.

'You're just going to disappear into the bathroom and take a shower *now*?'

Sally gazed at him in disbelief. 'Am I supposed to make an *appointment*?'

'No.'

'You want me to say *please*? Is that it?'

A muscle was thudding away in Gabe's jaw. 'No, I don't want you to say please. I just don't want you doing what you've just done.'

He was off his rocker. Would he prefer her not to breathe? Bewildered, Sally said, 'I don't know what you're talking about.'

'This!' He pointed to the dumped carriers, and to her coat and umbrella on the chair. 'This.' Her handbag on the coffee table. 'Those.' Her shoes on the carpet. 'And them.' Her silver earrings on the window ledge. 'And *those*.' The armful of glossy magazines she'd tried to put on the arm of the sofa, which had slithered off and landed in a heap on the floor. 'You came into this flat one *minute* ago and look at the mess!'

'Oh. Sorry.' Was that really what was upsetting him? 'I'll pick them up later,' Sally said nicely, to humour him. 'I promise.'

'No you won't, you'll pick them up now.'

'But I'm just—'

'Now,' Gabe repeated firmly.

'But—'

'Or I throw them out of the window into the street.'

God, talk about neurotic. But since he clearly wasn't going to give in, she rolled her eyes and retraced her steps around the living room, picking everything up. Even though it was a complete waste of time because she was going to need *all* these things when she left for work tomorrow morning.

'Good. Well done,' said Gabe when she'd finished.

You had to pity him really.

Sally said sarcastically, 'Thank you, Mr Anal.'

'My pleasure, Miss Slob.'

★ ★ ★

'Where's Sally? Have you strangled her yet?' Having followed the smell of cooking up the stairs, Lola gave Gabe a hug.

'Give me a couple more days.'

'Ooh, Alfredo. My favourite.' She inspected the pans on the hob. 'So apart from the tidiness thing, how d'you think the two of you'll get on?'

'God knows. If I met her in a bar I'd think she was fine,' said Gabe. 'But that's because I wouldn't know what she's really like.' He paused. 'She doesn't have a boyfriend, right?'

Lola pulled a face. 'No. Bit of a disastrous history with men. One of them jilted her practically at the altar.'

'And we don't have to wonder why.'

'That's mean. You've just been dumped yourself.'

Gabe shrugged and tipped fettuccine into a pan of boiling water. 'I'm just saying, she could get a crush on me. I don't need that kind of hassle. Platonic flat-sharing only works as long as one person doesn't secretly fancy the pants off the other.'

Enthralled, Lola said, 'You think she fancies you?'

'I don't know. Maybe.' Another pause. 'It's happened before. And let me tell you, it's the last thing I need right now.'

Lola pinched a slice of parmesan; she loved to tease Gabe about his effect on women. 'Serves you right for being so gorgeous. What did Sally do to give herself away then?'

'Oh, you know those looks girls give you. She was doing it earlier.' Gabe added a carton of double cream to the garlic sizzling in the pan. 'That kind of moony, pouty thing. I just thought, oh God, please don't start, I can't be doing with— *shit!*'

The hairbrush whistled past his ear and ricocheted off the kitchen wall. 'What the . . . ?' Gabe twisted round in disbelief.

'Sorry, but someone had to shut you up.' Sally was in the

doorway, wrapped in a brown silk dressing gown, her hair wet from the shower and her face the picture of outrage. 'You're talking rubbish, you're making it all up! You've been chucked by some girl in Australia who didn't find you irresistible so now you're fantasising that someone else likes you, to give your ego a bit of a boost. But you can't go around saying stuff like that.' Her eyes glittered. 'Because it's not *true*.'

'OK, I'm sorry. I got it wrong. You could have done me an injury with that hairbrush,' said Gabe.

'I meant to. I'm just not a very good shot.' Turning to Lola, Sally said, 'And you believed everything he was telling you!'

Lola shook her head apologetically. 'He's usually right. Most girls do fancy him. Gabe's a bit of an expert when it comes to that sort of thing.'

'Well, he's got it wrong this time, because I promise you I *don't* fancy him, and I *definitely* wasn't giving him any kind of moony pouty look.' Brimming with derision, Sally said, 'If anything, I was thinking that any man who makes such a big fuss about keeping his flat perfect is probably gay.'

Lola stifled laughter but Sally was clearly peeved.

'I'm not gay,' said Gabe.

'And I don't fancy you. *At all*.'

'Fine. I believe you.'

'Ha, you're saying that now, to be polite. But I bet you secretly still think I do.'

'I promise I don't think that. Cross my heart and hope to die. And in return you have to stop thinking I'm gay.'

'Could we call a truce and stop talking about you two now?' Lola had been patient but enough was enough. Plaintively she said, 'If nobody minds, I'd quite like us to talk about me.'

Chapter 22

Over dinner Lola brought them up to date with the Newfound Father situation.

'I phoned Mum today to try and casually drop Nick's name into the conversation, and she said, "Oh hello, darling, you just caught us, Malcolm and I are off to Cardiff." She told me they're spending the night with Malcolm's brother and his family. So I couldn't really say anything about Nick James, could I? I'll have to wait until she gets back. To be honest, I hadn't realised she and Malcolm were getting so serious, I thought they were just good friends, but Mum said he wants to introduce her to everyone.' Lola paused and tore into a chunk of focaccia. 'I don't know how I feel about that. I mean, it's not that I don't like Malcolm. He's just . . . well, not the kind of man I had in mind for my mum. He has this awful beard that makes you want to pin him down and hack away at it with nail scissors. And he wears weird baggy jumpers, and sandals with the hairs on his toes poking through . . .'

'Over the years I'm sure she's wished you'd chosen different boyfriends,' said Gabe, 'but there wasn't anything she could do about it. Besides, they're visiting his brother in Cardiff, not eloping to Gretna Green.'

Lola pulled a face. 'I really hope they're not sleeping together.'

Brightly Sally said, 'At least she's too old to get pregnant.'

Which was another mental image Lola could do without. Mopping up the last of the Alfredo sauce from her plate, she amused herself instead by watching Gabe pretend not to care that Sally had dripped Frascati from her glass onto the table.

'And how would you have felt if you'd met your father for the first time,' Sally went on, 'and he looked just like this Malcolm character?' Her tone was encouraging. 'It wouldn't put you off him then, would it?'

Oh crikey, it might. Especially the hairy toes. Lola went hot and cold at the thought. At least Nick James hadn't done that to her; she was almost sure he wasn't the type to get his toes out in public or wear—

'You've spilled a bit of wine,' Gabe blurted out.

Sally shrugged comfortably. 'Never mind, it's only white.'

Gabe sighed. Lola kept a straight face and watched him pointedly not saying anything.

'Oh, look at yourself.' Sally grinned and reached behind her for the magazine she'd been allowed to leave – *neatly* – in the magazine rack. She opened it out, turned it upside down and blotted up the wine. 'There, better now?'

'Yes. Although a normal person might have used kitchen roll.'

'This was closer.' Turning the magazine back over and studying the wet pages, Sally said, 'Anyway, it's only Jack Nicholson in his swimming shorts. He won't mind.'

'Ah, look at him.' Lola leaned across to peer at the shot. 'Got a bit of a belly on him now. I had such a crush on that man when I first saw *One Flew Over the Cuckoo's Nest*.'

'She has pretty strange taste in crushes.' Gabe reached for the Frascati bottle. 'More wine?'

'Yes please. Try not to spill it this time. Go on,' Sally flashed him a saucy smile, 'who else does she like?'

'Ricky Gervais.'

'Euww.'

'That's supposed to be a secret.' Commandeering the magazine, Lola riffled through in search of inspiration. 'I have normal crushes too.' She jabbed triumphantly at a photo on the next page. 'Heath Ledger, he's one. And Johnny Depp, obviously.'

'Not to mention Alan Sugar,' said Gabe.

'And my brother,' Sally chimed in. She wrinkled her nose. 'To me, that's even weirder than fancying Alan Sugar.'

'They're both mean. But in a sexy way. Ooh, that reminds me, Tom Dutton.' Lola's eyes lit up and she puffed out her cheeks in appreciation. 'Now *he's* mean and sexy. And wasn't he fantastic in *Over You*? I cry my eyes out every time I see it. Gabe came with me to the cinema and was laughing at me as usual . . . where are you going?' She swivelled round as Gabe jumped up and headed for his bedroom. 'Can't stand the competition? Feeling inadequate? Worried that no one will ever fancy you again?'

Gabe returned with his camera. 'I forgot to tell you. I saw him.'

'Alan Sugar?' Lola's heart gave a little skippety skip of excitement. It was one of her fantasies that Sir Alan would one day march into Kingsley's in a filthy mood because he urgently needed a certain book and no one in *any* of the other bloody useless bookshops in the whole of London had been able to bloody help him. Then he'd fix her with his challenging, pissed-off stare and bark out the name of the book and she, Lola, would say, 'Sir Alan, we *did* have a copy of this book in stock, but it was sold this morning. *Happily*,' she'd continue before he could explode with frustration, 'it was sold to me, and I have it in my bag, out in the back office. If you like, I'll get it for you now.' And the look of relief on Sir Alan's face — relief and *respect* — would be just fantastic. Naturally he would whisk her off at once in his limo and insist on treating her to lunch at the Oxo Tower—

'Not him. Tom Dutton.' Whilst Lola was joyfully running through her favourite daydream, Gabe had been busy with his laptop.

'What? Where? At the airport?'

'On the way to it. Hang on, nearly there.'

'You're so lucky,' wailed Sally. 'I never see anyone interesting. Bumped into Dale Winton once in a newsagents and that's about it. He was buying TicTacs and— ooh!'

'Let me see.' Lola joined them in front of the laptop and jostled with Sally in order to gaze at the photo Gabe had brought up on the screen. 'Wow, it *is* him. Who's he kissing?'

A second photo flashed up and Lola saw at once who it was. Next to her Sally let out a squeal of recognition and yelped, 'Jessica Lee!'

'I thought you'd like to see them.' Pleased with himself, Gabe clicked onto the third photo, the one showing Tom loping back to his car. 'They pulled up separately at this service station and disappeared together up a side alley. I just happened to have the camera in my hand. I knew you'd think I was making it up if I didn't have proof.' His fingers hovered over the laptop's touchpad. 'I could make this one your screensaver if you like. Or shall I just delete them?'

'Excuse me! Are you *mad*?' To be on the safe side Sally

grabbed his hand before he could press anything drastic and lose the photos forever. 'It's Tom Dutton and Jessica Lee!'

'I *know*.' Gabe looked aggrieved. 'That's why I thought Lola would be interested.'

He didn't understand. He didn't have a clue. Lola and Sally exchanged glances.

'This is two *major* Hollywood celebs we're talking about,' said Sally.

'Bloody hell, will you stop treating me like a three-year-old? I know that!'

Lola patted his shoulder. 'They're 'nogging.'

'So?'

'So, no one knows they're even seeing each other.'

'How do you know that?'

'Because if it *was* known, it would be in all the papers,' Sally patiently explained. 'Because those of us who aren't major Hollywood celebs are interested in things like that.'

'Ri-ight.' Gabe was still looking baffled. Gossip magazines simply didn't feature in his life.

It was time to treat him like a three-year-old. Sally tapped the photos on the screen. 'You can sell these, Gabe. For a lot of money.'

'Oh!' He frowned. 'What, to a newspaper?'

'To a picture agency,' Sally said promptly. 'They're the experts. They'll sell the rights to newspapers and magazines all over the world. It's money for old rope. We can phone one right now. These photos were taken how long ago? Three days? Wow, you're lucky no one else has caught them since then. This is what's known as a scoop.'

'Hold on, hold on,' Gabe protested. 'I'm not so sure about this. What if they don't want people to find out? They might already have partners.'

'Oh, aren't you sweet?' Sally looked at him as if he were a puppy, then said briskly, 'Number one, they don't. Jessica Lee broke up with Kevin Masterson six weeks ago and Tom hasn't had a girlfriend for months. Number two, it's not your job to protect celebs. If they're playing away and get caught out, that's not your problem. In fact it jolly well serves them right, and their other halves *should* know what's been going on behind their backs.'

Drily Gabe said, 'There speaks someone who's had it done to her.'

'Well, yes, I have.' Sally looked indignant. 'Not that I did *anything* to deserve it.'

'Has it ever occurred to you that they might not have been able to handle the way you live? Who knows, maybe if you'd been a bit tidier,' Gabe shrugged, 'you could have been down off that shelf by now.'

'Oh, for heaven's sake,' Sally exploded. 'I'm trying to help you here and you're being completely ungrateful. Go on then, press the delete button, just wipe those photos out. See if I care.'

'Will you two give it a rest?' complained Lola. 'I'm starting to feel like a Relate counsellor. Here you go.' She dumped a copy of the Yellow Pages in front of Gabe. 'Find a picture agency and give them a ring.'

'How do I know which one to choose?'

'That one.' Leaning over Gabe's shoulder, Sally pointed to a small box advert for the Carter Agency.

Gabe twisted round to look at her. 'Why?'

'I know Colin Carter. He's married to my friend Janey. That's how I know about picture agencies,' said Sally. 'Colin's a good bloke and he wouldn't rip you off. I can give him a ring now if you like, tell him what you've got.'

'Great.' Gabe passed her his phone.

But Sally hadn't completely forgiven him yet. As she began keying in the number she said crisply, 'Not that you deserve it. I can't imagine why I'm being so kind to you when you're always so horrible to me.'

Chapter 23

The photographs appeared in the *Daily Mirror* two days later. They were also sold to newspapers and magazines all over the world. Colin Carter had just phoned Gabe and told him that he had a good eye for a picture; if he came up with any more photos he should be sure to give him a call.

It was Christmas Eve and without ever having considered it, Gabe now found himself with the possibility of a brand new career as a member of the paparazzi.

He gazed at the newspapers spread out on the coffee table in front of him and frowned. 'I couldn't do it. Everyone hates the paparazzi.'

'It might be fun. All those celebs,' Lola said encouragingly. 'All that fresh air.'

Gabe hesitated. He really didn't want to go back to being a chartered surveyor. 'But you know what I'm like. I wouldn't recognise half the people I was supposed to be photographing.'

'God, listen to you.' Sally emerged from her room, her arms loaded with gift-wrapped presents. 'You old fogey! You don't say photographing, you say *papping*.' Never one to pass up the opportunity to have a dig, she said gleefully, 'You'll be playing *records* next, on your wind-up *gramophone*, whilst puffing away on a *Woodbine*.'

Gabe rolled his eyes. 'Are you off? Don't let us keep you.'

'Oh, are you leaving now?' Lola jumped up; it was seven in the evening and each of them was heading home to spend Christmas day with their families. 'Are you getting a cab to Barnes? Give everyone my love.' Well, Dougie. She didn't want Adele appropriating any of it; more to the point, couldn't imagine Adele *wanting* any of her love.

'No, I'm catching the tube to Doug's then we're going in his car. If you like,' Sally told Gabe, 'you can borrow my magazines and start learning who everyone is.'

'Maybe next week. I'm not spending Christmas doing homework.'

Doug lived in Kensington. 'You can't carry all those presents on the tube by yourself,' said Lola. 'Why don't I give you a hand? Kensington's practically on the way to Streatham.'

Sally frowned. 'But you've got loads of stuff to carry too.'

'Less than you have. Wouldn't it be easier for me to help you?'

'OK, better idea,' said Sally, 'how about if I give Doug a call and ask him to come and pick me up. I'll just say I've got too many bags.' She paused, looked at the expression on Lola's face. 'What's wrong with that?'

'I don't know. It just doesn't seem fair on him . . .'

'But he won't mind!'

Lola looked doubtful. 'He might *say* he doesn't.'

'Well, I don't get this.' Sally shook her head, baffled. 'I thought you'd have liked the idea of Doug coming over. Don't say you've gone off him.'

Gabe grinned at her. 'Are you serious? Try turning it around.

The reason Lola doesn't want your brother driving over is because . . . hmm, let me think, she'd far rather see where *he* lives and have a good look around *his* flat. Because she's nosy.'

'Is that why?' Sally turned to Lola, surprised. Lola shrugged evasively; Gabe knew her too well.

'Might be.'

'For heaven's sake! Why didn't you just say so, then? What am I, a mind-reader?' Sally rolled her eyes. 'Get your coat on and let's go.'

Lola didn't need to be asked twice. Since sobbing all over Dougie the other evening he'd been occupying her thoughts even more than before. He'd been so nice to her and being back in his arms – albeit briefly – had felt so right. She'd been dreaming about those arms. And for the first time she'd seriously begun to wonder if it might be possible to win Dougie back.

Doug lived in the ground floor flat of a huge Victorian pillar-fronted house in Onslow Gardens. If Lola thought she'd done pretty well for herself property-wise, his flat was several rungs further up the ladder. Then again, he was a management consultant with a super-successful company he'd built up from scratch; it had to pay well.

'Phew, here we are,' panted Sally, climbing the white marble steps and ringing the bell with her shoulder.

'I'm feeling so Christmassy! Wouldn't it be great if it could start to snow now?' Lola hugged the bags of presents and felt her stomach tighten with excitement. For so many years she'd felt this way about the thought of seeing Father Christmas; now she was feeling it at the prospect of seeing Dougie again.

What's more, she'd watched *Love, Actually* enough times to know that magical things *could* happen on Christmas Eve. Her cheeks were glowing and her hair was fetchingly tousled. She was wearing her favourite white fluffy scarf. And her mouth was slicked with a subtle but sparkly Guerlain lipstick that looked like pink frost and tasted delicious. If Doug wanted to throw caution to the wind and kiss her, she could guarantee he wouldn't be disappointed.

'Come on, come on, *hurry up*,' Sally urged through chattering teeth.

Well, he wouldn't be disappointed if only he'd come and open the door. Checking for CCTV cameras, Lola suppressed the less than welcome thought that Doug could have seen her on his doorstep and was now pretending to be out. He wouldn't do that, would he? Had he never watched *Love, Actually*? Didn't he know how romantic Christmas Eve could be, if only he'd relax into it, let bygones be bygones, and just let fate take its natural course?

Then the front door opened and there he was, barefoot and wearing a blue and white striped shirt over frayed jeans. Unable to help herself, Lola took a quick intake of breath and began to cough as the ice-cold air hit the back of her throat. One day, *one day*, she'd learn to be elegant and in control.

'Bloody hell, about time too,' Sally complained, bustling past him. 'It's freezing out there.'

'OK, two things. It's not even eight o'clock yet. I said to come over at nine.'

'You said eight.'

'Nine. Definitely nine.'

'Oh well, never mind. I'm early!'

'And secondly,' Doug's dark eyes narrowed, 'what's Lola doing here? Because I'm fairly sure our mother hasn't invited her to spend Christmas Day with us.'

Lola's heart sank. So he *hadn't* ever watched *Love, Actually*.

'Don't be sarcastic. Lola's here because she's doing me a favour,' said Sally. 'I had too much stuff to carry so she offered to help me out.'

'See? I'm a nice person really.' Lola beamed hopefully. 'And don't panic, I'm on my way to my mum's. I just saw that Sal was struggling with all her parcels so I said I'd lend her a hand getting them here.'

'Fine. I'll take them off you, shall I?' Having seized the bags containing the presents, Doug stepped back. 'There we go. Thanks. Have a good Christmas.'

He was a man. He probably only watched testosterone-fuelled, action-packed films like *Mission: Impossible* and *The Great Escape*.

'Don't be so *rude*,' Sally exclaimed. 'Honestly, I'm *so* ashamed of you sometimes. I was going to ring earlier and ask you to come and pick me up, but Lola said I mustn't do that, you were far too busy and important to have time to drive over to us, and that she really didn't mind struggling onto the tube and fighting through the crowds and *trudging* through the streets . . .'

Lola cleared her throat; Sally was getting carried away now.

'Anyway, the least you can do is invite her in for a drink to say thank you.'

Doug gave her a long-suffering look, then turned and said, 'Lola, thank you for helping my sister. Won't you come in for a drink?'

'Doug, that's so kind of you.' Checking her watch, Lola broke into a delighted smile. 'I shouldn't really, but . . . oh, go on then. You've twisted my arm!'

The living room was blissfully warm, L-shaped and comfortably furnished. Lola, greedily taking in every detail, noted that Doug – thank God – was neither as chaotically untidy as his sister nor as obsessively neat as Gabe. Charcoal-grey curtains hung at the long sash windows, contrasting with the deep crimson walls. There were magazines beside the sofa, DVDs next to the TV, a dark blue sweater left hanging over the back of a chair, various prints and paintings on the walls, two discarded wine glasses on the coffee table . . .

Oh, and a blonde in the kitchen doorway. Now there was an accessory she could have happily done without.

'Hi,' said the blonde.

'Hi.' Lola felt as if she'd just stepped into a lift that wasn't there.

'Well, well, this is a surprise.' Sally, never backward in coming forward, said, 'Who are *you*?'

'This is Isabel. A friend of mine.' The way Doug moved towards her was oddly protective, almost as if he was preparing to defend an innocent gazelle from a couple of boisterous lion cubs. 'Isabel, this is my sister Sally.' In throwaway fashion he then added, 'And her friend Lola.'

Just to make crystal clear to everyone in the room how completely unimportant she was, how utterly irrelevant to his life.

To compound it, Isabel smiled widely and said, 'Sally. I've heard all about *you*. Doug's always talking about you!'

'Is he? He's kept *very* quiet about you.' Sally unwound her lime-green scarf, flung aside her handbag and plonked herself down on the sofa. 'So, how long have you two known each other?'

'Glass of red?' Evidently keen to be rid of her ASAP, Doug appeared in front of Lola with the open bottle and a clean glass.

Talk about brisk. What could she ask for that would spin things out a bit longer?

'Actually, I'd love a coffee.'

'Well, we've known each other for ages.' Across the room, Isabel flipped back her ironed blonde hair and sat down cosily next to Sally. 'We work together,' she confided. 'But we've only recently become . . . you know, *closer.*'

It hadn't been love at first sight then. That was something to be grateful for. Although it would be nice if she could have been a bit less pretty.

'I was seeing someone else,' Isabel went on, 'but we broke up. After that, Doug and I just ended up getting together.'

Lola looked at Doug, sending him a telepathic message: *we could do that, you and me . . .*

'Coffee.' Doug's tone was brusque; he didn't appear to be telepathic. 'Why don't you sit down and I'll make it.'

'Actually I'll come with you.' Lola flashed him a sunny smile. 'Then I can make sure you don't palm me off with instant.'

As she followed Doug into the kitchen, Isabel was saying cheerily, '. . . and I'm going down to Brighton tonight, to stay with my parents. That's what Christmas is all about, isn't it? Mind you, I'm going to miss Doug! I can't wait to see what he's bought me. He wouldn't let me open it tonight.'

The kitchen was nice, black and white and boasting, among other items, a huge chrome Dualit toaster.

'Still keen on toast, then,' said Lola.

'What are you *doing*?'

'Inspecting the cupboards. What happened to the Pot Noodles? You used to love Pot Noodles.'

Exasperated, Doug said, 'When I was seventeen.'

'I bet you still secretly like them. Once a Pot Noodler, always a Pot Noodler.' Lola carried on opening and closing drawers and cupboards; finding a secret stash of Hot'n'Spicys would bring her *so* much joy. 'I bet you put on a hat and dark glasses, sneak off to some supermarket miles away, praying you won't bump into anyone you know, and buy up trolley loads at a time. And then you have to smuggle them back to Kensington – imagine the shame if the neighbours found out!'

'Will you stop riffling through my cupboards?'

'Why, am I getting warm?'

'Here, just take your coffee.' Having sunk the plunger on the cafetière in record time, Doug shoved a small cup into her hands.

Lola peered into the cup. 'Bit weak.'

'Too bad. Shall we head back through?'

'What did you buy Isabel for Christmas?'

Doug looked exasperated. 'I'm not telling you *that*.'

Sally, whose eavesdropping skills were second to none, said, 'You're not telling her what?' when they returned to the living room.

'I was wondering what he'd bought you for Christmas,' said Lola, 'that's all.'

'Anything's fine by me.' Sally beamed at Doug. 'So long as he's kept the receipt.'

'Oh poor Dougie! I wouldn't *dream* of taking back anything he bought me,' trilled Isabel. 'Whatever it was.'

'Remember when we bought each other the same CD? *Parklife*,' Lola fondly reminisced without thinking. 'God, we used to play that album non-stop. I can still remember the words to every song.'

'Hang on, you mean you and *Doug* bought each other the same CD?' Isabel looked confused. 'Oh, I'm sorry, I didn't realise . . .'

Lola shrugged and managed a smile that was both carefree

170

and tinged with regret; it seemed a bit mean to announce that Dougie had been her first love.

'Oh yes,' Sally said helpfully. 'They were boyfriend and girl-friend.'

'That was a long time ago,' Doug cut in. 'Back in the days when I still ate Pot Noodles. As I was just explaining to Lola,' he added pointedly, 'our tastes change over the years.'

Isabel let out a high-pitched shriek of laughter. 'You used to like Pot Noodles? Oh my *God*!'

Lola was extremely fond of Pot Noodles and felt as protective as a new mother whenever anyone made fun of them. She said evenly, 'I like Pot Noodles. They're brilliant. Chicken and Mushroom's my favourite.'

Chapter 24

'How are things going with Gabe?' In order to spare Isabel's blushes, Doug swiftly changed the subject.

'Hideous.' Sally shuddered. 'Talk about pernickety. He's *so* gay, just won't admit it.'

'He's not gay.' Lola hadn't yet managed to convince Sally but she kept saying it anyway. 'If Gabe was gay, he'd *be* gay. He's Jack Lemmon, you're Walter Matthau and you drive him insane, that's all it is. Some people leave tea bags in the kitchen sink,' she told Doug, because there were times when you couldn't help feeling sorry for Gabe. 'Yesterday your sister left hers on the coffee table.'

Sally shrugged. 'Not on purpose. Only because I hadn't realised it was still in my mug.'

Lola had been making her coffee last as long as possible. Finally she was down to the lukewarm grounds.

'Finished? Good.' Doug whisked away her cup, clearly keen to see the back of her.

Which – and here was her optimism rushing to the fore again – could mean that her presence was disturbing him *in a good way*.

'Could I use your bathroom before I go?' It was freezing out there; even Doug couldn't banish her and her bursting bladder to the vagaries of the great outdoors, surely?

Although he looked as if he'd quite like to.

'Out in the hall. Second door on the left.'

It was actually a tricky exercise, walking the length of the living room in a natural manner, super-aware of Dougie's eyes upon her. What was he really thinking? Was he mentally comparing her with Isabel? Come to that, how *did* she compare with Isabel? Her rival — the rival she hadn't known existed before now — was a cool sleek blonde with high-maintenance hair and a hint of the ice princess about her. She was probably more classically beautiful but was she as much fun? Pretty was all very well but Lola felt she might have the edge when it came to character. She was the playful spaniel whereas Isabel was more of a pampered feline; Isabel was Grace Kelly while she was Doris Day; Isabel had the kind of high-pitched laugh that could easily start to get on a man's nerves after a—

'I said second door on the left.' Out in the hall Doug's voice behind Lola made her jump. 'That's the second on the right.'

But he was a split second too late; she'd already opened the door and walked into his bedroom.

Bingo!

'Sorry. I'm always getting my left and right mixed up. Wow, this is nice!' Taking another step into the room, she drank in the burnt-orange walls, the duvet and pillowcases in bitter chocolate, the polished oak floorboards and mahogany furniture. This was where Doug slept, this was *his bed*. Lola did her best to picture him in it, except there was one small but vitally important detail missing. She couldn't *see* any pyjamas but . . .

'Do you still sleep naked?'

There, she'd said it.

Doug shook his head. 'You don't change, do you?'

Oh well. She shrugged. 'I like to know these things.'

'Even though "these things" aren't any of your business?'

But he wasn't sounding entirely pissed off. Encouraged, Lola said innocently, 'I just wondered if you'd turned into the kind of man who wears stripy cotton pyjamas all buttoned up to the neck, like Kenneth Williams in *Carry On Nurse*.'

His mouth twitched. 'Oh yes, that's me. That's what I wear.'

'You don't.'

'I definitely do.'

'You still sleep naked.' Lola exhaled with relief; *now* she was able to picture him in his king-sized bed. Even better, ice queen Isabel wasn't in there with him.

Hmm, ice queens probably had cold feet.

'OK, you've had your snoop around,' said Doug. 'Now I'll show you where the bathroom is.'

She couldn't help herself; the question was bubbling up. 'Do you really like her?'

'Do I really like who?'

'Isabel.'

As he steered her out of the bedroom and pointed her in the direction of the door opposite, Doug said, 'Again, not actually any of your business. But if it helps,' he paused, causing Lola's heart to expand with hope, 'then I suppose I'd have to say yes, I do.'

The pause had been deliberate. He knew exactly why she was asking and now he was getting his own back. Recklessly Lola said, 'Is sleeping with her as much fun as it was with me?'

There, *there* was that flicker again. God, she loved that flicker behind the eyes.

174

'Lola, you're talking about ten *years* ago. I don't even remember what sleeping with you was like.'

Which, if she'd believed him, might have counted as a put-down. Luckily Lola didn't for a minute.

'You know what I think? I think I must be having an effect on you if you're having to say stuff like that.' There was a warm glow in the pit of her stomach that had nothing to do with needing the loo. With a playful smile Lola said, 'Because I know you're lying now. I remember every detail of every minute of every time with you, Dougie. And I still will when I'm ninety. Because it was the most important thing in the world to me. It meant everything. And I know you remember it too.'

Another pause. He took a step closer and leaned forward, causing her to suck in her breath . . .

'It was *almost* the most important thing in the world to you.' Doug whispered the words in her ear. 'Remember? It came in second, behind money.'

Which put a bit of a dampener on a potentially promising moment. Doug turned and headed back to the living room and Lola paid her visit to the bathroom, which was white and modern and thankfully devoid of girly toiletries. Careful not to clink the bottle against the glass shelf, she unscrewed the top of Doug's aftershave and inhaled. It never failed to astound her that smells could be so evocative. Christmas trees, her mum's chocolate cake, fireworks, Ambre Solaire . . . so many smells, each triggering a different memory, and now she had Doug's distinctive aftershave added to the list, one more unique scent with the ability to transport her back to the night she'd met him again, the power to make her knees go weak with longing.

And it would still be happening when she was ninety.

OK, better put the bottle back on the shelf before she dropped it into the sink; that *would* be a giveaway. Time to say her good-byes and leave. Gazing at her reflection in the bathroom mirror, Lola pinched her cheeks and jooshed up her hair. With a bit of luck, what with everyone being jolly and wishing each other Happy Christmas, she might get the chance to give Doug a festive hug and a fleeting kiss on the cheek.

Not much to pin your hopes on, maybe. But every little helped.

'Oh, come here, don't you look gorgeous, where did you get that *scarf*?' Blythe flung open the front door and enveloped her daughter in her arms. As the car pulled away and disappeared up the road she said, 'Did somebody give you a lift? Why didn't you invite them in for a drink?'

Lola closed her eyes and revelled in being in her mother's arms; at least it wasn't going to be a completely hug-free evening. And yes, she *was* looking gorgeous, not that it had had the desired effect.

'I would have,' she fibbed, 'but they were in a hurry. It was Doug.'

'Doug? You mean Dougie Tennant?' Blythe exclaimed. 'Oh, he was always *such* a dear boy – I'd love to have seen him again. You should have forced him to come in!'

Oh yes, and wouldn't that have been relaxing? Earlier, as they'd all been preparing to leave Dougie's flat, Lola had briefly cornered him and murmured, 'By the way, my mum doesn't know about the money thing, OK? I'd rather she didn't find out.'

Doug had given her one of his withering looks, the kind that made her insides curdle with shame. 'I'll bet you don't.'

It was horrible but there was nothing she could do. And she

hadn't been able to risk not warning him, because there was always the chance that Blythe could have come rushing out of the house, blurting out *anything*. As far as she was aware, Lola had known that Dougie's mother disapproved of their relationship but that was all. The decision to finish with Dougie and move to Majorca had been Lola's alone, typically impetuous and possibly foolhardy, and based on Lola's decision that a long-term, long-distance relationship with Dougie could never work out.

'But if he gave you a lift over here, that's a good sign, isn't it?' Now, studying her daughter's face, Blythe said hopefully, 'Do you think he might be starting to forgive you yet?'

'Mum, stop it, don't get carried away.' Phew, just as well Doug had driven off at the speed of light; Lola envisaged her mother telling him that there were worse things in life than a bit of wounded pride. Hurriedly she nipped her mother's fantasies in the bud – it was bad enough being disappointed by her own. 'He's with his girlfriend. I went over to his flat with Sally. He only gave me a lift because she forced him to.' Maybe she was being extra-suspicious but Lola also wondered if Doug had done it in order to avoid the festive goodbye hug-and-a-kiss. When she'd clambered out of the back of the Mercedes with her bags of presents, he'd pretty much made reaching him a physical impossibility by remaining in the driver's seat with Isabel next to him.

Had that been deliberate?

'Oh well, never mind. Men and their silly egos.' Blythe was nothing if not supportive. 'Come on inside, it's freezing out here. We're going to have such a lovely time,' she went on proudly. 'I've got smoked salmon and Madagascan king prawns from Marks and Spencer. Your favourites.'

★　　★　　★

It was the not knowing how her mother might react that was causing Lola to hesitate. On the one hand she wanted, more than anything, to talk about her father.

Not her stepfather, Alex. The biological one, Nick.

On the other hand, it was Christmas morning and the very last thing she wanted to do was upset Blythe. Their family Christmases had always been extra-special, but since Alex's death five years ago, she and her mother had made even more of an effort, drawing closer still, both of them treasuring this time together and cherishing all the shared happy memories that meant so much.

Which was why, despite longing to raise the subject of Nick James, every time she geared herself up to do it Lola felt her stomach clench and the words stick in her throat. She had the number of his mobile keyed into her phone. Was he wondering why she hadn't contacted him yet? It was Christmas Day and the schmaltzy, happy-ever-after side of her – the kind that wept buckets over the festive films shown on Hallmark – had dared to fantasise about blurting everything out to her mother, followed by Blythe getting all emotional and admitting that she'd made a terrible mistake all those years ago, and that she'd never stopped loving Nick. Cut to Nick, sitting alone in his flat on Christmas Day, gazing blankly out of the window at small children having a boisterous snowball fight outside in the street – because in Hallmark films it *always* snows on Christmas Day. A look of regret crosses his face; he made a mistake and has spent the last twenty-seven years paying for it. Blythe is still the only woman he's ever loved, but it's all too late now, she's—

The phone rings, brrrrrr brrrrrr. Nick hesitates then answers it. His eyes widen in wonder as he whispers, 'Blythe?'

Cut to: a sunny, snowy hill overlooking an insanely picturesque

London. Lola, wearing her beautiful sparkly white scarf, sends Blythe up the hill ahead of her and sits down on a bench to wait. At the top of the hill, Nick paces nervously to and fro through the snow. Then he sees Blythe and everything goes into warm and fuzzy slow motion until somehow they're in each other's arms, spinning round and round in that way that can make you feel dizzy just watching them . . .

Well, it *could* happen, couldn't it?

'Okey dokey, that's the parsnips done.' Wiping her hands on her blue striped apron, Blythe counted the saucepans and consulted her list. 'Stuffing, check. Bread sauce, check. Chipolatas, bacon, baked onions, check check check. How are those carrots coming along?'

'Finished.' It was a ridiculous amount of work for one meal but that was tradition for you. They both enjoyed the whole cooking ritual. In fact, Lola discovered, while she'd been lost in her happy Hallmark reverie, she'd managed to peel and chop enough carrots to feed the entire street.

'Ready for a top-up?' Blythe took the bottle of sparkling Freixenet from the fridge and gaily refilled their glasses. 'That skirt's wonderful on you. And the belt's perfect with it. Oh, sweetie pie, I love you so much, give me a hug.'

Mum, guess whose number I've got stored on my phone . . . ?

Mum, remember when I was born . . . ?

Mum, you know how sometimes you bump into someone you haven't seen for *years* . . . ?

Still the words wouldn't come. As Blythe wrapped her in a Fracas-scented embrace, Lola decided to wait until lunch was over. Maybe this afternoon, when they were relaxing together in front of the fire eating Thornton's truffles, she could casually slide the conversation round to the opposite sex in general, then old boyfriends in particular and how they might have changed since they'd last seen them—

'Ooh, I'll get that.' Blythe darted across the kitchen as the phone began to ring. 'It's probably Malcolm, calling from his sister's in Cardiff.'

It was Malcolm. Lola popped a chunk of carrot into her mouth, tipped the rest into a pan of sugared and salted water, and went upstairs to the bathroom. By the time she came back down, her mother was off the phone.

'What's wrong?' said Lola.

'Nothing's wrong.' Blythe's freckles always seemed to become more prominent when she was feeling guilty. 'That was Malcolm.'

'I know. He's staying with his sister's family in Cardiff.' Malcolm was a divorcee whose son was serving overseas in the army.

Blythe leaned against the dishwasher. 'He was. But now he's back. His sister's mother-in-law had a heart attack yesterday afternoon and they all had to rush up to the hospital in Glasgow. She's in intensive care, poor thing, and it's touch and go. But poor Malcolm too,' Blythe went on pleadingly. 'He had to drive back from Cardiff last night and now he's all on his own at home.'

Lola experienced a sinking sensation in her stomach, like water spiralling down a plughole.

'Can you imagine?' Blythe's eyes widened. 'On Christmas Day.'

It was so obvious what was coming next. Lola wanted to wail 'Noooo' and hated herself for it. She wished she was less selfish, more generous, one of those genuinely kind people who wouldn't hesitate for a second to suggest what she knew perfectly well Blythe was about to suggest.

'On his own,' Blythe prompted.

The frustrated ten-year-old inside Lola was now stamping her foot and yelling, But it's not *fair*, this is *our* Christmas and now it's all going to be *spoiled*.

The grown-up, rational 27-year-old Lola fiddled with a teaspoon and said, 'Doesn't he have any other friends he could spend the day with?'

'I don't suppose he wants to be a burden.' Her mother tilted her head to one side, the diamanté clip Lola had bought her from Butler and Wilson glittering in her coppery hair. 'Everyone has their own families.'

So he has to pick on ours, bawled the bratty ten-year-old Lola. No, Mummy, make the nasty man go away, I don't *want* him here!

God, she was horrible. How could she even think that? Awash with shame and self-loathing, Lola forced herself to say brightly, 'So he's coming over?'

'Is that all right, love? You don't mind, do you?' Which meant the invitation had already been extended and accepted. 'Dear Malcolm, if it was the other way round he'd be inviting us to stay. He's an absolute sweetheart. If ever anyone needs any help he's there like a shot.'

'Of course I don't mind.' Disappointment hit Lola like a brick. Bang went the opportunity to raise the subject of her real father.

'Thanks, love.' Beaming with relief, Blythe slotted a new compilation CD into the hi-fi. 'You're an angel. We'll have a lovely day together.' Then she clapped her hands as, in his familiar raspy voice, Bruce Springsteen began to sing 'Merry Christmas, Baby'. 'Oh, my favourite! Did I ever tell you I used to lust after Bruce Springsteen? Those skintight jeans, that sexy red bandanna, those beautiful dark *eyes . . .*'

Yeek, and now she was dancing around the kitchen in a scarily early eighties way. This was her mother; once upon a time she had lusted after snake-hipped gypsy-eyed Bruce Springsteen and now she was involved with Malcolm Parker who sported patterned sweaters, hideous sandals and the world's bushiest beard.

This was what getting older did to you, Lola realised. Your priorities shifted and you truly began to believe that things like hairy-hobbity toes weren't so bad after all.

Please, God, don't ever let that happen to me.

Chapter 25

'Ho ho ho! Happy Christmas one and all!' In celebration of the day, Malcolm was wearing a bright red, Santa-sized sweater over his plaid shirt and bottle-green corduroys. As he made his way into the house he grazed Blythe's cheek with a kiss and beamed at Lola. 'Well, this is a treat! How kind of you both to invite me. I hope it's not too much trouble.'

'Of course it isn't.' Lola felt ashamed of herself; he was a sweet man, if not what you'd call a heart-throb. And at least he wasn't wearing sandals today, so the hairy toes weren't on show.

'The more the merrier,' Blythe gaily insisted. 'Come on through to the living room. We're going to have a lovely day!'

Lola watched Malcolm sit down and realised that for the rest of the day, instead of sharing the comfortable squashy sofa with her mother, she was relegated to the slightly less comfortable armchair with its less good view of the TV.

'I didn't know if you had a Monopoly set, so I brought my own.' Triumphantly Malcolm produced it from his khaki haversack. 'Nothing like a few games of Monopoly to get Christmas going with a swing! Those people who just sit around like

183

puddings watching rubbish on TV . . . what are they like, eh? They don't know what they're missing!'

Lola, who couldn't bear Monopoly and had been banking on sitting like a pudding watching TV, said brightly, 'What can I get you to drink, Malcolm?'

And it *wasn't* rubbish.

Evidently detecting the bat-squeak of panic in her voice, he looked anxious. 'Unless you don't like playing Monopoly?'

'Of course we do, Malcolm.' Blythe rushed to reassure him. 'We love it!'

The day was long. Verrrrrry lonnnnnng. Being relentlessly nice and having to pretend you were having *so much fun* had been exhausting. By ten o'clock, with Malcolm still showing no sign of leaving, Lola conceded defeat. Faking a few enormous yawns, she made her excuses and kissed Blythe goodnight.

'Sure I can't tempt you to one last game of Monopoly?' Malcolm's tone was jovial, his eyes bright with hope.

'Thanks, Malcolm, but I just can't stay awake.' Poor chap, it wasn't his fault he was boring. 'I'm off up to bed.'

'Let's hope it's not because I'm dull company, ha ha ha!' Crumbs from the slice of fruit cake he'd been eating quivered in his beard as he beamed at Blythe. 'You'd tell me if I was, wouldn't you?'

The thing was, people *said* that, but they didn't actually *mean* it; if you told them how staggeringly dull they were, they'd be shocked and hurt.

'Don't be daft, Malcolm.' Cheerily Blythe said, 'How about a nice drop of Scotch to go with that fruit cake?'

Upstairs in her old bedroom Lola sat up in bed with a book and tried hard to feel more like Mother Teresa, less like a selfish spoilt brat. Malcolm's last words to her had been, 'Thanks for being so welcoming, pet. I tell you, this has been one of the best Christmases of my life.'

Which had brought a bit of a lump to her throat. Because Malcolm was a sweet, genuinely good man who had given up his Sundays for years to do volunteer dog-walking, and who would never say anything unkind about anyone. He would never hurt Blythe.

But he was no Bruce Springsteen either. He wasn't even Bruce Springsteen's older, grizzled, weatherbeaten uncle. Lola really, *really* hoped he wasn't going to spend the night here . . . oh God, how did other people with parents-who-were-dating-again cope when their parents chose partners who just weren't . . . well, *right*?

The book wasn't holding her attention. After a couple of chapters Lola gave up and listened to the murmuring voices of Malcolm and her mother downstairs in the living room. She couldn't make out what they were saying but at least the fact that they were saying something meant they weren't . . . urrghh, snogging on the sofa.

Reaching for her mobile, Lola scrolled through the address book until she found Nick James's number.

As it began to ring at the other end she felt her chest fill with butterflies and, panicking, pressed Cancel.

OK, this was ridiculous. He was her father. It was allowed.

Taking deep breaths she rang again. Had he spent the last five days waiting for this moment, getting all jumpy every time his phone burst into life, then being disappointed each time it wasn't her?

Or, *or*, what if she'd been a disappointment to him and he'd decided he didn't need a daughter like her in his life after all?

What if he'd hastily changed his number? Oh God, what if it had been a fake one all along?

Five rings. Six rings. Any moment now it was going to click onto answerphone and she'd have to decide whether to leave a—

'Hello?'

Whoosh, in a split second all Lola's nerves vanished. His voice was as warm and friendly as she remembered.

'Nick?' She couldn't call him Dad, that would feel too weird. 'Hi, it's . . . um, Lola.'

'Lola.' She heard him exhale. Then, sounding as if he was smiling, he said, 'Thank God. You don't know how glad I am to hear from you. I was beginning to think I wouldn't.'

She waggled her toes with relief. 'And I was just wondering if you'd given me a made-up number.'

'You seriously thought I'd do that?'

'Well, I was dressed as a rabbit. It could put some people off.'

'I'm made of sterner stuff than that. Hey, merry Christmas.'

Lola grinned, because her actual biological father was wishing her a merry Christmas. How cool was that? 'You too. Where are you?'

'Just got home. Spent the day with friends in Hampstead. How about you?'

Thank goodness he hadn't been on his own; that would have been just awful.

'I'm at Mum's house.'

He sounded pleased. 'You mean you've told her?'

'Um, no.' Realising that he thought Blythe was in the room with her now, Lola said, 'I wanted to, I was going to, then this friend of hers turned up and I couldn't. They're downstairs. I'm up here in bed. Too much Monopoly takes it out of you.'

'God, I can't stand Monopoly.' Nick spoke with feeling. 'Sorry. So how do you think she'll react when you do tell her?'

'That's the thing, I just don't know.' She hesitated, hunching her knees under the duvet. 'But I'm a bit worried that she might refuse to see you. And once Mum makes up her mind about something she can be a bit, well . . .'

'You don't have to tell me.' Nick's tone was dry. 'OK, let me have a think about this. What are you doing tomorrow?'

'Working.' Lola shuddered, because tomorrow was going to be hell on wheels; when she was crowned Queen of the World, opening shops on Boxing Day wouldn't be allowed.

'Friday?'

'Working.'

'Saturday?'

'I'm not working on Saturday.'

'How about Blythe? Would she be free then?'

'As far as I know.'

'OK, now listen,' Nick said slowly. 'How about this for an idea?'

But before he could tell her what it was, there was a knock at the bedroom door and Blythe poked her head round. When she saw Lola's mobile, she said, 'Well, that's a relief, I thought you were talking to yourself! Who's that you're on the phone to?'

Um . . . 'Gabe.'

Her mother, who was fond of Gabe, said brightly, 'Say hi to him from me!'

'Mum's here.' Lola gripped the phone tightly as she spoke into it. 'She says hi.'

'Am I Gabe?' Nick sounded amused. 'Say hi back. And wish her a merry Christmas from me.'

OK, this was seriously weird now. 'He says hi, and merry Christmas.'

'Tell him I hope he's had a good day.' Blythe smiled broadly.

'Tell her very good, thanks,' said Nick. 'All the better for hearing her voice.'

'And I hope he's been behaving himself,' said Blythe.

'She hopes you've been behaving yourself.' OK, enough now.

Nick sounded as if he was smiling. 'Oh yes. Tell her I haven't been arrested in years.'

If there was anything more manic than working in the West End after Christmas when the sales were in full swing, it was shopping in the West End after Christmas when the sales were in full swing. Elbows were out, toes and small children were getting trampled on and everyone was carrying bags of stuff they'd either just bought or had been given for Christmas and were about to take back. And it was worth queuing for forty minutes to return a load of clothes to Marks and Spencer's, because who but a fool would want to keep them, when the exact same items were now half price on the rails, enabling you to buy – ha! – twice as many? This was Blythe's favourite bit.

'Mum, we've been shopping for three hours. My feet hurt. My back's starting to ache.'

'Lightweight!'

'And I'm thirsty,' Lola said whinily.

'We'll buy you a bottle of water.' Her mother was in the grip of buying fever; her eyes were darting around, greedily taking in sequinny sparkly tops, dresses awash with flowers and frills, things with spots and stripes and fringes . . . OK, some of the colours might be iffy, but they were *reduced in the sale* . . .

'And I'm hungry,' Lola pleaded. '*Sooo* hungry. Mum, if you

make me carry on shopping now, I'll last another hour. But if we stop for a proper rest and have something decent to eat, I'll be set up for the rest of the day.'

Blythe heaved an impatient sigh. 'You were easier to take shopping when you were in a pram. OK, we'll eat. Where d'you want to go?'

'Marco's,' Lola said promptly. 'We always go to Marco's.'

'Are you sure? It's a ten-minute walk from here. We could just go to the café downstairs.'

'Oh no, *no*.' Lola shook her head. 'Because then you'll just try and fob me off with orange juice and a prawn baguette. We're going to Marco's and we're going to have chicken cacciatore and a nice glass of red, just like proper ladies who lunch.'

The restaurant was busy, warm and welcoming. Lola slipped her shoes off under the table and took a big sip – OK, maybe slightly bigger than a big sip – of Merlot. 'Oh, this is better. My feet thank you. My stomach thanks you. Are we both having the chicken?'

'Fine by me. Steady with that wine, love. You're glugging it down like water.'

It was one o'clock. Lola felt the butterflies start up in earnest; any time now, her mother was going to find out why.

She saw him twenty minutes later through the full-length front window, making his way across the street. Blythe, sitting with her back to the entrance, was chattering away about holidays. Lola took a deep breath; in an ideal world her mother's hair would be just brushed and she'd be wearing rather more make-up, but short of lunging across the table and forcibly applying a fresh coat of lipstick to her mouth, there wasn't a lot she could do about it. Yeek, and now the door was being pushed open, here he came, it was really going to happen.

'. . . so I said I'd think about it, although I'm not sure it's really my thing.' Blythe wrinkled her nose. 'I mean, hill walking in Snowdonia. In big clumpy hiking boots. Sleeping in a tent, for heaven's sake! Would you say I was the tenty type? It's all right for Malcolm, but where would I plug in my hairdryer? And what happens when I need to . . . to . . .' Her voice trailed away and the piece of chicken she'd been about to eat slid off her fork. All the colour abruptly drained from her face, leaving only freckles behind.

Nick, standing behind Lola's chair, said, 'Hello, Blythe.'

Chapter 26

Blythe was in a state of shock. For a split second Lola thought she might bolt from the restaurant. Then, visibly gathering herself, she managed a fixed smile. 'Nick, what a surprise. How nice to see you.' Even her voice sounded different. 'How are you? Looking well.' Her shoulders were stiff, her jaw clenched with terror; mentally she was screaming *go away, go away, please go away.*

'I'm fine, thanks. And you haven't changed at all. It's incredible.'

Lola said, 'Mum—'

'Oh, sorry, love, this is Nick.' Blythe jumped in before Lola could ask any awkward questions. 'We knew each other years ago . . . well, nice to see you again, we mustn't keep you . . . heavens, is that the time already? We're going to have to rush if we're—'

'Mum, it's OK.' Desperate to explain, Lola blurted out, 'I know who Nick is. And this isn't a coincidence; he knew we'd be here today because I told him. We met up before Christmas. He's my father. And we really like each other.' Hopefully, because her mother was staring at her as if she'd just sprouted an extra pair of ears, she said, 'So that's good, isn't it?'

Blythe's hand trembled as she took a gulp of wine. Then

another gulp. 'You planned this.' Her voice rose in disbelief. 'You met up before *Christmas*?'

'I was going to tell you,' Lola said hurriedly, 'but I didn't know how you'd react. And then Malcolm turned up on Christmas morning . . .'

'OK if I sit down?' Nick indicated a spare chair.

'My God, this is too much to take in.' Clutching her head, Blythe said, 'Just turning up like this, out of the blue . . . how did it happen? Who found who?'

'Well, it wasn't me,' said Lola. 'It couldn't have been me, could it? Seeing as you told me my father was an American who never even told you his real name.'

Her mother rubbed her forehead with both hands and said nothing.

'Because that wouldn't have exactly given me a lot to go on.' Lola's tone was dry.

'Which is why I said it. And it worked,' Blythe retaliated. 'It did the trick perfectly well.' Pointedly she added, 'For twenty-seven years.'

'I saw Lola being interviewed on the local news.' Nick pulled out the chair and sat down. 'Just for a few seconds, but it was enough. I had to find out if she was my daughter. And she is.' His eyes softening, he slid one hand across the table towards Blythe then withdrew it as she snatched hers out of reach. 'You've done a fantastic job, Blythe. She's an absolute credit to you.'

Lola felt ridiculously proud. Her father thought she was pretty good, possibly even fantastic.

'And to Alex. Her stepfather,' Blythe said stiffly. 'He's the one who helped to bring her up.'

Nick nodded. 'Of course.'

'I've told him all about Alex,' said Lola.

'And did he tell you everything too?' Breathing rapidly, Blythe turned her attention to Nick. 'Hmm? Did you? *Every*thing?'

People at other tables were starting to pay attention. Maybe organising this surprise reunion in a restaurant hadn't been such a great idea. Lola, who had thought having other people around might help to keep things under control, said surreptitiously, 'Mum, sshh.'

Which was kind of pointless seeing as Nick didn't bother to lower his own voice when he said, 'Yes, Blythe, she knows I went to prison.'

Now it was the turn of the avidly eavesdropping woman at the next table to go *sshh* at her husband who was droning boringly on about golf.

'That was twenty-seven years ago,' Nick continued. 'I made a mistake and I paid for it a hundred times over. I lost you and I lost my daughter. And before you ask, no, I *haven't* been in trouble with the police since then. I am a normal decent law-abiding citizen.'

'Congratulations.' Frostily Blythe said, 'Some of us have always been that.'

'Hey. Blythe.' His smile crooked, Nick seized the bottle of Merlot and poured some into Lola's empty water glass. 'It really is fantastic to see you again. We don't have to fight, do we? Can't we just be friends?'

'What? I don't know. This has only just happened.' Blythe noisily exhaled, shook her head. 'I can't even *think* straight.'

'I never stopped thinking about you. About both of you.'

For a second her eyes flashed. 'And I never stopped thinking about the way you lied to me.'

'Mum, it's all in the past.'

'But it happened,' Blythe insisted. 'I was eight months pregnant when I got the phone call telling me my boyfriend was in prison. No warning, no hints, just . . . bam. It was like . . . God, it was like the whole world had exploded. I thought my life was over, I didn't know what to do, I was *desperate*. And now here you are, turning up again out of the blue, saying, hey, never mind all that, it's in the past, let's just put it behind us and be friends!' She paused, sitting back in her seat and raking her fingers through her hair. 'Because I don't know if I want us to be friends. I'm fine as I am, thanks.'

'I'm Lola's father,' said Nick.

'Not as far as I'm concerned. Alex was the one who was there for her.' Heatedly Blythe said, 'And guess what? He didn't go to prison once!'

Lola closed her eyes; not quite the Hallmark reunion she'd been hoping for. 'Mum, you lied to me about Nick, remember? You didn't tell me the truth because you wanted to protect me, you didn't want me to be hurt.'

Her mother said defensively, 'So? Was that wrong?'

'No! You did it because you loved me!' Spreading her arms wide, narrowly missing the groin of a startled passing waiter, Lola said, 'But that's exactly why Nick lied to you! He didn't tell you about being arrested and charged because he loved you and didn't want you to be upset!'

'And didn't *that* work well.' Bright spots of colour burned in Blythe's cheeks as she scraped back her chair. 'No warning, no nothing, just a phone call from some stranger letting me know you were in jail. Why on earth would I be upset about *that*?'

'What are you doing?' said Lola as Blythe made a grab for her bag.

'I'm going to the bathroom, then home.'

'Mum, don't!'

'It's OK.' Nick rose to his feet. 'I'll leave. I'm sorry.' He rested his hands on Lola's shoulders as Blythe, blindly ricocheting off chairs, hurried to the loo. 'We got that a bit wrong, didn't we? Give her a while to calm down. Maybe I'll see you later.'

Lola nodded, unable to speak.

Some time later her mother returned to the table.

'You don't have to tell me,' Lola said at once. 'I made another mistake.'

'Sorry, love. Talk about a shock.' Freckles glowing, Blythe energetically fanned her face. 'Maybe next time you magic a father out of thin air I could have a few minutes' warning. I've never been much of a one for surprises.'

Was it any wonder? Lola pushed away her plate and divided the last of the wine between their glasses. Of course her mother had been shocked but had she also, deep down, been just a teeny bit impressed by how Nick had turned out? Tentatively she said, 'Our eyebrows do the same thing.'

Blythe hesitated, then managed a brief smile. 'I know.'

'He's very good-looking.'

'Oh yes, he always had that going for him. And he knew it. Nick was a charmer, all right.'

Valiantly, Lola carried on. 'Nice clothes too. He dresses well.'

Her mother's smile changed, grew faintly mocking. 'And that makes all the difference.'

Which was unfair, because it didn't make *all* the difference. It was just that when you compared Malcolm's external appearance, his woolly, unkempt, hairy-toed appearance, with Nick's smooth metropolitan one, well, it made quite a lot.

And was that really so wrong? When it was, after all, the

reason why there were more posters of Johnny Depp on bedroom walls across the country than there were of Johnny Vegas?

'I like him,' said Lola.

'Of course you do.' Blythe shrugged. 'Look, I'm sorry if you think I've deprived you of your father all these years, but—'

'Mum, that's OK, you thought you were doing the right thing. But we've found each other now. He's back in our lives. And we can take it slowly, all get to know each other properly. You liked him once, you can like him again.' Lola raised her glass with a surge of hope and a flourish. 'Same as me and Dougie.'

'I think you're forgetting something.' Signalling a waiter for the bill, Blythe said, 'You still like Dougie. But from what you've told me, he doesn't seem to be too crazy about you.'

Mothers could be cruel. 'He'll change his mind,' said Lola. 'I haven't given up on him yet.'

Chapter 27

Across the hallway Lola's doorbell was ringing. Sally, engrossed in the ice skating on TV – and the bowl of Ben and Jerry's in her lap – wiggled her toes and imagined herself in a sparkly, hot-pink figure-hugging outfit twirling across the ice.

Ddddrrrrrrinnnggggg. Whoever was at the front door wasn't giving up. As the skating routine drew to an end, Sally put down her ice cream and clambered off the sofa.

She hauled up the sash window and leaned out. 'Hello? Lola's not at home.' Then she almost lost her balance and toppled out, because the man gazing up at her was just . . .

Wow.

Let's just say he was a definite cut above your average carol singer.

'Any idea when she'll be back? I've tried her mobile but it's switched off.' His dark hair gleamed in the light from the street lamp. Even at this distance his eyes were hypnotic. Effortlessly hypnotised, Sally said, 'She could be back any time now. Do you want to come in and wait?'

His teeth gleamed white. 'Are you sure?'

With a smile like that? Was he kidding? Praying Lola

wouldn't be back too soon, Sally called out, 'Hang on, I'll buzz you up.'

'Thanks.' His smile broadened when she opened the door to her flat. 'I don't want to be a nuisance. But it's pretty icy out there.'

No worries, come here, I'll soon warm you up!

Thankfully she managed to keep these words inside her head. Oh, but he was to die for, really he was, with those expressive eyebrows and chiselled cheekbones, and that dark swept-back hair curling over the collar of his coat. This was definitely lust at first sight. And wasn't there something familiar about those eyebrows?

'Come on in, I'll make us a cup of tea . . . *oops*.' In her excitement she almost kicked over the bowl on the carpet. 'Don't step in the ice cream! I'm Sally, by the way.'

'I know. Lola's told me all about you.'

'*Has* she?' Ridiculously flattered, Sally turned to look at him as she filled the kettle at the sink. *Whooosh*, ice-cold water promptly ricocheted off the spout, drenching her from neck to navel. When you were in the grip of lust it was hard to concentrate.

'Why don't I make the tea?' Amused, he said, 'You'd better go and change out of those wet things.'

Which was how real life differed from the movies because if this *hadn't* been real he might have offered to help her.

By the time she re-emerged in dry clothes she'd figured it out. 'I've heard all about you too,' Sally announced as he carried the tea through to the living room. 'You're Lola's dad.'

'Nick James.' His humorous dark grey eyes crinkled at the corners. Gorgeous eyes, gorgeous corners. And the way he dressed . . . well, that was right up her street too. A dark green shirt, black trousers and black shoes, you couldn't get plainer than that, but they were of excellent quality and so well-cut, and he wore them like a Frenchman. The glamorous citified kind you saw sitting at pavement cafés on the Champs Elysées, not the gnarled leathery farmer types with strings of onions slung around their necks.

Unlike grungly Gabe with his bleached T-shirts and disintegrating jeans, this was a man with *élan*, with *savoir faire* . . . a man who knew how to dress. He even – *mais naturellement!* – smelled fantastic. And he was Lola's father. Would this make things tricky or awkward?

Sally considered the facts then decided there was no reason why it should. If Lola was allowed to have a crush on her brother and yearn for him shamelessly, it seemed only fair that she should be allowed a shot at Lola's dad. Crikey, if Lola married Doug and she married Nick, she'd be Lola's stepmother *and* her sister-in-law; wouldn't that be a turn-up for the books? It was the kind of thing that got you invited onto TV shows and . . . um, OK, maybe getting a teeny bit carried away here, just the weeniest bit ahead of herself . . .

'The ice cream had pretty much melted,' said Nick. 'So I put the bowl in the sink.'

'Right. Um, thanks.' Oh God, please don't say he was going to turn out to be another neurotic-obsessive-compulsive-tidier-upper. But he hadn't cleared away anything else, so that was good. He had lovely hands too, capable-looking fingers and clean, well-shaped nails. Ooh, and if we all had children they'd be simultaneously each other's cousins *and* uncles and aunts . . .

'What are you thinking?' Nick was regarding her with interest, his dark head tilted to one side.

Again, probably best not to tell him. 'Just wondering if I'm allowed to ask how it went today, meeting up with Lola and her mum.'

'Not brilliantly. It wasn't a fairytale reunion.' He paused, stirring his tea. 'Hardly surprising, I suppose. Bit of a shock for Blythe. That's why I came over to see Lola, to find out how things are now. Relationships are . . . complicated.'

'Ha, tell me about it.'

Nick grinned. 'Lola did happen to mention you'd had your share of bad luck with men.'

Oh Lola did, did she? Cheers, Lola. Then again, maybe it had been fate all along, nature's way of forcing her to wait until Mr Right – no, Mr Absolutely Perfect – turned up.

And since he already knew, there was no point trying to deny the past.

'That's a very polite way of putting it,' Sally said ruefully, 'but I think you mean my share of bastards.' On the TV a groan of disappointment went up from the audience and she pointed to the pair of skaters sprawled on the ice. 'It's like that, isn't it? One minute it's all going so well, you're twirling and flying through the air and actually starting to think you're in with a chance of gold. And the next minute, *splat*, you're flat on your face. That's why I love watching my old video of Torvill and Dean doing Bolero. Because I know it doesn't go wrong, nobody falls over and they carry on being perfect right to the end.' She paused then said with a lopsided smile, 'Wouldn't it be great if our lives could be like that?'

Oops, had that been a bit too heartfelt? Did it make her sound needy and desperate? Was he going to make fun of her now?

But that didn't happen. Instead, nodding in agreement, he said, 'It's what everyone wants, if they're honest. We just can't help buggering things up. But the right man's out there some-where, I know he is.'

Sally looked innocent. 'For you?'

He smiled easily. 'For you. It's just a question of tracking him down.'

They carried on chatting for another hour. He was so wonder-fully easy to talk to. She learned about his career in advertising and told him about her own job — you couldn't really call it a career — as a receptionist in a busy doctors' surgery in Wimbledon.

Nick was surprised. 'And this is NHS? I wouldn't have had you down as a doctors' receptionist.'

'Because I'm not tidy?' Hurt, Sally said, 'I'm *very* organised at work.'

'I actually meant you look too glamorous.'

She flushed at the compliment, smoothed back her hair. 'I love my job. OK, it's not high-powered and it isn't glamorous, but the doctors I work with are great. Really friendly. It's never boring. And I'm good at what I do,' she added with pride. 'Dr Willis says I'm the most efficient receptionist they've ever had.'

'So this surgery then, is it not a good place to meet men? What are these doctors like?'

'Old and married.' Hastily, because she knew Nick was forty-eight, Sally said, 'I mean, *ancient*. Sixties. Much older than you.'

His mouth curved at the corners. 'Glad to hear it. How about the patients, then? Must be a few promising ones there.'

'Well, yes, until you look through their medical notes.' Sally pulled a face. 'And read all about their stomach upsets, their erectile dysfunction, the excessive sweating and eczema in their skin folds, not to mention their problems with excessive wind and snoring . . . I don't know, somehow all the magic goes out of them after that.'

He looked appalled. 'Jesus, who d'you have coming to your surgery? A bunch of trolls?'

'They don't have all those things. And not all at once. It's just when you type a name into the computer, the whole medical history comes up on the first page. Say it's an ultra-respectable bank manager,' Sally explained. 'He might look really nice, he might sound really nice. But one glance at the screen and I know he caught a sexually transmitted disease when he was nineteen, had a stubborn fungal infection between his toes when he was twenty-eight and for the last three years has been seeing a specialist at a centre for gender reassignment.'

'I take your point. What's more,' said Nick, 'I'll never try and chat up my doctor's receptionist again.'

Chapter 28

'You missed Nick. He left twenty minutes ago.' Sally beckoned Lola into the flat, eager to tell her everything. 'Isn't he great? He's been waiting here for you to get back. In the end he had to leave, but we've had a lovely couple of hours getting to know each other. He's just so—'

'Oh no, he waited a couple of *hours*? Why didn't he ring me?' Distracted, Lola scrabbled for her phone. 'Damn, when did I switch that off?'

'It wasn't a problem. We've been chatting non-stop. In fact—'

'Hang on, let me just give him a quick call.'

Sally waited impatiently for Lola to get off the phone; she was longing to tell her how well they'd got along together and what an attractive man her father was. Not that Lola could have any reason to mind, but to be polite she was going to jokily ask her permission before making a proper play for him.

'Damn, now his phone's switched off.' Lola shook her head, then straightened up and broke into a dazzling smile. 'Sorry, not concentrating. What a day! So you met Nick. Did you like him?'

Ha, just a bit! 'He's great,' Sally said eagerly. 'I *really* liked him; in fact—'

'Oh God, I'm so glad, because when you think about it, what would you do if you met your real father and he turned out to be awful? Wouldn't that be just the worst thing in the world? But he isn't awful, and we get on so well together, I couldn't—'

'So did we. Get on well together,' Sally blurted out.

'See? That's it exactly, he's a genuinely nice person. That's why I know I can do it.'

'Do what?'

Lola looked smug. 'Get them back together.'

Do *what*?

'But, but . . .'

'Wouldn't that be perfect?' Lola, her eyes shining, unwound her scarf and collapsed onto the sofa. 'And I've made up my mind now. I'm going to make it happen. OK, it didn't get off to the best of starts, but that was just the shock factor. I went home with Mum this afternoon and we had a proper talk about everything. It was amazing, hearing all this stuff for the first time. And look what she gave me.' Lola took an envelope from her bag and carefully slid out a photograph. 'It's the two of them together, before I came along.'

Feeling numb, Sally gazed at the photograph. Lola's mother, her red-gold hair swinging around her shoulders, was wearing a purple and white sundress, a stripy green cardigan and clumpy white platform shoes. Nick, sitting on the wall next to her with a proprietorial arm around her narrow waist, grinned into the camera. He was twenty years old, cocky and good-looking in a denim shirt and jeans, with everything going for him. Lola's mother looked like a young Jane Asher – minus the dress sense – and Nick was her Paul McCartney.

'This is how I know I can do it,' said Lola, tapping the old photo. 'My mum kept it all these years. That means she still cares about him.'

Sally exhaled slowly. The disappointment was crushing. Why did stuff like this always have to happen to her? Struggling to sound normal, she said, 'Maybe she just forgot it was there. I've got photos at home of my seventh birthday party but it doesn't mean I care about the kids I was at infants school with. I can't even remember their names.'

'That's completely different.' Lola shook her head. 'You were seven years old. When it's boyfriend-girlfriend stuff, you don't hang on to photos of the ones you don't like any more. You just don't want those pictures to exist! But if you *do* still care about the other person, you keep the photos. Like I've still got all mine of me and Dougie.'

'Maybe, but has he still kept his ones of you? Anyway,' Sally was defensive, 'it's a personal thing. Some people keep all their photographs regardless.' Meaning that *she* had. Crikey, if she were to tear up all the photos of her with the exes who'd chucked her, she wouldn't have any left. Dammit, and now she wasn't even going to be allowed to have a shot at Lola's father because Lola – *completely* selfishly – had decided that she wanted him to get back together with her mother.

Bum.

The door swung open behind them and for a split second Sally's foolish heart leapt, because what if it was Nick rushing back to tell her he couldn't bear to be without her, that it had been love at first sight for him too, that he had *no* interest in getting back together with Blythe . . .

Oh, and that he'd secretly had a spare key cut, which was how he'd been able to burst back into the flat.

'They do it deliberately,' Gabe announced, tipping Lola's feet off the sofa and throwing himself down with a groan of despair. 'I swear to God, their mission in life is to officially do my head in. Celebrities.' He exhaled, pushing his hands through his floppy blond hair. 'Couldn't you just roll them up in a big red carpet and tip them over a cliff?'

'Not a good night?' Lola was sympathetic.

'Bloody useless. Complete waste of time. I waited three hours for this actress to come out of a hair place in Primrose Hill. I was getting thirstier and thirstier, but I stuck it out because I knew she had to be finished soon. Then finally I couldn't stand it a minute longer and raced into the shop across the road. I was in there for fifteen *seconds*, no more than that. And when I came out, her limo was pulling away. I tell you, I felt like throwing rocks at it.'

'Poor you.' Lola gave his arm a squeeze. 'Yeurgh, you're freezing. What's all this stuff in your pocket?' She had a quick rummage, pulling out sandwich wrappers, crisp packets and a folded sheet of A4 paper.

'Homework. Colin gave it to me.' Gabe shook his head wearily. 'It's a list of car registration numbers belonging to celebs. If you spot one in the street, you know they're in the vicinity. I'm supposed to learn the whole list. Oh hell, I can't do this job. How am I supposed to recognise all these people when there's so damn many of them? And when it comes to the girls with blond hair extensions, well, they're even worse. They all look exactly the same!'

'You'll get the hang of it.' Lola's tone was consoling. 'What about the other paps, are they friendly?'

'They're OK,' grumbled Gabe. 'But they're taking the mickey out of me because I keep getting things wrong. I thought I'd spotted Britney Spears coming out of Waterstones with an armful of dictionaries but it wasn't her. And this morning I got a great shot of George Clooney pushing a pram in Hyde Park, except it turned out to be some bloke from last year's *Big Brother*. I'm a laughing stock. They keep pointing to old homeless guys in the street and saying, "Quick, Gabe, it's Pierce Brosnan!" and "Hey, Gabe, isn't that George Bush?"'

'But your photos of Tom Dutton and Jessica Lee were in *Heat* this week,' said Lola. 'Look how much money you made from those shots. They're just jealous.'

'That was a fluke. I could work for the next five years and not get another chance like that.'

'Or it could happen again tomorrow,' Sally chimed in. 'That's the thing, you never know. It's like panning for gold.'

'We'll see. This isn't as great as I thought it might be. And I have to work on New Year's Eve,' grumbled Gabe. 'What a lousy way to spend the night, hanging around *outside* all the best parties, freezing my nuts off.'

Sally looked smug. 'You can take my photo if you like. I'm off to a fantastic glitzy do on New Year's Eve.'

'That's three days away.' Eyeing the plates with crumbs on, the dirty cups, the pistachio nut shells and the basket of make-up on the coffee table, Gabe said evenly, 'Any chance of clearing this mess up before you go?'

'See what I'm up against?' Sally rolled her eyes and grinned at Lola. 'Totally neurotic!'

It was seven o'clock on New Year's Eve. 'You won't believe what's happened,' wailed Sally, bursting into Lola's flat. 'My bloody boss has only been and gone and stood me up.'

Lola, hopping around with one shoe on and one shoe off, said, 'For your posh do? You can come along to the White Hart with us if you like. It won't be posh and you'll definitely get beer spilled over you, but it'll be a good night.' It would actually be a sweaty, crowded, extremely rowdy night but Tim from work had bullied everyone into buying tickets and Lola hadn't had the heart to refuse. Persuasively she added, 'A tenner a ticket and all the burgers you can eat.'

Sally looked horrified. 'My God, I can't imagine anything more horrible. My ticket for the Carrick cost a hundred and fifty pounds.'

'Blimey, I'd want gold-plated, diamond-encrusted burgers for that price.'

But it was for charity, Lola learned. And they certainly didn't serve burgers at the five-star, decidedly glitzy Carrick Hotel overlooking Hyde Park. The event was dinner and a quiz, with tables of ten forming teams who were to compete against each other. Dr Willis, Sally's boss, had been due to partner her for the evening – in a platonic way, naturally, what with him being sixty-four years old and keen on astronomy – but had just phoned to apologise that he couldn't make it after all, his daughter having begged him to babysit his grandchildren instead.

'So the ticket's already been paid for,' Sally finished. 'Seems a shame to waste it. Wouldn't you rather come with me to the Carrick than squeeze into some scuzzy, sticky-carpeted pub?'

Weakening, Lola pulled a face; she hated letting people down. 'Tim's expecting me to be there. I don't want to disappoint him.'

'Sure? It'll be fun.' Sally played her trump card. 'Doug's on our table.'

Oh well, everyone else from Kingsley's was going along to the White Hart; it wasn't as if Tim would be all on his own. 'Go on then.' Lola's heart began to beat faster, because this could be her chance to really impress Dougie. 'You've twisted my arm.'

Chapter 29

Having changed out of her beer-friendly black lycra top and frayed jeans into an altogether more suitable peacock-blue dress with spaghetti straps and swishy sequinned hem, Lola entered the Carrick's ballroom feeling quite the bee's knees. Moments later those same knees quavered with excitement as, through the crowds, she spotted Dougie over by the bar, looking even more handsome than ever in formal black tie. Heavens, how could any girl resist him? He was gorgeous. Giving herself time to mentally get her act together, Lola hung back as Sally approached the group at the bar.

'Hey, you're here.' Doug turned when she tapped him on the shoulder. 'Everyone, this is my sister Sally, specialist subjects fashion and shopping. And rather more usefully she's brought along her boss who's a doctor, so any medical questions and he's our man. He's also excellent on astronomy, which . . . which is . . .' As he was speaking, Doug's gaze had veered past Sally, searching for someone who would fit the description of aged, avuncular, planet-watching Dr Willis. When he spotted Lola his voice trailed off, his welcoming smile faded and he said, 'Oh for heaven's sake, I don't believe it. You *again*?'

Which was, frankly, more than a little hurtful.

'Honestly.' Sally rolled her eyes at the rest of the group. 'Is this what he's like at work? Frank couldn't make it, he has to babysit his grandchildren tonight, so I asked Lola if she'd come along in his place. Otherwise we'd have been a team member short for the quiz.'

Doug shook his head. 'So Lola's our medical expert for the evening. Perfect. Let's just hope no one needs an emergency tracheotomy.'

'Doug, calm down. I'll answer the medical questions,' said Sally.

The tall man next to Doug said intently, 'Are you a doctor too?'

'Well, no, not exactly, but I'm a GP's receptionist.' As the man's lip began to curl into a sneer Sally said, 'Do you know what papilloedema is?'

He looked startled. 'No.'

'See? I do. I know where the medulla oblongata is. I know about systolic and diastolic blood pressure measurements. I can tell you what talipes are.' Airily Sally added, 'And I can tell you exactly what to do with a sphygmomanometer.'

The man took a gulp of his drink. Lola stifled a grin. Touché.

'Fine.' Doug looked resigned. 'Just don't try and take out anyone's appendix.'

'Sally, *hiiii*!' Yeeurgh. Isabel joined the group, flicking back her silky ice-blond hair and clutching Sally's arms as if they were long-lost friends. Moments later, spotting Lola, she said with rather less enthusiasm, 'Oh, hello again.'

'I'm Tony, history and politics,' the tall man announced. Gesturing towards the others he said, 'Alice is biology and Greek mythology. Jerry's Egyptology and maths. And this is Bob, whose speciality is—'

'Trying to swim the Channel with his arms and legs tied up?' Lola couldn't help herself; when she was nervous, stupid stuff just came out of her mouth.

Tumbleweed rolled past. Quite deservedly, no one laughed. Tony cleared his throat and said, 'No, Bob's speciality is classical music.'

'And cricket,' said Bob.

'Great,' said Lola.

'How about you?'

Crikey, how about me?

'Um . . . well, literature.'

'And?' Tony eyed her beadily; it appeared everyone was required to be an expert in two subjects.

'And . . . er, sumo wrestling.' That would be safe surely?

'Excellent, excellent.' As he rubbed his hands together they made a rasping, sandpapery sound. 'So which should we be hoping for this evening, hmm? *Kachikoshi*? Or *makekoshi*?'

Bugger. And his lip was curling again. He *knew*.

'OK,' said Lola, 'I was lying. I don't know anything about sumo. I only have one specialist subject and I'm sorry if that's not enough, but I'm only here as a last-minute replacement. It's either me or an empty chair.'

'Don't worry about Tony, he's a pompous twit.'

'Is he? I mean, I know he is.' To Lola's relief, not everyone in the group was unfriendly. With the quiz due to start in five minutes, she beamed at the girl redoing her make-up in the ornate gilt mirror in the cloakroom. 'I just didn't realise people would be taking it so seriously.'

'Don't worry, you'll be fine. God, this skirt's killing me.' The girl, whose name was Elly, straightened up and gave her stomach a disgruntled prod. 'I've put on almost a stone over Christmas, nothing fits any more. I'm going to have to join a gym before I turn into a complete hippo.'

'I hate gyms.' Lola pulled a face.

'I thought of giving Doug's a go. He says it's all right.' Disconsolately tugging down her corrugated skirt, Elly said, 'But they'll still make you suffer, won't they? What I really need's a magic wand.'

Lola carefully untwiddled a strand of hair from around one of her silver earrings. 'Is that Holmes Place?'

Yhooooosh, Elly sprayed Elnett Ultrahold wildly around her head like a cowboy twirling a lasso. 'No, Merton's in Kensington – ow, sod it!'

She'd sprayed Elnett right in her eye. 'Here,' Lola passed her a clean tissue; the thought of Dougie working up a sweat on a rowing machine was enough to send any girl's aim wonky.

'Thanks. And just ignore Tony.' Elly's smile was encouraging. 'We'll still have fun; you don't have to try and impress him.'

'You're right.' Lola didn't tell her that the person she really wanted to impress was Doug.

Their table was doing well in the first round; everyone was getting their chance to shine. Rivalry between the thirty or so teams in the banqueting hall was intense. Having answered a fiendish question about the last rugby World Cup, Doug (specialist subjects sport and economics) was so elated he actually grinned across the table at Lola before realising what he was doing and abruptly reaching for his drink instead. But the moment was already imprinted in Lola's mind; for a split second there, it had been just like old times. Fresh hope surged inside her; please *please* let him be weakening, let him realise that the attraction was still there. From what she could tell, this thing with Isabel was pretty shallow, hardly the romance of the century. Isabel might be beautiful but her personality wasn't exactly dazzling; in fact she was like an irritatingly chirpy child, tugging Doug's arm for attention, giggling and endlessly whispering in his ear. Basically she was nothing but an airhead . . .

'And now,' boomed the question master, calling the noisy room to attention, 'the penultimate question in Round One. Pay close attention, ladies and gentlemen, because every point counts.' He paused for effect. 'And this question is in two parts. The first part is this. What is the speed of light?'

Lola's spirits sank; she was desperate to show Doug she wasn't a deadweight, that she could be a useful member of the team, but how was *anyone* supposed to know—

'Three hundred thousand kilometres per second,' Isabel whispered.

What?

What?

'Good girl.' Tony wrote down the answer without blinking.

'And now for the second part,' the question master announced. 'In order for any object to escape the earth's gravitational pull, it must be flying at or above the earth's escape velocity. The question is, what is that velocity?'

Everyone at the table turned their gaze on Isabel. *No*, Lola wanted to yell, *no, you can't know the answer to that, you just can't* . . .

With a self-deprecating smile Isabel murmured, 'Eleven kilometres per second.'

Smirking, Tony scribbled down the answer on their table's card.

'OK, time's up, please raise your cards.'

All across the room, cards were lifted and checked. The question master announced, 'The answers are three hundred thousand kilometres per second and eleven kilometres per second.'

A great cheer went up around their table. Isabel took a sip of iced water and continued to look modest. 'And Table Sixteen, the Sitting Tennants, were the only ones to get both parts of that question right. Well done, you Sitting Tennants!'

Lola, leaning over to Elly on her left, said incredulously, 'How did she know that?'

Elly said, 'Who, Isabel? Oh, she's mad about stuff like that. She went along to evening classes last year, just for fun. Got an A in A-level physics.'

Lola's stomach clenched as she observed Isabel, with her dinky little nose and perfect smile. Geeky boffins were supposed to look like geeky boffins, not swan around like Grace Kelly in slinky sea-green silk with strappy Gucci sandals on their feet.

'And now, the final question of the first round.' Up on the dais, the question master tapped a knife against his glass to regain everyone's attention. 'Ready? This is one for all you book lovers out there.'

Lola's heart promptly broke into a gallop. Now *she* was the centre of attention. Adrenaline buzzed through her veins and her knees began to judder. Across the table, only *slightly* patronisingly, Isabel said, 'Come on, Lola, you can do it!'

'Right, ladies and gentlemen, your question is this.' As the question master paused for further dramatic effect, Lola concentrated on looking serious, focused and super-intelligent. 'What word appears one thousand eight hundred and fifty-five times in the Bible?'

Oh, for bloody *crying* out loud.

'Lola?' demanded Tony when she shook her head and sat back. 'Come along now, what is it?'

'How am I supposed to know the answer to that?'

He looked at her as if she were an imbecile. 'Because it's a literature question and books are your speciality.'

'It's the Bible!' Stung by the unfairness of it all, Lola cried, 'Even if I *had* read the Bible, I promise you I wouldn't have counted how many times each word appeared!'

'Quick!' shouted Jerry.

'Um, OK . . . "and".' Lola blurted the word out in a panic, aware that across the table Isabel was writing something on the back of one of the programmes.

AND, Tony scrawled on the answer card.

'Time's up,' called the question master. 'Raise your cards please. Ah, I see lots of you got it right this time. Well done, all of you who knew that the correct answer is Lord.'

'Oh, bad luck, Lola.' Isabel smiled sympathetically.

The others didn't say anything. They didn't need to. Then Jerry, peering at the programme by Isabel's elbow, exclaimed, 'You wrote it down! You *knew* Lord was the right answer.'

'Shh, it doesn't matter. Questions about books are Lola's field of expertise. I didn't want her to feel I was muscling in.'

Intrigued, Sally said, 'But how did you know it was Lord?'

'Same way as everyone else who got it right, I expect.' Isabel dimpled prettily – dammit, she even had dimples. 'It's a Trivial Pursuit question. Once you've been asked it, it's not the kind of answer you forget.'

Chapter 30

The four-course meal, each course served between rounds of questions, was sublime. The glittering ballroom with its mirrored walls, opulent décor and hundreds of tethered gold and white helium balloons, was beautiful in every way. By concentrating on the good parts and reminding herself that she never had to see the ultra-competitive contingent again, Lola chatted to Elly and Sally and began to enjoy the evening. It was, after all, a far cry from warm beer and burst eardrums at the White Hart.

By the beginning of the fifth and final round they were joint leaders along with the Deadly Dunns, a team from another management consultancy. The rivalry was intense now; there might be laughter on the surface but, deep down, reputations were at stake.

Sally got them off to a flying start by knowing the whereabouts in the body of the islets of Langerhans, which Lola privately felt should be found not in the pancreas but somewhere off the west coast of Scotland in the vicinity of Barra, Eriskay and Skye.

The questions continued and their table's points continued to mount up. Bob knew something ridiculously obscure about the composer Dmitri Shostakovich and earned himself a round of applause. Jerry the Egyptologist preened, having correctly answered a question about the identity of the tekenu. Elly dithered a bit but finally guessed correctly that David Hockney had attended Bradford Grammar.

Lola began to wonder if she was actually the least intelligent person in the entire room. Even people who didn't look remotely clever were getting things right whilst she was still struggling to break her duck.

Isabel let out a shriek of delight and smothered Doug in kisses when he correctly answered that David Campese was the player who'd scored the most tries in test rugby.

Lola helped herself to more wine. One booky-type question, that was all she asked, a question that nobody else knew the answer to. And when she answered it correctly, everyone would break into wild applause and Dougie would give her one of his heart-melting smiles . . .

Finally it was the penultimate question of the quiz. Doug's table and the Deadly Dunns were still neck and neck. It's only a game, Lola told herself, it's only a game. But she felt sick anyway; it felt more important than that.

'Right, here we go,' said the question master. 'James Loveless, George Loveless, John Standfield, Thomas Standfield, James Brine and James Hammett are the names of . . . ?'

Lola, busy knocking back wine, froze in mid-glug. She knew who they were. Bloody hell, she actually knew an answer!

Everyone else looked blank. Sally whispered, 'Is it the Arctic Monkeys?'

'Soldiers who won the VC?' guessed Bob.

History was Tony's specialist subject. He was shaking his head, gazing in turn at the others in search of enlightenment.

'Are they footballers?' hazarded Jerry the Egyptologist.

Tony looked at Isabel, then at Doug, before glancing briefly in Lola's direction. Hastily swallowing her mouthful of wine and keen not to let anyone at nearby tables overhear, she mouthed the answer at him.

Tony frowned and mouthed back, '*What?*'

Tingling with excitement, Lola mouthed the words again, more slowly this time. '*The Tolpuddle martyrs.*'

Tony turned away as if he hadn't seen her. Reaching for the answer card he scrawled a few words and, leaning across to Isabel, whispered in her ear.

Lola watched open-mouthed as she cried, 'Oh Tony, you're *brilliant.*'

'Everyone raise your cards,' called the question master. 'And the correct answer . . . is . . . the Tolpuddle martyrs!'

'Yayyyy!' Everyone else on the table let out a huge cheer. Bob and Jerry clapped Tony on the back and Lola waited for him to announce that, in fact, *she*, Lola, was the one who'd known the answer.

But he didn't. He just sat there looking smug and lapping up all the congratulations. Lola gazed around wildly; had none of them *seen* what had happened? Not even Doug?

'Damn, the Deadly Dunns got it too,' said Doug. 'We're still level. It's right down to the wire.'

Bloody Tony, what a cheater! Lola was so busy being outraged and glaring at him that she barely listened to the final question.

'. . . famous writer died in eighteen eighty. Her *nom de plume* was George Eliot. But what was her real name?'

This was it. Lola sat up as if she'd been electrocuted. Ha, *and* it was a trick question! Everyone else was going to think the answer was Mary Ann Evans. More importantly, the Deadly Dunns were going to think that. But the clue was in the way the question had been phrased, and seven months before her death at the age of sixty-one, Mary Ann Evans had married a toyboy by the name of John Cross. So the question being asked was, in fact, what was her real name *when she died* . . .

'Well?' said Bob. 'Do you know it?'

'Of course I know it.' Lola signalled for the answer card and a pen. With a flourish she wrote Mary Ann Cross. Oh yes, was that a flicker of respect in Doug's eye? About time too! She was about to win his team the competition!

'Raise your cards, ladies and gentlemen.'

Trembling with excitement, Lola held it above her head.

'Hmm.' Doug was looking at the other raised cards.

Oh Dougie, have faith in me, would I let you down?

'And the correct . . . answer . . . is . . .' the question master strung it out *X Factor* style, '. . . Mary . . . Ann . . . Evans!'

'For fuck's sake,' groaned Bob.

'*No*,' Lola heard herself blurt the word out, shock prickling at the base of her skull. Shaking her head in disbelief, she said, 'That's wrong!'

Jerry's tone was bitter. '*You're* wrong.'

'YEEEAAAHHH!' Realising they'd won the competition, the Deadly Dunns were cheering their heads off.

'But I'm not wrong. Mary Anne Evans married a man called John Cross . . . she *did* . . .' The words died in Lola's throat as she realised it no longer mattered; the game was over and she'd lost it − irony of ironies − by trying to be too clever.

Bam, went the cork as it flew out of the Deadly Dunns' triumphantly shaken bottle of champagne. Everyone else in the room was applauding them. They rose to their feet and bowed, before breaking into a boisterous chorus of 'We Are the Champions'.

Bob shook his head in disgust.

Tony said, 'Shit, they're never going to let us forget this.'

Lola was bursting for the loo. If she left the table now, they'd all talk about how rubbish she was. Oh well, who cared? If she didn't leave the table now she'd really give them something to talk about.

The ladies' loo was blessedly cool, a calm ivory marble haven from the babbling crowds in the ballroom. Having touched up her make-up and enjoyed five minutes of peace and quiet, Lola was just putting away her lipstick when the door swung open and Doug said, 'There you are.' His miss-nothing gaze checked out her face. 'Are you OK?'

'Fine.' As one of the loos was flushed behind her, Lola said, 'You aren't allowed in here.'

'Come outside then.' He held the door open and ushered her past him. In the corridor he said, 'I thought you might have been upset.'

'You mean crying?' Lola was glad the whites of her eyes were still clear and white. 'I wouldn't give your friends the satisfaction. And I'm not upset, I'm just sorry I let you down.'

Doug shook his head. 'Hey, it doesn't matter. It was only meant to be a bit of fun. I had no idea Tony was going to take the whole thing so seriously. They're not my friends either,' he added. 'Tony works for me. Jerry and Bob are friends of his. Tony was the one who persuaded me that coming here tonight would be good PR. He can be a bit of an arse. Well, quite a lot of an arse. Tony takes his quizzes very seriously.'

'He's a cheating arse,' said Lola; it was no good, she couldn't not tell him. 'I gave him the Tolpuddle martyrs answer. I *did*,' she insisted when Doug look amused. 'That was me! He just couldn't bear to admit it.'

'OK. Well, I'm glad you're all right. And I'm sorry about Tony.'

Touched by his concern – that had to be an encouraging sign, surely – Lola smiled and said, 'Thanks. Not your fault.'

Doug hesitated. 'I was going to ask you, how's it going with your father?'

Yay, another encouraging sign! 'Pretty good. I'm trying to fix him up with my mum but she's digging her heels in. I won't give up though. When you know two people would be perfect together, if one of them could just forgive the other for some silly mistake they made years ago, you have to persevere. Otherwise it would just be a terrible waste,' Lola said innocently. 'Don't you think?'

Dougie gave her that look she knew so well. 'Maybe your mother really isn't interested.'

'Ah, but that's the thing. Deep down, I think she still is.' Lola gazed at him, longing to touch his face. 'Remember that weekend we went to Brighton and you took loads of photos of me on the beach?'

Doug paused, clearly wondering if there was any point in trying to say no. He shrugged. 'Vaguely.'

Vaguely, right. Which meant he was definitely lying. He'd been eighteen, she'd been seventeen and they'd made love at midnight on a lilo on the beach. How could any red–blooded male fail to remember a weekend like that?

'I'd love to see those photos again.'

His mouth twitched. 'You don't give up, do you?'

Lola smiled back, realising that he wasn't going to tell her whether or not he still had them. That was the trouble with trying to outsmart someone smarter than yourself. On the other hand, reminding him of the existence of the photos might prompt him to dig them out and the sight of her cavorting in the sea in her pink bikini might in turn remind him of how happy they'd been, and how happy they could be again.

'Well,' Dougie cleared his throat. 'I suppose we'd—'

'Yes, better get back.' She dived in, saying the words before he could say them himself. 'Don't want people starting to wonder where we've got to. Just one thing first.' Her heart beating faster, Lola rested a hand on his arm. 'Seeing as it's New Year's Eve and I probably won't get the chance later, can I wish you a . . .' *move towards him* '. . . happy . . .' *slide your free arm around his neck* '. . . New . . .' *half close your eyes, half open your mouth . . .*

'Year,' said Doug, planting a brisk kiss on her cheek before stepping back.

Damn, foiled again. So near yet so far. This was a man with *way* too much self-control.

What a job. What was he doing here, freezing his nuts off outside a club, listening to everyone on the inside counting down to midnight?

Next to Gabe, Jez muttered, 'Hey, man, happy New Year.'

'Yeah, you too.' Gabe huddled further inside his fleece, his breath puffing out in front of him, his hands so cold he could barely grip the camera.

'It's midnight. They're all in there, going crazy.' Shivering, Jez jerked his head. 'Fancy a cup of tea in that café up the road?'

Gabe nodded; this had to be the best time to get one.

Ten minutes later they made their way back to the club.

'Bloody hell,' cried one of the other paps, 'you missed it! That *EastEnders* guy ran out; all he was wearing was his cowboy boots.'

'You're having us on.' Jez paled.

'Naked as a baby, I swear to God. And he did a handstand. Not a pretty sight.' Chuckling, the pap showed them the shots on his camera. 'That's my work done for the night. Picked the wrong time to leave, you lads. Look out for these pictures in the *News of the World*.' He left, crowing with delight.

Jez said with feeling, 'I bloody hate this bloody job.'

'Me too.' But the annoying thing was, it had its addictive side. Balanced against the cold and the tedium and the endless hanging around was the knowledge that the next big picture might be only a click away. It was like shark fishing: one minute you were bored out of your mind, the next you were firing on all cylinders because at any second anything *could* happen . . . like this stretch limo heading down the street towards them now, slowing down. Getting his camera ready, Gabe experienced the now-familiar rush of adrenaline as a blacked-out window slid down. He moved into position alongside Jez. Because this could be *anyone* – Jack Nicholson dressed as a nun, Mick Jagger with Lily Allen, Simon Cowell with—

'What the *fuck*?' yelled Jez as half a dozen yellow plastic bazookas fired torrents of ice-cold water at them. Shaking his dripping hair out of his eyes, almost dropping his camera, Gabe cursed and watched the limo accelerate away. The occupants were roaring with laughter, delighted with their prank, and no one even knew who they were.

'Happy New Year, losers,' one of them bellowed through the window.

Gabe was soaked to the skin. Four interminable hours and he hadn't managed so much as a single decent photo. This was possibly the very worst New Year's Eve of his life.

Chapter 31

'I'm not sure this is such a good idea,' said Lola. 'Remind me again why we're here?'

Because I've got the most enormous crush on your father and I'm longing to show off in front of him, knock him dead with my dazzling footwork and spinny twirls!

Sally didn't actually say this out loud. Turning to Lola she explained, 'Because it's fun and it's something you've never done before. I mean, look at this place! Did you ever see anything so pretty?'

Lola followed the expansive sweep of her arm, dutifully taking in the flaming torches and architectural lighting illuminating the courtyard's classical façades. 'I'm going to fall over and break my ankles.'

'You won't. I'll show you how to do it properly. Besides, falling over's all part of the fun.' Personally Sally felt her choice of Somerset House ice rink, off the Strand, had been inspired. 'And it's only here for a couple more weeks – ooh look, there's Nick!'

Luckily the sub-zero temperatures meant that her cheeks were already pink. In her white fake-fur hat and matching gilet, worn over a red cashmere sweater and black jeans, Sally was ready to impress the hell out of Lola's dad. When Lola had idly wondered what father-daughter things she and Nick could do together on their road to getting to know each other, it had taken her . . . ooh, all of two seconds to think of something that could include her as well.

Even if it meant having to sacrifice Lola's ankles to do it.

OK, that was just a joke; it wouldn't really happen anyway. Oh God, look at Nick, he was *so* gorgeous, she could just—

'Over here,' Lola called out, windmilling both arms to attract his attention.

'Hey, you two.' Joining them, he gave Lola a hug and a kiss.

She beamed, clearly delighted to see him again. 'Look at you, so *brown*.'

Nick, just back from ten days in St Kitts, in turn greeted Sally with a kiss on the cheek that made her quiver like a terrier on a leash. Even his polite kisses were thrilling.

Nick grinned. 'So you're going to be teaching us all the moves tonight.'

Was that an unintentional double entendre or was he saying it like that on purpose?

'Absolutely. You're both going to love this.' Her eyes shining – just in case he was flirting with her – Sally said, 'By the time I finish with you two tonight, you'll be whizzing round like pros.'

'And by this time next year we'll be going for gold in the Olympics.' Inspired, Lola said excitedly, 'Can we get out onto the ice now?'

'Lesson one.' Sally yanked her back. 'Always best to queue up first and hire some skates.'

Lola was a revelation on the ice, more spectacularly useless than Sally would ever have guessed. She had no sense of balance whatsoever. Clinging to the barriers and wailing, 'This is really slippy!' she was edging her way round the outside of the rink at the speed of a lame tortoise.

Happily this meant Sally was free to coach Nick, who might not be any great shakes on the ice but who was fifty times better than Lola. At least he could stand up and – more or less – manage circuits, so long as Sally was there to hold on to his hands. Which was heaven, almost as good as when, upon losing his balance and wobbling crazily in the centre of the rink, he had flung both arms around her waist.

Oh yes, that had definitely been a highlight, a moment to treasure. Maybe later she'd make it happen again and this time allow herself to stumble and fall on top of him in a laughter-filled tangle of arms and legs. When Lola wasn't looking, of course.

Leaning closer and breathing into her ear, Nick protested, 'This can't be much fun for you.'

Was he serious? This was the most fun she'd had in years. 'I'm fine.' Sally experienced a frisson of excitement as his left thigh brushed against hers, then another as the right thigh followed suit.

Was that an accident?

'No, it's not fair.' Nick shook his head. 'Why don't I have five minutes' rest, then you can do some proper skating without having to hold me up. I'll just watch from the side and admire the way you experts do it.'

Oh dear, nobody liked a show-off. But his eyes were glittering and she couldn't resist. Having guided him to the barriers then skated back to the less crowded centre of the rink, Sally struck a pose then pushed off into an impromptu routine. God, skating was so brilliant, it was one of the few things she was really good at. And she was *gliding* across the ice now, as accomplished and elegant as a swan, with the stars twinkling overhead in an inky sky and hundreds of admiring eyes upon her . . . if she went into a fabulous spin or launched into a triple salchow, would everyone gasp with delight and break into a spontaneous round of applause?

OK, a triple salchow was too ambitious, but how about a double axel? Was Nick watching? Would he be suitably impressed by her technique? Yes, there he was, Lola had managed to hobble-skate over to him and they were both hanging on to the barriers, watching her. Right, here goes . . .

'*OW!*' bellowed Sally, crashing to the ice like a felled tree. 'OW, OW, OW, who did *that?*'

Because someone had come up behind her and delivered a vicious kick to the back of her calf. Letting out a shriek of pain she clutched her left leg as melted ice soaked into her jeans. What kind of psychopath would sneak up like that and kick a complete stranger so *hard*? Ow, God, she couldn't breathe, she could barely think straight, it hurt so *much* . . .

'Are you OK?' Nick and Lola slithered up to her, having somehow managed to weave their way through the crowds of skaters. For heaven's sake, did she look OK?

'Did you see who kicked me?' Sally felt perspiration breaking out on her forehead.

'Nobody kicked you.'

'They did! I felt it!'

'There was no one near you.' Lola pulled an apologetic face. 'If it felt like being kicked by a donkey, you've probably snapped an Achilles tendon.'

Damn, she was right. 'Nooo!' Sally sank down in despair and

rested her face against the ice, because this was a nightmare. 'I don't want it to be my Achilles tendon!'

Lola, valiantly attempting to help her into a sitting position, promptly lost her balance and gasped, 'Oof!' as she tumbled back like an upturned beetle on to the ice.

'What's going on?' Puzzled by the commotion on the stairs, Gabe emerged with dripping wet hair and a dark blue towel draped around his hips.

'What does it look like?' Sitting on her bottom, inelegantly hauling herself up one stair at a time, Sally was huffing and puffing and looking fraught.

'Ice skating went well, then.' Gabe looked at Lola and her father, who were following her up the stairs carrying a pair of crutches.

'It's not funny,' Sally wailed. 'We've just spent three hours in casualty. When they told me I'd torn my calf muscle I thought I'd just be limping a bit for a few days. I was actually relieved because I thought it was better than snapping an Achilles tendon, but it's not better at all, it's going to be a complete *nightmare*.' Finally, laboriously, she reached the top step, raised both arms and demanded imperiously, 'Don't just stand there. Help me up.'

Gabe's heart sank. Was his luck ever going to change? 'Sorry, *who's* going to be a complete nightmare?'

Nick, struggling to keep a straight face, said, 'She has to rest the muscle completely, keep the leg elevated at all times. She's going to need some serious looking after.'

Oh God.

Lola said helpfully, 'You'll have to lift her in and out of the bath.'

Fat chance of *that*.

'No you won't,' Sally hurriedly chipped in before he could say anything about cranes. 'I can still manage a shower.'

'So long as you don't fall over.' Lola winked as she held open the door for Sally to go through.

Gabe winced as one of the aluminium crutches clunked against the door frame. 'Look, wouldn't it be easier to go and stay with your mother? Then she could look after you.'

Crash went the other crutch against the skirting board as Sally lurched inside. 'Whoops, these are tricky things to get the hang of.'

Gabe took a deep breath. 'The thing is, I'm going to be out working a lot of the time.'

'But if I went to my mother's house I'd be on my own *all* the time.' Over her shoulder Sally said, 'Because she and Philip are off on holiday tomorrow. So that wouldn't be very good, would it?' There was a crash as she stumbled into the coffee table, sending flying the cups and plates she hadn't cleared away earlier. With a sigh of relief she lowered herself onto the sofa and stretched out across it, propping her leg up on a couple of cushions. 'There, that's better. All comfy now. Ooh, I'd love a cup of tea.'

Chapter 32

Sometimes a name simply didn't register on your personal radar but it turned out that everyone else knew at once who it belonged to. Such was the case with EJ Mack, whom Lola had never heard of. But when his publishers had announced that he'd be available during the third week of January for signing sessions, everyone else at Kingsley's had got as over-excited as if Al Pacino had offered to turn up.

'But how can you know who he is?' Bemused, Lola had studied the publisher's press release. 'He's only a music producer.'

Cheryl, Tim and Darren had exchanged despairing looks. 'He's *huge*,' said Darren. 'He's worked with everyone who's anyone.'

'And he's so brilliant, all his female artists get crushes on him,' Cheryl chimed in with relish. 'He's very discreet but I bet he's slept with loads of them.'

'Fine, we'll let him come here then.' Still unconvinced, Lola said, 'But it'll still be your fault if nobody turns up.'

It was always embarrassing when that happened. Watching the poor authors' faces fall as they sat there behind their teetering piles of books, gradually realising that not one single person was going to come along and buy one. Their smiles faltered;

230

sometimes they pretended they'd never wanted to sell any copies of their book anyway. Other times they feigned illness and escaped early. On one memorable occasion an author had reacted particularly badly, launching into a major temper tantrum and flinging his greatest rival's books all across the shop.

Anyhow, it didn't seem as if this was a problem they were likely to encounter tonight with EJ Mack. Loads of customers had been thrilled to discover he was coming to Kingsley's. As Lola unloaded boxes of his books and arranged them in spiral towers around the signing table, people were already starting to gather in the shop. Too cool to form an orderly queue but not cool enough to turn up at seven thirty, which was when EJ Mack was scheduled to arrive.

And he wasn't even good-looking, according to Cheryl. Turning over one of the hardbacks, Lola scrutinised the arty, grainy black and white portrait that gave away hardly anything at all. The face was averted from the camera and further obscured by the brim of some weird trilby-style hat.

Oh well, he'd be here soon. Hopefully to sign two hundred copies of his book in double-quick time so they could all be home by nine thirty. OK, maybe not home by nine thirty on a Friday night if you were a super-successful uber-cool cutting-edge music producer, but definitely if you were a knackered bookshop manager with a drastically empty stomach and hot achy feet.

'He's here!' squealed Cheryl twenty minutes later.

Lola scanned the crowded shop, absolutely none the wiser. 'Where?'

'That's him, the one in the blue anorak.'

Oh good grief, how could anyone be cutting-edge in a turquoise anorak?

Then her gaze stuttered to a halt and her eyes locked with those of EJ Mack.

'God, man, this is wicked,' gushed Darren, appearing out of nowhere. 'Look at him, he's so brilliant.'

Tim, next to him, breathed enviously, 'And he's slept with some of the most beautiful women on the planet.'

Lola opened her mouth but no sound came out. Flanked by his publisher's balding rep and blonde PR girl, EJ Mack approached them.

'Well, this is a coincidence.' Smiling, he stuck out his hand. 'Who'd have thought we'd be bumping into each other again? How's your partner?'

Lola tried her best to come up with an answer. Tim, keen to bridge a potentially awkward silence, leapt in with, 'Hi, I'm Tim! She doesn't have a partner.'

'God, sorry. You mean you broke up? What's going to happen with the baby?'

Funny how someone could look like a geeky speccy accountant-type one minute and not quite so geeky and accountanty the next, even if he was still wearing spectacles and that bizarre anorak. Although now that she knew who he was, Lola could see that the silver-rimmed rectangular spectacles were probably trendy in an ironic postmodern kind of way.

'It's all going to be fine,' she told EJ Mack.

'*Baby?*' Cheryl stared in disbelief at Lola's stomach. 'What baby?'

EJ Mack gave her a speculative look.

'Right,' Lola said hurriedly. 'Let's get this show on the road, shall we? Can I take your coat? And welcome to Kingsley's! You've got lots of fans queuing up to meet you! And can I just say how much I enjoyed your book . . .'

'That's very kind.' EJ Mack slowly removed his anorak and passed it over to her. 'Which chapter did you like best?'

'Oh, um . . . all of them.'

'So that means you haven't read it.'

'Sorry, no, but I definitely will.' Lola blinked as someone took a photograph. 'Can I get you a drink? Coffee, water, anything else?'

'Did my publisher not send you my list of needs? Bourbon biscuits,' E J Mack said gravely. 'Peeled grapes. And a bottle of Jack Daniels.'

Cheryl was still frowning. '*What baby?*'

The signing session had been a great success. In the music world EJ was a 31-year-old legend and devotees of his work were thrilled to have this chance to meet him. EJ in turn didn't disappoint them, he was charming, witty and interested in talking about music. He had worked with everyone who was anyone and plenty of tonight's book-buyers were keen for him to work with them too. By the time they'd finished, EJ had been saddled with a stack of CDs pressed upon him by starry-eyed wannabes.

'Occupational hazard,' he said good-naturedly.

'I'll get you a carrier bag,' Lola offered.

'I'd rather have a private word, if that's all right. In your office?'

Bum, so he hadn't forgotten. Lola felt herself go pink, glanced awkwardly at her watch. 'Um . . .'

'Just for a couple of minutes.' Turning to the rep and the PR girl, EJ said, 'That's OK, isn't it?'

'Of course it's OK,' the PR girl exclaimed. 'Take as long as you like! Take a couple of hours if you want to!' Because being lovely to her company's authors was her job.

The light glinted off EJ's steel-rimmed spectacles as he smiled briefly at the enthusiastic blonde. 'Don't worry, a couple of minutes will be fine.'

Once inside the office Lola said, 'OK, I'm sorry, I told a fib.'

'More than one, at a guess.' He leaned against the chaotic desk, counting off on his fingers. 'The pregnant woman isn't – never *was* – your partner. Was she even pregnant?'

Shamefaced, Lola said, 'No.'

'And the smell?'

'We boiled an awful lot of cabbage.'

'You really didn't want me moving into that flat, did you?'

'Oh, please don't take it personally. We didn't know who you were. Whoever turned up, we were just going to do everything we could to put them off. Like playing that music . . .' Lola's voice trailed away, because they'd been playing Eminem. Damn, hadn't she overheard a fan earlier, gushing about the album EJ had worked on with Eminem?

'Hmm.' EJ raised an eyebrow. 'The music was fine, it was the dancing that worried me. So who lives there now?'

'Um, Sally. The one who wasn't pregnant. And the guy who was meant to be letting the flat unexpectedly came back from Australia so they're both in there now, driving each other nuts.' Eagerly Lola said, 'So in fact you had a bit of a lucky escape . . .'

'Look, it's not that big a deal.' He shrugged and helped himself to a liquorice allsort from the bag on the desk. 'I live in Hertfordshire and staying in hotels whenever I'm up in town gets tedious. I just thought it'd be easier to have a base here, somewhere to crash when I can't be bothered to drive home. I'm renting a place in Hampstead now.'

Lola was just glad he'd taken it in his stride. 'Well, I'm sorry we messed you about.'

'Don't worry about it.' His gaze slid downwards to where, having eased off one shoe, Lola was surreptitiously flexing her aching toes. 'Been a long day?'

'Just a bit. I can't wait to get home and run a bath.' Relieved to have been forgiven, she confided, 'My feet are killing me and I'm completely shattered.'

'Shame, I was just about to ask if you fancied a drink. Ah well, never mind.'

'Oh!' Lola's eyes widened.

'Doesn't matter. Thanks for this evening anyway, I enjoyed it.' EJ had reached the office door now. 'Shall we go?'

'But . . . but . . .' Wow, that was an invitation she hadn't expected, a bolt from the blue. Following him, Lola said, 'Well, maybe a drink wouldn't be so—'

'No, no, you're too tired.' He turned back, his thin clever face pale beneath the overhead fluorescent strip lighting. 'Forget I asked. You get yourself home and jump into that hot bath.' With a glimmer of a smile he added, 'You do look exhausted.'

Ouch. Or maybe touché. Talk about getting your own back.

Chapter 33

The advance proof copy of EJ Mack's book, given to her months ago by the publisher's sales rep, was lying under her bed unopened and covered in dust. Wiping it clean on the carpet, Lola raced barefoot across the landing to 73C. Oh, for heaven's sake, Gabe was bound to be out and he hadn't thought to leave the door on the latch; how long was she going to have to wait for Sally to hobble across and unlock it?

Impatiently she hammered on the door. 'Sal, quick, just roll off that sofa, crawl over here and let me in this minute because you are not going to *believe* who I met tonight!' Then, as the door began to open, 'And by the way, everyone at work was *agog* when they heard you were my pregnant lesbian lover— ooh!'

Of course it hadn't been Sally answering the door that quickly. Of course it had to be Doug, whom Lola hadn't seen for three weeks, not since New Year's Eve at the Carrick when she'd made such a dazzling impression. *Bloody Mary Ann Cross.*

'So now you're having a lesbian affair with my sister.' Doug shook his head in resignation. 'My God, you really do want to give my mother a heart attack.'

'Sorry. Hi, Doug, I didn't know you were here.' Otherwise I'd have quickly redone my make-up and *definitely* not just made myself that cheese and pickled onion toasted sandwich.

'You know, I wish I was gay,' complained Sally, lying in state across the sofa. 'We're far nicer people. It's got to be easier fancying women than fancying men.'

'Not when they reek of pickled onions,' said Doug.

Ouch.

Then again, speaking of fancying men. Doing her best not to breathe near him, Lola said, 'No Isabel tonight?' and for a split second allowed herself to get her hopes up. ('Isabel, I'm sorry, it's not you I love, it's—')

'Yes, I'm here too!' Emerging from the kitchen with a tray, Isabel said gaily, 'Hi, Lola, look at us, meals on wheels!'

'I ran out of milk.' Sally eased herself into more of a sitting position, wincing with pain as she shifted her leg a couple of inches on its pile of cushions. 'Gabe's been gone for hours and he gets cross with me when I keep phoning him, so I gave Doug a call instead.'

To be fair to Gabe, Lola had heard about last night's debacle when, whilst queuing at the pharmacy for Sally's ibuprofen capsules, he had missed a headline-making punch-up between two A-listers outside Nobu.

'Poor lamb, stuck here all on her own with no milk for a cup of tea,' Isabel trilled. 'Then when we said we'd pop over with a couple of pints she mentioned how hungry she was and asked us to bring her a takeaway.'

The poor starving lamb had the grace to look faintly ashamed at this point, as well she might. Lola said indignantly, 'What happened to the lasagne I brought over this morning? All you had to do was heat it up.'

'It's still in the fridge,' Sally admitted. 'Sorry, I was just in the mood for a Chinese.' Hastily she changed the subject. 'So who did you meet tonight?'

Lola's stomach was still rumbling, baying for attention, despite the toasted sandwich. Oh well, if Sally didn't want the lasagne – the delicious home-made lasagne she'd put together completely from scratch – she'd jolly well eat it herself. 'Remember the geeky speccy guy who wanted this flat? Him!'

'Yeek, you mean he came into the shop and saw you? Was it embarrassing?'

'Just a bit, seeing as he was doing a signing. By the way, he asked after you and the baby.'

Sally patted her stomach. 'We're doing great, thanks.'

Lola, still clutching the book in her hand, said, 'Have you ever heard of EJ Mack?'

'The music bloke? Worked with Madonna last year?' Popping a forkful of chicken Sichuan into her mouth, Sally shrugged. 'Kind of.'

'EJ Mack's a genius,' Isabel exclaimed. 'He's worked with *everyone*.'

'Well, it was him,' said Lola.

Sally almost choked on a mushroom. 'What? EJ Mack's the speccy geek? Oh my God, he's like a mega-millionaire and we didn't even *know* . . .'

'Sounds like you missed your chance there, girls!' As she said it, Isabel slipped her arm around Doug's waist and gave it a proprietary squeeze, signalling, oh you poor creatures, here I am with the perfect man and there's you two with not even a half-decent one to share between you . . . gosh, don't you just wish you were as pretty and lucky as me?

Honestly, who did she think she was? Cinderella? More to

the point, who were the ugly stepsisters? Inwardly nettled – for heaven's sake, she was *still* clinging on to Doug – Lola said airily, 'Who says I missed my chance? EJ and I got on brilliantly. He asked me out.'

Oh yes, that made them sit up and take notice!

'Seriously?' Isabel's eyebrows shot up.

Even Doug looked impressed.

Sally squealed, 'The geek asked you out!'

'Actually, he's not as geeky as we thought.' Lola rushed to EJ's defence. 'He wears those clothes because he doesn't want to draw attention to himself. And behind those glasses his face is really quite interesting . . . and he has these amazing cheekbones . . .'

'So what you're saying is, the more money he has, the better looking he becomes,' Doug drawled with just a hint of eyeroll.

'Last time we saw him he hardly said anything at all.' Reaching over to pinch a handful of Sally's prawn crackers, Lola said defiantly, 'Tonight I found out he has a really nice personality.'

Doug's mouth twitched. 'Of course you did.'

'So you're actually going out with him?' Sally was so excited she dropped her fork. 'On a *date*?'

'Let's hope he doesn't forget to bring along his platinum Amex,' said Doug.

'Could somebody pick my fork up, please?'

'He asked me out tonight,' said Lola. 'But I was worried about Sal being stuck here all on her own, so I turned him down.' There, ha, *now* who was the most selfless, thoughtful and downright saintly person in this room?

'Aah, isn't that nice?' Sally beamed. 'Then again, I bet your feet were killing you in those new shoes you wore to work today. And far nicer to have some notice to get yourself tarted up. So when are you seeing him instead?'

Lola flushed. 'I'm not. He asked me out and I said no thanks. We left it at that.'

'Are you mad? You can't not see him again! He's EJ Mack!'

'Well, it's too late now.' Throwing up her hands, Lola said, 'At least I can say I turned him down.'

Doug's face was deadpan. 'Either that or he never asked her out in the first place.'

'Oh Doug, you are *wicked*.' Isabel gave him a pretend slap. 'You can't call Lola a liar!'

'You'd be surprised what I can call Lola.' He scooped up his car keys from the coffee table and raised a hand in farewell. 'When it comes to scruples and honesty she's in a class of her own. Right, we're off . . .'

'I can't imagine why I'm in love with your brother,' Lola said crossly when Doug and Isabel had left. 'He's a complete arse.'

'You're not doing terribly well, are you?' said Colin Carter of the Carter Agency.

Gabe sighed and shook his head. Was he about to be told he should give up the day job? He hadn't had much luck during the past few weeks.

But Colin was a kindly soul. 'Don't be too downhearted. You're only ever one photo away from the next worldwide scoop. Look, we've had a tip-off that Savannah Hudson's holed up in a cottage in the wilds of Gloucestershire. She's been keeping a low profile lately. Here's the address.' He handed over a scrap of paper and said, 'No one else knows about it, so this could be your big chance. Don't bugger it up.'

'Right, thanks, I won't.' Gabe was torn because he'd been short with Sally this morning – she'd woken him at five o'clock, calling out from her bedroom to ask *him* to turn off *her* beeping, run-down mobile phone – yet he knew she was the only reason Colin was giving him this break. He owed her for that, but at the same time she was doing his head in.

'You do know who Savannah Hudson is,' Colin double-checked, because last night Gabe had mistaken George Galloway for Des Lynam.

'Don't worry. I know who she is.' Gabe nodded vigorously to prove it as he tucked the address into his wallet. 'I won't let you down.'

Chapter 34

London had been cold, grey and a tad breezy. Out in the Cotswolds the weather was rather less subtle; huge clouds raced across a gunmetal sky and there was a howling gale. Driving across Minchinhampton Common, high and brutally exposed, Gabe half expected to see the cows and sheep being swept off their feet and whisked into the air. Even the players on the golf course were struggling to stay vertical.

Which wasn't great news as far as Gabe was concerned because it meant there wasn't a huge incentive for Savannah Hudson to venture outside.

The cottage was perched on the side of a hill, only slightly set back from the narrow lane winding its way down from the common towards the small country town of Nailsworth. There was a nondescript green Peugeot parked in the driveway and a couple of lights on in the cottage, indicating that she was probably in there. Needless to say, there was nowhere to park outside the cottage; the lane was single-track with passing places dotted along its length. No sooner had Gabe pulled into one than a tractor came chugging up the hill as a yellow Fiesta appeared behind him, forcing him on. Which meant he was going to have to leave his warm car further down the hill and spend the afternoon lurking in a wet hedge. It was probably one of the reasons Savannah Hudson had chosen to hide out in this cottage. Honestly, these camera-shy celebrities were so selfish.

Having parked in Nailsworth, Gabe stocked up in the bakery with a selection of pies and cakes to keep him going and stave off the tedium. He put a can of Coke and a bottle of water in the pockets of his Barbour. Back at the car he took out his camera, careful to keep it hidden from view, and slung it around his neck under the waxed jacket. Please God, make today the day he got a decent shot and could prove to Colin he wasn't a complete waste of space.

Two hours later Gabe had cramp in his legs. He was going out of his mind with boredom. It would be getting dark soon, he'd eaten all his food and it was obvious Savannah Hudson wasn't going to emerge from the cottage. The only good thing about the afternoon was that the pies from the bakery had been excellent.

Bugger, he wasn't going to be able to impress Colin after all. Unless he knocked on the door of the cottage, fell to his knees and begged Savannah Hudson to take pity on him. Maybe she would, and he could just take a couple of quick faux-candid shots . . .

What the hell, it was worth a try. He unfolded his long legs, brushed himself down and headed for the cottage. There was definitely someone inside, he could see their outline through the drawn curtains as they moved about in the lit-up living room.

Putting on his most charming face – the one that didn't seem to be getting a lot of use these days – Gabe braced himself and rat-tatted the black wrought-iron knocker.

The door was opened by a middle-aged woman in a purple velour tracksuit, clutching a duster and a can of lemon Pledge.

'Oh, hi,' charming smile, charming smile, 'I'm here to see Savannah.'

'Sorry, duck, she's not here. Friend of hers, are you?'

Gabe knew he should say yes, then he might be invited into the cottage. He sighed inwardly; this was why he was so crap at this job. 'No, not a friend exactly . . .'

'Off you go then, duck.' The woman's expression changed.

'Wait, do you know when she might be back?'

'Maybe tomorrow or the day after. Bye.' The door was closed firmly in his face.

That was that then. If the woman had been lying and Savannah Hudson was inside the house, she wouldn't be coming out now.

Terrific. No photos *and* it was starting to rain. He may as well get back to the car before the heavens opened.

At least it was downhill.

As he set off down the lane, Gabe tried to work out what time he'd be home. His social life had taken a serious nosedive lately, what with work and having to look after Sally-the-whingeing-cripple and getting over the whole bloody soul-destroying business with Jaydena. Maybe a night off was what he needed, a few hours of mindless drinking and clubbing with old friends, chatting up girls, possibly even getting some long-overdue sex . . . Ha, so long as they could go back to her place, because if he brought someone home to Radley Road they were bound to be interrupted in mid-shag by Sally banging on the wall that separated their bedrooms, bleating, 'Gabe, I'm really thirsty and my leg hurts too much for me to get out of bed, could you bring me a glass of water *pleeease*?'

Oh yes, her leg was definitely a pain. The only good thing

244

about it as far as Gabe was concerned was that having Sally physically confined to the sofa all day meant the mess she created was confined to that area. The rest of the flat, practically undisturbed, was really quite tidy and—

Bloody hell.

Having rounded a bend, Gabe saw a figure hurrying up the lane towards him with a bag of shopping in one hand and a dog on a lead in the other. His brain shot into overdrive as he took in the oversized jacket, the skinny legs in skinnier jeans, the blonde head almost hidden beneath the hood of the jacket and the thick grey scarf wound round her neck . . . Bloody hell, it *was* her, Savannah Hudson was heading straight for him, this was his big chance.

Then her head tilted up and she saw him, her actress's antennae on instant alert. As her hood blew back she stopped in her tracks, like a deer hearing the click of the hunter's rifle. Gabe, already reaching for the camera slung around his neck, realised she was about to bolt and called out, 'Please, could I just take one picture of—'

But the wind whipped his words away. Savannah was backing off, dragging the dog with her. The dog, a black and tan Jack Russell, began barking furiously, leaping up on its back legs. Tugging harder to keep it under control, Savannah almost dropped her bag of shopping. Then a ferocious blast of wind knocked her off balance and sent her staggering sideways into the verge. She let out a shriek of alarm as the hedge bordering the lane bent and swayed, grasping at her with branches like mad spiky fingers.

'Look, I'm sorry,' Gabe yelled above the noise of the wind, advancing towards her. 'I just wanted to . . .'

The words faded in his throat and he stopped dead, gazing

in disbelief as the furiously waving branches clawed at her hair and, having yanked it free, waved it like an ecstatic contestant on *Supermarket Sweep*. Savannah Hudson let out a whimper of anguish and dropped the shopping as she attempted to shield her exposed head – click – from Gabe. Letting go of the dog's lead, she used her other hand to grasp helplessly – click click – at the blonde wig caught up on the spiky branches.

Jesus Christ, she was as bald as an egg. This was a major scoop, bigger even than his petrol station exposé of Tom Dutton and Jessica Lee. Appalled, Gabe hastily sidestepped as the dog raced up to him barking furiously.

'Sshh, it's OK, don't do that.' Reaching down, he grabbed the dog's lead before a car could come along and mow it down. Together they made their way over to the verge where Savannah Hudson was still battling to free the wig. It was a hawthorn hedge and the spikes were needle-sharp. Tears swam in her eyes and she ducked her face away at Gabe's approach, flinching as a thorn scratched her wrist.

'Here, let me. I'm sorry, I'm so sorry. I'll do it,' said Gabe. 'You just hold the lead.'

'Please,' her voice broke, 'just leave me alone. Bunty, *shh*.'

Bunty, what a name for the world's yappiest terrier. The yaps were actually making his ears hurt. Ignoring the scratches his hands were amassing, Gabe grimly disentangled strands of hair from the vicious branches and finally managed to liberate the blonde wig, although it did look as if it had just been dragged through a . . . no, no, definitely not the moment to make a joke.

'Thank you.' Tears slid down Savannah Hudson's white face; angrily she dashed them away.

'Sorry,' Gabe said again as she crammed the wig onto her head, covering her naked scalp and pulling up the hood of her jacket for good measure. He retrieved the dropped carrier of shopping from a clump of dead stinging nettles in the ditch and handed that back too.

'Sorry? Really? I doubt that.' Savannah's lip curled with derision. 'I should imagine you're jumping for joy. You've got just what you wanted, haven't you?' She indicated the camera around his neck and said sarcastically, 'I hope you're proud of yourself.'

Gabe reached for the camera; earlier, Pavlovian instinct had taken over and he'd barely been aware of taking the photos. But – he checked – yes, there they were, clear as day on the screen, ready to reveal Savannah Hudson's secret to the world.

She'd now turned and was already hurrying on up the lane with her shopping and her ridiculous yippy-yappy dog.

'*Wait*,' Gabe called out. He caught up within thirty seconds and put a hand on her arm to slow her down.

'Please, just leave me alone.' Snatching her arm away Savannah said evenly, 'And don't touch me either or I'll have you for assault.'

'OK, OK, just stop for a moment and watch me.' Closing his mind to what he was about to do, Gabe waited until he had her attention. His hands trembled as he showed her the photos on the camera screen. 'OK, see the delete button? You press it.'

If he'd expected Savannah Hudson's rosebud mouth to fall open, for her to turn to him in wonder and whisper, 'Seriously? Do you mean it? Are you really sure?' he'd have been disappointed. In a nano-second her index finger had shot out, pressing the button and deleting the images forever.

Dink, dink, gone. Just like that. And if Gabe had been expecting her to fling herself at him in gratitude crying, 'Oh God, my hero, thank you, *thank you*,' well, he'd have been sorely disappointed there too. Instead she turned away, muttering, 'And don't tell anyone either.'

He watched Savannah Hudson trudge up the hill with Bunty still yapping at her side. Then they rounded the bend and disappeared from view. A smattering of icy rain hit Gabe in the face and he shivered at the realisation of what he'd just done.

Damn right he wouldn't be telling anyone. If he did, they'd only call him a prat.

Chapter 35

In retrospect, Lola was able to acknowledge that she'd made a big mistake in confiding to the others at work – OK, *boasting* to the others at work – about having been asked out – OK, *practically* asked out – by EJ Mack. Now, at least half a dozen times a day someone would clutch their chest and exclaim, 'Oh my God, here he is! Lola, EJ's here to beg you to go out with him . . . quick, look, he's crawling on his knees through the shop . . . he's saying, "Pleeeease, Lola, *pleeeeease* will you go out with me?" . . . Oh look, and now he's crying, there are tears dripping all over his lovely blue anorak.'

Which might have been mildly amusing the first couple of times but was altogether less hilarious now.

Anyway, concentrate on the books that needed to be ordered. In the back office, huffing her hair out of her eyes, Lola returned her attention to the computer screen and double-checked a list of ISBNs.

Across the desk, after hastily swallowing the last mouthful of her lunchtime prawn sandwich, Cheryl picked up the ringing phone.

Seconds later, windmilling her free arm in front of Lola, she squealed, 'It's for you! You'll never guess . . . it's *him*!'

'Who?' Lola couldn't help herself; her ever-hopeful heart leapt at the idea that it might be Doug.

'EJ Mack!'

God, weren't they sick to death of playing that game yet? Cross with herself for even thinking it could have been Dougie, Lola said, 'Well, tell him sorry, but I don't want to speak to someone who has the nerve to go out in public wearing a turquoise anorak. Tell him to bugger off and pester Madonna instead.'

Hastily covering the receiver, Cheryl hissed, 'You berk, I'm serious. It really *is* him.'

'She's right,' EJ confirmed when Lola took the phone. 'It really is.'

'Oops. Hello.'

'And I'll have you know, the anorak is Jean Paul Gaultier.'

'OK,' said Lola. 'Sorry. I'm nothing but a fashion heathen.'

'The trouble is, you think I dress like a trainspotter because I can't help myself. Whereas in fact I *choose* to dress like a trainspotter because I am a leading proponent of cutting-edge, postmodern, pseudo-supergeek fashion, as featured by Jean Paul in his last Paris collection.'

Shit. 'Right. Sorry again.'

Gravely, EJ said, 'That's perfectly all right. You can't help being a heathen. How are your feet now?'

'*What's he saying?*' mouthed Cheryl frantically, her eyes like saucers.

'They're . . . much better.' Lola ignored her.

'And you're not feeling too shattered?'

'No, I'm fine, thanks.'

'So if I were to ask you if you'd like to meet me tonight, do you think you might say yes?'

Yeek! Cautiously – because he'd caught her out last time – Lola ventured, 'I might.'

'Shall we do that, then?'

It was like, Are you dancing? Are you asking?

'If *you* want to,' said Lola.

'You don't sound very enthusiastic. Do you really want to see me?'

'Sorry, I'm playing it cool. Deep down I'd really like to see you.'

'Progress at last. Do you play snooker?'

'Er . . . crikey, not very well.'

'Great, more chance of me winning. Can I ask you something else?'

'Fire away.'

'If I looked like me and dressed like me but my job was collecting trolleys in a supermarket, would you still be agreeing to see me?'

Lola thought about it. Finally she said, 'No, I wouldn't.'

He laughed. 'Good for you. A bit of old-fashioned honesty does it for me every time. When shall I pick you up?'

'Um, eightish?' How long did it take to play a game of snooker? 'I live at—'

'Don't worry,' EJ cut in, sounding amused. 'I know where you live.'

When Lola had put the phone down, Cheryl let out a parrot-like shriek of excitement. 'He actually rang! You're going out on a date with EJ Mack! What was it he asked you when you said no you wouldn't?'

'Oh, nothing much.' Lola shrugged and studied the computer

screen. 'He just wanted to know if I'd sleep with him while he was wearing his geeky anorak.'

'My leg looks as if it's gone fifty rounds with Mike Tyson,' Sally complained. 'The sight of it's starting to make me feel sick.'

She had a point. In the ten days that had passed since the accident, her leg from the knee down had morphed into something grotesquely discoloured – it was *literally* black and blue – and so swollen it looked ready to burst. Lola, feeling faintly queasy herself, finished gingerly unstrapping the bright blue gel pack from Sally's overheated calf and said as the doorbell rang, 'It's defrosted, I'll get the other one out of the freezer. Who's that?'

'Oh,' Sally looked at her watch, 'is it seven already? Mum and Philip said they'd pop over. Could you buzz them in?'

Adele, super-svelte in a pale grey wool suit and a cloud of Arpège, acknowledged Lola with the kind of distant smile one might bestow on a friend's uninteresting five-year-old grandchild. Crossing to the sofa, she gave Sally a kiss and said, 'Darling, how horrendous! Did you get our card?'

'Hello there, Lola.' Philip, far more friendly, nodded at the defrosted gel pack in her hand. 'Got you working overtime, has she?'

Lola grinned. 'Don't worry, she'll get a shock when she sees the bill.' Oops, possibly not the most diplomatic thing to say, given the circumstances.

'Hmm.' Her tone dry, Adele addressed her daughter. 'Well, just don't let her haggle the price up. Anyway, darling, now that we're back we can have you at home with us.'

'Thanks, Mum, but I'm fine here. Everyone's been great, Lola and Gabe are looking after me really well. And Doug and Isabel have been helping out too.'

Adele beamed and said serenely, 'Oh, isn't Isabel an absolute angel? I'm so glad Doug's found someone wonderful at last! We couldn't be happier for him, could we, Philip?'

For a split second Philip and Lola exchanged glances. Lola struggled to keep a straight face because Adele was definitely doing it on purpose. Philip cleared his throat. 'Whatever makes Doug happy, dear. That's good enough for me.'

'And she's from *such* a good family,' Adele exclaimed. 'Her father's a cardiac surgeon, you know.'

Wouldn't it be nice, thought Lola, if he could whip out the old, mean, unforgiving heart in Adele's chest and replace it with a lovely warm new one.

But no matter how much she knew Doug's mother wasn't going to change her mind about her, a small, ever-hopeful part of Lola couldn't bear to give up trying. Returning from the kitchen with the frozen gel pack for Sally's leg, she said, 'I like your necklace, Mrs Nicholson. It's beautiful.'

'Why thank you.' Delighted with the compliment, Adele reached up and stroked the silver and onyx necklace. 'It was a present from Isabel. She has the most exquisite taste.'

The Groucho Club, that was where they'd be playing snooker. Lola had now read EJ's book – not an autobiography as such, but the story of his experiences in the music industry – and there had been a couple of mentions of playing snooker at the Groucho, where he was a member, so she was pretty sure this was where he'd be taking her. Which was unimaginably exciting because everyone knew the Groucho was stuffed with celebs. Imagine being able to boast to everyone at work that you'd spent last night potting pinks with Damien Hirst and Will Self and . . . ooh, Madonna and Guy, Stephen Fry, the boys from

Blur . . . and she'd be witty and wonderful and make them all love her, then— ooh, doorbell.

The car was, frankly, a bit of a disappointment.

'Is this yours?' Lola hesitated as EJ opened the passenger door for her.

'Yes, that's why we're driving off in it. Otherwise it would be called stealing.'

Oh well, maybe the car only looked like a grubby cherry-red Fiesta. Maybe it was actually a gleaming scarlet Ferrari Marinello in disguise.

'Where are we going?' Please say the Groucho, please say the Groucho, *please* don't say some grotty dive in the back-streets of Bermondsey.

EJ's mouth was twitching; had he read her mind? 'Wait and see.'

'Well?' said EJ forty minutes later. 'What d'you think?'

'I think blimey.' The house was lit up from the outside like Buckingham Palace. In fact it looked a bit like Buckingham Palace. They were in Hertfordshire, out in the depths of the countryside but only a few miles from Hemel Hempstead.

'I think blimey too,' EJ said cheerfully. 'Every time I see it. I grew up in a council flat in Chingford. Now I live here. Pretty cool, eh?'

So this was what he spent his money on. 'Better not let the Beckhams see this place,' said Lola. 'They'll be jealous.'

'Come on, we've got a snooker match to play.'

Security lights zapped on as they crunched across the gravel. In the distance a couple of dogs began to bark. The front door, black and solid, looked as if it would keep out an army of marauders.

'Did your anorak really come from Jean Paul Gaultier?' Lola eyed its nylon sheen.

EJ grinned. 'Nah, Millets.'

As evenings went, it was an experience. The house was vast and Lola got the full guided tour. EJ beat her at snooker on the purple baize-covered table and she managed to shoot the yellow ball clear across the room, narrowly missing a mullioned window. There were nine bedrooms, each one with an en-suite. He showed her his offices and recording studio, and the gold and platinum discs lining the bottle-green walls. There was also a home cinema complete with plush plum-velvet seats, a fully equipped gym, a stadium-sized living room and a kitchen bigger than Belgium.

'Are you hungry?' said EJ, reaching for his phone. 'I can give Myra a call and she'll make us something.'

Myra was the cook/housekeeper who lived with her husband Ted the handyman/gardener in a cottage in the grounds.

'I'm starving. No, don't drag her over here.' Having nosily inspected the fridge, so packed with food it resembled a Tesco Metro, Lola stopped him dialling the number. 'I'll do us both a frittata.'

At one o'clock in the morning EJ drove Lola back to Notting Hill and said, 'Thanks, I really enjoyed this evening.'

'Me too.' In the dim orange light from the street lamps overhead, Lola could see the lines and shaded angles of his thin, clever face. He still wasn't conventionally good-looking but it was definitely the kind of face that the longer you studied it, the better it got.

'Want to do it again?'

'Maybe.' She paused. 'If you do.'

His cheekbones grew more pronounced. 'Hedging your bets.'

'I didn't know if it was a trick question. What if I said ooh, yes please, and you said oh well then, good luck with finding someone to do it with.'

'Hey.' Taking her hand, EJ said, 'I like you. And I'd like to see you again. I'm off to New York tomorrow, but can I give you a ring next week when I get back?'

'Fine.' Lola liked him too; he had a dry sense of humour and was good company. Plus he'd eaten all his frittata despite her having accidentally tipped in far too much chilli powder, causing it to be mouth-explodingly hot.

'At this point, as a general rule, I'd give you a goodnight kiss.' EJ paused. 'But we're being watched.'

Gosh, he was observant. Peering up, Lola saw he was right; the lights were off but there was a face pressed avidly to the window.

'It's my pregnant lesbian lover.' Evidently Sally's bad leg wouldn't allow her to get up to make a cup of tea, but hobbling over to the window to spy on other people's nocturnal goings-on was another matter.

'Being nosy.' Waving up at Sally, EJ said, 'On the bright side, at least with her gammy leg she can't dance.'

Sally waved back. Seconds later, Lola's phone began to ring.

'Is he nice?' Sally demanded. 'Have you had a good time? Where did he take you? You can bring him up for a coffee if you like. Are you going to have sex with him? And why's he driving such a godawful car?'

'I'm *very* nice.' EJ, who'd grabbed the phone, said, 'And yes, we had a great time thanks. We played snooker at my place. I won. And my car isn't awful, it's reliable and doesn't get vandalised in town like the Lamborghini.'

'Sorry,' giggled Sally. 'Are you coming up for coffee?'

'Can't, I'm afraid. Early flight to catch.'

'How about sex?'

'Thanks, generous of you to offer, but aren't you supposed to be giving that leg of yours a rest?'

'OK, stop that.' Lola seized control of the phone.

'I like him,' Sally said delightedly. 'You should definitely sleep with him.'

'He can still hear you,' said Lola. 'I'm going to hang up now.' Before Sally could ask if she had any idea how big EJ's willy was.

'Tell her to move away from the window,' EJ added.

Into the phone Lola duly repeated, 'Move away from the window.'

'Why?'

'Because I want to kiss Lola and I can't do it if you're watching. I'm very shy.'

Chapter 36

Coming to Malcolm's house to celebrate his birthday hadn't been Lola's idea of a fun-packed way to spend a Saturday afternoon but it was part of the deal. Blythe had finally, reluctantly agreed to meet Nick again – and this time be civil to him – on condition that Lola first returned the compliment and met Malcolm's family and friends.

'But why?' Lola protested. 'What's the point of me being there?' Apart from anything else, they were bound to be a load of beardy, lentil-eating, Scrabble-playing old fogeys.

'Because everyone's heard all about you,' Blythe said patiently, 'and they'd love the chance to meet you properly. Come on, it'll be fun.'

Hmm, that was debatable. In truth it was all a bit too meet-the-in-laws for Lola's liking. She didn't want her mother's relationship with Malcolm to be progressing in this direction. Why would Blythe even want to carry on seeing Malcolm now that Lola had found her such an infinitely more desirable alternative? How could she possibly prefer bumbling teddy-bear Malcolm to someone as sleek and stylish as Nick?

But a deal was a deal and maybe Blythe just needed a bit

more time to venture out of her comfort zone, to get used to the idea that Nick James was back in her life. Lola vowed to be utterly charming to Malcolm's family and friends no matter how bearded and dull they might be, and then her mother would be forced to do the same when she came over to Radley Road next week to meet up again with Nick.

Oh God, please don't let anyone this afternoon suggest a nice game of Monopoly.

After two hours of being relentlessly charming, Lola was beginning to flag. She'd talked – well, bellowed – about books to Malcolm's ancient deaf neighbour from across the road. Then she'd chatted some more about books to one of his other neighbours, who was very keen on gardening. The drawback of her job was that when strangers were making polite conversation they invariably started talking about their favourite books and authors. She now knew that the ancient deaf lady was a fan of Daphne du Maurier, that the gardening fan liked books about . . . um, gardening, and that Malcolm's ruddy-faced friend Miles was immensely proud of the fact that he was capable of quoting great swathes of P. G. Wodehouse he'd learned by heart. Even when nobody was remotely interested in hearing him do it.

It almost came as a relief when Miles's boisterous son – 'Can you ask J.K. Rowling to put me in her next book?' – accidentally knocked a slice of pepperoni pizza down the front of Lola's cream shirt. Resisting the urge to reply, 'You mean squashed between the pages like a beetle?' she excused herself and escaped to sponge off the stain.

In the kitchen she found Annie, Malcolm's plump daughter-in-law, busy taking trays of quiche and stuffed peppers out of the oven.

Annie chatted away as Lola sponged the front of her shirt.

'It's so lovely to meet you at last. Malcolm's told us so much about you.' Her bosom jiggling as she carved up the quiches, she added jovially, 'That's when he isn't telling us about your mum!'

'Poor you.' Lola pulled a sympathetic face.

'Oh we love it, it's so sweet! They get on so well together, don't they? Just like a couple of teenagers!'

OK, they definitely weren't like a couple of teenagers.

'Mm.' Lola kept her voice neutral. Talk about getting carried away.

'It's wonderful for both of them. Malcolm's such a lovely person,' Annie prattled on. 'And of course your mum is too! And now it's just so perfect that they've found each other. I'm a sucker for a good old romance, aren't you?'

Lola said cheerfully, 'Old being the operative word!' Yuk, please let Annie be wrong.

'Oh dear, that mark isn't coming out.' Annie eyed the orange pizza stain Lola had been scrubbing at on the front of her shirt. 'And now you're all wet!'

'Don't worry, I'm fine. And definitely don't offer to lend me one of Malcolm's jumpers to wear instead.' Flippantly Lola added, 'Or one of his lumberjack shirts!'

'Oh but—'

'Honestly, I'd rather stay wet. I'm sure Malcolm's lovely, but the geography teacher look isn't quite me.' Lola pulled a complicit face because Annie was herself wearing a stunning navy silk dress and jewelled Karen Millen shoes, so would understand.

Annie paused and gave her an odd sideways look. 'Malcolm's just Malcolm. Clothes aren't his number one priority.' Tipping

260

frozen rosti onto a baking tray she went on, 'Why, does that bother you?'

Damn, she didn't understand. Hastily, Lola said, 'No, it was just a joke.'

'He might not dress like Prince Charles,' Annie said stiffly, 'but he's still a nice person.'

Oh God, now she'd offended Annie. 'Look, I'm sorry, I didn't mean to—'

'And it's not as if your mum's a great style queen anyway.'

Now it was Lola's turn to be offended. She might be allowed to criticise Blythe's dress sense but no one else was.

'See?' Evidently reading her mind, Annie raised an eyebrow. 'Not very nice, is it?'

'I just want my mum to be happy.' Lola dabbed furiously at her wet shirt with a fresh wodge of kitchen roll.

'And you don't think Malcolm's up to the job? You don't think he's good enough for her, is that it?'

Honestly, all this kerfuffle because she'd said Malcolm dressed like a geography teacher.

'Not at all,' Lola ventured carefully. 'I just wonder if they're as compatible as you think they are. They might enjoy each other's company, but how much do they really have in common?'

'They don't have to have anything in common! People are different! You love books,' Annie retorted. 'I think books are boring! But that's just me and it doesn't matter. My husband's a motorbike fanatic and I love slushy movies. I like listening to Barry Manilow, he's crazy about Meatloaf. But we're still happily married. It doesn't mean we don't love each other.'

'You might go off him if he made you play endless games

261

of Monopoly.' Lola couldn't help herself; the words popped out.

But Annie didn't take offence. Instead she handed Lola a tray of hot mini-samosas and said drily, 'OK, you may have a point with the Monopoly. Could you be an angel and take these through?'

At least at a film premiere you could safely assume that anyone turning up wouldn't object to being snapped. Gabe, who had high hopes for this evening, marvelled at the fact that the air temperature was minus several degrees and he was freezing his nuts off in his leather jacket, yet the endless parade of starlets doing their beam-and-pose bit on the red carpet were wearing dresses the size of your average J-cloth.

Maybe the layers of fake tan kept them warm.

'Tania, over here!' bellowed a gaggle of paparazzi as a slinky brunette in a shimmering purple scrap of nothing emerged from the next limo in the queue. Gabe wasn't entirely sure who she was – one of the *Coronation Street* girls possibly – but he clicked and snapped along with the rest of them and wondered briefly what it must be like to wear six-inch strappy stilettos. Oh well, with a bit of luck he'd never find out. Poor old Tania was developing a fine pair of bunions; soon all she'd be able to fit those feet of hers into would be flip-flops.

'Matt, Matt, give us a smile,' yelled the paps as the next celebrity sauntered up the carpet. OK, Gabe was pretty sure he knew this one, he was a Channel 4 TV presenter . . . or maybe a member of that boy band with the reputation for unzipping their trousers and flashing their—

Eurgh, right second time. What these boys didn't seem to realise was that where the sight of their backsides was concerned, familiarity bred contempt. Once you'd seen one spotty adolescent bottom, you'd seen them all.

'What a tosser,' murmured the photographer next to Gabe. 'Their last single only just scraped into the top forty. They're getting desperate now, terrified their record company's about to dump them. By this time next month they could be back working in Burger King.'

'Me too.' Gabe spoke with feeling. Let's face it, he hadn't exactly set the paparazzi world alight since his fluke photo back in Sydney. As the next limo drew up he polished the lens of his Leica Digilux, ready for whoever might be about to—

'Hey, Savannah, this way!' The paparazzi lurched into a frenzy of action, galvanised by the unexpectedness of her appearance. With a jolt, Gabe saw her emerge from the car behind a huge security guy in a too-tight dark suit with the look of a debt collector about him.

This was the public face of Savannah Hudson. Tonight she was in full-on film-star mode. Her blond hair was carefully styled, her make-up perfect. Around her narrow shoulders she wore a silvery velvet wrap; the rest of her body was draped in bias-cut white satin. She looked like an infinitely fragile, stunningly beautiful goddess. Not a plastic carrier bag, not a pair of Wellington boots in sight.

No bald heads either, unless you counted the shaven one belonging to the security gorilla.

Savannah posed for the photographers, showcased her outfit and dutifully smiled while turning this way and that. Having taken a few pictures, Gabe stopped and put his camera down in order to watch her. Maybe it was his stillness amongst the frenzied screaming horde that attracted her attention but moments later she spotted him. Their eyes met for a second. Gabe nodded, acknowledging her with a brief smile, but there was no flicker of acknowledgement in return. Savannah's gaze slid past him, the smooth professional smile moved on to dazzle the next gaggle of photographers and after a few more poses she was off up the red carpet to cheers of delight from the assembled fans.

Well, what had he expected? For her to wave and yell out, 'Hey, everyone, there's the guy over there who papped me when my wig came off!'

Gabe got on with the business of snapping the next wave of celebs, standing his ground as the other paparazzi pushed and shoved around him. Several minutes later, just as he'd bagged a telling shot of a husband and wife giving each other the kind of look that hinted their marriage might be on the rocks, he felt a hand grasp his shoulder.

It was a firm hand and – bloody hell – an enormous one. Looking round, Gabe saw that it belonged to the security guy in the too-tight suit.

'What's wrong?' Gabe took in the grim expression on the man's face, the interest of the photographers around him. Shit, was he about to be beaten to a pulp on the pavement?

'You've been pestering Miss Hudson.' The words were accompanied by a menacingly jabbed finger. 'My advice to you, *sonny*, is to leave her alone. Got that?'

For a split second Gabe thought he was being targeted by a pickpocket. Then he realised his wallet wasn't being stolen, something was being pushed *into* his jacket pocket.

He murmured, 'Got it,' and – out of sight of the other paps – felt the huge man give his pocket a meaningful pat.

'Glad to hear it.'

'Bloody hell,' said one of the paps when the incredible hulk had stalked off. 'I thought he was going to hammer you into the ground.'

'Me too.' With a grimace Gabe raked his fingers through his hair. 'Close call. In fact I'm going to get myself a drink to celebrate still having a neck.'

Chapter 37

Around the corner, away from the crowds and the noise, Gabe pulled a folded cinema flyer from his pocket. In the semi-darkness he had to turn it over twice before spotting the mobile number scribbled diagonally across one corner.

Mystified, he called the number. It was answered by the incredible hulk.

This was getting more Dan Brown by the minute.

'It's me.' Feeling stupid, Gabe said. 'The photographer.'

'That's a polite way of putting it.' The hulk sounded amused. 'You could call yourself paparazzi scum.'

'If there weren't any of us,' Gabe retorted, 'you'd be out of a job. Why am I ringing you anyway?'

'The boss wants to see you.'

'Who?' Why ever would his boss be asking to see him?

Evidently sensing his confusion, the hulk explained in a caring, gentle fashion, 'Savannah, you dozy pillock. Wait on the corner of Irving Street and Charing Cross Road. We'll be there in ten minutes.'

This was downright weird. Looking around to see if he was having an elaborate prank played on him – was Get Back at the Paps some new reality TV show? – Gabe zipped the Leica inside his jacket and headed away from the crowds. Lost in thought, he made for Irving Street. Was he out of his mind, even going there? If the hulk turned up with a couple of ready-for-trouble friends he could end up getting more than his camera broken.

Thirteen minutes later a limo with the obligatory blacked-out windows slowed to a halt beside Gabe. The door slid open and the hulk said, 'Get in.'

'You must be joking,' Gabe retorted. 'Do I look stupid?'

The hulk grinned, flashing a gold incisor. 'Now you come to mention it . . .'

'Oh, *stop* that,' exclaimed a despairing female voice and Gabe's mouth fell open as Savannah Hudson's face came into view. Beckoning to Gabe she said, 'Ignore him. Just please get into the car.'

It was something of a novelty, checking there were no paps lurking around the entrance to the Soho Hotel before diving out of the limo, through reception and into the lift.

The hulk waited downstairs in the bar. Up in her suite Savannah disappeared into the bedroom to change out of the liquid silk gown and into one of the hotel's oversized towelling robes. When she returned Gabe sat in a chair over by the window and she perched cross-legged on the vast bed.

'I wanted to say thanks properly,' she ventured at last, 'for doing what you did.'

'That's OK.' Gabe was nursing a bottle of tonic from the minibar.

'And for not doing what you could have done.' As she spoke, Savannah's hand fiddled nervously with a tendril of styled blond hair. 'I should have thanked you when you deleted those pictures. I was just in such a panic at the time, you have no idea. Then when you'd gone I was convinced you'd only pretended to delete them. But it's been over a week now. If you'd still had them they'd have been everywhere by now.'

'I deleted them. Actually,' Gabe pointed out, because it had been her index finger on the button, '*you* did.'

Savannah shrugged. 'You didn't tell anyone, either. My manager's been bracing himself for a barrage of phone calls about my health and there haven't been any. Not one.'

'When I make a promise I keep it.'

'I didn't trust you. I'm really sorry.'

'That's all right. To be honest, I don't think I'm cut out for this paparazzi business. Can I ask you two questions?'

Savannah took a deep breath then exhaled like a diver. 'Go on then, fire away.'

'Aren't you supposed to be sitting in that cinema watching the film?'

For a moment Savannah looked nonplussed. Then the corners of her mouth began to twitch. 'You're new, right? We might turn up at a premiere but it doesn't mean we watch the film. Most of us walk up the red carpet, disappear into the cinema and then head straight out again through the back door.'

'Oh.'

'That's so sweet. If it's any consolation,' said Savannah, 'I love it that you didn't know that.'

'There's lots of things I don't know about this stupid job. Can I ask my other question now?'

She nodded, took a sip of water.

'Do you have cancer?' said Gabe.

Flushing, Savannah shook her head. 'No I don't. And thank

goodness I don't, I'm *truly grateful* I don't. But if I was bald because I had cancer at least people would feel sorry for me.' She put the bottle of water down on the bedside table and said, 'But I don't, I have alopecia, which is something actresses like me aren't supposed to get because it's not glamorous and it's not attractive, and p–people would make f–fun of me . . . oh God, and my career would be over . . .' As she spoke, the tears spilled out and rolled down her cheeks. Shaking her head, she buried her face in her hands and began to sob, great heaving sobs that shook her tiny, towelling-clad frame.

'Oh don't do that.' Appalled, Gabe jumped to his feet.

The next thing he knew, she was in his arms, as fragile as a baby bird, weeping helplessly and soaking the front of his grey sweatshirt. A spider appeared and Gabe brushed it away in horror then realised when it landed on the white carpet that it was a clump of false eyelashes.

'You're so k–kind,' Savannah hiccupped, her eyes now bizarrely lopsided.

'Here, let me just do something . . .' Gently Gabe peeled the strip of lashes from the other eye. With a handful of tissues he wiped away the dregs of the professionally applied make-up. It was surreal, doing something as intimate as this to a face he'd seen so many times on cinema screens. Everyone in the country knew Savannah Hudson from her TV and film roles. She was beautiful, talented, fragile. And he was sitting with her on a king-sized bed, consoling her as she wept. To lighten the mood he said, 'I was just thinking I can't believe this is happening. But I bet you *never* thought you'd be here doing this with someone like me.'

She managed a watery smile. 'Not in a million years.'

'Everyone hates us,' said Gabe. 'We're right up there with

traffic wardens, tax inspectors and those people who club baby seals to death.'

'And bitchy journalists,' Savannah added, 'who always manage to find something horrible to say about you, like how knobbly your knees are, or how unflattering your trousers. One of them wrote a piece last year about my eyebrows looking ragged. The headline was "Savannah Needs a Damn Good Plucking".' She paused and tapped her wig. 'Can you imagine the field day they'd have if they knew about *this*?'

'But it's not your fault.'

'They don't care about that.' Two more tears popped out. 'All they want is a good laugh and to sell a few more copies of their rotten magazine.'

'Listen to me,' Gabe said firmly, 'you're beautiful.'

Savannah shook her head. 'Not without hair I'm not. My agent told me I looked like a wing nut.'

'That's not true. I *saw* you,' Gabe insisted. 'And you didn't.'

'You must have caught me at a flattering angle. Trust me, I do.'

'You *don't*.'

In response, Savannah reached up and peeled off her wig. She sat before him on her knees and gazed steadily at him.

How had he not noticed before? Minus the hair, her ears stuck out. She looked exactly like a wing nut. A weary, fearful, deeply ashamed wing nut.

'See?' whispered Savannah.

Gabe did the only thing he could possibly do. Reaching forwards, he cupped her damp, tear-stained face between his hands, drew her towards him and kissed her on the mouth.

He'd meant it to be a brief, reassuring kiss but Savannah clung on, wrapping her arms around his neck. Time stood still for Gabe; bloody hell, this was Savannah Hudson he was kissing and now she was the one making sure it carried on. All he'd wanted to do was stop her crying. Then again, he wasn't going to be the one to pull away . . .

Finally Savannah did, but only by a couple of inches. Touching his cheek she whispered, 'Do you really like me?'

'You're beautiful. Why wouldn't anyone like you?' Gabe stroked her head, as warm and smooth as a new-laid egg.

'No wedding ring.' She reached for his left hand, double-checked it was unencumbered. 'Girlfriend?'

'No girlfriend.'

'You're very good-looking.'

Gabe smiled. 'Should have seen me before the plastic surgery.'

'Oh no, you definitely haven't had that. When it comes to men having plastic surgery, trust me, I'm an expert. Are you really single?'

He nodded. 'Since just before Christmas.'

'I haven't been with anyone for over a year.' Savannah's smile was wry. 'Isn't that pathetic? My manager says it's no wonder my hair's dropped out. But it's so hard to trust people, you never know what they're going to do or say. And now with all this business going on . . .' she indicated her head, 'it's even worse. It just seems like everyone lets you down, they can't help themselves. Every last one of my exes has done a kiss and tell. In the end you just think it's easier not to bother.'

'Right.' Gabe realised he was still stroking her face. 'Complicated.'

'It *is* complicated. Nothing's ever straightforward. You have no idea.'

'My God, I'm glad I'm not a stunning, Oscar-nominated actress.'

Savannah broke into a smile. 'I'm glad you're not too.' Then she kissed him again. Longingly.

And this time it didn't stop.

'Hey, Gabe, any joy?'

Gabe stopped dead as he emerged from the hotel at nine o'clock the next morning. Lenny, one of the other paparazzi, was leaning against a wall smoking a roll-up and keeping his camera out of sight.

'What?' Aware of the eyes of the bellboy on him, Gabe prayed he wasn't giving himself away.

'Any sign of Savannah Hudson? She's meant to be staying here.' When Gabe hesitated, Lenny said, 'Isn't that who you were looking for?'

'Oh right, I didn't know.' His pulse racing, Gabe gestured vaguely behind him. 'I just called in to use the loo.'

Lenny rolled his eyes and grinned. Gradually Gabe's heart slowed down. The bellboy, less amused, murmured, 'Well, don't do it again.'

Back at Radley Road by nine thirty, Gabe found Sally already ensconced on the sofa with an open packet of biscuits, a pile of magazines and *Friends* on the TV. It was the one where Rachel discovers Ross's list of criticisms about her. Rachel, beside herself, was stamping her foot and yelling, 'You think I'm SPOILT?'

'Morning, cheap tart.' Sally greeted Gabe jauntily through a mouthful of chocolate caramel digestive. 'What time do you call this to crawl home?'

'I call it time to Sellotape your mouth shut. Don't do that,' said Gabe as she flicked biscuit crumbs off her skirt and onto the rug.

'I'm a poor helpless invalid who can't even carry a cup of tea. What else am I supposed to do with crumbs? If I leave them on me I'll just end up sitting on them. And I can't exactly get the Hoover out. Anyway, don't change the subject.' Sally tapped her watch. 'I still want to know where you've been.'

'What are you, my probation officer?'

'I'm interested!'

Avid, more like. 'I'll make you a cup of tea,' said Gabe.

In the kitchen he rubbed his face and exhaled slowly. Of course he wanted to tell Sally that he'd spent the night with Savannah Hudson but he wasn't going to. Nor Lola; neither of them would be finding out about it from him. When Savannah had anxiously asked him if he'd told *anyone* about their traumatic encounter last week, he'd been able to answer truthfully that no, he hadn't.

Back in the living room Gabe handed Sally her mug of tea, put the biscuits on a plate and tidied up the slew of books and magazines on the floor.

'Don't put them where I can't reach them.' Sally's tone was querulous.

On the TV, Rachel snapped, 'I do *not* have chubby *ankles*.'

The penny finally dropped. Ha, that's who she reminded him of.

'You still haven't told me.' Sally adjusted the cushions supporting her leg.

'Lenny and I were working late, staking out the Soho Hotel.' Gabe shrugged, yawned widely. 'Waste of time, didn't get anything. And it was freezing too. In the end we went back to Lenny's place to thaw out. I crashed out in a chair, woke up at eight o'clock this morning.'

'Do you know, I almost feel sorry for you.' Sally gave him

273

a pitying look. 'You could be in the running for Most Useless Pap on the Planet.'

'Thank you,' said Gabe. 'And to think I was about to make you a bacon sandwich.'

'The bacon in the fridge? Oh no, you can't cook that.'

Gabe was both tired and hungry. 'But that's why I bought it.'

'I know, but I promised it to Lola for her dinner party tonight.' Sally said generously, 'You can have Weetabix instead.'

Chapter 38

Lola had fulfilled her part of the bargain. Now it was her mother's turn. Tonight she was hosting a proper grown-up dinner party in her flat and Blythe and Nick – her actual *parents!* – were jolly well going to be nice to each other.

In fact if all went well, there would be some serious rekindling going on. Even if Blythe had got the wrong end of the stick and exclaimed, 'Ooh, lovely. Can I invite Malcolm along too?' Tactfully Lola had been forced to say, 'Actually, Mum, he might feel a bit awkward. Would you mind if he wasn't here?'

God, though, cooking proper grown-up food was hard work. She'd been slaving away for ages and there was still heaps to do, never mind getting herself ready and—

Crash went the kitchen door as Sally bashed it open with one of her crutches and came clunking through. 'Crikey, done enough stuff? I thought there was only five of us.'

'There is. I hate it when I ask for seconds and there aren't any, so when I'm cooking for other people I always make . . . well, quite a lot.'

'Enough for twenty-five, I'd say.' Hobble-clunking her way over to the plate of chilli-infused king prawns, Sally said, 'I'd better just check these are all right. *Mmm.*' She leaned against the worktop. 'So, how do I look?'

'Like someone who hasn't had anything else to do today except get herself dolled up.' Pausing with a saucepan of mangetouts in one hand and a tray of roast potatoes in the other, Lola said, 'You look great. I can't believe you're wearing that dress. What if you spill something on it?'

'It'll dry-clean.' Sally patted her favourite pale yellow dress. She had fastened her hair up with silver, crystal-studded combs and her make-up was flawless.

Lola was touched that she'd gone to so much trouble. 'And you're not even going to have anyone to flirt with. I should have invited someone nice along for you. Here, at least help yourself to a drink – oh Lord, that can't be one of them already.'

Sally, already helping herself to wine from the fridge, said cheerfully, 'You never know, maybe it's someone gorgeous for me to flirt with.'

She was half right. It was Doug.

Lola's heart did its usual floppity skip-and-a-jump; he looked even more irresistible when he hadn't shaved. What she wouldn't give for a bit of stubble-rash.

'I called in on Ma earlier and she asked me to drop this off with you.' He dumped a light blue, leather-trimmed holdall on the table in front of Sally. 'Apparently you asked her for them. What is it, more clothes?'

'Better than that.' Sally clapped her hands and unzipped the holdall. 'Old photos!'

Lola, busy chopping courgettes, was entranced by the look on Doug's face. 'Only you could pick up a bag, wonder what's in it and not even think to take a sneaky look inside.' Thinking that this was why she loved him so much – OK, it was one of

276

the many reasons along with the stubble – she went on, 'If I ever need something smuggled through customs, I'll know who to ask.'

Dougie shot her a look that suggested he didn't love her in return, before turning back to Sally. 'Why did you want them?'

'Lola's mum's bringing loads of photos over tonight to show Lola's dad. I thought it'd be nice to have some of mine here too, so I could join in. Don't worry, I won't pass round any embarrassing ones of you. Well, apart from that one of you naked in a paddling pool with a plastic bucket on your head.'

'I won't let her,' Lola hastily assured him, before Doug could seize the holdall and race off into the night. On an impulse she said, 'You could stay if you want.'

'What?'

'For dinner.' Adrenaline sloshed through Lola's body. 'I've made mountains of food. You can see my mum again, and meet my dad . . . the more the merrier, honestly. It'd be great if you were here too.' Then I can sit next to you and accidentally brush my thigh against yours, we can play footsie under the table, I'll feed you spoonfuls of chocolate pudding and you'll realise how perfect we are together—

'Thanks,' Dougie cut into her happy fantasy, 'but I can't.'

Oh. Unable to hide her disappointment, Lola blurted out, 'But I've made chocolate pudding with real custard!'

He smiled, just slightly, and shook his head. 'Sorry. I'm seeing Isabel tonight.'

Bring her up here, thought Lola, we can drown her in home-made custard. God knows, we've got enough of the stuff.

'Shall I get that for you?' Seeing that Lola's hands were wet, Sally picked up the ringing phone. 'Hi . . . no, this is Sally . . . oh hello, you! Yes thanks, the baby's fine!' Beaming, she said,

'Where are you, still in New York? Oh, right. No, she's busy cooking, we're having a dinner party this evening . . . hey, why don't you come over? Don't be daft, of course you can – Lola's just invited my brother but he's busy.' Covering the receiver Sally whispered, 'That's all right, isn't it?'

What else could Lola say? 'Fine by me.'

Sally hung up a couple of minutes later. 'There, all sorted, EJ's on his way.'

'Great.' Lola forced a smile because she'd have preferred Dougie.

'And I'm off.' Doug took out his car keys and headed for the door. 'Have a good time.'

'Damn,' exclaimed Sally, rummaging through the blue holdall. 'Did you see him do it?'

Lola was busy frying shallots in butter. 'Do what?'

'There was a small dark green photo album in here five minutes ago. And now it's disappeared. Bloody hell, my rotten sneaky Artful Dodger of a brother has only gone and sodding well half-inched it.'

By ten o'clock everyone had eaten as much as they physically could and there had been no culinary disasters. On the surface it seemed like a successful dinner party, buzzy and fun, but as far as Lola was concerned it wasn't going according to plan. Nor could she help wondering what EJ was making of it. Gabe, despite being as charming as ever, was definitely distracted and quieter than usual. He'd been checking his watch all evening, as jumpy as a cat. Sally wasn't behaving normally either; possibly in an attempt to make up for Gabe's air of distraction she was talking and laughing with that bit more enthusiasm than usual, gesturing vivaciously with her hands as she chatted away, laughing more loudly than usual and generally behaving like an over-excited teenager in the grip of a girlie crush.

Which was slightly weird, seeing as there wasn't anyone here for her to have a crush on. Mystified, Lola reached for the jug and poured herself another glug of custard. Unless Sally secretly fancied EJ . . . crikey, could that be it? Was that possible? When he was wearing *those* trousers?

Damn, why couldn't Doug be here now? That would help take her mind off the realisation that, across the table, her wonderful plan to get her parents back together wasn't going according to . . . er, plan.

It was deeply frustrating, trying to keep an eye on them and listen to what they were saying, but doing it subtly so they didn't notice.

And now they weren't even chatting to each other; her mother was talking to EJ and Gabe, while Nick and Sally were trading holiday stories. Honestly, it was as if neither of her parents was even *trying*.

Chapter 39

'Do you know what might be helpful?' said Blythe when Lola tackled her in the kitchen. 'If you could just stop *watching* us all the time.'

'But I can't help it! I want to watch you!'

'Well, it makes us feel like two giant pandas in a zoo, with everyone waiting for us to mate.'

'Mum! Eeuuw!'

Blythe smiled faintly. 'See? That's how I feel too.'

'About Nick? But he's my father. You were in love with him,' Lola protested. For heaven's sake, they'd mated at least *once*.

'Twenty-eight years ago,' Blythe reminded her.

'And now he's here again!' Lola couldn't understand how her mother could be this uninterested in Nick. For herself, finding Dougie again had brought all the old feelings rushing back stronger than ever. Yet for Blythe it simply wasn't happening, which was frustrating beyond belief.

'Look, if your father and I had gone ahead and got married back then, we'd have been divorced by the time you were three. I know that now.' Blythe went on as Lola opened her mouth to protest. 'I'm old enough to know it for a fact. Look at your father and look at me.' She gestured at herself, at her wild red hair and pink glittery blouse, the crinkled leaf-green skirt that so strongly resembled a lettuce. Then, flipping a hand towards the living room, she said dismissively, 'And there's him in his trendy clothes, with his hair cut by Gordon Ramsay.'

Startled, Lola said, *'What?'*

'Oh, you know who I mean.' Her mother's tone was scornful. 'Some celebrity hairdresser chap off the telly. You see, that's the difference between us, love. Nick went in one direction, I went in the other. Neither of us are the same people we were back then. And now he's turned into the kind of person who thinks it's normal to spend a hundred pounds on a haircut. I mean, can you imagine? Talk about a fool and his money soon being parted!'

For heaven's sake, would you listen to her? 'Mum, you can't *say* that.'

'I can say anything I like, love.'

'About me?' Nick appeared in the doorway, causing Lola to clatter coffee cups into their saucers.

'About your hair,' Blythe said cheerfully.

'Sorry,' said Lola. 'My mother's turning into a bit of a delinquent.'

Nick shrugged. 'That's OK, Blythe's entitled to her opinion about my hair, just as I'm allowed to have an opinion about her skirt. Would you like me to carry that coffee through?'

'Thanks.' Lola passed him the tray.

'Maybe I wore this skirt because I knew it would annoy you.' Blythe beamed.

Lola said, 'And maybe you're about to get a pot of coffee tipped over your head. Could you please be nice to each other or should I put you at opposite ends of the table?'

'Hey, we're fine.' Nick's tone was reassuring. 'Just having fun.'

'Of course we are.' Giving Lola a conciliatory hug, Blythe said, 'Don't take any notice of us. Dinner was gorgeous, by the way. And I do like EJ, *very* much.'

Lola wondered if Sally did too.

'He's a good chap.' Nodding in agreement, Nick said, 'Is he wearing those trousers for a bet?'

Back in the living room, Lola poured out the coffee. Gabe drained his in one scalding gulp and jumped to his feet. 'Right, I'm off to work.'

'Now?' Lola said. 'But it's nearly midnight.'

'Colin wants me to get some shots outside Bouji's. It's somebody's birthday there tonight.'

Sally the Queen of *OK!* magazine said eagerly, 'Ooh, whose?'

'Um . . . can't remember.' Combing his hair with his fingers and shrugging on his battered suede jacket, Gabe said his good-byes, gave Lola a thank-you kiss on the cheek and headed for the door.

'Um . . . Gabe?'

He turned, eyebrows registering impatience. 'Yes?'

Lola cleared her throat. 'Aren't you forgetting something?'

'What?' He looked blank.

She pointed to the coffee table behind him. 'Might help if you took your camera.'

'OK,' said Lola an hour later when it was only the two of them left. 'On a scale of one to ten, and I know he's an older man so it isn't easy, but how attractive would you say my father is?'

Ten! No, twelve! No, six hundred and ninety-eight! Whoops, better not say that. Mentally reminding herself that she was several glasses of wine beyond sober, Sally gave the matter serious consideration and said carefully, 'Well, he does have his own hair and teeth, so I would say . . . sevenish. And nice clothes . . . OK, maybe seven and a half.'

'Exactly.' Lola thumped the dining table in agreement. 'That's what I think too. And for an older man, seven and a half's perfectly respectable, it's a good score. But when I asked Mum earlier, she said three! I mean, *three*. And she wasn't being horrible, it's what she really genuinely thought.'

Hooray.

'He's not fat, he's not a skinny rake,' Sally went on. 'Maybe even an eight.'

'OK, now you're getting carried away.' Dismissively Lola shook her head. 'He's only my father. But the point is, how can my mum not fancy him? All those feelings she once had – where did they *go*?'

'No idea. Maybe they evaporated.' Sally shrugged and dripped wine down her chin. 'Just vanished. Like Doug's feelings for you.'

Lola winced. 'Don't say that! Do you have any idea how much it hurts to hear you say that?'

'But it's true. Once it's gone, it's gone. You can't force Doug to change the way he feels about you. And you can't make your mum fall back in love with your father.' *Especially when I want him.*

'You're being mean. OK, how many marks out of ten would you give EJ?'

There was an odd, intense look in Lola's eyes as she asked the question. Sally, topping up their glasses, sensed that this was important to her. Lola must be keener on EJ than she was letting on.

And he was good fun . . . in a speccy, nerdy, wealthy kind of way.

In a generous mood – and because it was in her best inter-ests to make Lola happy – Sally said, 'Honestly? Nine.'

'Nine!' Lola looked incredulous.

'Why not? He's lovely. Oh my God, what is that on your *head*?' Having been idly flipping through one of the albums Blythe had brought along to show Nick, Sally was distracted by a photo of Lola, aged about seven, wearing a black leotard and unflattering black skullcap with huge pink and black ears attached.

'I was a mouse in the school play. Don't make fun of me – I was the star of the show. Do you like EJ?'

'I just told you, of course I do.' Turning to the next page, Sally snorted with laughter at a snap of Lola on a trip to the zoo, leaping back in fright as an elephant investigated the ice cream in her hand with its trunk.

'No, but do you *like*-like him?'

Sally looked up; it was on the tip of her tongue to say no, the only man she *like*-liked was Nick. She could say it, couldn't she? Just blurt it out, then Lola would know and she wouldn't have to hide her feelings any more . . . Oh God, but what if it caused an upset? Lola hadn't yet given up on the idea that she could get her parents back together. Maybe tonight wasn't the best time . . .

'Who, EJ?' Dimly aware that the pause between question and answer was too long and terrified that Lola might somehow be managing to read her mind, Sally took another glug of wine and said over-brightly, 'Of course I don't. Oh look, I love this one of you in a wig!' Hurriedly she pointed to a snap of Lola dressed as John McEnroe during his red headband era. 'Was that for a fancy dress party?'

'That's not fancy dress, those were my best shorts.' Her mouth twitching, Lola aimed a pudding fork at Sally's injured, propped-up leg. 'And I wasn't wearing a wig.'

Sally made her wibbly-wobbly way across the landing shortly afterwards, careering off walls and giggling wildly as she exclaimed for the fifteenth time, 'You can*not* be *serious*!'

Leaving the washing-up for tomorrow, Lola headed for bed and took Sally's photo albums with her. Doug might have made off with the album containing the most photos of him – spoilsport – but he still featured in the others often enough to make them interesting. Having had to pretend to be fascinated by the pictures of Sally earlier, she could now concentrate unashamedly on Doug. God, he'd been a beautiful baby . . . and an irresistibly angelic toddler . . . there he was at a school concert with his hair all neat, his knees all knobbly and one grey sock falling down . . . here were ones of him as a teenager, aged thirteen or fourteen, with a mischievous look in his eyes and a cheeky grin . . .

Lola wiped her cheek as a lone tear escaped. Dougie riding his bike with no hands, Dougie diving into a swimming pool, Dougie about to tip a bucket of seawater over Sally while she sunbathed on a beach, Dougie – older now, possibly eighteen or nineteen – cavorting in a park with a group of friends she didn't know.

More tears dripped off Lola's chin, because these were his university years now, the ones she could have shared with him, *should* have shared but hadn't.

Everything would have been so different and you could drive yourself mad wondering how your life might have turned out if only you'd done this or that.

And wondering was irrelevant anyway. At the time she hadn't had any other choice.

Lola jumped as the phone began to ring, causing the album

to slide sideways off the bed. It was gone one o'clock in the morning; who could be calling her now? Unless it was Dougie, who had been looking through the dark green photo album he'd made off with earlier and been overcome with longing and regret . . .

'Hello?' Lola said breathlessly, her palms damp with hope. Her imagination conjured up a split screen of the two of them in their own beds flirting over the phone with each other like Rock Hudson and Doris Day in *Pillow Talk* . . . or Meg Ryan and Billy Crystal in *When Harry Met Sally* . . .

'Ello, eez Carlo zere to spik wiz?' It was the gruff voice of an elderly Italian woman.

All the hope inside Lola plummeted like a rock dropped into a well. 'Sorry. You've got the wrong number.'

'*Ach.*' The old Italian woman clicked her tongue and heaved a sigh of annoyance before abruptly hanging up.

Lola switched off the phone. Of course it hadn't been Doug. What did she expect?

'Do you trust me?'

'I trust you.'

'Go on then. Take it off,' said Gabe.

Savannah flushed and double-checked that the bedroom curtains were drawn shut. Not even the most persistent paparazzo could sneak a peek into the cottage. She was safe from prying lenses, safe from discovery. Reaching up, she removed the wig and put it on the dressing table in front of her.

'Maybe a bit of powder,' Gabe suggested. 'Just to take off the shine.'

She did as he said, then took a steadying breath and turned on the seat to face him.

'Round to the left a bit. I don't want you full on.' Keen to avoid the wing-nut effect, he wanted to minimise her ears. A three-quarter shot would be most flattering. 'And tilt your head slightly . . . relax your shoulders, I'm not about to rip your teeth out. Now give me a hint of a smile . . . perfect, that's *perfect* . . .'

Afterwards Savannah hugged him. Together they watched as the series of images emerged from the printer on high-gloss photographic paper. Gabe was pleased with the results; as their session had progressed, the tension in Savannah's muscles had dissolved. Towards the end of the sitting she had begun to relax and enjoy herself. Her smile had broadened and lost its I'm-posing-for-the-camera-without-my-wig-on anxiety. The final few had achieved what he'd been aiming for; a beautiful woman who happened to have no hair was gazing into the lens without fear. She was wearing natural make-up, silver hooped earrings and a simple white camisole top over jeans.

'Thank you.' Savannah couldn't stop gazing at them. She shook her head in wonder. 'Thank you so much. You don't know what this means to me.'

'My pleasure.'

'You're incredible.' She turned and kissed him.

Gabe grinned. 'You're not so bad yourself.'

'Maybe if I keep looking at them, I'll get more used to them.'

'Let's hope so.' He watched her slide the glossy colour photographs into the wall safe, where no one else could get at them.

'You do the rest,' said Savannah, and Gabe set about deleting first the images from the memory card, then the files from the laptop itself.

'All done.' There was data recovery software on the market capable of retrieving deleted images but he didn't mention this to her.

'Thank you.' If she was aware of this she didn't mention it either. The point was that she had trusted him to take the photographs, which was good enough for Gabe. Slowly, slowly, Savannah was gaining in confidence.

She was also besotted with him, which was a pretty flattering thing to happen, even if it meant that for the last week or so he'd been getting less sleep than a new mother of twins with colic.

'You're doing it again,' Savannah chided.

'Doing what?'

'Looking at your watch. I hate it when you look at your watch like that.'

Gabe smiled and kissed the tip of her nose. 'I know, I'm sorry, it's called being a part of the real world. We can't all be A-list movie stars taking a few months off between films. Some of us have to get back to London, earn a living.'

'But I don't want you to go. I'll be all on my own.' Pouting, Savannah slid her hands beneath his holey pink T-shirt.

Gabe gently removed them; thanks to her insecurity she was exhaustingly clingy. 'Just a quick coffee, then I really do have to leave.'

He leaned against the Aga and watched Savannah make the coffee. Her actions were delicate, precise, as neat and organised as the kitchen itself, always wiping away wet mug rings with a J-cloth and cleaning up crumbs on the worktop. She was more than capable of keeping the cottage immaculate without Pauline the housekeeper – and owner of Bunty the yappy terrier.

'Would you like to stay, if you could?'

Here came the rush of neediness again. To reassure her, Gabe said patiently, 'Of course I would.'

'OK. In that case, stay.' Savannah tilted her head. 'I'll pay you what you would have earned. How about that?'

'How about that?' echoed Gabe. 'How about *no*?'

'Why not?'

'Because I'm not a gigolo. Don't take it personally.' He held up his hands. 'It's just not something I could do. Look, I need to work tonight and tomorrow. But I can come down on Sunday.'

'Or I could come up tomorrow.' Savannah looked hopeful. 'Book a suite at the Ritz.'

'Sunday's better. I'll see you here.' Gabe shook his head; in London there were paparazzi everywhere and being holed up in a hotel wasn't his idea of fun. At least down here in the depths of the countryside they could go out for walks, although Savannah's preferred form of exercise was more bedroom-related. Not that he was complaining about that, and it wasn't as if it would last forever. Next month she was off to the States to make two films back to back and their brief fling would be over.

'Two whole days. I'm going to *miss* you.' She threw her arms around him.

'I'll miss you too,' said Gabe. He must give Sally a call on the way back, see if there was anything she wanted him to pick up. Reaching for his cup, he spilled a couple of drops of coffee on the flagstoned kitchen floor. Before he could reach for the J-cloth, Savannah had grabbed it and wiped up the drips, rinsed the cloth under the tap and squeezed it dry.

Gabe smiled to himself. Sally would never have done that. At best she would have casually scuffed at the drips with the sole of her shoe.

Chapter 40

Blythe loved to watch Lola at work in the shop, helping customers and making them smile. To the rest of the world Lola might be a capable 27-year-old but as far as Blythe was concerned she'd always be her little girl.

Spotting her, Lola waved and called over, 'Hey, Mum, what a coincidence. Dad was in here just now! You missed him by five minutes.'

Blythe smiled and nodded, noting that Lola had stopped calling him Nick. She was happy for Lola that the two of them were getting on so well; she just wished Lola would stop trying to—

'Ooh, why don't you come with us tonight? We're going along to the opening of a new exhibition at the Simm Gallery, then on to dinner at Medici's.' Eagerly Lola said, 'How about the three of us going together? We can pick you up and drop you home afterwards.'

Correction, Lola would always be her persistent, never-give-up, endlessly hopeful little girl. 'Thanks, love, but I won't. You and Nick have a nice time. Art galleries aren't really my thing.'

That was putting it politely; art galleries bored her witless.

Lola looked disappointed. 'Oh well, what if we give the gallery a miss? We could just go to Medici's instead, is that a better idea?'

Never-*ever*-give-up . . .

'Lola, it's fine, I'm seeing Malcolm tonight. It's quiz night at the Feathers and we're going along to that. I don't dislike your father, it's just that we have our own lives to lead. Trust me, we're both happier this way.' Blythe hadn't told Lola – had no intention of telling her – what had happened on the night of Lola's dinner party when she and Nick had left at midnight and shared a taxi home. When it had arrived at her house in Streatham and Nick had invited himself in for a coffee, she'd gone along with the suggestion just to be polite. They'd chatted amicably enough for half an hour before Nick kissed her.

It should have been romantic but Blythe had felt nothing. *At all.* He'd done his level best but she hadn't been able to summon so much as a goosebump of excitement. It was like being kissed by a packet of cornflakes.

Poor Nick, it hadn't been his fault; he was undoubtedly a more than competent kisser, and with all the practice he'd undoubtedly had over the years possibly an Olympic-level one. But had he had any effect on her? No, he hadn't. Once upon a time he'd meant everything in the world to her, but now she was completely immune to his charms.

Nul points.

It was a mystery how these things happened. But they did.

'We could go upstairs,' he'd murmured, all seduction guns blazing. 'For old time's sake.'

'Oh Nick. Thanks for the offer.' Blythe had smiled and given his arm a regretful pat. 'But I don't think so.'

He'd done the eyebrow thing then, that instantly familiar

combination of surprise and disbelief. It was the look she'd seen on Lola's face when at the age of seven she'd opened a drawer and found, hidden away in a matchbox, all the baby teeth that hadn't been magically whisked away by the tooth fairy after all.

'Why not?'

'I don't want to.'

More eyebrow action. Something told Blythe he wasn't often turned down.

'Is it because of this other chap of yours? What's his name . . . ?'

'Malcolm.'

'Malcolm.' For a split second Nick's mouth twitched as if he might be on the verge of saying something disparaging about his rival. Evidently thinking better of it, he reined himself in and said instead, 'Sweetheart, it's *us*. You and me. Malcolm doesn't have to know.'

Blythe gave him a long look. 'Oh Nick. I wouldn't do that to Malcolm. And you shouldn't ask me to.'

He had the grace to look ashamed. This time his expression uncannily echoed Lola's on the morning of her first-ever hangover when, at fifteen, she had gone along to a friend's party and ended up falling asleep in her friend's parents' bed.

Nick shook his head. 'Blythe, I didn't mean to—'

'I know, I know, it doesn't matter. And I'm not saying no because of Malcolm,' Blythe told him. 'I'm saying it because of me.'

He half smiled, accepting her decision. 'Fair enough. That's absolutely your prerogative.' He paused, then added with a complicit glint in his eye, 'It might have been fun though.'

Amused, Blythe showed him to the front door. 'I daresay. I'm just not curious enough to need to find out.'

'Mum? Hello?' Lola's voice snapped Blythe back to the present. 'What are you daydreaming about now?'

OK, probably best not to say sex with your father. 'Sorry, love, just wondering whether Malcolm would like a nice book about World War Two for his birthday next week. He likes that sort of thing.'

'I thought you'd decided to buy him a sweater.'

'Oh, I already have. A lovely stripy red and yellow one with an eagle on the front.'

'In that case, better come with me.' Lola steered her in the direction of the history section. 'Sounds like poor old Malcolm's going to need a book about World War Two to cheer him up.'

The weather had taken a distinct turn for the better in the last week; temperatures rose and the sun shone, drying out the ground and encouraging the first primroses to peek through the tangled undergrowth. Avoiding the public footpaths where they might bump into other walkers, Gabe and Savannah strolled arm in arm through the woods on the hill below Minchinhampton Common. Savannah was talking about her experiences of working with other actors and the fights that ensued when they discovered their co-stars had negotiated bigger Winnebagos than they had. Even when you were an A-lister, evidently, size mattered.

'. . . he said if he couldn't have one as big as George's, he was walking off the set. And the director said from what she'd heard— *whoops.*'

'Careful.' Gabe caught Savannah as she tripped over a tree root.

'All strong and masterful. I love being rescued by you.'

'Don't need any more invalids in my life just now. One woman crashing around on crutches is plenty, thanks.'

Savannah gazed up at him then reached up and pulled his head down to meet hers. There was new urgency in her kiss. Finally she let go and leaned back again, her chest heaving and her eyes almost feverishly bright. 'Gabe, come with me.'

'Come where?' Gabe hesitated, he couldn't help himself; did she mean back to the cottage for yet more unbridled sex? He was as heterosexual as the next man but his heart sank slightly at the prospect. He wasn't sure he had the energy for another bout.

'To LA. Why not? We want to be together, don't we?' Savannah gripped the sleeves of his faded blue sweatshirt. 'Well, what's to stop us?'

'Hang on, you mean Los Angeles? In California?' It was necessary to ask. Gabe had learned this lesson the hard way years ago when he'd asked a girl if she wanted to go to *Grease* with him and she'd joyfully assumed he was inviting her on holiday. For all he knew, LA could be the name of some uber-trendy new London restaurant.

Savannah beamed. 'No, Los Angeles in Iceland. Of course Los Angeles in California!'

This time Gabe's heart didn't so much sink slightly as go crashing down like a lift with its cables cut. She was making it sound like a spur of the moment idea but he knew it wasn't; this was something she'd been waiting to spring on him.

'Um . . .'

'Don't say *um*, say yes! And there's no need to look so worried.' Savannah shook her head. 'When you think about it, it's the obvious answer. My agent's rented a house for me in Bel Air so that's all taken care of. And I know you'd feel funny about coming out just to keep me company, but that's the beauty of your job – you can work as easily over there as you can here!'

'Savannah, listen—'

'So basically it's perfect in every way! The answer to all our prayers,' she rattled on. 'We can be together, we can even go public as a couple because I completely trust you now!'

'Hang on a—'

'And it'll get you away from that messy flatmate of yours . . . I mean, I'm sure she's a nice enough person and all that but, yeuch, I have to say she sounds a complete nightmare to live with. Plus, *she'll* be relieved to see the back of *you.*'

'Sav, listen—'

'So, talk about tough decisions, is it going to be picking used tea bags out of the sink in a disgusting bombsite of a flat in Notting Hill, or being waited on hand and foot by the live-in staff at an eight-bedroomed mock-Grecian mansion in Bel Air, complete with home cinema and infinity pool?'

Gabe looked at her and said nothing. He didn't need to; Savannah read it in his eyes.

Finally, hesitantly, she said, 'So . . . is that a no?'

He nodded. 'Yes.'

Hope flared. 'Does that mean yes it's a no, or yes it's not a no, it's a yes?'

Gabe hastily shook his head. 'Sorry. It means I can't come to LA with you.'

'Can't? Or won't?'

Oh hell, he hated it when girls got pedantic.

'Can't, I suppose.' He rubbed the back of his neck. 'I'm sorry, but it wouldn't be fair on you. You're an amazing girl and I think the world of you, but there's just . . . something missing.'

'Like, my hair?'

295

Shit. 'No. God, *no*.' Vehemently Gabe shook his head. 'Don't even think that.' Fuck, was she really thinking that?

'It's all right, I believe you.' Savannah managed a ghost of a smile.

'Well, good, because your hair has nothing to do with it. If anything I'm thinking there must be something seriously wrong with me. I mean, you're Savannah Hudson,' said Gabe. 'And I'm nobody at all. The lowest of the low. Lower than that, even. I'm a street pap.'

She picked at a loose strip of bark on the tree trunk beside her. 'And now you're turning me down. Does that mean you'll sell your story to the papers?'

'I won't do that. I'd never do that. You can still trust me.' Gabe's voice softened. He felt sorry for her. It couldn't be easy being Savannah Hudson.

'You know who I feel like?' She made a brave stab at levity. 'Like the Baroness in *The Sound of Music* when she gets dumped by Captain Von Trapp.'

Was this an embarrassing film to admit to being familiar with? Oh well, never mind.

'Except I'm not about to run off with an irritating ex-nun and seven caterwauling children.' When a shocked Lola had discovered last year that Gabe had never seen her all-time favourite film she had sat him down and forced him to watch it. Personally he'd have gone for the Baroness every time; what had Julie Andrews been *on* when she'd let them cut her hair like that?

Back at the cottage for what they both knew was the last time, Gabe collected together his few belongings. Upstairs, having picked up his toothbrush and aftershave, he looked around the clinical white bathroom and Savannah's equally immaculate bedroom. He wouldn't miss this place; for all its traditional exterior, the inside of the cottage was modern and sparsely furnished, minimalist bordering on sterile . . .

Hang on a minute. That couldn't be right, surely? Taken aback, Gabe looked around again. He *liked* sterile, didn't he? Cool, clean lines and no clutter was his thing, had *always* been his thing. And this was what he was seeing here; design-wise, he and Savannah couldn't be more perfectly matched. Yet somehow all these clean lines suddenly seemed a little bit . . . well, empty.

OK, this was too weird, like an alien invading his brain and taking over. An alien with shocking taste at that, and a predilection for gaudy knick-knacks.

Unable to face searching through pristine drawers for the dark grey sweater he knew was in here somewhere, Gabe left it and hurried down the staircase.

Savannah, pale but composed, was waiting in the kitchen with her back to the Aga.

'So you're off then.'

'I should be getting back.' Thank God she wasn't crying.

'Sure you don't have a chirpy ex-nun and seven caterwauling kids waiting for you at home?'

Gabe smiled briefly. 'Trust me, all I have is a stroppy invalid waiting to give me an earful because she asked me to pick up a box of tea bags before I left the flat last night and I forgot.'

'And you really don't have another girlfriend waiting on the horizon?'

'I really don't.'

'I just wasn't right for you, is that it?'

'Hey, you'll be perfect for someone else. You know that.' Gabe folded her into his arms and she clung to him.

Against his chest Savannah mumbled, 'I just have to find someone who likes bald girls. Mr Spock, maybe.'

'Don't think like that.' He dropped a kiss on her forehead. 'You're beautiful with hair or without it. Be proud.'

She smiled. 'I'll do my best. And if I ever decide to go public, you can be the one to take the photos.'

Gabe gave her one last kiss. One last hug. 'Sweetheart, it'd be an honour.'

Chapter 41

'I don't believe it,' cried Sally. 'Another living breathing human being! After months of being marooned up here all alone, I finally have the chance to speak to someone – that's if I can remember *how* to speak . . .'

'You're doing just fine.' Nick grinned up at her from the pavement. 'Want to buzz me in?'

Did she want to buzz him in? Was he kidding? Hastily clonking through to the bathroom and slapping on a bit of powder and lipgloss, Sally clonked her way back through the flat and pressed the buzzer. Somewhat embarrassingly – but at the same time rather excitingly – she'd had a dream about Nick last night in which he'd taken her to the Summer Exhibition at the Royal Academy, flirted with her endlessly and ended up showing her into a room containing a stunning sculpture of two life-sized bodies intertwined. Then, in front of all the other visitors milling about, he had begun to demonstrate exactly *how* the bodies were intertwined, whispering into her ear as he did so, 'You bend your left leg like *this* and put your right arm around my waist *like this* . . .'

Tap tap tap.

Nick was now knocking on the door. All of a fluster, Sally fast-forwarded through the rest of the dream, where he'd started kissing her and running his hands over her body and a stroppy uniformed security guard had stomped up and announced that they couldn't do that sort of thing here and Nick had said, 'But, it's *art . . .*'

'Sally? Have you fallen over in there?'

'Sorry.' She opened the door, let him in. 'I was just having a quick tidy-up.'

Which was so ragingly obviously untrue, it was a wonder a thunderbolt didn't strike her dead on the spot. But Nick, ever the gentleman, simply greeted her with a kiss on the cheek and said cheerfully, 'How are you?'

'Fed up. I feel like Robinson Crusoe. Gabe buggered off yesterday, God only knows where because *he* won't tell me, and Lola's gone out for the day with EJ. Gabe was supposed to pick up some tea bags yesterday but he didn't, so I went all the way to the corner shop on my crutches . . . and when I got there they were shut! So then I had to hobble what felt like fifty miles down the road to the next shop and when I finally got *there*, they didn't even sell PG Tips, only horrible cheap tea bags that taste of dust. I tell you, I'm so fed up with this stupid leg of mine I just want to *chop it off*.'

'Oh dear.' Nick was doing his best to keep a straight face.

'And I've got blisters on my hands from using the stupid crutches.' He was wearing his navy cashmere crew-neck sweater over a white shirt and cream chinos. With a jolt Sally realised that he'd been wearing the same sweater last night in her dream . . . well, until she'd pulled it off over his head.

'So, not the best of days.'

'You could say that.' She broke into a smile to show she wasn't a complete grump. 'Not the best of weeks. See that?'

'See what?' Nick followed the direction of her gesturing hand.

'That empty mantelpiece.'

He frowned. 'It's not empty. There's loads of things on it. Fairy lights, photos, candles . . .'

'But no Valentine's cards,' said Sally. 'That's where I'd put my Valentine's cards if I'd been sent any. But I haven't been, so I couldn't put them there. Because nobody sent me any. Not even *one*.'

'I didn't get any either.'

'Didn't you?' Hooray for that. Mischievously she said, 'Not even from Lola's mum?'

Nick laughed. 'Especially not from Blythe. It's OK, I think Lola's come round at last to the idea that she's not going to get us back together. Sweet of her to try, but let's face it, we're poles apart. That Disney happy ending was never going to happen.'

Better and better. Sally began joyfully concocting an alternative happy ending starring . . . *ta daa!* . . . herself.

'Anyway, this is the reason I dropped by.' Nick took a couple of rolled-up leaflets from his pocket. 'Lola's got it into her head that we should be taking up badminton, so I've been to look at a couple of sports centres. I can leave these with you or slide them under her door.'

All this way just to drop off a couple of leaflets? Was that true, or was he using it as an excuse to see her when he knew Lola wouldn't be here?

'Leave them with me. I'll give them to her when she gets home. Where are you off to this afternoon? Somewhere nice, I expect. Having fun, meeting friends . . .'

'The truth? There's an account I should be doing some work on, but to be honest I'm not in the mood.' Pausing to study

301

her for a moment, Nick said, 'How about if I invited you out to lunch, would that cheer you up?'

'Really? Are you sure?' Sally was barely able to conceal her delight.

'Why not? Decent food, a few drinks and good company.' Nick's grey eyes crinkled with amusement. 'What could be nicer than that?'

This was everything she'd hoped for and more. Every nerve ending zinging with possibilities, Sally said, 'I can be ready in ten minutes.' God, talk about fate bringing together two people who were perfect for each other. What a fantastic day this was turning out to be.

Nick grew better and better looking as lunch progressed. By the time coffee arrived he was irresistible. The food had probably been good too but what with all the excitement and batting back and forth of scintillating one-liners interspersed with more deep and meaningful conversation, Sally hadn't actually got around to eating much of it. Her stomach had shrunk to the size of a thimble and adrenaline production was in overdrive. It no longer mattered that Nick was Lola's father because – thank God – he and Blythe had no intention whatsoever of getting back together. The hurdle had been removed as deftly as Paul Daniels might whisk away a card during a magic trick. And along with the hurdle, Sally felt her inhibitions disappearing too, possibly helped along by the bottle of wine she appeared to have played a large part in demolishing. Every time Nick topped up her glass and she half-heartedly protested, he reminded her that he was driving and it would be a shame to let it go to waste.

Which it most certainly would have been. And now she was bathed in a delicious, warm top-to-toe glow. Semi-accidentally brushing her hand against his, Sally said, 'So did you not want any more children or did it just never happen?'

Nick looked momentarily startled at this about-turn. OK, they *had* been in the middle of a conversation about killing time at airports when your flight's been delayed, but she was interested. It was always a nice thing to know.

'Well, my ex-wife was never keen. She was a career woman, not really interested in kids. I couldn't really force her to have them against her will.' There, that was it, the last box ticked. Sally's heart melted at the thought of this wonderful man wanting children and being cruelly denied them by his cold-hearted career-driven harridan of an ex.

OK, he was now officially perfect. All her life she'd been getting herself involved with men who ran a mile if you so much as mentioned babies. And everyone knew that older men made better fathers. Look at Michael Douglas, he *doted* on his gorgeous children and dazzling young wife.

'Whoops, hang on, let me just . . .'

Sally gave up the struggle to haul herself out of the passenger seat and allowed Nick to do the honours, providing a shoulder to lean on as she and her crutches navigated their way onto the pavement. By some miracle she didn't trip over them. Gathering herself, she handed the front door key to Nick and said, 'Coming in?'

It was a rhetorical question. Of course he was. Nick said cheerfully, 'I think someone has to make sure you don't fall down the stairs, don't you?'

Sally took deep breaths; this was it, she knew it. Gabe was out, they had the place to themselves and the situation couldn't be more perfect. Well, OK, it would have been a teenier bit more perfect if she didn't have her gammy leg to contend with, but it certainly wasn't going to stop them.

Finally they reached the flat. Somewhat unromantically, Sally discovered, all the wine she'd drunk had found its way to her bladder and she was forced to excuse herself in order to visit the bathroom. Returning, she found Nick gazing out of the living-room window. Lit from behind, he had a profile like a Greek god.

He turned, indicating the kitchen. 'I put the kettle on. Thought you might like a coffee.'

OK, it was time. He wanted her to be the one to make the first move. And he was smiling, waiting for her to make it. Approaching him – *clunk* – and taking care – *clunk* – not to bash into the coffee table, Sally smiled back then deliberately took her arms out of the crutches and propped them against the wall. Facing Nick, she said, 'I don't want a coffee.'

'No? Well, that's all right. You don't have to have one.' Amused, Nick said, 'It's not compulsory.'

'Can you believe this is happening?' Without the support of the crutches Sally felt herself beginning to sway.

'Steady.' He reached for her. 'You're not a stork.'

Who wanted to be a stork? 'It's the last thing I expected.' Sally gazed at him. 'Is it the last thing you expected?'

He looked bemused, frowned slightly. 'Well, yes, but ice skaters do injure themselves, so I suppose there's always a chance . . .'

'Doesn't matter.' They appeared to be talking at cross purposes but Sally was beyond caring. 'It won't make any difference, I promise.' Curling her arms around his neck, unable to hold back a moment longer, she lunged forward and kissed him passionately, full on the mouth.

Chapter 42

Making his way along Radley Road, Gabe slowed and looked up at the window of the flat. Puzzled by the sight of what appeared to be two people locked in a passionate embrace, he reached instinctively for the camera around his neck and peered through the long lens, adjusting it until it slid into focus.

What the . . . ?

Gabe's heart began to thud in his chest. Jesus. Sally and Lola's father. Sally, wrapped around him like a scarf. Lola's father . . . for crying out loud, how long had this been going on? How long had they been carrying on behind his back? And not only his back, Lola's too, because she absolutely definitely didn't know about this.

Unable to watch any more, Gabe put down the camera and turned away. His hands were trembling and he felt as if he'd been punched hard in the stomach. Talk about sly, underhand, deceitful . . . How *dare* they? He swallowed and turned back; yes, they were still there, no longer kissing but only inches apart, holding each other and gazing into each other's eyes, murmuring sweet nothings . . . So this was the kind of man

Nick James was, nothing but a sleazy Lothario. How *fucking* dare he?

Something truly horrible was happening. When Nick jerked away, Sally said, 'Sshh, it's OK, you don't have to worry about Lola any more. *She understands.*'

But Nick wasn't looking relieved. More like horrified. Eyes wide with disbelief, he said, 'This isn't to do with Lola.'

'Wh–what do you mean? I d–don't understand.' It came out as a whisper. 'I thought you liked me.'

'I do like you.' Nick shook his head. 'Of course I do,' he insisted. 'You're Lola's *friend.*'

This was a nightmare. Sally felt sick and suddenly, hideously sober. In a lifetime of faux pas, this one took the biscuit. Never before had she made quite such a prize dick of herself as this.

'I'm so sorry.' Nick was clearly mortified. 'I had no idea.'

That only made it worse.

'No, *I'm* sorry. I thought you were flirting with me.' At least she could be honest – there was no point in trying to pretend the kiss had been some kind of accident.

Vehemently Nick shook his head. 'I was just being friendly. I was glad we seemed to be getting on so well. I want my daughter's friends to like me.'

Humiliation was washing over Sally in waves; she'd liked him so much she was mentally already pregnant with their first child. How could she have got it so utterly, completely wrong? How was she ever going to erase the memory of that kiss from her brain? She'd never be able to forget the moment she launched herself at his mouth and felt him freeze in disbelief . . . oh, oh *God* . . .

'Come on, sit down.' Nick skilfully steered her away from

the window and lowered her into a chair. 'And don't be upset. I'm incredibly flattered.'

But not flattered enough to reciprocate her feelings, obviously.

'You're a beautiful girl. Any man would be proud to have you as his girlfriend.'

Any man except you, *obviously*.

'Look, I have to leave.' Nick checked his watch, clearly lying but desperate to escape. 'Why don't I make you that coffee now, then I'll be off.'

Because I don't want bloody coffee, I want a gallon of weed-killer.

'And don't worry, we'll just pretend this never happened. Lola doesn't need to know. I won't tell her,' Nick said gently. 'I won't breathe a word to anyone. That's a promise.'

It took Gabe half a minute to reach his car. He zapped open the door and sank into the driver's seat, appalled by what he'd learned about himself in the last thirty seconds. Because he genuinely hadn't had any idea, not even the remotest inkling, that the sight of Sally with another man could make him feel like this.

Yet . . . it had. Despite the fact that she drove him insane on a daily basis, that she lived her life surrounded by clutter and chaos and that domestically they were about as compatible as Tom and Jerry, in the space of just a few seconds Gabe discovered that he was capable of white-hot jealousy where Sally was concerned. Because he didn't *want* her to be seeing someone else.

Oh God, now he knew he was going stark staring mad. Sally, of all people. Gabe groaned aloud and rubbed his hands over his face. This couldn't be happening; he didn't *want* to want her. She was the last person on the planet he needed to get involved with.

Except . . . well, that wasn't going to happen anyway, was it? It wasn't as if it was even an option, because she was already involved with someone else.

Bloody hell, Lola's dad. How long had *that* been going on? And they'd been keeping it very quiet, although this was hardly surprising given the circumstances. Lola was currently doing her damnedest to get her mum and dad back together. If Nick and Sally were prepared to take the risk of her discovering that one of her best friends had pinched him instead . . . well, it had to be serious.

Gabe felt sick. First Savannah, then a puncture on the M4 on the way back to London, and now this. What a ridiculous situation to be in.

Seeing as he couldn't go back to the flat for a while, Gabe switched on the ignition. The car radio came to life, belting out an REM classic. Michael Stipe, never the cheeriest of souls, sang mournfully, 'Eeeeeeeeeverybody huuuuuuurrrrrts . . .'

Hmm, with Sally's track record the chances were that she was the one who'd end up getting hurt.

'Eeeeeeeverybody huuuuuuuurrrrts—'

Oh, do shut up. Impatiently Gabe jabbed the off button, cutting Michael Stipe off in mid-warble. Who was he trying to kid? Right now, *he* was the one hurting. Jealousy was a new sensation and it was gnawing away in his chest like battery acid.

He didn't like this feeling one bit.

Sally was in the kitchen when Gabe arrived home at midnight. Hobbling out in her dressing gown clutching a packet of Kettle chips, she watched him shrug off his jacket.

'Where have you been? You look awful.'

Gabe glanced at her. 'Not looking so fantastic yourself.'

'Thanks.' Sally already knew she looked like poo. Feeling sorry for yourself and having a good old two-hour blub in the bath was capable of doing that to you. She'd tried to scrub away the shame of having made an idiot of herself but it hadn't worked. Basically, as far as men were concerned, she always had been and always would be a walking disaster.

OK, a limping one.

But at least Gabe didn't know about this afternoon's debacle with Nick. Attempting normality Sally said, 'Been working all this time?'

He shrugged. 'Yes.'

'Any good shots?'

'No.' Gabe was standing stiffly by the window gazing out into the darkness, his streaky blond hair dishevelled and his hands now stuffed into the pockets of his ancient jeans.

Annoyed by the fact that he hadn't even noticed, Sally said, 'Spot the difference?'

His jaw was taut. 'What?'

'Oh, for heaven's sake, if this is how observant you are it's no wonder you miss out on all the best photos! How does this room look to you?'

This time his gaze swept over the floor, the sofa, the coffee table. 'Have you tidied up a bit?'

'A bit?' Incredulous, Sally exclaimed, 'I tidied up a *lot*. Even with my bad leg! I cleared stuff away, put a load of magazines out for recycling, polished the table with Mr Sheen . . . I took *all* my lipsticks and hair things off the window sill . . .'

'What brought this on?'

She flushed. A mixture of guilt, shame and displacement

therapy had spurred her into action. Keeping busy meant she didn't have time to keep going over all the bad stuff buzzing around in her brain.

Aloud Sally said, 'I just thought I should try and start making a real effort. I know it annoys you when I'm untidy.'

'And you suddenly decided to do it just for me?' There was a discernible edge to Gabe's voice. He raised an eyebrow in disbelief. 'Or is it for the benefit of people in general?'

'People in general.' Sally bristled at his tone. 'Why are you being like this?'

For a split second he opened his mouth and looked as if he was about to retaliate. Then he shook his head instead and said, 'OK, forget it, I'm just tired. It's been a hell of a day.'

You could say that again. And Sally knew her ordeal wasn't over yet. Since it would look suspicious if she suddenly started avoiding Nick, she was going to have to put on a brave face and pretend everything was fine whenever they encountered each other . . . oh God, maybe it would be easier to emigrate . . .

'Look, I'm sorry I snapped.' Gabe's voice softened. 'Why don't you sit down and I'll open a bottle of wine?'

More wine, after all the trouble it had got her into at lunchtime? Shuddering at the memory and only too aware that if Gabe were to turn sympathetic she could end up blabbing out everything – oh yes, and wouldn't *that* help matters – Sally shook her head. 'No thanks, I'm off to bed.'

Chapter 43

Lola had just finished serving a customer when she glanced up and saw a vision entering the shop.

OK, not an *actual* vision. Doug.

It really was him. In person. Incredible.

What's more, she hadn't even realised she'd said his name aloud, but she must have done because Cheryl, next to her, followed the line of her gaze and said, '*That's* Doug?' She sounded duly impressed. As well she might.

Lola nodded.

'Great suit.' Cheryl, a sharp dresser herself, always noticed other people's clothes. She said approvingly, 'Made to measure.'

Every last drop of saliva in Lola's mouth disappeared. Because if he was coming into her store to buy a book, that was a good sign, surely? Choosing to shop at this particular branch of Kingsley's had to mean he liked her. Gosh, he looked edible in that dark suit, all lean, mean and . . .

'Hi!' squeaked Lola as Doug approached the desk, clearly in a hurry. 'Well, this is a nice surprise! What can I—?'

'Sally's been trying to get hold of you. Your mobile's switched off and there's something wrong with the phone line here.'

Lola knew this; a brace of telephone engineers were in the back office working on it as they spoke. 'It's being fixed. What's wrong with Sally?'

'Nothing. She says you have to get to a TV. Now.' Doug was slightly out of breath. 'She rang me at work twenty minutes ago. Do you have a TV in this place?'

'A TV? This is a bookshop! What did Sally say it was about?'

'She didn't, just said to make sure you saw it. From the sound of things, it's important. It had better be,' Doug went on. 'Because I had to leave a meeting to come here and tell you about it.'

Her heart racing and her mouth drier than ever, Lola whispered, 'Is it something bad?'

Cheryl took charge. 'He's already told you he doesn't know. Off you go,' she said briskly, pushing Lola out from behind the desk. 'There's only one way to find out.'

Televisions, televisions . . .

Out on the pavement Lola pointed across Regent Street. 'Dover and May, fourth floor.'

Doug said, 'I thought we'd look for a bar with a TV in it.'

'This is closer.' Dover and May was one of Lola's favourite department stores and they had dozens of TVs, rows and rows of them, *hundreds* in fact. 'Quick, after this bus— *oof* . . .'

Yanked back by Doug in the nick of time, Lola bounced off his chest. The taxi driver shook his head in disgust.

'After the bus *and* the taxi,' Doug said evenly. 'OK, now we can cross the road.'

Through the doors of Dover and May, they raced past the perfume counters and islands of make-up, dodging sales girls waiting to pounce and spray scent at anyone who couldn't dodge out of the way fast enough. Together they ran up the escalator. On the first floor they zigzagged past dawdling shoppers in the homeware department. Up the next flight of escalators and through ladies' clothes and shoes – Lola spotted a stunning pair with black glittery heels – then more escalators, followed by racing through menswear and almost knocking over a display of mannequins in stripy sweaters . . . God, this was like getting in training for the marathon . . .

'We'd have been better taking the lift,' panted Lola.

'Never mind, we're here now.'

Belatedly she realised something. 'You're still here. Don't you need to get back to your meeting?'

They'd reached the fourth floor. Leaping off the escalator, Doug expertly steered her through the electrical department, past hi-fis and kettles and every kind of laptop. 'Are you serious? After all this, I want to know what it's about.'

The super-expensive high definition TVs were all showing a recorded wildlife programme. Over at the bank of more afford-able models, Channel 4 racing was on, horses galloping towards the finish line on every screen.

Evidently attracted by the sight of a pair of customers looking as if they were keen to buy, a salesman materialised out of nowhere.

'Good morning, sir, madam. Can I help you in any way?'

'Oh thank you! You most certainly can!' Lola clutched his arm with relief. 'We need the channel changing.'

The flashing pound signs faded in the salesman's eyes but he put a brave face on it. 'The channel changer. Certainly, madam, the remote control units are over here, if you'd like to follow me—'

'No, no, I want you to change *this* channel.' Jabbing a finger at the screens filled with horses, Lola said agitatedly, 'Please!'

The salesman frowned. 'Um . . . which of the TVs are you interested in?'

'None,' Doug intervened. 'Not today, but my friend desperately needs to see something on one of the other channels and we'd be incredibly grateful if you could just—'

'Please please *please*.' Lola's voice rose as she hopped from one foot to the other. 'I'm begging you! I'll just die if I miss it!'

'OK, keep your hair on.' No longer quite so polite now he knew there was no sale in the offing, the salesman disappeared behind the counter where a bank of switches was situated. Glancing over at Lola before addressing Doug under his breath, he said, 'I saw a film with this kind of thing in it once. *Rain Man*.'

The channels began to change. Lola held her breath. Then she saw him, on every screen, multiplied a hundred times over. 'Stop,' she croaked before the salesman could flick past. 'This is the one.'

Much as the family of strangers in *Rain Man* had regarded Dustin Hoffman when he'd pitched up on their doorstep, the salesman regarded Lola warily and said, 'I'll leave you to it then. Just don't . . . touch anything, OK?'

Lola didn't hear him. She was gazing transfixed at the screen where the makeover segment of a popular daytime show was in progress. The female presenter, gesturing cheerfully to a life-sized photograph, said, '. . . so this is how he looked when he arrived at the studio first thing this morning . . .'

Lola realised she was trembling. Next to her Doug said doubtfully, 'Is that your father?'

She shook her head.

'No? So who is it?'

'Shh.'

'. . . and this is how Blythe looked . . .'

314

Lola let out a bat squeak as a photograph flashed up on screen of her mother, looking typically frazzled and flyaway and wearing . . . yikes . . . her favourite pink sparkly waistcoat over a turquoise paisley blouse and well-worn tartan trousers.

'My God, that's your mum.' Doug shook his head in wonder.

'Well, that was the two of them a couple of hours ago,' the jolly, voluptuous presenter exclaimed. 'So let's see how they're looking now!'

'I *remember* those tartan trousers.' Incredulously Doug pointed at the screen.

The shimmering curtains parted and Blythe and Malcolm made their entrance.

Chapter 44

'Oh my GOD!' shouted Lola, startling several browsing shoppers.

'Shh.' Doug gave her a nudge. 'Stay calm or we'll get chucked out.'

Stay calm?

Lola whispered, '*Oh my God*,' and clapped her hands over her mouth. On the TV screen her mother, self-consciously attempting to pose for the camera, looked like a Stepfordised version of herself and the effect was positively eerie. Her delinquent hair had been cut, blow-dried and ruthlessly straightened, her lipstick was deep red and glossy and her complexion had an airbrushed, plastic quality to it. She was also wearing eyeliner for the first time in her life. To complete the transformation, the batty-mother clothes had been replaced by a chic, leaf-green shift dress with matching fitted jacket and darker green high-heeled shoes.

'Oh my word,' gushed the presenter, 'don't you look fabulous!'

And in one way she did; Lola could see that other people might look at the made-over version of Blythe and feel that it was a huge improvement. It was just that the made-over version no longer looked anything like her mother. In a daze she watched the makeover experts step forward and explain how they had achieved the miracle of Stepfordisation. Blythe continued to look embarrassed. Then it was Malcolm's turn.

With a jolt Lola noticed him properly for the first time. OK, now this really *was* a transformation. Gone was the hideous bushy beard for a start. Malcolm was now clean-shaven, his hair had been cut and slicked back from his face and, in place of the awful bobbly sweater and baggy corduroys, he was wearing – good grief! – a really well-cut dark suit.

In fact, wow. Malcolm was looking years younger, like a completely different person. Now that you could actually see his face it was revealed as not so bad after all. Why on earth had he ever grown such a horrible beard in the first place?

Next to her Doug said, 'I can't believe your mum's doing this. Whose idea was it?'

Lola frowned, because in the shock of the moment it hadn't occurred to her to wonder the same thing. And now that she *was* wondering, it did seem a bit odd. Blythe wasn't the type to write into programmes like this and she'd never had a hankering to appear on TV.

'. . . so Malcolm, coming here today was all your idea,' the presenter said cosily, 'because you felt you needed to smarten up your image.'

A crackle of alarm snaked its way up the back of Lola's neck; was the presenter reading her mind?

'Well, yes.' Malcolm looked bashful. 'I suppose I wanted to make a better impression on people . . . or rather I was keen for them to have a better opinion of me . . .'

317

'He's too polite to say so,' Blythe chimed in, 'but he's actually referring to my daughter.'

'Oh!' gasped Lola.

'Who, I gather, has strong opinions when it comes to clothes.' The presenter gave Blythe a sympathetic look.

'That's one way of putting it. Trinny and Susannah rolled together, that's what she is,' said Blythe. 'With a touch of Simon Cowell. Always telling me I look like a dog's dinner.'

'I am *not*,' cried Lola. 'Not always!'

'I mean, it's water off a duck's back as far as I'm concerned. Sometimes I'll take her advice,' Blythe went on, 'and sometimes I won't. But that's because I'm her mother. I'm used to her.'

'Whereas it hasn't been so easy for you, Malcolm, has it?' The presenter's voice softened. 'Criticism like that can be quite hurtful, can't it?'

Stunned, Lola said, 'But I didn't criticise him! I *didn't*!'

'Oh no, no, Blythe's daughter has never criticised me. At least not to my face,' Malcolm said hastily. 'She's a lovely girl, very polite. I just felt a bit lacking in the, um, sartorial department, I suppose. Getting dressed up and making the most of myself has never been my forte. And I want Lola to think well of me because . . . well, because I think a great deal of her mother.'

Lola's throat tightened. She couldn't speak, couldn't swallow.

The twinkly-eyed presenter, addressing the camera, said, 'So, Lola, I know you aren't watching at this moment because you're at work and Malcolm and Blythe didn't tell you they were going to be doing this today, but if you do happen to see a recording of this programme I'm sure you'll agree that Malcolm and your mum have scrubbed up a treat! They both look wonderful. If you ask me, your mum's a lucky lady to have found herself such a very caring and thoughtful man.'

'Here,' murmured Doug. Lola took the handkerchief and wiped her eyes.

'And after the break,' the presenter continued cheerfully, 'we'll be talking to a husband and wife who have both undergone sex changes, and who'll be joining us here in the studio with their daughter who until two years ago was their son!'

'There you go.' Doug half smiled. 'Things could be worse.'

'I'm so ashamed.' Lola sniffed hard, because being lent a hankie and dabbing away tears was one thing but blowing your nose in it was altogether less dainty.

'So that's your mum's boyfriend, the one you don't like.'

'I don't dislike him. I just thought Mum could do better.' Sniff. 'I thought she was settling for Malcolm because he was easy.'

She didn't mean easy in *that* sense – yeuch, perish the thought.

'He seems like a nice chap.'

'He is. I just couldn't s-stand the beard.' Lola gave up and blew her nose noisily into the hanky. 'And now everyone knows how shallow I am. They're all going to think I'm a really horrible p-person.'

For a moment she thought Dougie might put his arms around her, reassure her that she really wasn't horrible, maybe even drop a consoling kiss on her forehead. Instead the annoying salesman reappeared and said to Doug, 'Is she finished here? Can I change the channel back now?'

'Sorry, yes, thanks very much.' Realising that most of the customers in the vicinity were watching them, Doug gathered himself and checked his watch. 'Come on.' He gave Lola's shoulder a tap and said lightly, 'Let's get you back to the hospital before the nurses find out you've escaped.'

★　　★　　★

319

Blythe had washed her hair and changed out of the grown-up leaf-green suit. In her purple flowery top and pinstriped skirt and with the glossy, poker-straight blow-dry a thing of the past, she looked like herself again.

'Wasn't it awful? I felt like a clone!' Hugging Lola, she said, 'And the eyeliner! Never again!'

Malcolm, following Blythe into Lola's flat, said, 'She's been going on about that blessed eyeliner all day.'

'It's all right for you,' Blythe retorted, 'you didn't have to wear it.'

'Maybe not, but I still had to go into make-up, didn't I? *Base*, they put on my face.' Malcolm shook his head in bafflement. 'And powder! That was a first, I can tell you. Felt like Danny La Rue!'

'Malcolm, I'm so sorry.' Lola moved past her mother to greet him with a hug and a kiss on his freshly shaven cheek. 'I never meant to make you feel bad about yourself . . . I'm so *ashamed . . .*'

'Oh, there there, no need to apologise.' Embarrassed, Malcolm said bashfully, 'The thing is, you were right. I even knew it myself, just didn't have the nerve to try and change things on my own. When you've had a beard for twenty years you kind of get used to it. If anything,' he told Lola, 'I'm grateful to you for telling your mother I looked a fright.'

Ouch.

'You look fantastic now.' She stepped back and gazed at him, meaning every word.

'He does, doesn't he?' Blythe nodded in agreement.

'I've got rid of all my old jumpers,' Malcolm said proudly. 'The fashion woman told me to throw out anything with a pattern on it, and I have.'

'She said that to me too,' Blythe chimed in. 'And I told her to take a running jump.'

'We went to Marks and Spencer's this afternoon and bought loads of new clothes. The fashion woman wrote me out a list. She said I shouldn't wear sandals any more either.'

Lola decided she loved the fashion woman with all her heart. 'Well, anyway, thank you for being so nice about it. And why are we still standing out here in the hallway? Come on *in*.'

'Sorry, love, we can't stop.' Blythe beamed. 'We only dropped by to show ourselves off to you. Well,' she amended, 'so that Malcolm could show himself off to you and I could let you see that I'm back to normal. We've got to get to the pub – it's quiz night and everyone's dying to hear about our time at the TV studios.'

It was on the tip of Lola's tongue to ask her mother if she preferred Malcolm the way he looked now. But she already knew the answer. Malcolm might be pleased with his makeover but it wouldn't make an ounce of difference to the way Blythe felt about him, because external appearances were simply irrelevant as far as she was concerned. What counted was the person within.

Worse, Lola knew she was right. Maybe it would help to get Dougie out of her system if she could try a bit harder to fancy EJ instead.

Chapter 45

'That's thirteen-three,' Nick called out. 'Ready? Or do you want to stop for a couple of minutes to catch your breath?'

Catch her breath? *What* breath? There was none left in her lungs, that was for sure. Lola shook her head, determined not to give in. This was *badminton*, for crying out loud. If it had been tennis or squash she could have understood being this exhausted, but badminton wasn't anywhere near in that league, everyone knew it was one of those namby-pamby games played by children and old people where you flicked a silly little shuttlecock back and forth over a net. As a child she'd played badminton in the back garden and it hadn't been remotely like this.

'Oof,' Lola gasped, lunging after the shuttlecock as it whistled past her ear. Stupid, *stupid* racquet . . .

'Fourteen-three.' Grinning, Nick prepared to serve again.

'*Oof*.' Fuck.

'Game. Well done.' He came round to her side of the net, patted her on the back.

'You can't say well done when it wasn't.' Clutching her sides where two stitches were competing to see which of them could hurt most, Lola panted, 'I was rubbish.'

'No you weren't, you were actually pretty good. But I was better.'

'That's so unfair. I'm your daughter. Aren't you supposed to let me win?'

He looked amused. 'Not when you're twenty-seven.'

Lola leaned forward, hands on knees, then realised people watching outside the badminton court would see her knickers and hurriedly straightened up. To add insult to injury it had all been her idea to come here tonight because she'd found out that Merton's Sports and Fitness Club in Kensington was where Dougie was a member and last Thursday Sally had mentioned in passing that he was playing squash that night. Working on the assumption that Thursdays at Merton's might be a regular thing, Lola had called up the club and asked if she and her father could come along and try out the facilities before deciding whether or not to join.

And yes, Merton's did indeed seem like a great place to socialise and expend a few calories if you were so inclined, but there was one small drawback.

No Doug. Anywhere at all. They'd been given the full guided tour of the club and there was no sign of him. Plus, having been generously given a free, hour-long slot on this badminton court, they were now morally obliged to carry on using it.

Still panting like a pervert, Lola glanced up at the clock on the wall. Nine minutes down, fifty-one to go.

She looked at her father, who wasn't even remotely out of breath. 'OK, we'll have another game. But this time pretend I'm six and let me win.'

Never had an hour passed so slowly. By the end of it, Lola was puce in the face, wheezing like a steam engine and staggering around on legs like overcooked spaghetti. Badminton wasn't namby-pamby after all. Battle-hardened members of the SAS could hone their fitness levels playing this game. Thank goodness Dougie hadn't been here to witness her humiliation.

'Ready for a drink?' said Nick as she shakily wiped her face and neck with a towel.

'Ready for loads of drinks.' How could she ever have thought that coming to this place tonight would be a good idea? As soon as they'd showered and dressed they were out of here.

'You've dropped your hairband,' said Nick as Lola just about managed to haul the strap of her sports bag onto her shoulder.

'I can't pick it up, it hurts too much.'

She waited as Nick went back to retrieve the pink hairband, then turned and wearily pushed through the glass swing doors.

Dougie was standing on the other side, watching her.

'Oh!' So much for thanking her lucky stars he wasn't here. If there was a god, he really did have it in for her. A trickle of sweat slid down her forehead for that extra-glamorous finishing touch.

'Lola, what's going on?' Doug shook his head. 'Are you stalking me?'

Lola swallowed, suddenly realising that this was exactly what she was doing. Instantly on the defensive she said, 'What are you talking about? Of course I'm not stalking you! Who says you're not stalking me?'

'I've been a member of this club for the last three years. I thought maybe my sister happened to mention it.'

'Well, she didn't.' Technically this was true; Elly who worked for him had been the one who'd mentioned it. But shame crept up and Lola felt her pulse quicken. Oh God, he was right, she was turning into one of those deranged females incapable of accepting rejection, madwomen who end up shouting in the street and getting arrested for harassment.

'Here's your hairband.' Catching up with them, Nick eyed Dougie coolly and said, 'What's this about stalking? I was the one who suggested we try this club. It wasn't Lola's idea to come here.'

And now she had her father covering for her, lying to protect his deranged-stalker daughter. Mortified, Lola gazed down at her feet and felt the trickle of sweat drip down to her chin.

'Sorry, I was just surprised to bump into her. Didn't have Lola down as the badminton-playing type.'

'Why wouldn't I be?' Defiantly Lola said, 'We had a fantastic game.'

'Really?' Dougie's mouth was twitching. 'When I looked through the window half an hour ago you didn't appear to be having much fun.' He turned to Nick. 'Hi, I'm Doug Tennant. You must be Lola's father.' Shaking Nick's hand, he said, 'You were wiping the floor with her.'

Nick relented. 'I was rather, wasn't I?'

Oh terrific.

'I'm going to get showered and changed,' said Lola.

'Me too. See you in the bar afterwards.' Nick nodded cheerfully at Doug. 'Nice to meet you.'

Ten minutes later Lola screeched to a halt at the entrance to the bar. Doug was standing with his back to her, talking to a couple of women with toned brown thighs. There was no sign of Nick. She retraced her steps and waited for him to emerge from the men's changing room.

He looked surprised when he did. 'What are you doing here? I thought we were meeting in the bar.'

'I don't want to stay for a drink. Doug's in the bar. He'll only think I'm stalking him again.'

'Hey, that's OK, it doesn't matter.'

'Yes it *does* matter.' Lola wearily shook her head. 'Because he's right, I have been stalking him. And it's time to stop.'

They went to Café Rouge in Lancer Square. Over red wine she'd ordered but no longer had the heart to drink, Lola told Nick the whole story from beginning to end.

'So that's it, I've basically made the world's biggest fool of myself but it's all over now. Doug's not interested in me and I've finally accepted it. I gave it my best shot and I failed. Time to give up and move on. As everyone always loves to say, there are plenty more fish in the sea.' Lola curled her lip. 'Although whenever they say that, it really makes me want to get hold of a big fish and smack them round the face with it.'

'I won't say that then. Oh, sweetheart, I do feel for you.' Reaching across the table, Nick gave her hand a squeeze. 'I can't believe you haven't told me any of this before.'

'I didn't want you thinking you'd got yourself a scary daughter. You might have run for the hills.'

'I wouldn't.'

'OK, but you might have thought I was pathetic.' Lola shrugged. 'I wanted to impress you, make you think you had a daughter to be proud of.'

'Sweetheart, I *am* proud of you.'

Lola blinked back tears; he was being so nice to her and it felt lovely being called sweetheart. 'Yes, but I have behaved pretty stupidly. I mean, throwing myself at a man who kept telling me he didn't want me, it's hardly the brightest thing to do. *Anyway*,' hastily she drew a line with her free hand, 'I won't be doing that any more.'

'I wish there was something I could do to help.' Nick thought about it for a couple of seconds. 'Do you want me to have a word with him?'

Lola smiled, because that brought back memories. Once, when she'd been ten, a boy in her class had been teased about his ginger-ness and frecklediness. The teasing had carried on for a few days and the novelty had been about to wear off, until one morning the boy's mother had turned up at the school, gathered together the group of culprits and given them a good talking-to. The entire school had listened, enthralled. Sadly, she'd been even gingerier and freckledier than her son, so from that day on he'd had to endure *months* of merciless mickey-taking directed at both himself and his mother.

'Thanks, but there's no need.' She imagined Nick giving Doug a good old ticking-off, telling him not to be so mean and ordering him to be nice and give his daughter another chance. 'It's over. He's with Isabel now.'

'And you've got EJ.' Nick's tone was encouraging. 'You like him, don't you?'

Lola shrugged. Of course she liked EJ, but only as a friend. They kissed – which was fine – but hadn't slept together. He was great company and a nice person but the magic wasn't there. It wasn't fair on EJ and she was going to have to tell him. It was time to finish that relationship too – if you could call it a relationship when you weren't even having sex.

As they were leaving Café Rouge Nick said, 'So, what happened to the money Blythe mustn't know about? What did you spend it on?'

'I can't tell you.'

He laughed. 'Tell me!'

Lola spotted an approaching taxi. 'Really, I can't.' She stuck out her arm and flagged down the cab. 'Sorry, Dad, but I can't tell anyone. Ever.'

Chapter 46

Sally had done something to annoy Gabe and she had a pretty shrewd idea what it might be.

The tidiness issue − or rather the lack of it − had over the last couple of weeks become a real bone of contention.

OK, even more of a bone of contention than it had always been. She could tell because the difference in Gabe was pronounced. He had withdrawn mentally, almost as if he couldn't be bothered to argue with her any more. He was also distancing himself physically, working all hours and spending less and less time at home. At first she'd been thrilled that he'd stopped nagging her to clear up after herself but after a while she'd kind of begun to miss it. As her torn calf muscle gradually repaired itself and she grew less reliant on crutches, Sally had even found herself once or twice doing the washing-up *while there were still clean plates in the cupboard.*

Not that Gabe had noticed or shown signs of being remotely grateful when she'd pointed it out to him; he'd been so distant and off-hand recently that she'd almost given up trying to please him.

Almost, but not quite. Because Gabe was being a grumpy

sod but Sally still wanted to cheer him up, get the old relaxed smiley Gabe back.

And today was her last day of being an invalid. At midnight, Cinderella-style, her sick note expired. Tomorrow she was going back to work at the surgery and she was looking forward to it. Inactivity had bred boredom. She'd watched too much TV, read too many magazines, eaten far too many biscuits. In fact, she could do with expending a bit of energy now. Gazing around the flat, Sally decided to spend the day tidying up and . . . oh God, could she do it? . . . *de-cluttering* the flat she'd devoted so much time to cluttering up.

Yes, she *could* do it and she was *going* to. Feeling energised already, Sally pushed up her sleeves and limped over to the ornate stained-glass mirror over by the window. She knew her passion for coloured fairy lights drove Gabe to distraction. OK, fine, she could live without fairy lights. Reaching up, she unwound the ones draped around the mirror and threw them onto the sofa. Then, because the mirror was now looking naked, like a Christmas tree brutally stripped of decorations, she took it down too.

Breathe in, breathe out, no need to panic. And that pink lampshade with the glittery fringing was another culprit; Gabe had always hated it. Sally unplugged the lamp and added it to the mirror and the fairy lights on the sofa. She was on the verge of hyperventilating now but that was OK, no need to panic, it was only *stuff*. It didn't make a difference to her life.

Cushions next. She'd keep her silver sequinned star-shaped cushion – in her bedroom – but the rest could go. And all the tea-light holders, which she knew Gabe found unbelievably pointless. And the vase of peacock feathers on the floor next to the TV. And any magazines more than two months old. Right, start with the cushions, then move on to—

329

Sally stopped in mid-fling at the sound of the letterbox clattering downstairs. The post had arrived an hour ago, so what was this? Hobbling over to the window, expecting to see a spotty teenager delivering flyers, she peered down and saw instead the rear view of a slender blonde disappearing into the back of a black cab. The door slammed shut and the taxi pulled away.

Curious enough to go and investigate, Sally wrestled the armful of cushions into a black bin bag then made her way downstairs. Reaching the front door, she bent down and retrieved the envelope from the mat.

It was a plain, pale blue envelope with Gabe's name on the front. Just that, Gabe, no surname, written in black ink with enough of a curly flourish about it to indicate that it had been penned by a girl.

Was this why he'd been so distant lately? Was Gabe embroiled in a tempestuous relationship that for some reason he hadn't mentioned to her or Lola? As she slowly made her way back up the stairs, Sally itched to know what the envelope contained. Could she do that holding-it-over-the-kettle thing and steam it open? OK, maybe not; she'd tried that once during her miserable time with Toby the Tosser. Not only had the letter not been incriminating – it had been a dental appointment – the steam had turned the envelope all crinkly, making it glaringly obvious what had happened to it. And hadn't Tosser Toby enjoyed getting his money's worth out of that little slip-up? He hadn't let her forget it for weeks.

Back in the flat Sally heroically put the letter down on the table. No snooping; instead she'd get on with the job in hand. Rummaging through one of the kitchen drawers she located an advertising card she'd kept – how spooky was that? – from a small local charity asking for items to sell in their shop. *Can't Deliver? We'll Collect!* promised the card, which was jolly helpful of them. She called the charity's number and booked them in for four o'clock. There, now she couldn't chicken out. Once everything was gone, it was gone for good.

Clean, clear lines might actually be nice. De-clutter your surroundings, de-clutter your life. As she energetically dragged magazines out from under the armchair, Sally began to feel better already. She could become a style icon, a champion of minimalism and space creation.

Blimey, and she'd always thought style icons were boring! She'd be turning into Anouska Hempel next.

Gabe stopped dead in the doorway, taking in the scene.

Finally he said, 'What's going on?'

'Ta-daaa! Just call me Anouska Hempel.' To match the cool, clean lines of the flat, Sally had even changed into a floaty white dress.

'Who?' As he studied the living room, devoid of . . . well, pretty much everything, Gabe said flatly, 'So that's it, you're off.'

'What?' It was Sally's turn to be confused.

'Leaving, taking all your stuff with you. Moving out, moving *on* . . .'

'No!' She shook her head, dismayed by the realisation that this was probably what he'd been praying for. 'I'm not going anywhere. I just tidied up. I thought you'd be pleased! I started doing a little bit then I got carried away. And guess what? I think I like it!'

Gabe exhaled audibly – with relief or disappointment, she couldn't tell. He put down his camera and said evenly, 'So where is everything?'

'Gone.' Sally's spirits plummeted; she'd been so proud of herself. Why couldn't Gabe be proud of her too?

'Gone where?'

'Charity shop.'

'Why?'

'Because I'm turning over a new leaf!' If her leg hadn't still been hurting she'd have stamped her foot. 'Gabe, why are you *being* like this?'

He shrugged. 'Probably because I'm wondering why you're being like this. It isn't *you*.'

'Oh, for God's sake!' Sally's voice rose in frustration. 'All my life people have complained about how untidy I am, and now I'm doing something about it you're being all *weird*.'

'I'm not being weird,' said Gabe, who definitely still was. 'I'm just wondering who you're trying so hard to impress.' He eyed her white dress and make-up and said with an edge to his voice, 'Off out somewhere tonight?'

Like she was some kind of prostitute or something.

'Yes.' Sally stared back at him. 'Is that allowed?'

'Who are you seeing?'

Honestly, damn cheek. In actual fact she'd been invited over to dinner by her lovely boss Dr Willis and his wife Emily to celebrate her return to work. Annoyed by Gabe's attitude, Sally said, 'What are you, my mother?' and flounced into her bedroom. If he was going to be this stroppy and horrible, so was she.

When she returned ten minutes later with a black and white checked holdall, Gabe raised an eyebrow.

'So you won't be home.'

Having earlier turned down the Willis's kind offer of a bed for the night in order to save her the tube journey into work the next day, Sally had now changed her mind. Maybe by the time she returned tomorrow evening, Gabe would have snapped out of his mood. 'Well done. You should be a detective. Oh, by the way, you've got a lett—'

'What?' Gabe looked up from his laptop when she abruptly stopped in mid-sentence.

Sally's brain shot into overdrive, replaying the last eight hours at warp speed. The letter . . . where had the letter gone? She'd left it on the coffee table before launching into her tidying frenzy and now it was no longer there. Somewhere along the way it had got swept up in the whirlwind and deposited good-ness knows where.

'Come *on*.' Gabe sounded like Jeremy Paxman only more impatient. 'I've got *what*?'

OK, she definitely didn't need him shouting at her, which was what he'd do if she told him the truth.

'A lettings agent after the flat. He called earlier, wondered if you were still interested in renting it out.' As she spoke, Sally limped over to the magazine rack and began feverishly flicking through the few magazines she hadn't despatched to the charity shop.

'A lettings agent? What are you doing now?'

'Just looking for the . . . um, piece of paper. I wrote down their name and number in case you wanted to call them back.'

'Why would I call them back? I don't want to rent the flat out.'

'No? Well, you know, I thought I'd take their number anyway, I'm sure it's here somewhere.' Bloody buggering hell, this was the last time she *ever* tidied anything up. 'Let me just check in the kitchen bin.'

'Leave it.' Gabe waved her away from the kitchen door. 'Don't bother. If I want to speak to a lettings agent I'll look in the Yellow Pages.'

'OK.' She'd definitely thrown the letter out. And now she'd lied to him too, but he'd been so arsey he deserved it. Feeling guilty – but not guilty enough to confess – Sally picked up her holdall and headed for the door. 'Bye.'

Gabe was bent over his laptop, scrolling through the day's photographs. He muttered 'Bye,' without looking up.

Bastard. He hadn't even wished her luck for her first day back at work tomorrow.

Reaching for her stick and limping more heavily than she needed to, Sally clumped out.

Gabe let out a groan and sat back on the sofa. He hadn't even wished her good luck for tomorrow. The last ten days had been a journey to hell and back. All he could ever think about was Sally and, clearly, all Sally could think about was Nick James. Equally clearly, Nick must have passed some comment about the mess she surrounded herself with, prompting this afternoon's out-of-the-blue blitz on the flat.

Gabe rubbed his face then ran his hands over his messed-up hair in defeat. And what had that business with the phone call from the lettings agent been about? Was that Sally's way of dropping a hint, subliminally indicating that before long she'd be gone? Shit, and to think that for the first few weeks of her being here he'd *wanted* her out.

The phone rang.

'Hi, it's me.' Lola, finishing up at Kingsley's, sounded in a flap. 'Just to let you know I'm going over to EJ's so I won't be home till late. But if anyone feels like cooking anything and saving some for me, they could leave it in my fridge for when I get back.'

'Sorry. I'm working and Sally's already gone out,' Gabe said evenly. 'She didn't say where.'

There was a moment's silence, then Lola said, 'Oh, that's right, her boss invited her over for dinner. She mentioned it yesterday.'

Hmm, lying to her friend, covering her tracks. Gabe wondered how Lola would react if she knew who Sally was really with.

'She took an overnight bag.' Jealousy welled up; it was on the tip of his tongue to tell her.

'Really? Well, it's probably easier for work. No need to sound so disapproving.' Lola sounded amused. 'I'm sure Sal's not having an affair with him. He's a bit old for her.'

Gabe took a deep breath. Should he say it?

'Anyway, wish me luck,' Lola babbled on. 'My stomach's churning like an ice-cream maker. I'm finishing with EJ tonight. God, I hope he takes it well, I don't want him to be upset.'

That was it, Gabe realised he couldn't do it. If he told Lola now, she was the one who'd be upset. She had enough on her plate for one evening; let her get the EJ thing dealt with and out of the way first.

Chapter 47

It was like being on a really strict diet and having someone present you with a year's supply of Thornton's truffles. Lola had never actually been on a really strict diet owing to her inability to give up . . . well, Thornton's truffles, but she just knew this was how it would feel. Toby Rowe was a multimillionaire music mogul and an old friend of EJ's. It had been thrilling enough being invited along to his fortieth birthday party, held at the kind of private members club Lola had only ever dreamed of visiting, but now Toby was offering something more.

Life just *wasn't fair.*

'Come on.' Toby's tone was cajoling. 'It's only for a week. You can take a week off work, can't you? EJ, work your magic on this girl, make her say yes.'

There were people in this room so famous they'd make your head spin, and rumours swirling around that Bono was going to be dropping in later. If that happened, Lola knew her head would swivel right off.

'Say yes,' EJ joined in. 'It'll be fantastic. If I can take a week off, surely you can too.'

Toby already had a party of ten friends flying out in the first week of April to stay at his villa on St Kitts. Evidently it was large enough to accommodate two more. From the sound of things it could hold another twenty. And the people joining Toby and his girlfriend were all major players in the music business. Lola would be practically the only civilian. Just the thought of sunbathing around the pool in the company of singers with triple platinum albums to their names was almost too exciting to bear.

'Go on,' Toby added with a persuasive wink, 'you know you want to.'

Lola bit her lip; of course she wanted to, more than *anything*. Imagine Robbie Williams asking if she'd mind rubbing suncream into his shoulders . . .

Oh God, this was torture. 'I have to check the staff rota. I'm not sure if I can take the time off.'

'Couldn't you just phone in at the last minute,' said Toby, 'and tell the boss you've got flu?'

Wouldn't that be nice?

'Except I am the boss.' Lola pulled a face. 'And I wouldn't believe me. I'm always suspicious when people phone in with a croaky voice and tell me they have flu.'

Toby said, 'Or when they ring in with a croaky voice to tell you they've sprained an ankle.'

'What I really hate,' said EJ, 'is when we're recording an album and they phone up with a croaky voice to tell me they've got a croaky voice.'

Lola's heart sank as he grinned his quirky, lopsided grin. He was such good company, the kind of person anyone would love to have as a friend. And he had buckets of money . . . why, *why* couldn't she look at him and feel a frisson of lust?

But there you go, she couldn't and that was that. She wasn't being fair to him. Checking her watch, Lola saw that it was midnight and she had to be at work by eight tomorrow morning. It was time to do what she had to do. She touched EJ's arm and said, 'I need to get home. If you want to stay on, I can get a cab.'

But EJ was far too much of a gentleman to do that. He shook his head and put down his orange juice. 'It's OK. I'm pretty shattered too.'

They said their goodbyes to Toby and his friends. As EJ drove back to Notting Hill, he told her more about Toby's villa on St Kitts, about the view over Half Moon Bay, the golf course, the scuba diving, the spectacular Black Rocks—

'I'm sorry,' Lola blurted out, 'I can't go.'

'Don't say that. You haven't checked with work yet.'

Her fingernails dug into her palms as she squeezed her fists tight. 'It's not work.'

'No?' EJ pulled up at traffic lights, glanced sideways at her. 'Is it the plane tickets? Because that's not a problem. I'll pay for those.'

The lights from the Burger King opposite were reflecting off his glasses. He was such a thoughtful person. Mental images of Half Moon Bay floated tantalisingly in front of Lola – tropical palms, a glittering turquoise ocean, herself tanned and magically thinner than usual in a pink bikini . . .

'OK, here's the thing.' Gearing herself up, Lola wished he could be driving the battered old Fiesta tonight; she didn't want to be responsible for him pranging his beloved Lamborghini. 'EJ, I really like you but we're going to have to stop seeing each other.' The lights changed and they moved forward; flinching and praying he wouldn't go careering into the bus ahead of them, she said hastily, 'But you're a fantastic person.'

EJ remained in control of the Lamborghini. Drily he said, 'But not quite fantastic enough.'

'Oh, don't say that! I'm sorry! It's not you, it's me, I just – mind that cyclist!'

'Don't worry, I'm not going to hit the cyclist.'

'But I don't want you to be upset.'

'Lola, it's OK. It's not your fault.' He steered skilfully around a couple of drunks staggering across the road, then indicated left and pulled into a side street. 'Would it help at all if I said I'd kind of guessed this might be coming?'

The streetlights illuminated the angles of his face. Behind the spectacles Lola glimpsed sadness mixed with stoicism.

They'd never even slept together.

'I'm sorry,' she said again. 'You're so *nice . . .*'

'I know I am. I also know I'm not the world's best looking guy, but I was kind of hoping to win you over with my brilliant personality.' He shot her a lopsided smile, seemingly able to read her mind. 'That's why I never tried to get you into bed, in case you were wondering. Because I knew you hadn't reached the stage yet where you really wanted to. I thought if I was patient . . . well, that the right time would come along and everything would be perfect. But there was always the risk that you'd bale out before it had a chance to happen.' He pulled a wry face. 'And guess what? I was right, you're baling out. Maybe I'm psychic.'

'But you've slept with so many incredible girls,' Lola protested. 'Famous ones! Loads more glamorous than me!'

'Maybe I have.' He shrugged, half smiled. 'Maybe they don't mean so much.'

'Oh God, don't say that.' Lola felt terrible now.

'Sorry, I don't want you to feel guilty. Hey, it's OK. Really.

Can't make chemistry happen if it isn't there. It's a shame, but I'll survive.'

'You deserve someone fantastic.' Lola really meant it.

'Thanks.' EJ started the Lamborghini up again and drove her home.

Before she climbed out of the car, Lola hugged him hard and said, 'Have a great time in St Kitts.'

He smiled, sad for a moment, then gave her waist a squeeze. 'I have to say, all credit to you for telling me tonight. A lot of girls would have waited until after the five-star, all-expenses-paid holiday.'

'I know.' Lola wondered if she'd live to regret it. 'I think I'm probably mad.'

As he planted a goodbye kiss on her cheek, EJ said with affection, 'That's probably why I liked you so much in the first place.'

Chapter 48

What a shame you couldn't fall in love with a man as easily as you could fall in love with a coat.

'This is it.' Lola hugged herself and did a happy twirl in front of the antique, rust-spotted mirror propped against the side of the stall. 'This is the one. It's perfect!'

'Fabulous.' Sally nodded in agreement.

Blythe, ever practical, said, 'How much?'

But Lola didn't care. It was love at first sight. The moment she'd clapped eyes on the coat, fuchsia-pink velvet, long and swirly, she'd known it was the one for her. And they'd be happy together; the coat wouldn't reject her. It wouldn't haughtily announce that it didn't want to be her coat. It would never let her down, stand her up or make her cry.

Plus it had an iridescent parma violet satin lining; how many men could boast that?

Oh yes, when everything else around you was going pear-shaped, there was always Portobello Market, with its bustle and colour and endless treasure trove of shops and stalls, to cheer you up.

Just as there was always someone to nag you about money.

341

'Lola. Tag,' Blythe prompted, pointing to the sleeve.

This was the downside of having a mother who went for quantity rather than quality every time. Blythe lived for the sales. Her idea of heaven was rummaging through the bargain rails in charity shops where you could buy a whole new outfit for six pounds fifty.

'Um . . . forty-five.' Lola attempted to hide the tag up the coat's sleeve as her mother approached.

Too late. Blythe peered at the tag then dropped it as if it had barked at her. 'Two hundred and forty-five!' She gazed at Lola and Sally in disbelief. '*Pounds!*' Just in case they'd thought she meant Turkish lira.

'But Mum, it's a coat.'

'It's a second-hand coat.' Blythe was indignant.

'Vintage,' said the stallholder.

'If this was in a charity shop you'd be able to buy it for twenty pounds!'

'But this coat isn't in a charity shop,' the stallholder patiently explained.

'Not any more it isn't. I bet that's where you found it, though. You probably bought it for a tenner and now you're selling it for silly money! Lola, offer her fifty pounds and not a penny more. Barter with the girl.'

'Mum, sshh, look at the label. If this coat was on sale in Harvey Nichols it would cost thousands.'

'But see how thin it is. You can hardly call it a coat – it won't even keep you warm!'

Lola briefly considered pretending to give up, carrying on along the road and secretly scuttling back this afternoon. But how could she risk leaving such a beautiful thing for even a few minutes? What if someone else came along and snapped it up? It would be like leaving George Clooney on a street corner and expecting him to still be there waiting for you hours later.

Besides, she was twenty-seven years old, not seven. She looked the stallholder squarely in the eye and said, 'Two hundred.'

The stallholder, who knew a pushover when she saw one, shrugged and said, 'Sorry, I can't go below two thirty.' The subtext being: because I know how badly you want this.

Lola took out her purse and began counting out twenties.

'Lola, you can't buy it.'

'Mum, I love this coat. It'll make me happy. And it's my money, I can spend it how I like.'

'I don't know where she gets it from,' Blythe tut-tutted as Lola rolled her eyes at the stallholder. 'Two hundred and thirty pounds for somebody else's old cast-off. That's shocking.'

At last the transaction was complete and they moved on. Sally, after a week back at work, was relishing her day off and getting along quite niftily now with the help of her walking stick. Blythe stopped at a stall selling patchwork waistcoats and said, 'Now these are fun, and they're only fifteen pounds!'

'They're horrible,' said Sally.

'Oh. Are you sure?' Blythe looked to Lola for a second opinion.

'Really horrible,' Lola confirmed.

'At least they're new. Ooh, how about this?' Excitedly Blythe waved a peacock-blue scarf adorned with silver squiggles. 'Seven pounds!'

Lola nodded. What harm could a scarf do? The sooner her mother bought something, the sooner she'd stop going on about the coat. 'Yes, buy it.'

'No, don't buy it!' Sally let out a snort of laughter and waggled her hands in a bid to draw Lola's attention to something on the scarf.

'Honestly, you two,' Blythe grumbled. 'It's like going shopping with Trinny and Susannah. What's wrong with—'

'My God! Lola!'

Everyone turned in unison at the sound of the girl's voice. Next moment Lola found herself having the breath hugged out of her lungs as market-goers swirled around them on the pavement.

At last Jeannie put her down and Lola said, 'I don't believe it. Look at you! You're so *brown*.'

'That's because I'm living in Marbella now! We're just back for a few days visiting my mum.' Jeannie's hair was sunbleached, her skin was the colour of a hazelnut and she was wearing faded, hippyish clothes and flip-flops. 'And you aren't brown,' she said cheerfully, 'so that must mean you live in unsunny Britain.'

'I do. I live right here in Notting Hill. And this is my mum.' Lola indicated Blythe. 'And my friend Sally. Mum, this is Jeannie from school.'

'Oh, the Jeannie you went off with to Majorca! How lovely to meet you at last,' Blythe exclaimed. 'And what a coincidence – fancy bumping into you like this!'

As things had turned out, Lola hadn't ended up spending more than a few days with Jeannie. Shortly after her arrival in Alcudia, Jeannie had hooked up with a boy called Brad who was moving on to work in a restaurant on a surfer's beach in Lanzarote. Jeannie had gone with him the following week and that had been the last she and Lola had seen of each other. Lola, aware that her mother and Alex would have been worried sick if they'd known she was out there on her own, had discreetly glossed over that snippet in her postcards home.

'Such a coincidence!' echoed Jeannie. 'I was just looking at

Sarah's jacket, admiring it from a distance, then I saw who she was talking to and I was just, like, ohmigod!' She ran her fingers over the sleeve of Sally's caramel leather jacket and said appreciatively, 'It's even better close up.'

'Sally,' said Sally.

'Huh? My name's Jeannie.'

'I know. You just called me Sarah. I'm Sally, Sally Tennant.'

'Oops, sorry! Brain like a sieve, me!' Jeannie tapped the side of her head, then stopped and began wagging her index finger in a thoughtful way. 'Although not always. Hang on a minute, wasn't Tennant the name of that boyfriend of yours?'

The index finger was now pointing questioningly at Lola.

'Doug Tennant.' Sally gave a yelp of excitement. 'That's right, he's my brother!'

Lola experienced a sensation of impending doom, like an express train roaring out of a tunnel towards—

'You're kidding!' Her eyes and mouth widening in delight, Jeannie looked from Sally to Lola. 'So you and Doug got back together? My God, I don't believe it! That's so romantic! What happened about the money? Did his witch of a mother make you pay it all back?'

Lola's first instinct was to clap her hands over her ears and sing loudly, 'Lalala.' Her second was to clap her hands over her mother's ears and go, 'Lalala.' But it was too late; Blythe was frowning, looking as bemused as if everyone had suddenly started babbling away in Dutch.

'Oops, sorry!' Jeannie smacked her forehead and turned back to Sally. 'I just called your mother a witch!'

'What money?' said Blythe.

'Dougie and I didn't get back together,' Lola blurted out. 'Sally's my next door neighbour.'

345

'Oh crikey, I'm getting everything wrong here, aren't I?' Jeannie shook her head dizzily and burst out laughing. 'Well, except for the bit about your mum being a witch. You have to admit, that was a pretty beastly thing she did. I mean, that's messing with people's lives, isn't it?'

'Excuse me.' The bored stallholder nodded at the scarf being twisted in Blythe's hands. 'Are you going to be buying that or what?'

'So did Doug ever find out about the money?' Jeannie said avidly.

Blythe carried on twisting the scarf. 'What money?'

Lola closed her eyes and breathed deeply; when she'd gone out to Alcudia she'd made a point of explaining to Jeannie that her mother didn't know about the money thing. How, *how* could Jeannie forget something as important as that, yet remember a detail as small and irrelevant as Dougie's surname?

'Yes, Doug found out.' Sally, attempting to ride to the rescue, said hastily, 'But that's all in the past, everyone's moved on, it's—'

'Oh, don't try and change the subject, I've always wanted to know what you spent all that money on. God, I wish someone would've given me ten grand to dump any of the loser boyfriends I've hooked up with over the years.' Apologetically, Jeannie touched Sally's arm. 'Not that your brother was a loser. I met him a couple of times before they broke up and he was totally fit.'

He still is. Desperate to get away — although it was too late now, the cat was out of the bag — Lola grabbed the blue and silver squiggly scarf from Blythe. 'Mum, are you going to buy this?'

'No she *isn't*,' Sally repeated, earning herself a glare from the stallholder.

346

'Why not?' Lola gave the scarf a flap to try and get the creases out. 'It's pretty!'

Useful too. She could strangle blabbermouth Jeannie with it.

'It's obscene.' Jeannie pointed to the silver squiggles, which Lola hadn't realised were scrawled words. 'Rude Spanish word. Rude Spanish word.'

Sally helpfully pointed out another squiggle. 'Very, *very* rude Spanish word.'

God, it was too. Lola hurriedly put down the scarf.

'That's disgusting.' Rounding on the hapless stallholder, Blythe said, 'You should be ashamed of yourself, selling something like that.'

'I don't speak Spanish.' The man shook his head in protest. 'I didn't know.'

Nobody was listening to him, nobody cared. Blythe had already swung round and pointed an accusing finger at Lola. Her expression intent and her voice scarily controlled, she said, 'But he shouldn't be as ashamed of himself as *you*.'

'I can't believe this.' Blythe's cup of coffee sat in front of her untouched. She shook her head and gazed across the tiny café table at Lola. 'I can't believe you did something like that. In God's name, *why*?'

Lola felt sick with shame. She'd never imagined her mother would find out about the money. She wished she still had Sally here to be on her side.

'Well?' Blythe demanded.

'I've told you. Because Dougie's mother hated me and Dougie was moving up to Scotland. We were so young, what were the chances of us staying together? I mean, realistically?' Lola's coffee cup rattled as she tried to lift it from the saucer.

Her whole life, she'd loved earning praise from her mother, making her happy and proud of everything she did. Blythe's approval was all that mattered and until today she'd known she'd always had it, unconditionally.

Until an hour ago. The coffee tasted bitter and she'd tipped in too much sugar. What were the chances of bumping into Jeannie and the whole sorry story spilling out like that?

'And the money,' said Blythe. 'The ten thousand pounds. What happened to it?'

Lola shifted in her seat. She wasn't completely stupid, she did have a plausible lie put by in case of absolute emergencies.

And now appeared to be the time to drag it out.

'OK, it wasn't ten thousand pounds. It was twelve and a half.' May as well get as many of the facts correct as possible. 'And I used most of it to buy a Jeep so I could get around the island.'

'A *Jeep*? Dear God! But you hadn't even passed your test!'

'I know. That's why I didn't tell you. It's also why I couldn't get it taxed and insured.' Her palms growing damp, Lola forced herself to carry on with the lie she'd concocted years ago and hoarded for so long. 'Which is why, when it was stolen a week later, I couldn't do anything about it. I'd spent the money on a Jeep then, *boom*, it was all gone. I was back to square one.'

'No you weren't.' Blythe was shaking her head again. 'At square one you had Dougie. Oh Lola, what were you thinking of? I thought we'd brought you up better than that. Relationships are more important than money! Look at Alex and me, we were happy whether we had it or not. If you love someone, money's irrelevant. You sold your chance of happiness with Dougie for a . . . a Jeep! That's a terrible thing to do.'

'I know. I know that now.' Lola was perilously close to tears, but she wasn't going to cry. She forced herself to gaze around the crowded, steamy café, listen to Dexy's Midnight Runners playing on the radio, concentrate on the jaunty music.

'It's like that coat today. It cost far too much but you just didn't care, you had to have it.'

'OK, Mum, can we stop now, please?'

But Blythe hadn't finished yet.

'And you know what? If you were capable of doing that to Dougie, you don't deserve him. How could you be so stupid? I feel like phoning that boy up and apologising to him myself, I really do.'

Oh God. Her mother's disappointment in her was too much to bear. Telling herself not to cry hadn't worked. Tears rolled down Lola's cheeks as she clenched her fingers and blurted out, 'I was seventeen, I was stupid and I did a terrible, *terrible* thing. I don't blame you for hating me,' she shook her head in despair, 'because I know it was wrong. And I'll regret it f–for the r–rest of my l–l–life.'

Blinded and sniffing helplessly, she fumbled in her pocket for a tissue. None there. The next moment she felt her mother's arms go around her and a paper napkin being pushed into her hand.

'Oh sweetheart, of course I don't hate you. You're impetuous and you don't always think things through, but you're my daughter and I love you more than anything in the world. There, shh, don't cry.' Blythe rocked her, just as she'd always done as a child. 'You made a mistake and you've learned your lesson. And you'll never do anything like it again, that's the important thing.' Pulling away, she smiled and tenderly wiped rivulets of mascara from Lola's wet face with her finger. 'My God, the antics you've got up to over the years. Just you wait, one of these days you'll have children of your own and then you'll know how it feels when they do things that shock you.'

Chapter 49

Sally, who still didn't have the faintest idea what she'd done to upset Gabe, was getting more and more frustrated.

'The omelette pan's missing. You were using it yesterday. What have you done with it?' He was crashing around the kitchen, banging cupboard doors open and shut, as exasperated as if she'd deliberately tipped the contents of the bin all over the floor.

Which Sally was quite tempted to do, what with all the fuss he was making.

'I washed it up, dried it and put it away.' Biting her tongue, she opened the final cupboard door and took out the omelette pan. 'There, panic over.'

Gabe looked irritated. 'It's never been kept in that cupboard.'

Every time she felt bad at having lost the letter that had arrived for him – and not mentioning it – Gabe said something to make her feel less guilty. Like now. Evenly Sally said, 'Gabe, up until a couple of weeks ago, I'd have left the omelette pan on the stove or dumped in the sink and I wouldn't have got this much grief about it. Why are you being like this?'

Didn't he realise that she might sound in control but inside she was finding his attitude deeply upsetting?

'Sorry.' Gabe didn't sound remotely sorry. 'Will you be coming straight home from work?'

'No, I won't. So don't worry, I won't be here to put the wrong cup on the wrong saucer.'

He switched on the gas ring, ignoring the jibe. 'Where are you going?'

'Having dinner with Roger and Emily.'

'Who?'

'Dr Willis and his wife.'

Gabe said sarkily, '*Again?*'

He never used to be sarky.

'Yes, *again*,' Sally mimicked him.

'Why?'

Why indeed? She hadn't the foggiest. But Roger had said they had something they wanted to tell her so she'd agreed. 'I don't know.' Pointedly Sally said, 'Maybe they enjoy my company.'

Gabe exhaled heavily and began breaking eggs into a bowl. Sally picked up her keys and limped out of the kitchen.

They'd always got on so well together. How had it come to this?

'Ten o'clock, love, with Dr Burton.'

Sally dragged her attention back to the elderly woman on the other side of the counter, checked the lists on the computer screen and said, 'That's fine, Betty, take a seat.'

'You all right this morning, love? Looking a bit peaky.'

Sally forced a smile; it was always a joy to know you looked as rubbish as you felt.

'I'm OK, Betty. Just a bit . . . tired.' Tired of being criticised, tired of hearing she looked peaky, tired of being nagged at

351

because she'd put the omelette pan away in the wrong sodding cupboard.

'Oh hello, Maureen, didn't see you there.' Betty beamed at Maureen, sitting over by the magazines with her knitting.

'How're you doing, Betty? I'm not so bad myself. Feet still playing up but I'm trying some new tablets, so fingers crossed. And our Lauren's expecting again, that's cheered us all up.'

'Ooh, lovely. What d'you think of Sally over there, then? Reckon she's looking a bit peaky, do you?'

Oh, for crying out loud.

'Probably too many late nights,' said Maureen, peering over the top of her glasses at Sally perched on a stool on the other side of the reception desk. She winked saucily. 'Got yourself a new boyfriend, love? Burning the candle at both ends? Too much canoodling and what-have-you, that's my guess. Am I right, hmm?'

'That's not what I meant,' said Betty. 'I was thinking more along the lines of morning sickness.'

Oh, for *crying out loud* . . .

Across the waiting room the old regulars, Maureen and Betty, were chuckling away. Half a dozen other patients were all watching expectantly too, waiting for her to come out with some chirpy reply.

To her absolute horror Sally realised that she was actually *physically* about to start crying out loud. Her vision blurred with tears and her throat tightened from the inside. Attempting to duck down out of sight behind the computer screen, she almost toppled off her stool. Her walking stick was out of reach, propped up against the filing cabinet. If it hadn't been for her leg she would've made a dash for the bathroom but she was too clumsy and too slow. Even Maureen with her gammy feet and Betty with her lumbago were faster, peering over the counter and clucking with concern.

Since they'd already seen the tears, Sally let them slide down her face. 'S-sorry, I'm not pregnant. Just having a b-bit of an off day.'

'Oh, love, go on, let it all out. Here, have a tissue, don't go dripping mascara on that lovely shirt of yours. There there, don't worry. So, boyfriend trouble, is it? Is he giving you the runaround?'

Everyone in the waiting room was agog and staring. All the magazines had been put down. Mortified but unable to help herself, Sally sobbed noisily for a couple of minutes before blowing her nose and shaking her head. 'I'm so embarrassed.'

'Good,' a middle-aged man said crisply. 'Now you know how we feel, having to sit here knowing that you know all our shameful secrets.'

'Like piles,' mused the older man next to him.

'Speak for yourself,' a girl in a purple sweater retorted. 'I don't have piles.' As several people smiled she said, 'I have an irritable bowel.'

'And my boyfriend isn't giving me the runaround.' Sally took yet another tissue from Betty and wiped her eyes. 'Because I don't have a boyfriend. And my flatmate's being really mean . . . I don't think he w-wants me there any more but I d-don't know why and I just feel like such a *f-f-failure . . .*'

'Men are nothing but trouble. You're better off without them.' The girl in the purple sweater said, 'My last boyfriend broke my nose. He hit me across the bedroom then told me it was my fault for brushing my hair in an annoying way.'

Sally shook her head. 'I'm useless with men. I bought my last boyfriend a course of tooth-whitening treatment and he ended up running off with the dental nurse.'

'My husband's a drinker,' Betty chimed in. 'Drinking's all he ever does. Forty years we've been married and he's never managed to hold down a job for more than a week.'

Competitiveness stirring inside her, Sally wiped her nose and said, 'One of my exes drank too. And another one jilted me practically at the altar!'

The girl in the purple sweater, not to be outdone, blurted out, 'I came home from work once and my ex was in the garden pegging out the washing.'

Everyone in the waiting room looked at her. Maureen said, 'Isn't that a good thing?'

'He was doing it wearing my best bra and knickers.'

God, that was something she'd never even considered. Sally said mournfully, 'I'm better off on my own.'

'Come on, not all men are awful.' Maureen rose spiritedly to their defence. 'My son's a lovely lad. He'd make any girl happy. In fact, you two would make a wonderful couple. I could introduce you to him if you like.' She was nodding eagerly at Sally.

Next to her, leaning back, Betty was mouthing, 'Gay.'

Sally stammered, 'Um . . . thanks . . .'

'The thing is, even when you think people are happy together, chances are they aren't. Everyone just likes to pretend.' Holding up the copy of *Hello!* she'd been reading, the girl in purple declared, 'This magazine's six months old. Look at these two on the cover, wrapped round each other like a couple of eels. But are they still together now? No they're not. And it's the same all the way through the magazine! Everyone's split up since then, split up and sold their stories about how hellish their lives together really were, and you've wasted all that time envying them . . . I mean, what is the *point*?'

'By 'eck, love, steady on.' An elderly man in a flat cap spoke for the first time. He shook his head and said good-naturedly, 'There's plenty of happy marriages out there, trust me.'

The girl in purple cocked a disbelieving eyebrow. 'Could have fooled me.'

'You've just got off to a bad start, pet.' The man's eyes crinkled at the corners; he sounded like the voice-over in the Hovis ads. 'Everyone has someone who's right for them. It's just a question of keeping going till you find them.'

'I'd have better luck finding the Loch Ness monster,' said the girl in purple.

'You'll get there in the end.' His smile was genial. 'And let me tell you, it's worth it. You might not think it to look at me now, but I were a bit of a jack-the-lad in my day. I had my share of girlfriends. Never saw the point in settling down, I were having too much fun. Then I met Jessie. She worked in a bakery in Bradford and the moment I walked into that shop and saw her behind the counter I knew she were the one for me. Eyes like stars, she had. Before I even heard her speak I fell for her, hook, line and sinker. We started courting and after a month I asked her to marry me. Nobody could believe it, not the family, not me mates down the pit, not the lasses I'd been out with before Jessie came along. But I knew it were the right thing to do, you see. I'd found the girl I wanted to spend the rest of my life with.'

The whole of the waiting room was on the edge of their seats, listening to him tell the story in his simple heartfelt way.

'And?' prompted the girl in purple.

'We've been married forty-nine years, pet. And happier together than I ever thought possible. My Jessie means all the world to me.'

It all sounded too perfect. Sally frowned. 'Don't you ever argue?'

'Argue?' The man chuckled. 'Of course we argue! Hasn't been a single day when we haven't had a fight about summat. And let me tell you, I wouldn't have it any other way.'

BRRRRR went the buzzer, making everyone jump.

'Mr Allerdyce, please, to room four,' Dr Willis's voice came over the intercom.

'That's me.' Having leaned heavily on his walking sticks in order to haul himself to his feet, Mr Allerdyce tipped his cap to everyone in the waiting room.

When he'd made his way out and the door had closed behind him, the middle-aged man said, 'His wife probably can't stand the sight of him.'

Everyone in the waiting room turned and gave the man a stony look.

'Sorry.' He flinched under the glare of their disapproval. 'Just a joke.'

'Are you divorced?' said the girl in purple.

He looked surprised. 'Yes, I am.'

The girl nodded. 'I thought so.'

Chapter 50

'You're leaving the practice?' Sally couldn't believe it; she loved working for Dr Willis. Her whole world was crumbling around her. What had she done to deserve this?

'Isn't it exciting? We can't wait.' Emily beamed across the dinner table at her. 'Skipton's where I grew up, all my family are there, it's just such a wonderful place to live. Everyone's so friendly, not like down here. Do you know the Dales?'

'Not really.' Sally was still struggling to take in the news. The other doctors were OK, pleasant enough, but Roger Willis was her favourite. The practice wouldn't be the same without him.

'It was Emily's idea.' Roger refilled their wine glasses. 'She spotted the ad in *Pulse*, organised a trip up to Skipton, even dragged me round the estate agents before I knew I'd got the job. We'd always planned to retire up there,' he went on. 'But this way we've got a few years of me working in the area first, becoming a real part of the community.'

'That's why we asked you over here this evening. We wanted you to be the first to know. Here, take a look at the place we're buying.' Bursting with excitement, Emily produced a glossy brochure. 'All my life I've dreamed of living in a house like this.'

They were moving to Yorkshire and they expected her to be pleased about it. Sally's heart was in her boots but she forced herself to take the brochure and look interested.

The place was spectacular, a sprawling converted farmhouse on a hillside with lovingly tended gardens and stunning views across the valley. There were five bedrooms, three of them en-suite, and a kitchen the size of a tennis court. There was even a granny annexe, a snooker room and – crikey – an *actual* tennis court.

Sally said, 'It's fantastic. Can I come with you?'

Emily paused, a forkful of fish pie halfway to her mouth. 'Really?'

Oh no, it was like the middle-aged divorced chap attempting humour in the waiting room this morning. 'I was joking,' said Sally.

'Oh.' Emily's face fell. 'Shame.'

'Sorry?'

'No, my fault, you got our hopes up there for a minute.' Emily waggled her free hand. 'It's just that the current recep-tionist is the wife of the chap Roger's replacing. They're moving down to Cornwall. So the practice needs a replacement . . . but of course you wouldn't want to leave London, silly of me to even think it! Although you're welcome to come up and stay with us whenever you like. In fact you must! You'll fall in love with the place, I know you will. The people are so warm and sociable, it's like a different world up there.'

Sally gazed again at the photographs in the glossy brochure. Was this a sign?

Was Yorkshire a different world?

Was it fate that had brought Mr Allerdyce into the surgery this morning with his heart-warming tale of true love? She had looked through his medical notes after his visit and discovered that the wife he adored was crippled with osteoporosis and confined to a wheelchair, but that with the help of the family Mr Allerdyce was able to care for her devotedly. Reading this and picturing the two of them together had sent Sally into the loo for another little weep. Honestly, it was a wonder she was able to see out of these eyes, they'd squeezed out so many tears today.

'When we wake up in the morning we'll look out of our bedroom window and see all that.' Roger Willis proudly tapped the photograph of rolling green hills dotted with sheep.

Sally drank it in. Sheep. How many people could look out of their window in London and see sheep?

All Creatures Great and Small. That had been one of her favourite TV programmes. And she'd always had a secret weakness for Postman Pat. There were hills and sheep galore in Greendale.

Was this all simply a coincidence or could it be a sign that she was meant to live somewhere hilly and popular with sheep? Where men were men and true love still existed? Where people called you lass and made you welcome?

Heartbeat. Was that set in Yorkshire? Yes it was.

Where the Heart Is? Tick, ditto.

The Royal. Ha, yes, so was that. And there was a *reason* why so many feel-good cosy Sunday evening dramas were set in Yorkshire. It was because Yorkshire was a cosy feel-good place to live.

And there was a Harvey Nichols in Leeds . . .

'Hello? Sally?' Roger was holding the dish of fish pie, waving the ladle to attract her attention. Having caught it, he said jovially, 'What are you thinking? You're miles away!'

'I'm not.' Sally moved her fork to one side, allowing him to spoon another helping of delicious fish pie onto her plate. 'But you never know. I could be.'

'I've got some good news for you,' said Sally.

'Oh?' Gabe halted in the doorway, clearly surprised to see her still up at one o'clock in the morning.

'Great news. Happy news. You're going to be thrilled. It might even make you crack a smile.' Sally was drinking Pernod and water, which was unbelievably disgusting but she'd been in need of Dutch courage and there hadn't been anything else alcoholic in the flat. Talking things through with Lola would have helped but Lola was away for the night, being wined and dined at a publisher's dinner being held in a hotel in Berkshire.

She had to do this on her own. Well, with the aid of Pernod.

'Go on then,' said Gabe. 'Thrill me.'

Having psyched herself up to tell him, Sally abruptly lost her temper.

'See? *See?* You're still doing it!' Her eyes narrowed and her voice rose as Gabe chucked his jacket over the back of the chair. 'Even now! I'm trying to tell you something that you'll want to hear and you're being all distant and sarcastic.'

'I'm sorry. Right, I'm listening. See?' Gabe made his face deliberately blank. 'Not being sarcastic at all.'

And now he was treating her like a child. Her stomach in knots, Sally blurted out, 'Well, don't worry, soon you can be as sarky as you like because I won't be here to see it. I'm moving out.'

A muscle was going in Gabe's jaw. For a couple of seconds he just stood there looking at her. Then he turned away. 'Right. Good for you.'

'Is that it?' Adrenaline was sloshing through her body. 'Is that all you're going to say?'

'What else do you want me to say? OK, I've got something. Have you told Lola yet?'

'What?' Sally took a step back. 'No, because she's not here. I'll tell her tomorrow when she gets back.'

Gabe raised an eyebrow. 'And how do you think she'll react?'

'Oh, come on, it's not that big a deal!'

'Sure about that?'

'We're all adults!'

'But you haven't mentioned it before now, have you?'

'Because I only decided tonight! My God, why are you *being* like this? I'm leaving.' Pernod flew out of Sally's glass as she flung her arms wide. 'Isn't that enough? I thought you'd be delighted to have me out of here. And what's *this* about?' Agitatedly jabbing a finger at his discarded jacket, she cried, 'You spend your life nagging me but it's OK for you to act like a slob. Would it kill you to hang that up?'

Slowly and deliberately, Gabe picked up the jacket. As he made his way past her he murmured, 'Poor sod, does he know what he's letting himself in for?'

'Will you shut up? I've worked for him for the last two years, haven't I? So I can't be that unbearable!'

Gabe stopped dead. 'Worked for who?'

'Dr Willis!'

He gazed at her in utter disbelief. 'You're having an affair with Dr Willis?'

'What?' Sally let out a shriek. 'For crying out loud, what are you *on*? How could you *think* I'm having an affair with Dr Willis?'

'But . . . but . . .'

'He's *old*.' Sally wailed. 'And he's *married*.'

'So who are you moving in with?'

'Dr Willis. And his wife. But I won't be living *with* them, not in the same house. It's a self-contained annexe.' Sally mimed self-containment with her hands. 'When I wake up in the morning I'll see sheep.'

Gabe was gazing at the almost empty glass of Pernod. 'How many of those have you had?'

'One. It's vile. And can we please stop arguing now, because I'm not moving out tonight. I'm going to be here for another four weeks yet.'

He shook his head in confusion. 'I don't understand the bit about the sheep. At all.'

'There's loads of them, all over the hills.'

Gabe said evenly, 'Where are these sheep? Where is this house?'

'Near Skipton. In Yorkshire. That's where I'm going to be living.' As she said the words, Sally wondered if she really wanted to go. 'Living and working. It's a fresh start.'

'Why?'

'Why? Because I'm hoping it's going to be nicer than living in London. My boss is moving to Yorkshire and he offered me a job in his new practice. You don't want me here in this flat, you've made that perfectly obvious. Of course I'll miss Lola, but it's not going to stop me . . . Skipton's a really friendly place, I'll meet loads of new people, the views are—'

'So what happened? You and Nick broke up? Or is he moving up there too?'

For a split second she couldn't work out who he meant. 'Nick who?'

Gabe gave her a look. 'Come on. I know.'

Sally didn't know what he knew, but she felt herself flushing anyway. Great waves of heat and shame swept over her. If Gabe knew, that meant Nick must have told him. Except . . . oh God . . . it was far more likely that Nick would have told Lola who in turn had told Gabe, so basically they'd *all* been laughing at her behind her back.

'OK, I get it.' As her flush deepened Gabe said dismissively, 'You're moving up there together.'

'What are you *talking* about?' Sally stared at him; how could he even think this? 'I'm not having an affair with Lola's dad!'

'You mean it's over?'

'I mean it never happened!'

'No? Take a look in the mirror.' Gabe's tone was triumphant. 'If it's not true, tell me why you've gone redder than a traffic light.'

'Oh, I'm sorry, are we in court?' That was it; Sally lost the last vestige of control. 'Are you the lawyer for the prosecution? Not that it's *any* business of yours, but just to shut you up and get you off my back, the reason I've gone red is because, OK, I *did* have a bit of a crush on Lola's dad a while back and I did make a complete idiot of myself one afternoon telling him I liked him. But he was very nice about it and turned me down really gently, and I don't know what makes you think it ever went any further than that, but it definitely didn't. And if you don't mind, I'd really prefer it if Lola never found out.' Unable to meet his gaze, she said, 'Can we stop talking about this now? It's humiliating.'

No reply. Sally carried on staring at the floor. Finally she heard Gabe say, 'There's nothing going on between you?'

Her hands clenched in frustration. 'For God's sake! Isn't that what I just *said*?'

'Sorry. Just checking. The afternoon you made a bit of an idiot of yourself . . .'

'An awful lot of an idiot of myself.' In fact, actually admitting it out loud felt quite cathartic.

'OK, but was it a Sunday afternoon?'

Sally nodded and gritted her teeth, cringing at the memory. The ridiculous thing was, she no longer even thought about Lola's dad. The crush had died as quickly as it had sprung up, almost as if subconsciously she'd always known it would never turn into anything more. 'Yes, it was a Sunday. Lola was working. You were off out somewhere.'

'And you and Nick were standing over there, by the window.' As he pointed, a glimmer of a smile appeared at the corners of Gabe's mouth for the first time in what felt like months.

'I suppose so. Yes.' Admittedly she'd been slightly the worse for drink at the time but not so far gone that she couldn't remember the way the winter sunlight had streamed through the window, lighting up the glints in Nick's dark hair . . . *oh!* The penny dropped. 'You were outside the flat!' Her mouth fell open. 'You were watching me make a prat of myself!'

'I didn't know you were making a prat of yourself. He had his arms around you.'

'He was keeping me upright. And I don't know if I ever mentioned this, but I've had a bit of a bad leg.' Sally couldn't believe what she was witnessing; before her very eyes Gabe was metamorphosing from the tetchy grump of the past few weeks back into the old sparkly-eyed *human* Gabe she'd missed so desperately since the evil twin had taken his place.

Chapter 51

'I thought you were shagging him.' Gabe's whole face had changed, cleared. He was smiling now with what appeared to be relief.

Glad the misunderstanding had been cleared up but mystified by the relief, Sally said, 'Is that why you've been so stroppy and weird?'

He hesitated, then nodded. 'You could say that.'

'All because you thought I was having a thing with Nick? Would Lola really have hated it that much?'

There was that old familiar smile again, as if he knew something she didn't. Shaking his hair out of his eyes, Gabe said, 'No idea.'

'But that's why you were so iffy.'

A longer pause this time. Much longer. Finally he raked his hair back with his fingers.

'Actually, that wasn't why I was . . . *iffy*. I just didn't think you should be seeing him.'

'You didn't approve? Because of the age difference?' Sally hazarded. Blimey, who'd have thought it? 'But he's only twelve years older than me.'

Gabe grinned, shook his head and looked . . . well, to be honest she wasn't absolutely sure how he looked. If it had been anyone else she might have said embarrassed.

Finally he took a deep breath. 'OK, I can't quite believe I'm standing here saying this, but the reason I wasn't happy about it—'

'Not happy about it? Ha, that's an understatement!'

'Don't interrupt,' Gabe ordered. 'Let me get this out before I lose my nerve. The reason I was bloody furious about it was because I was . . . I was . . .'

Encouragingly Sally said, 'Spit it out.'

'Oh, for crying out loud, it was because I was jealous.' He threw both hands up in the air. 'There. Said it. Now you know.'

Sally stopped dead in her tracks. Surely not, *surely not* . . .

Gabe shrugged. 'Sorry.'

'Oh my God. Gabe! That explains so much,' Sally blurted out. 'I even guessed! I asked Lola and she said I was wrong, but I *knew*, right from the word go!'

'You did?' It was Gabe's turn to look stunned.

'I knew before I even met you.'

'What?'

'The whole tidiness thing.' She was triumphant. 'Dead give-away. Keeping everything neat and always nagging me to clear up my stuff. All that hassle about not leaving my plates on the carpet. Forever complaining when I forget to hang up the towels in the bathroom. It's so *obvious*.'

'You really think I'm gay?'

Flummoxed, Sally said, 'Isn't that what you're telling me?'

'*No*.' Gabe clutched his head, looking as if he was on the brink of tearing his hair out. His eyes, wide with disbelief, fixed on hers. The next moment he reached out and grabbed her.

Before Sally knew what was happening, she was being kissed. His warm mouth covered hers, her whole body was pressed against Gabe's, her skin was zinging like sherbet and . . . *cut*.

Just as abruptly as it had begun, the kiss ended. Gabe let her go and she was left standing there like a cartoon character, dazed and panting and with confusion in the form of giant question marks exploding out of her head.

'I can't believe you thought I was gay.' Gabe was breathing heavily too.

'But . . .'

'Oh shit, this is all going wrong. I thought I could do it but I can't.'

Before she could react, he was gone. The door of the flat slammed shut behind him and Sally heard his footsteps clattering down the staircase. She sank down onto the sofa and clutched her hands tightly together to stop them trembling. Her palms were damp too; desperate though she was for a glug of Pernod she knew the glass would slip through her fingers and crash to the floor.

OK, concentrate. Gabe had jumped to the wrong conclusion. And so had she. He wasn't gay, she was certainly convinced of that now. And if he wasn't jealous at the thought of Nick being involved with someone else, then it stood to reason that he had to be jealous at the thought of *her* seeing another man . . .

Shaking now, Sally replayed the incredible thought in her mind. But how could this be happening, exploding like a bomb in front of her with no warning at all?

And why was she feeling, amongst all the confusion and disbelief, as if it was something she'd been longing to happen for months?

But so secretly that she'd barely even acknowledged it, because it was simply *the* most unlikely scenario on the planet.

Sally wrapped her arms around her waist, rocking back and forth in order to think more clearly. Had she, deep down, been seriously attracted to Gabe since the first time she'd clapped eyes on him?

Yes.

Had she ever considered doing anything about it?

No.

Never.

Because it was like fancying George Clooney from afar. Millions of women did, it was an absolutely harmless pastime. But they also knew that if they happened to bump into George Clooney, the chances were that he probably wouldn't fancy the pants off them in return and pester them for a date.

And that was pretty much how it felt, inwardly acknowledging that Gabe was gorgeous and funny and pretty damn fanciable – if a bit over-zealous in the tidiness department.

However – and it was a big however – you didn't expect for a millisecond that anything would ever come of it because you knew so categorically you weren't Gabe's type.

Stumbling awkwardly to her feet, Sally headed for the chair over which he'd flung his leather jacket. Her heart flip-flopping like a landed fish, she felt in the inside pocket and pulled out his keys. His wallet and phone were in there too. He wasn't going to get far without them.

But she couldn't bear to sit here waiting for Gabe to come back. She had to find him before he had time to change his mind about her. Limping across to the window and flinging it open, Sally leaned out and searched the street below.

It was one thirty in the morning and there was no one in

Radley Road. How much of a start had he got on her? Lifting her head, she called out, 'Gabe,' as loud as she dared. Then, louder still, '*Ga-aaaaaabe,*' like a lone wolf howling in the forest.

After a few seconds she heard a window being thrown open somewhere close by and a male voice bellow, 'Shut the fuck up.'

But it was OK, it didn't matter, because the voice didn't belong to Gabe. (That *would* have spoiled the moment.) Sally reached for her walking stick and hurried out of the flat. Where was Gabe? It was a cold night and all he was wearing was jeans and an old polo shirt. Clunk-step, clunk-step went the stick against the stairs, interspersed with the sound of her rapid breathing. Then halfway down the staircase she saw the outline of a figure in the shadows, a scruffily dressed figure with messy hair leaning against the far wall of the darkened hallway.

Sally abruptly stopped. Now that she'd found him she didn't know what to say. 'I heard the front door. I thought you'd left.'

Gabe shook his head. 'I was going to. Then I realised I didn't have my keys.'

'Or your jacket. You'd have been cold.'

'That too.' The whites of his eyes gleamed in the darkness.

'You could have stayed upstairs,' said Sally.

'I couldn't. Too scared. I told you, I never expected to feel like this.'

'Me neither.'

She saw him nod. 'Bit of a shock?'

'Quite a lot of a shock.' Gathering her courage, Sally said, 'But a nice one.'

He was watching her carefully. 'Really?'

'Really. I thought I drove you mad. That's why I've been trying so hard to be tidier.'

This time she caught a flash of white teeth. 'I thought you were doing it to impress Lola's dad.'

Sally shook her head, wondering if he could hear the frantic thud-thud-thud of her heart from down there. 'No, not him. You.'

'I'm impressed.'

'Well, don't be. It's not going to last.' Sally felt it was only fair to warn him. 'I gave it my best shot but the novelty's wearing off.' She paused. 'Is that going to make a difference?'

'I don't know. Not if you're moving up to Yorkshire.'

How could everything change so drastically in a matter of minutes?

'I suppose I don't have to move up to Yorkshire. Seeing as the main reason I was planning on doing it was to get away from the miserable old git I was sharing a flat with.'

Gabe stepped out of the shadows, came to stand at the foot of the staircase. He touched his chest. 'Me?'

'Yes, you.' Feeling braver, Sally said, 'Come here.'

He climbed the stairs separating them. This time she knew he was going to kiss her. What she hadn't expected was for her trembling knees to give way, mid-kiss. Smiling broadly, Gabe gently lowered her onto the stairs and carried on kissing her. God, he was so good at it and his neck smelled so gorgeous, he was . . . *whoops* . . .

The walking stick she'd left propped against the banister toppled over and went clattering down the staircase. Sally squeaked, 'Oh no!' and attempted to muffle her laughter against Gabe's shoulder.

Gabe whispered, 'Don't worry, he's asleep.'

He wasn't. The door to the ground floor flat was wrenched open and Mr Kowalski, his white hair standing up like a cockatiel, bent down and picked up the walking stick. He turned, in his green and white striped flannel pyjamas, and eyed Sally and Gabe balefully.

'You two! Vot arr you doing, huh? Making sex on ze stairs in ze mittle of ze night?'

'Sorry, Mr Kowalski. Didn't mean to wake you.' Gabe grinned apologetically. 'We weren't . . . um, making sex on the stairs.'

'Ha. Pretty close, if you ask me.' Shaking his head, the old man skilfully threw the stick up to them, Gene Kelly style.

Equally skilfully Gabe caught it. 'Thanks.'

'Off, off you go! You make sex in your own beds and leave me to sleep in mine.' Having gestured extravagantly at the ceiling he shuffled back into his flat muttering, 'Too much noise, too much sex, *tuh.*'

Sally buried her face in Gabe's chest.

'Sounds good to me,' Gabe murmured, standing and helping her to her feet.

By the time they reached the flat, Sally was light-headed with lust, dizzy with joy and minus her shoes. As Gabe lifted her into his arms to carry her through to the bedroom, his mobile burst into life.

He shook his head. 'Don't worry, just leave it.'

Fretfully, Sally said, 'I hate not answering a phone.'

'It's not your phone.'

As well as ringing, the mobile was switched to vibrate. When Sally had taken it from his jacket pocket she'd left it, along with his keys, on the glass coffee table. Now it was buzzing and jiggling ever closer to the edge.

'It's going to fall, it's going to fall off, I hate it when that happens.' Sally flapped her free hand agitatedly and Gabe, still carrying her, veered back across the living room.

She scooped up the phone and answered it. 'Yes?'

'Oh hi, it's Maurice, is Gabe there?'

'Hi, Maurice.' Sally knew this was one of Gabe's fellow paps. 'I'm afraid Gabe has his hands full at the moment. Can I give him a message?'

'Right, sure. The thing is, I'm down in Brighton at the moment but I've just heard from a reliable source that George Clooney was spotted twenty minutes ago sneaking into a house in Notting Hill with a classy-looking redhead. Nobody else knows about it and I owe Gabe a favour so I thought he might like a chance at an exclusive. The address is 15 Carmel Villas.'

'OK, got that.' Sally's heart sank; what rotten timing. 'Thanks, Maurice, I'll tell him. Bye.'

'George Clooney?' said Gabe, who had been listening in. 'Mystery redhead? Notting Hill?'

'Fifteen Carmel Villas.' It was the perfect tip-off; Carmel Villas was less than a minute away on foot. When she'd been leaning out of the living room window just now yelling Gabe's name, George might actually have heard her. He might even have been the one who'd yelled at her to shut the fuck up. No, surely not, George would never be that rude.

'Put me down,' said Sally. 'You have to go.'

But Gabe was shaking his head, grinning that devil-may-care, easy-going grin she hadn't seen for so long. 'No I don't.'

'Gabe. You can't miss a chance like this.'

'Switch the phone off. Stop thinking about George Clooney.' Kicking open the door to his immaculate bedroom, Gabe said, 'Just this once, why don't we let the man have his fun without being interrupted?'

He was about to lower her onto the crisp, spotless, geometrically aligned white duvet. Sally, her arms entwined around his neck, whispered, 'I'm warning you, I'm going to make your bed awfully untidy.'

Gabe's eyes softened as they sank down together. 'I'm counting on it.'

Chapter 52

Sometimes you went away for a couple of days and it felt like a couple of days. Other times you went away for a couple of days and when you got back everything was different.

Lola felt as if she'd been away for a year.

'What's going on?' She walked into Gabe's flat and saw the look on Sally's face. Total, *total* giveaway.

'What?' Sally half laughed in that way people do when they're trying so hard to appear innocent.

'Hey, you're back!' Gabe, emerging from the kitchen with a tea towel slung over one shoulder and a cold beer in his hand, said with delight, 'Come here,' and gave her a smacking kiss on the cheek.

Ha, confirmation if any was needed. He'd been like a bear with a sore brain for weeks. And now he was kissing her. What's more, the atmosphere in the room was positively zingy.

'We've missed you,' Gabe went on cheerfully – and he definitely hadn't been cheerful for weeks. 'How did the book thing go?'

'Great.' Lola indicated the bag she was carrying, emblazoned with the name of the publishing company that had hosted the event. 'They gave me lots of books. I was just asking Sal what's going on.'

'Hmm? In what way?' Now it was Gabe's turn to look innocent, like a six-year-old being asked what had happened to the last Jaffa cake.

'You and Sally,' said Lola. She narrowed her eyes at the pair of them. 'Shagging.'

'Oh my God!' Sally let out a shriek of disbelief. 'How did you know? How can you *tell*?'

'OK, three reasons. One,' Lola counted on her fingers, 'Gabe's stopped being a miserable old git. Two, you look so sparkly there's only one thing that can have caused *that*.'

'Sparkly? Do I really?' Sally rushed over to the mirror.

'And three, I just bumped into Mr Kowalski on his way out to the paper shop. He happened to mention you'd been making sex on ze stairs.'

'Oh *bum*!' wailed Sally. 'We wanted to tell you ourselves.'

'If you hadn't woken up poor Mr Kowalski, you could have.'

'OK, but we weren't actually doing it, not out there on the stairs. I just accidentally dropped my stick.'

Ha, not to mention her knickers! Lola was still struggling to take in the news, but in all honesty not as stunned as she could have been. It was one of those scenarios that was so bizarre it made sense, so wrong it was almost right. Hadn't she wondered from the word go whether Sally and Gabe would be drawn to each other, if they found each other physically attractive but were so at loggerheads that they simply couldn't bring themselves to admit it?

'I know what you're thinking,' said Gabe. 'But I'm crazy about her.'

'She'll drive you mad,' said Lola.

'Probably. OK, definitely.' He slid an arm around Sally's waist. 'But she's been doing that since the day she moved in. I'm used to it now.'

'She's never going to be tidy,' Lola warned.

'We're going to hire a cleaner.' Sally was glowing with happiness.

Gabe grinned. 'Isn't it great?'

What choice did she have? If it worked out, of course it was great. Lola knew she should be thrilled for them and on one level she was. But at the same time, and she was deeply ashamed to have to admit it even to herself, there was that niggling worry that the balance of the relationship between the three of them was about to tip. Before, the triangle had been more or less equal. Now it was changing shape, lengthening, drawing two of the points closer together and distancing the third. She was going to feel left out and unwanted and – oh God – *lonely* . . .

'Are you worried that we won't have time for you any more?' Effortlessly reading her mind, Gabe let go of Sally and gave Lola a reassuring hug. 'There's no need, we won't abandon you.'

'Don't be daft, of course I wasn't worried. We're all grown-ups.' Lola submitted happily to the hug; how could she have thought everything wouldn't be fine? 'Ooh, that reminds me, I just saw a sign outside the King's Head – that comedian you love is doing a show there on Saturday night. Johnny thingummy? I thought we could all go.'

She felt Gabe hesitate. Sally exclaimed, 'Oh, what a shame, we'd have loved to, but . . .' She pulled a face and looked over at Gabe to help her out, as if Lola were a child asking how babies got made.

'The thing is, we kind of decided to fly over to Dublin,' said

Gabe. 'And we can't really cancel now that the plane tickets have been booked.'

'And the hotel.' Sally shrugged apologetically.

Gabe said, 'But how about if we book another ticket? Then you can come along too.'

Zooouuuup, that was the sound of the triangle lengthening, like Pinocchio's nose. OK, it hadn't really made a noise but they all knew it was there.

'Thanks,' Lola shook her head, 'but I'll be fine.'

Of course she would. It didn't matter. She was happy for them, she really was. At the moment Gabe and Sally were besotted with each other but after a while the icky-yicky lovey-doveyness would wear off and they'd slide back to normality.

'You can at least stay for dinner.' Gabe was presuasive, eager to make amends. 'I'm doing a cannelloni.'

Lola smiled, because the last thing they really wanted was a gooseberry sitting at the table. 'It's OK, I've just eaten. And I'm shattered – all I really want is a shower and an early night.'

Which was probably top of their agenda too.

The following evening Nick came round to Lola's flat after work. She was just telling him about Gabe and Sally when there was a tap at the door.

'Hi, come in.' Nick, answering it because he was closest, grinned at Sally and said, 'Congratulations, I've just been hearing your news.'

'Th-thanks.' Sally tucked her hair behind her ears and looked flustered. 'Um, Lola, about this weekend.'

'Is something wrong?' Had their flights been cancelled after all?

Sally shook her head. 'No, no, it's just that I thought you might be at a bit of a loose end and Doug just called. His company's taken a table at another of those charity dinners and he wanted to know if we'd like to go along. Of course we can't make it because we'll be in Dublin, but I wondered if you'd be interested.' Sally looked pleased with herself, as if presenting the answer to a single girl's prayers and solving Lola's abandonment issues in one fell swoop.

Lola shook her head, funnily enough not even remotely tempted. Being at a bit of a loose end was one thing, but was any end really that loose? 'No thanks.'

'Oh, go on. It's at the Savoy! On Saturday night!' Sally's eyes were bright, her tone cajoling. 'And there isn't a quiz this time, so you don't have to worry about showing yourself up.'

Up until a few weeks ago, Lola knew, she would have leapt at the chance to spend an evening in the same room as Dougie. Just breathing the same air and being able to gaze adoringly at him across the dinner table would have been enough.

But that had been then, when she'd still had hope, and this was now. Besides, Dougie would be there with Isabel doing the adoring bit at his side, leaving her, Lola, stuck at the far end of the table with the unfriendly know-alls who didn't see why they should waste their time being polite to the brainless bigmouth who'd messed up the question about George Eliot and single-handedly lost them the New Year's Eve quiz.

Phew, when you put it like that . . .

'Well?' Sally was still doing her bright-eyed persuasive thing. 'Wouldn't it be fun?'

'I don't think it would be much fun at all. In fact I'd rather boil my own head.'

At Stansted airport on Friday evening Sally walked straight past W. H. Smith.

'Are you ill?' said Gabe.

'Why?'

'You didn't go in.' He waved an arm at the lit-up, colourful displays.

'There's nothing I need.' She held up her bottle of water, patted her lilac leather handbag.

'But . . . you haven't got any magazines.'

'You noticed.' Sally looked pleased. 'I decided I was reading too many. It's time to stop.' Proudly she said, 'I'm going cold turkey.'

Gabe kissed her. 'What will you do on the plane?'

Sally grinned and kissed him back. 'Thought we might join the mile-high club.'

But when they boarded the flight there were loads of nuns on the plane, which acted as a bit of a contraceptive. Instead, as they flew over the Irish Sea, Gabe found his attention caught by the magazine being read by a middle-aged woman sitting further up the plane. For a split second as she'd opened the magazine he thought he'd glimpsed a photograph that . . . except no, it couldn't be.

Frustratingly the woman was now engrossed in an article about celebs with cellulite and wasn't allowing him to get another look at the photo on the cover.

'Who are you ogling?' Sally's nudge almost sent Gabe tumbling into the aisle.

He pointed. 'No one. Just trying to see what that woman's reading.'

'Hey, I'm the addict around here. Thanks for being so helpful.' Leaning past him, Sally peered along the aisle. 'It's about cellulite. One of those things where they show you photos of people's legs and bottoms then point out the dodgy bits with whopping great arrows in case we're too stupid to know what we're meant to be looking at.'

'OK.'

Proudly – and loudly – Sally whispered, 'I don't have cellulite.'

God, he loved her so much. Gabe gave her knee a squeeze. 'I know.'

Thirty minutes later, as they were queuing to get off the plane, Gabe reached down to pick up the abandoned magazine.

'Ga-abe, you're worse than me,' Sally protested behind him. 'Put it down and step *away* from the magazine. I can't believe you're doing this. You never used to be interested.'

'I just want to know who took one of the photos.' He turned over the magazine and saw with a jolt that he hadn't been mistaken. There on the cover, staring up at him, was Savannah.

More to the point, it was one of the photographs *he had taken of her*. Bald and proud, smiling bravely. No Hair, No Shame! announced the headline, above the quote: 'This is me, take me or leave me.'

'Oh my God,' Sally let out a shriek of disbelief. 'That's Savannah Hudson! What happened to her *hair*?' She seized the magazine and flicked through it until she found the article inside. 'She's had alopecia for ages and was too ashamed to admit it!' Skimming the page at the speed of light she said breathlessly, 'She's been wearing a wig for almost two years and no one ever guessed. She felt ugly and thought people would laugh at her . . . oh bless! . . . then she met someone who gave her the confidence to . . . oops, sorry.'

The queue was moving. Sally was being jostled along the aisle by an impatient nun. Gabe, his heart quickening, said, 'Does it say who?'

'Hmm? Um . . . no, no name, she's being discreet. Probably one of the actors from her last film.' There was a rustle of pages behind him, then Sally said suddenly, 'Bloody hell!'

He braced himself. 'What?'

'I don't believe it!'

They'd reached the front of the plane; it was time to smile and thank the air hostess before disembarking via the metal staircase. The lively Irish wind was busy riffling the pages of the magazine and plastering Sally's hair to her freshly applied lipstick, but Gabe knew she was still bursting to share her startling discovery. Savannah must have given the game away. Aloud he said, 'You don't believe what?'

Sally clattered down the steps, leaning on her stick and shaking her head incredulously. 'Savannah Hudson's hair. Not her real hair, obviously, because she hasn't got any. But that blond wig she's been wearing. It cost seven thousand pounds!'

Savannah hadn't given the game away. When they reached baggage reclaim Gabe read through the article himself.

'Why are you so interested?' Sally rested her head against his shoulder.

'I snapped her a while back, at a premiere in Leicester Square. Just wondered who'd done the photo session.' His name hadn't been printed; there was no byline. But pride still surged up because these were *his* photographs. And they looked great.

'Oh sweetie, someone a bit more famous than you.' Sally gave him a consoling hug. 'Never mind, maybe one day you'll be doing proper photos too.'

Gabe half smiled, because there was no point in taking offence. It was the truth; half the people he photographed were prepared to tolerate him briefly, to spare him a few seconds as they emerged from a restaurant or paused on their way along the red carpet. The other half covered their faces or ran off in the opposite direction the moment they clapped eyes on him. It was fantastic that Savannah had used the photos he'd taken of her, but disappointing that she couldn't have given him the credit. Especially as she had promised he could be the one to take the shots of her big 'reveal'.

Gabe shrugged. Oh well, that was life. He'd hurt her feelings; what did he expect?

'It's so brave of her,' Sally was still gazing at the photo. 'I mean, she's Savannah Hudson. Poor thing, she looked amazing with hair. It must be awful to lose it.'

Gabe felt compelled to defend her. 'She still looks good.'

'Pretty good,' Sally conceded, tilting her head as she traced the outline of Savannah's ears. 'But you have to admit, these stick out a bit. A drop of Superglue might have helped. She does look a bit like a wing nut.'

Chapter 53

Nick stood by the mirrored doors at the entrance to the Savoy's Lancaster Ballroom. Everyone had enjoyed an excellent dinner and the babble of voices was deafening. Scanning the room, he spotted Doug Tennant at one of the circular tables close to the stage. Presumably those around him were the work colleagues who had given Lola such a hard time on New Year's Eve.

Nick weighed up the situation. Should he be doing what he was about to do?

Sod it, why not?

Doug was leaning to one side, laughing at something the girl next to him had just said, when he saw Nick making his way towards the table. Recognising him at once, Doug straightened and said, 'Hello there. On your own tonight?'

'Yes.'

Doug raised an eyebrow and smiled slightly. 'Don't tell me your daughter's got you following me now.'

'Is that what you think? Not at all,' said Nick. 'She doesn't even know I'm here.' The blonde girl at his side must be Isabel; oh well, couldn't be helped. Keeping his tone light, he went on, 'Anyway, she's given up on you. You had your chance and you blew it. It's your loss. I just hope you don't live to regret it.'

'Excuse me.' An older woman who'd only just begun paying attention put down her wine glass and demanded, 'What's going on? Who *is* this man?'

'My name's Nick James.' If this was one of Doug's employees she was knocking on a bit. 'My daughter knows Doug. I just came over to say hello, and to tell him that in my view he's made a big mistake. Sorry,' Nick added, addressing the girl at Doug's side, 'but it's something that needed to be said. I can't help myself; I think she's had a rum deal.'

'Doug?' The older woman was sitting there, stiff-backed like a judge, clearly dissatisfied with the answer. 'Who's this person talking about?'

Doug said flatly, 'Lola.'

'What? Oh, for heaven's sake!' The woman stared at Nick in disbelief. 'You're the father?'

Instantly Nick realised his mistake. 'I am. And you're Doug's mother. How very nice to meet you at last.'

They both knew he didn't mean it. Adele Nicholson looked as if she'd swallowed a pickled chilli. 'And you seriously think my son made a mistake?'

Nick flashed her his most charming smile. 'I do.'

'The only mistake he made was getting himself involved with your daughter in the first place,' Adele flashed back. 'Do you *know* what that girl did to him?'

'Yes, I know exactly what she did. And she made a mistake too, I'm not denying that. But she had her reasons. My point is, we all make mistakes,' said Nick, 'but there's such a thing as forgiveness. I made a huge mistake twenty-eight years ago, but Lola's forgiven me. So has her mother. And we're all here

384

tonight for the same reason. To help people who've made mistakes.' Noting the look of incomprehension on Adele's carefully made-up face he picked up one of the glossy embossed programmes from the table. 'This is a charity dinner in aid of the Prince's Trust. Some of the money raised this evening will go to help former prisoners who are being rehabilitated into the community.'

Adele clearly hadn't thought this through, had only come tonight because of the royal connection. She now looked as if she'd swallowed a frog.

'Anyway, lecture over. It seems that some people are more easily forgiven than others. I'll leave you in peace.' Nick looked at Doug. 'As I've already said, Lola's accepted that you aren't interested and she's moving on. Personally, I still think you're making a mistake. I may not have known Lola for long but she's an amazing girl, loyal and generous, one of a kind. And I'm proud to be her father.' He paused then said evenly, 'One last thing. I wonder if you've ever asked yourself why she needed that money?'

Nobody spoke. Up on the stage the MC was preparing to introduce the band.

Nick nodded fractionally at Doug. 'I'll leave you to enjoy the rest of the evening. Bye.'

He was upstairs in the bar when Doug appeared beside him twenty minutes later.

'I thought you'd left,' said Doug.

'Just had to get away from that bloody awful music. Not my thing.' Nick signalled to the barman. 'Can I get you a drink?'

'Scotch and water. Thanks. I was rude earlier,' Doug dipped his head, 'and I apologise. I shouldn't have made that remark about Lola sending you here to follow me. That was below the belt.'

'Look,' said Nick, 'I love my daughter to bits, but I can admit that she's done her fair share of chasing after you. Up until a few weeks ago she might well have tried that trick. But it's over now.' He paused, paid for the drinks and said, 'I'm sorry too. It probably wasn't very sensitive of me to say all that stuff in front of everyone.'

Doug smiled slightly, shrugged it off. 'Never mind. It's this business with the money that I'm interested in.'

Thought you might be.

'Did you ever ask Lola why she took it?' said Nick.

'Of course I did. She said she couldn't tell me.' Doug waited, took a sip of his drink, then said with a trace of impatience, 'Well? I'm assuming she told you.'

'No. I asked her but there was no way of getting it out of her. She said she was sorry, but she could never tell me.'

'Same here.' Doug looked disappointed; he'd clearly thought he'd been about to find out the truth.

'Sorry. But something interesting happened last week. You know Lola never *ever* wanted her mother to find out about the money thing?' Nick waited for Doug to nod before proceeding. 'Well, Blythe *did* find out about it. You can imagine how shocked she was. She even called me to tell me about it. She couldn't believe Lola had done such a terrible thing to you.'

'And?' Doug was gazing at him intently.

After a pause, Nick said, 'Blythe asked Lola what she'd spent the money on and Lola told her. A fancy Jeep, apparently. Which was stolen a week later. She hadn't insured it, so that was it, the money was gone.'

'Really? A Jeep?' Doug frowned.

'That's the story.' Nick held his gaze for a long moment before knocking back his Scotch in one go. 'Think about it,' he added, ready to leave and wondering if Doug Tennant was smart enough – *surely* – and cared enough – *hopefully* – to work it out. 'Then ask yourself whether you think the story Lola told her mother was the truth.'

Chapter 54

Going cold turkey was proving harder than Sally had imagined. This was a magazine habit they were talking about, after all, not crack cocaine.

Oh, but she had a long-standing habit to kick and she badly missed turning those glossy, exciting-smelling, brand new pages. She was doing her best to keep herself entertained instead with a copy of *Pride and Prejudice* lent to her by Lola but it just wasn't doing the trick. Apart from anything else the pages weren't glossy and there was no mention in it anywhere of *Coronation Street*. What's more, the print was so tiny she had to screw up her eyes to read it, which made her realise she was probably on the verge of needing reading glasses which in turn made her feel *old*.

'Oh shut *up*,' Sally wailed at the TV as an advert for the latest edition of *Heat* came on. Chucking *Pride and Prejudice* at the screen only caused the craving to intensify.

She tried changing channels and folding her arms. Oh yes, great help. OK, but how about if she didn't *buy* a new magazine, just had a little look through an old one instead? That would take the edge off the cravings, wouldn't it? Except she'd have to contain herself until she got to work and nabbed one of the tatty old germ-laden cast-offs in the waiting room and she wasn't working this afternoon . . . oh now, hang on, unless there were still a couple lurking around here somewhere that had managed to escape the cull . . .

A light bulb went on inside Sally's head and she launched herself off the sofa. Because the sofa was the answer! In the bad old days when she'd been forced to tidy up at a moment's notice, as much excess mess as humanly possible had been *squashed* into that narrow space between sofa and carpet. Furthermore, because out of sight was *completely* out of mind, it had never occurred to her to clear the stuff out.

And thank goodness for that! On her hands and knees Sally peered into the dark gap and saw shoes, empty crisp packets, plates, socks, one of her all-time favourite devoré velvet scarves – yay! – and, oh joy, a scrumpled-up magazine. She reached under the sofa for it, stretching her fingers to the limit—

'What are you doing?'

Sally paused, bottom up in the air. 'Just looking for my pink scarf.' She dragged it out, said triumphantly, 'And here it is! Why, what are you doing?'

'Admiring the view.' Gabe grinned and gave her bottom a pat. 'I'm off for a shower, got an appointment with a Page Three girl in Hyde Park.'

'Lucky you. Will she be naked?'

'Clothes on. Her agent set it up; it's for a snatch pose. Which is *not* what it sounds like.' He gave her a look as she started to snigger. 'It means you use a long lens and make the shots look as if they've been snatched from a distance. The girl's going to have a huge fight with her boyfriend at eleven o'clock on the bridge over the Serpentine. If it rains, we'll shoot it in the café.'

Sally smiled and watched Gabe disappear into the bathroom. The moment the door closed behind him she was burrowing back under the sofa for the magazine . . . *reeeeach* . . . oh dear, was this the equivalent of someone who's given up cigarettes scrabbling about in the gutter for somebody else's abandoned dog end?

She fell on the magazine with a cry of relief. Dog-eared and battered it may be, but it was only a few weeks old. Still kneeling on the floor, Sally lovingly turned the pages. There was an interview with Nicole Kidman about her latest film. Kate Moss was wearing purple micro shorts and pink polka-dotted Wellingtons – as you do – as she shopped in Knightsbridge. Leonardo di Caprio was photographed playing volleyball on the beach, here was the montage of cellulite shots, there the snaps of unshaven armpits, the soapstars making holy shows of themselves at a party after an awards ceremony. OK, it wasn't intellectual but it was entertaining and during her darker days she'd drawn huge comfort from knowing that even super-glamorous celebrities could have disastrous love lives too. Not that this applied to her now, ta dah, she no longer needed to surround herself with other people's misery because she had Gabe and he was everything she'd ever— oh.

Sally's stomach clenched with recognition as she turned a page and the envelope dropped out of the magazine into her lap. So that was what had happened to it during her fit of frenzied tidying the other week.

She put down the magazine and examined the envelope with Gabe's name on it. In one way it was nice to have the mystery of its disappearance solved. But it also presented her with a dilemma because she'd never actually mentioned the letter to Gabe.

The temptation was to rip it to shreds and stuff it in the

bottom of the kitchen bin. After first reading it, naturally. She knew it was from a female, and that around the time of its delivery Gabe had been in a seriously iffy mood. There was a distinct possibility that the non-arrival of the letter could have had something to do with that.

Tear it up.

Read it first.

No, just tear it up and throw it away, it's better not to know.

OK, stop, *stop*. Sally closed her eyes. She loved Gabe and that meant she had to be honest with him.

Fear beat like a bird inside her chest. Over the years, being honest hadn't always come naturally to her. As she pushed open the bathroom door it crossed her mind that this could be the last time she saw his body naked. And she'd only just got to know it. Oh God, could she do this?

'Gabe?' She opened the shower cubicle an inch, experienced a little frisson of lust at the sight of him and said, 'I've got something for you.'

Steam billowed out of the cubicle. Gabe turned, shampoo streaming down his face as he rinsed his hair. With a grin he opened the door wider and in one movement pulled her into the shower. The next moment she was minus her sodden dressing gown. 'That's a coincidence,' he said playfully, 'I've got something for you too.'

Honestly, what a wasted opportunity; if she'd taken the envelope in with her, the ink would have run and the letter would have been rendered illegible, neatly solving all her problems in one go.

Except she hadn't thought of that, had she? Instead, like a complete durr-brain, she'd dropped it onto the tiled floor as Gabe was yanking her into the shower. And here it was, patiently waiting for them when they eventually emerged, twenty highly pleasurable minutes later.

'OK, don't be cross with me.' Sally retrieved the envelope and handed it to him. 'This arrived a couple of weeks ago, then it went missing. And that was your fault because you made me tidy the flat.' She kissed him hard on the mouth. 'I just found it under the sofa inside a magazine.'

Gabe, who found her self-imposed ban hilarious, said affectionately, 'Not that you'd ever look inside one of those.'

'I lapsed. I'm only human. Anyway, read your letter.' Grabbing a white bath towel and wrapping it around herself, Sally hastily left the bathroom.

Mystified, Gabe shook back his hair then opened the envelope. The letter was handwritten in turquoise ink.

Dearest Gabe,

I deleted your number from my phone to stop myself from becoming your nuisance caller, hence this letter.

Well, I've decided the time has come to show the world the real me. And I want to use the photos you took. Hope that's OK with you. If you want me to give you the credit and a byline, get in touch. If I don't hear from you I'll be discreet and won't use your name. I shall also donate the fee for the article and your photos to Alopecia UK.

All love

Sav

xxx

Gabe smiled and wondered how much money he'd missed out on. He could have used it to leave the papping life behind him and start afresh in a studio . . . Oh well, never mind, too late to worry about it now. The charity wouldn't be too thrilled if he were to ring them and demand his share of the fee back. And in time he would set up on his own, specialising in portrait photography. At least Savannah had made the effort to contact him, which was good of her.

He was glad she'd thought of him.

Sally was outside the bathroom, waiting for him and visibly bracing herself. 'Well?'

She'd probably had her ear pressed up against the door. 'It's fine. Nothing important.'

He saw her exhale. 'Really? Oh thank God. You're not cross that I didn't tell you?'

Gabe shook his head. 'No.'

Sally hugged him. 'Sorry. I love you.' She leaned back, gazing into his eyes. 'You're sure it's OK?'

'I love you too.' Kissing her, Gabe said, 'And I'm sure. It was just someone wanting me to take a few photos of them. I'd probably have said no anyway.'

'Girlie handwriting.'

'That would be because it was written by a girl.'

'Pretty?'

'Yes.'

'Girlfriend of yours?' Sally ventured.

Had Savannah ever really been his girlfriend? Not if he was honest. Gabe shook his head. 'No, just a friend. And I won't be hearing from her again now.'

'Well, good. Especially if she's pretty.' Sally eyed the letter folded in his hand. 'Can I read it?'

'Why? Don't you trust me?' Then, when she hesitated, 'Look, I know you've had a rotten time with men in the past, but I'm not like them.'

'I know.'

Gabe held up the letter. 'Here, you can read it if you want.'

Sally visibly relaxed. 'It's OK. I don't need to. You can throw it away.'

'Trust me?'

'I trust you.'

Gabe softened. Slowly but surely he would convince her that he'd never let her down, that she was the most important person in his life. Dropping the letter into the loo, he pulled the flush and said, 'Good.'

Chapter 55

Lola was on the shop floor rebuilding a display of cookery books that had been casually demolished by a student's backpack. As she balanced Delia on top of Jean-Christophe Novelli – ha, it was all right for some – a woman with a bag-laden pushchair came racing into the shop. Flustered and clearly in a state of panic she rushed up to Lola. 'Excuse me, do you have a loo?'

The boy lolling in the pushchair glanced up at Lola, typical male, sublimely unconcerned by the problems he was causing. Feeling sorry for the woman – this was the joys of motherhood for you – Lola said, 'Yes, over there to the left of the biographies, right at the back of the shop.'

The perspiring woman gasped, 'Thanks so much,' picked up the carton of fruit juice her son had just chucked to the ground and yanked the pushchair to the left. 'Come on, Tom, let's go.'

Before she could scoot him away, the little boy beamed up at Lola and said in a loud, conspiratorial voice, 'Mummy's got to do a *big* poo.' Which hugely entertained everyone else in the vicinity. Sniggers abounded as the poor mortified woman scurried off. Normally an event like this would have made Lola's day. Instead she carried on propping up books.

'Are you all right?' Cheryl arrived with another box of hard-backs to add to the display.

'I think I need something to look forward to.' Lola's stomach rumbled as she said it. Checking her watch and realising it was twelve fifteen, she said impulsively, 'Like a really nice lunch. How about coming with me to Rossano's? My treat.'

But Cheryl was already looking awkward and shaking her head. 'Today? Sorry, can't make it. I've got an appointment.'

'Oh.' Why didn't that sound believable – apart from the fact that Cheryl was the world's most feeble liar?

'Sorry! But some other time, definitely!'

Lola nodded. 'Who's your appointment with?'

'Um . . . a doctor.'

Well, how about that? Untruthfuller and untruthfuller. Lola looked concerned. 'Are you ill?'

'N-no.'

'Pregnant?'

'No!'

This was fascinating. Her assistant manager was by this time the colour of a plum.

'I think I can guess,' said Lola. 'It's Botox.'

Cheryl's shoulders sagged with relief. 'Yes, Botox.'

'The time has come and you're giving it a whirl.'

'Well, you know.' Cheryl touched her forehead. 'I've been getting a bit . . . *frowny* lately.

Lola nodded. 'I've noticed that too. Look, why don't I come along and hold your hand?'

Cheryl said hurriedly, 'Oh, there's no need, it's just a prelim-inary appointment to have a chat about it. I haven't made my mind up quite yet.'

One o'clock arrived and there was only one thing for it.

Lola left the shop first with a cheery, 'Good Luck!' and melted into the crowds of shoppers on the opposite side of the road. In all honesty, there was nothing like a spot of harmless sleuthing to cheer a girl up on a Tuesday lunchtime.

When Cheryl emerged from Kingsley's five minutes later she turned left and headed up Regent Street at quite a pace. Lola tucked the collar of her black coat up around her neck, as all the good spies do, and followed at a discreet distance. Cheryl had re-done her make-up and taken her hair out of its pony-tail. She was wearing a swingy white jacket over her red dress and the flat grey pumps she wore for work had been replaced with crimson high heels. She looked lovely. Any syringe-wielding medic would have been impressed. Relieved she hadn't flagged down a cab, Lola stayed on her tail as she plunged down a side street. With fewer people around she'd be spotted if Cheryl looked back, might have to pretend to be engrossed in the eye-popping display – yeek! – in the window of this Soho sex shop.

But Cheryl didn't look back. She carried on heading deeper into Soho. Finally reaching Wardour Street, she paused outside a super-chic, green and silver-fronted restaurant. Lola hung back, watching with interest as she ran up the steps and disappeared inside.

Well, this was interesting. Cheryl was without question meeting a man and chances were that his interest in her wasn't medical. ('Why, Doctor, is that a Botox syringe in your pocket or are you just pleased to see me?')

The big puzzle was, why was she being so evasive about it?

OK, only one way to find out.

'Good afternoon,' said the charming blonde receptionist. 'May I help you?' The interior of the restaurant was pale green and silver, modern and expensive-looking and curvy.

'Hi there, I'm supposed to be meeting my friend,' said Lola. 'Her name's Cheryl Dixon.'

'I'm sorry, madam, we don't have a booking in that name.'

'I know, I'm so sorry, I can't remember the name of the other person.' Lola smiled, determined to out-charm the receptionist, and attempted to sneak a look at the list of names on the computer screen. 'My friend just came in a minute ago, she's wearing red stilettos.'

The receptionist swiftly swung the computer screen around so Lola couldn't see it.

'Sorry, madam, if you don't have a booking . . .'

'Oh please, I have to see them, it's urgent . . . her car's being towed away . . .'

The receptionist's smile was now a thing of the past. 'But that's not actually true, is it?'

Blimey, what was this place, Fort Knox? The tables were situated in booths, which meant you couldn't see who was seated at them. At this rate the restaurant had to be harbouring the Pope out on a hot date with Cilla Black.

'OK, I need the loo,' said Lola.

'Madam, the cloakroom facilities are for customers only.'

Why was this girl being so *obstructive*? 'Sorry, but I need the loo now. It's an emergency.' Lola gazed at her then raised her voice slightly. 'I have to do a big poo.'

She watched the receptionist wondering if she meant it. After a second – because what if she *did*? – the blonde pointed the way. 'Over there, up the stairs and on the left.'

'Thanks.' Lola set off across the restaurant, peering into each booth as she passed and earning herself some odd looks along the way. No Pope so far. No Cheryl either.

Then she saw them. So wrapped up in each other they

didn't even notice her standing there. Stunned, Lola observed the giveaway body language going on between the two of them; if that wasn't full-blown flirtation she didn't know what was.

Hell's bells, and she hadn't even had the slightest *inkling* . . .

On the other hand, thank God it wasn't who she'd subconsciously been afraid it might be.

Cheryl spotted her first. Her face changed in an instant from lit up to *oh fuck*. She promptly knocked over her glass of wine.

'Hi, Cheryl. I wouldn't let him inject your frown lines if I were you. I'm not sure he's a qualified doctor.'

'You followed me!' Cheryl bat-squeaked, the familiar flush crawling up her neck.

'I had to. You wouldn't tell me who you were seeing. Hello, Dad.' Lola gave her father a hug. 'I tried to ring you on Saturday night to see if you wanted to go to the cinema but your phone was switched off.'

'Boring works do.' Nick kissed her on the cheek then regarded her with concern. 'Sorry about this. Are you upset?'

'About you and Cheryl? God no, it's fantastic! I just can't believe it. How long has this been going on?'

'A few weeks.' Luckily the spilled wine was white; Nick used a pale green napkin to mop it up.

'So that's why you've been coming into the shop to buy so many books. I thought you were doing it so you could see me!'

'Sweetheart, I was.' Nick grinned. 'You were the number one reason.' He paused. 'Cheryl was the unexpected bonus.'

Lola pulled up an extra chair and sat down. 'Now I know how the star of the show feels when the understudy gets more applause than she does.'

'Then I came in one day when you were off and we got chatting.'

'I told him how nice you were to work for,' Cheryl said hopefully.

'Anyway, there was a spark between us, so I asked her out. We had a great time and it's gone on from there.'

'And you just forgot to mention it to your only daughter.'

'We didn't know how you'd react,' said Cheryl.

'You make it sound as if you're scared of me.' Lola shook her head in disbelief.

Cheryl pulled a face. 'I am.'

'Madam?' A waiter materialised at the table with their menus. 'Are you joining your friends for lunch?'

Lola's stomach gurgled. She looked from her father to Cheryl then back again.

'Is that your stomach? Are you starving?' Nick squeezed her arm. 'Of course you're staying for lunch.'

Touched by the offer when it was so obvious they'd rather be alone together, Lola pushed back her chair. 'It's OK, I'll leave you to it. And don't worry, I think it's great that you're seeing each other.'

She honestly genuinely truthfully did. And not just because Cheryl was lovely and deserved someone nice after her pig of an ex-husband had abandoned her three years ago. Lola hugged them both and left them to enjoy their lunch in peace. What she couldn't admit to anyone was the sensation of icy fear she'd experienced on realising that Cheryl didn't want her to know who she was seeing.

Of course it seemed ridiculous now, but just for a while back there it had crossed her mind to wonder if it could have been Doug.

The blonde receptionist raised oh-so-polite, perfectly sculptured eyebrows as Lola sashayed past the desk. 'Better now, madam?'

The receptionist who was so perfect, naturally, that she'd never been to the loo in her life.

Lola nodded and beamed at her. 'Yes thanks. Much.'

Chapter 56

The woman placing the order rested threadbare elbows on the counter and said, 'It's the most marvellous book, you know. Called *When Miss Denby went to Devon*. By Fidelma Barlow. Have you heard of it?'

'Sorry, no, that one's passed me by.' Lola typed the details into the computer.

'Oh, it's unputdownable, an absolute joy! I can't understand why it isn't a *Sunday Times* bestseller. It deserves to be made into a film!' The woman nodded enthusiastically. 'Miss Denby would be a wonderful role for Dame Judi Dench.'

Lola checked the screen. 'Okaaay, yes, we can get that for you by Friday.'

'Lovely!' The woman's face lit up. 'Can I order fifty copies please?'

'Fifty! Gosh.' Maybe it was for a book club. Hesitating for a moment, Lola said, 'You have to pay for them in advance, I'm afraid.'

'Oh no, it's OK.' The woman shook her head. 'I don't want to pay for them.'

'I know it's a lot of money. But somebody has to.'

'But not me! I just want you to put them on the shelves. Make a nice display like you do with the Richard and Judy books. Right at the front of the shop,' the woman said helpfully, 'so that people will buy them.'

By the time Lola had finished explaining the niceties of stock ordering to a disappointed Fidelma Barlow, it was almost eight o'clock, kicking out time. Fidelma, shoulders drooping, left the shop. Lola, who knew just how she felt, dispiritedly straightened a pile of bookmarks and wondered if she could bear to go along to the party tonight that Tim and Darren had invited her to . . . except she already knew she couldn't, which meant she was now going to have to come up with a convincing reason why not.

The next moment she looked up and almost fell over. There, standing six feet away like an honest-to-goodness mirage, was Doug.

Lola's heart, which never listened to her head and hadn't yet learned to stop hoping, went into instantaneous clattery overdrive.

'Hello.' She clutched the computer for support. 'What's this? Is my mum on the telly again?'

Doug smiled slightly. 'No.'

'My dad then? On *Crimewatch*?'

'Haven't spotted him on *Crimewatch*. Maybe he was the one in the balaclava.' Tilting his head, Doug said, 'But you're half right. I am here because of your dad.'

'You are?' She hadn't been expecting him to say *that*.

'We had a chat on Saturday night.'

'*You did?*'

'He didn't mention it? OK, obviously not. Well, we were at the Savoy.'

Lola boggled. 'My dad was *there*?' So that was why his mobile had been switched off. And to think he could have come along to the cinema with her instead.

'Well, we didn't communicate by telepathy. He spoke to me about you. Quite forcefully, in fact.' Doug paused, then glanced over at a nervously hovering Darren who was waiting to empty the till. 'Sorry, could you just give us a couple of minutes?'

'Um, but I need to get the—'

'Darren?' Lola murmured the word out of the corner of her mouth. 'Go away.'

'OK.' Defeated, Darren slunk off.

'I was watching you with that woman just now. The one who wanted you to stock her book,' said Doug. 'You were really nice to her.'

'That's because I'm a really nice person. Believe it or not. And you were eavesdropping.'

'Not eavesdropping. Listening. Like I listened to your dad on Saturday night.' He waited, gazing directly into Lola's eyes. 'I know why you took that money when my mother offered it to you.'

'*What?*' Lola felt as if all the air had been vacuumed out of her lungs. How could he know that? It wasn't physically possible, it just wasn't.

Doug gave an infinitesimal shrug. 'OK, I don't know *exactly* why. But I do know it didn't have anything to do with a Jeep.'

'How? Why not?' Anxiety was now skittering around inside Lola's stomach like a squirrel.

'Because you told me you could never tell me the reason you needed the money. And that's what you said to your father too.' Doug tilted an eyebrow at her. 'But if the Jeep story was true, there's no reason why you couldn't have told us that. Therefore it stands to reason that it wasn't.'

Lola felt dizzy. This was like being cross-examined on the witness stand by a barrister a zillion times cleverer than you. In fact this might be a good moment to faint.

'So basically,' Doug continued, 'you needed the money for something that meant far more to you than a Jeep. It was also something you were determined your mother was never to find out about.' Pause. 'Well, there was only one other person on the planet who was that important to you back then.' Another longer pause. 'And that was your stepfather Alex.'

Lola's eyes filled with tears. She blinked and realised the shop was empty. No customers, no staff. Everyone had gone, miraculously disappeared. *Thank God.*

'I can't tell you.' Helplessly she shook her head. 'I just can't. I made a promise.'

'That's OK, I'm not asking you to. No digging.' Doug's voice softened. 'I know who you did it for. I don't need to know why. I didn't understand before, but I do now. That's enough. It's all in the past.'

Was this how Catholics felt when they were absolved of all sin and forgiven by God? Lola, who hated crying in front of people but seemed to have been doing a lot of it lately, could feel the tears rolling faster and faster down her face. She couldn't speak, only nod in a hopeless, all-over-the-place, nodding-doggy kind of way.

'You know, you've been pretty lucky as far as fathers go. First Alex, now Nick. He's so proud of you,' said Doug.

For heaven's sake, how was she supposed to stop crying if

he was going to come out with stuff like this? Blindly Lola nodded again and wiped her sleeve across her wet cheeks.

'And he certainly made me think,' Doug went on, 'when he told me I'd missed my chance with you.'

'He really said that?' Lola sniffed hard. This was the thing she'd forgotten about fathers; how much they loved to embarrass their daughters in public.

'And the rest. As if it hasn't been hard enough these past few months, reminding myself why I should be steering clear of you. Then along comes your father giving me all sorts of grief, *then* explaining to me why I should think again. That knocked me for six, I can tell you.'

As if it hadn't been hard enough these past few months? Slowly, desperate not to be getting this wrong, Lola said, 'So that night when you first saw me again at your mother's house . . . does that mean you didn't hate me after all?'

'Oh yes I did. With all my heart. Absolutely and totally.' Doug half smiled, causing her heart to lollop. 'But at the same time the old feelings were still there as well, refusing to go away. Like *you* were refusing to go away. It drove me insane having you back in my life, because I wasn't able to control the way I felt about you. I wanted to be indifferent, to see you and feel nothing. But I just couldn't. It wouldn't happen.' He tapped his temple. 'You were in here, whether I liked it or not.'

Lola was trembling now, almost but not quite sure that his coming here tonight was a very good thing. 'Like a tapeworm.'

He looked amused. 'You always did have a way with words.'

'Oh Dougie, all this time you've been hating me, I've been trying my best to change your mind.' The words came tumbling out in a rush. 'In the end I just had to give up, told myself to stop before I made a complete prat of myself . . . except I already *had*, over and over again . . .'

'I quite enjoyed those bits. I think watching you try to play badminton was my favourite.' He grinned, moved closer to the counter. 'I waited in the bar afterwards, but you didn't turn up.'

'In case you accused me of stalking you again.'

'I'm sorry. I haven't behaved very well either.' Ruefully Doug said, 'I've lied to you, for a start.'

'About what?'

'The photos of us when we were young. Of course I kept them. They're at home, hidden away in a cupboard,' his eyes glinted, 'along with my secret stash of Pot Noodles.'

'I knew it!' Triumphantly Lola said, 'Once a Pot Noodler, always a Pot Noodler. Did Isabel know about this?'

Ach, Isabel . . .

'What's wrong?' said Doug when she winced.

'Isabel. Your girlfriend.'

He relaxed. 'She isn't my girlfriend. I finished with her weeks ago. On the night of your dinner party, in fact.'

'What?'

'I smuggled away the photo album. By the time I'd finished looking through the old photos of us, I realised Isabel couldn't compete. I told her I couldn't see her any more and she handed in her notice.'

'Poor Isabel.' Lola did her best to sound as if she meant it.

'I gave her a great reference. She's working in Hong Kong now.' Dougie moved towards Lola. 'You don't know how close I came to ringing you that night.'

Lola remembered the wrong number and her reaction when the phone had begun to ring. 'I wanted you to. So much. Oh

407

Dougie . . .' It was no good; having a counter between them wasn't helping at all. She came out from behind it and threw herself into his arms.

Oh yes, this was where she was meant to be. It was all she'd ever wanted. As he kissed her – *at last* – she knew everything was going to be all right.

Despite the odd potential drawback.

When he'd finished kissing her, Dougie smiled and said, 'What are you thinking?'

'That this is one of the happiest moments of my life.' Lola stroked his hair. 'And that your mother's going to be absolutely furious when she hears about this.'

'Don't worry about my mother. After Dad died, she became over-protective of us. When she made you that offer she thought she was doing the right thing. But it's OK, I've had a chat with her. All she wants is for me to be happy, and she accepts that now. She'll be fine.'

God, he was a heavenly kisser; no one else even came close. And there was so much more fantastic stuff to look forward to. Double-checking that they were safely out of sight – the lights were still on in the store but from here no one walking past in the street could see them – Lola allowed her hands to start wandering in an adventurous fashion.

'What are you doing?'

'What I've been wanting to do for a long, long time.' She smiled playfully up at him. 'Ever got intimate in a bookshop before?'

Doug surveyed her with amusement. 'Is that a dare? Are you trying to shock me?'

Lola gazed into his dark eyes. Then, slowly and deliberately, she reached out and unfastened his belt.

'Shouldn't do that,' Dougie murmured, 'unless you're sure you've got the nerve to go through with it. From start to finish.' He trailed an index finger down her chest until he came to the top button of her shirt. It came undone, exposing the top of her lacy lilac bra.

'Are you calling me chicken?' Lola retaliated by pulling his shirt out of his trousers.

'I think you might lose your nerve.' Deftly he undid the next button on her shirt.

Trembling now, Lola struggled with the fastening on his trousers. 'I think you know me better than that. If I say I'm going to do something, I'll— *aaarrgh!*'

'Lola?' The door at the back of the shop opened and Tim poked his head round. 'Oh sorry!' His eyes popped as he realised what he was interrupting.

'I thought you'd all left!' Flustered, Lola clapped both hands over her exposed bra.

'Everyone else has. I'm just off now. I wondered if you'd made up your mind yet about coming along to the party.'

Hmm, have sex with Dougie or go to a party with Tim and Darren. That was a tricky one.

'Um . . . I don't think so, Tim. But thanks anyway.'

'OK.' Hardly knowing where to look, Tim backed away. 'Well, have a . . . nice time.'

Lola nodded and somehow managed to keep a straight face. When the door had closed behind Tim, she looked at Dougie and said, 'OK, now I've lost my nerve.'

'Thank God for that.' Doug smiled his crooked smile and tucked his shirt back into his trousers.

'So, your flat or mine?'

He raised an eyebrow. 'I have Pot Noodles.'

Giddy with joy, Lola made herself decent. 'That settles it then. A nice time followed by Pot Noodles.'

Dougie put his arm around her. 'Who could ask for more?'